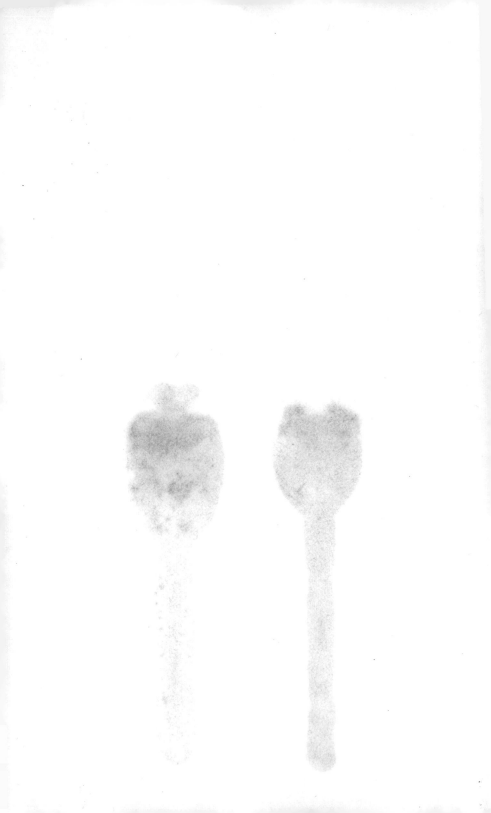

SOME DATA

and Other Stories

of Southern Life

Yours very truly
Sarah Barnwell Elliott.

SOME DATA

and Other Stories
of Southern Life

by
Sarah Barnwell Elliott

Edited and arranged
with an introduction by
Clara Childs Mackenzie

8981

Seaforth Publications
Bratenahl, Ohio

The following stories are published here for the first time: "The
Heart of It," "A Long Dream," "Old Ties," "A Speculation in
Futures," and "We People." © Seaforth Publications, 1981.

These stories first appeared in the following publications: In *Book
News*: "Hands All Round" (1898), and "Jim's Victory" (1897). In
Harper's Magazine: "Baldy" (1899), "An Ex–brigadier" (1896), "Faith
and Faithfulness" (1896), "An Incident" (1898), "Miss Maria's
Revival" (1896), "Readjustments" (1910), and "Without the Courts"
(1899). In *McClure's Magazine*: "Progress" (1899). In *Scribner's
Magazine*: "The Last Flash" (1915), and "Squire Kayley's Conclusions"
(1897). In *Youth's Companion*: "After Long Years" (1903), "Beside Still
Waters" (1900), "Some Remnants" (1901), and "The Wreck" (1907).
"Some Data" first appeared in a commemorative collection entitled
From Dixie, edited by Mrs. K.P. Minor (Richmond, 1893).

Library of Congress Cataloging in Publication Data

Elliott, Sarah Barnwell, 1848-1928.
    Some data and other stories of southern life.

    1. Southern States--History--Fiction.
I. Mackenzie, Clara Childs.   II. Title.
PS1589.E28S6   1981   813'.4   81-9203
ISBN 0-933496-01-X   AACR2

CONTENTS

INTRODUCTION

On August 31, 1928 *The New York Times* printed a brief obituary of Sarah Barnwell Elliott, author and suffrage leader, who had died the day before at Sewanee, Tennessee. The very brevity of the notice suggests that by the time of her death, Elliott was all but forgotten. Certainly most of what she had published was out of print. Meanwhile, a new generation of writers was starting to create what critics would soon proclaim a literary renaissance in the South. William Faulkner's first two novels, *Soldiers' Pay* and *Mosquitoes,* had just been published. The list of outstanding new writers grew—Wolfe, Tate, Ransom, Warren, followed by Welty and many more. One literary era had unmistakably ended and a new one had begun.

Sarah Barnwell Elliott had been part of the postwar generation of Southern writers which included George Washington Cable, Joel Chandler Harris, Thomas Nelson Page, Grace King, Mary Noailles Murphree and others, whose short stories and novels tried to capture oddities of their region, now defeated and humiliated, for readers nationwide, who were curious about the South's economic and social problems. Most of these writers turned out nostalgic and romantic pictures of former times, painting scenes of old plantation days, with dashing Southern Cavalier planters and docile slaves. Harris dealt with the freedmen's plight in "Free Joe" but in a sentimental way. Most of the local-color fiction, however, ignored whole groups of Southerners and traded, instead, on the literary myth of the Chivalric Southron. While the South was experiencing upheaval and enormous social change, its writers tended to retreat to a safer, calmer past, which they glamorized and sentimentalized. The old Jeffersonian landed aristocracy of cultivated and well-educated men became distorted to resemble characters of novels by Sir Walter Scott, the favored novelist of the day.

Unlike most of these writers, Sarah Barnwell Elliott had been born into that tidewater plantation society and knew it well. Both parents came from Beaufort, South Carolina, known as the home of the "Father of Secession," Robert Barnwell Rhett. Allied on both sides of the family to clans of wealthy rice and cotton planters, Sarah Elliott could claim descent from four colonial governors of South Carolina and Georgia. Elliott's father, aristocratic in outlook and moderate in politics, chose to remove himself from the public arena following the Nullification Crisis in 1832, fearing the hotheaded "Jacobins," who threatened to pull down the old ruling class which he represented. Entering the Episcopal ministry, he was elected first Protestant Bishop of Georgia. The family moved to Montpelier, Georgia, where Sarah was born in 1848, and later to Savannah, their home until 1864. Once a slave owner himself, Bishop Elliott put aside the ownership of land and slaves for economic and ethical reasons. He was dedicated to the cause of bringing blacks into the Christian fold, and foresaw a day when they would become wage earners, and might even re-colonize and Christianize Africa. He also devoted considerable energy to the educational needs of the young men and women of the South, his most notable accomplishments being the establishment of the Georgia Episcopal Institute for women, and later the founding of the University of the South at Sewanee.

Educated at home, Sarah began to write stories and a romantic novel at about the age of twelve. She and her sisters were avid readers, devouring volumes of history and philosophy, learning languages and music, and steeping themselves in the popular British novels of the day. The three older brothers, meanwhile, each studied for one of the professions. Had the opportunity been opened to her, Sarah might have done so as well; because of her determination to be self-supporting, she chose writing as her life work.

Scholarship was traditional in this family, and writing skill was handed down through two generations. Sarah's grandfather, Stephen Elliott, M.D. (1771-1830), a physician, banker, and an eminent botanist, published a two-volume botany of his region. He was also founder, editor, and contributor to the *Southern Review* (1828-1832). After his death, his editorial work was carried on by his son, Stephen Elliott, Sarah's father. Most of Bishop Elliott's published writings, however, consisted of sermons and position papers on church affairs. Yet another author in the family was an older cousin, William Elliott III (1788-1863). Though occupied with the operation of his many rice and cotton plantations (at one time he owned eleven), William Elliott wrote agricultural monographs from time to time and published a collection of realistic hunting and fishing sketches called *Carolina Sports,* as well as a drama in verse. *Carolina Sports* (1846) contains valuable glimpses into the life of the prosperous country squire in the South during the 1830s and 1840s. Popular from the beginning, the little book has gone through four editions and is still read by sportsmen today.

Despite this fortunate inheritance of learning and literary endeavor, Sarah's girlhood was not without cares. First came the Civil War, sending her brothers off to the army, followed in 1866 by the untimely death of her father, an event which left the family without home or livelihood. A serious illness that year had threatened Sarah's life. Their Beaufort relatives, to whom they might have turned for help, were all scattered; Federal troops had captured the area in 1862 and set up The Port Royal Experiment, a plan to break up the old estates and resettle the freed slaves on forty-acre farms. At first, Mrs. Elliott and her daughters found a temporary home with relatives in up-country Georgia. Then in 1870 they were reunited with her son John and his wife in a new home at Sewanee, Tennessee, where John had been appointed college physician and member of the faculty at the University.

Once settled at Sewanee, Sarah found opportunities for further study and she resumed writing. Eventually, in 1879, a first novel was published entitled *The Felmeres,* followed by a series of sketches and short travel pieces. These she sold to help pay for a European trip in 1886-87, accompanying her oldest brother Robert on a journey to the Holy Land.

While staying in Florence, Italy, part of that winter, Sarah was introduced to Constance Fenimore Woolson, the well-known local-color writer, who had published a series of stories about the Carolina low country called *Rodman the Keeper* (1880). This meeting with an experienced older writer set Sarah Elliott on the path which would soon bring her national recognition. Woolson advised her to write from personal experiences and memories of her own girlhood in Beaufort and Savannah, that heartland of the tidewater bluebloods; the hardships experienced by her family and friends after the Civil War; and in particular their response to the industrial expansion of the New South, for these were subjects of interest to the many readers of the popular magazines of the day. Wisely, Elliott adopted this course. She also chose to use the new techniques of Realism brought over from England and France. Instead of glamorizing the past, this new Realism focused on the present and dealt with the darker side of life. Writers employed considerable dialogue and sought to describe the environment in photographic detail. Instead of interjecting editoral comments on the characters' situations, the author discretely withdrew, becoming the omniscient teller, and allowing words and actions to convey emotions. Soon

Elliott's spare and carefully written stories based on her own firsthand experience, or those of her much-traveled brothers and other relatives and friends, began to appear in the national monthly magazines like *Harper's, Scribner's,* and *McClure's.*

From 1887 onward, Elliott encountered a steady demand for her work; she produced four more novels, two short novels, a biography of Sam Houston, more than thirty published stories, a successful stage play, and numerous essays, reviews, and some poetry. By 1895, when she moved to New York to be near the center of literary activity, her name was listed in *Who's Who in America* and her literary reputation was established.

In spite of these achievements, Elliott's work was never well known in the South. Her woman's rights and suffrage activities, begun in New York, eventually carried her to leadership of the suffrage movement in Tennessee, where she wrote manifestoes, addressed the legislature, lectured nationally, and lobbied in behalf of the Nineteenth Amendment. But Southerners were slow to warm to the idea of giving women the vote, and Tennessee proved to be the only Southern state that would ratify the amendment. The South was not eager to take "suffragettes" to heart. What is more, her stories giving realistic views of Southern manners and customs, describing racial strife and postwar hard times, were not what Southerners wanted to read about. Thus, while Elliott's books and tales were widely read elsewhere, and even though one best-seller had been published in England and Australia and even translated into German, she was largely unknown outside of the New York and Sewanee circles.

Elliott was probably far ahead of her time in attempting to publish stories on volatile issues like lynching, racial conflict, the outlawed custom of duelling, stories whose like would not be seen in work by Southern writers until Faulkner introduced his saga of Yoknapatawpha County to the world. Her best known work, *Jerry,* although not about the South, contains characters who had been born in the hills of Kentucky and Tennessee. *Jerry* takes place in the Colorado mountain gold fields and tells of labor battles, stock market swindles, railway land speculation, and mob violence. Her one collection of short stories, *An Incident and Other Happenings,* begins with an account of a black man who narrowly escapes an angry lynch mob. The collection was brought out by Harper's in 1899, just when the Negro Question was being hotly debated and race relations were most unstable.

It is not surprising, therefore, that five late stories dealing with controversial racial and social problems should have failed to be published in her lifetime. After Elliott's death, they were stored with her other papers and mementos in an old-fashioned hat trunk in the attic of her nephew's home on Edisto Island, SC. Here they remained until 1967 when Stephen Elliott Puckette, as her literary executor, entrusted them to me for use in writing a study of Elliott's work. The five stories are being published in this collection for the first time, almost a century after they were written. They are "A Long Dream," "A Speculation in Futures," "The Heart of It," "Old Ties," and "*We* People." Each reflects some aspect of Southern life that, while exceptional and sometimes melodramatic, must be taken into account for a many-sided understanding of that regional experience. Here are personal conflicts, strong hatreds, years-long deception, problems around miscegenation for which there are no satisfactory solutions, and what is more, provoke hot-tempered actions that end in tragedy. Here is a complex and static society, full of contradictions, so unlike the hopeful and innocent, energetic, and upwardly mobile society America projected as its image to the world in the last century.

Several of the stories in this collection are fictionalized accounts of actual events. Most notable is "Some Data," the opening story, about a former planter who tries to reclaim his land but is turned away by the "stranger people" who now occupy it; he is reduced to catching and selling fish for a living, an activity he once indulged in as a sport; finally, he dies of old war wounds, in despair at being unable to start over in the only work he knows. The story is based on the life of General Stephen Elliott, Sarah's cousin, an accomplished sportsman-turned-soldier, who commanded at the second defense of Fort Sumter, was wounded in 1864, and returned home, hoping to resume farming in Beaufort. He was never able to reclaim any of his land, which had become part of the previously mentioned Port Royal Experiment, and died in wretched circumstances in 1866. The four-part narrative is a fine example of the way Sarah Elliott worked with experience to shape a readable and moving short story.

Another example of thinly veiled family history comes in "*We* People." The main episode is historic fact, but the characters are developed to reflect typical attitudes, and the ending is changed to reinforce the theme of lawlessness and violence. The real-life story took place in 1903 in Columbia, SC, during the administration of Governor "Pitchfork Ben" Tillman. N.G. Gonzales, Sarah's cousin, was leading a crusade against the politics of Tillman in the pages of *The State* newspaper, which he had founded and edited. Grandson of William Elliott III, descendant of the old Bourbon moderates, Gonzales fought the so-called Populist Tillman and his nephew Jim Tillman on many fronts, but chiefly because they were lynch-prone racists, and were supporters of the corrupt State-operated Liquor Dispensary system. One day as the unarmed Gonzales crossed a street in front of the Capitol, he was shot by Lieutenant-Governor Jim Tillman and died several days later. A jury of Tillman's friends and political cronies acquitted him, despite his obvious guilt, on grounds that a man had a right to defend his name. "Shooting on sight" was the latest form of the old Code Duello. In real life, unlike the story, there were no night riders to even the score. What is unusual in this tale of violence is the reaction of friends of the wounded man and his brother. Even their black nurse thinks them cowardly for not fighting a duel with their enemy--they were not behaving like *we* people--not "one of us," the old guard and their retainers, for whom it was unthinkable that a man could refuse to defend his honor.

Not all the stories deal with violence. The old way of life Elliott remembers, as she describes her grandmother's Beaufort home in "Beside Still Waters," represented an intensely religious environment, where a strong sense of duty bound master and servant. In this paternalistic society, the slave had become an extension of the family, must be taught moral values and a work ethic. There were remarkable men like Anthony, the black overseer, who could read and write and was entrusted with important decisions and all record keeping, even though in South Carolina it was illegal to teach slaves to read. This settled, structured way of life is pictured in three more Elliott stories centered on Miss Maria, and her experiences before the war, and later with her former slave Kizzy, as a wartime refugee.

The agrarian South after the war adapted poorly to newfangled technologies and mercantile enterprises. In "Progress," Sam Long is generous to a fault with his friends, but his lack of business sense leads to bankruptcy. But there are other characters who do well in the New South. In one of Elliott's best stories, we meet sturdy survivors like "Ex-brigadier" Billy Stamper, a man who can laugh at his own escapades, determined to adapt to new ways.

These twenty-two stories and sketches represent about half of Elliott's story output. They have been selected because they share certain themes, and because all are about the Southern experience. Placed in a roughly chronological order, they offer a panorama of scenes, attitudes, philosophical differences, and character types that amount to a rambling social history of the Deep South from the 1840s to 1915, through three wars, and a vast amount of personal suffering and regional hardship.

Yet this recitation of seemingly unending gloom and tragedy is occasionally relieved with glints of humor. Together the stories offer "some data" for a composite portrait of a place and time.

Dr. James B. Meriwether, professor of English, University of South Carolina, was kind enough to read these stories, and it was he who suggested they ought to appear as a "Southern Collection." I am also much indebted to Dr. Lewis Pinckney Jones, Kenan Professor of History at Wofford College, for evaluating Elliott's work in light of his extensive experience with the writings of other members of the Elliott-Gonzales family. Dr. Arthur Ben Chitty, Jr., historiographer of the University of the South, has also shown great understanding and offered considerable encouragement in this and other projects related to the work of Sarah Barnwell Elliott.

Cleveland, Ohio   C.C.M.
10 March 1981

SOME DATA

I.

You want some data for a sketch of Ted's life. He was a very reserved fellow, but I suppose I knew him as well as any one did. I might give you facts and dates, but I can give you four scenes in Ted's life that will be better, I think. I was so vividly impressed at those times, that whenever he is mentioned they rise before me as clearly as if set down on canvas.

We were cousins, and I, an undersized, rather sickly orphan, knew no other father or mother than Ted's, nor any other home, nor wanted to know.

Ted broke the ponies—kept the fishing tackle and guns in order—and licked all the fellows who called me "Molly." I did his Latin and Greek when we sat side by side in the old town school, and later, when we went to college, the same division of labor took place. In the end, our debts were divided by two—Ted graduated creditably, and I was not a disgrace to the class as a sportsman. Not to be able to ride, to shoot, and to manage a boat, was on our course considered a true and deep disgrace, and from this Ted saved me.

He was never happy away from the water, and never away from it any longer than he could help. His father owned Head Island, and Headland was our home. It was a big, white, old-fashioned, Southern country house, with nothing fine about it save the avenue and the people. Comfort, and plenty, and peace, and good-will, and health—happiness came without seeking. Some things at Headland I will never forget; one was the view. Standing in the deep piazza, one looked out from under the shadow of the great live oaks, over a wide sweep of sun-lit or storm-swept water, clear out to Far Island, where the broad Atlantic roared and thundered. I have never seen any sky so blue, nor any water that sparkled so. Another thing was the jonquils—white jonquils—masses and masses of them that bloomed just before we moved into the town of Deep Haven for the summer—"As pure as the souls of children," Ted said once to himself, and I overheard him. He

1

would gather reckless quantities and put them in his boat when he went out. He would watch them withering in the sun, while they filled the air with sweetness. "What better death than sunshine, or what pleasanter grave than the water?" he would say, and scatter them overboard.

A third thing that Headland was famous for was the cooking. You see, all of one end of the kitchen was open fireplace. I have been in model kitchens with shining stoves, and trim pans arow, but for good cooking, with all flavors and juices preserved, give me the big open fireplace of the old Southern kitchen. They were necessarily disorderly, for the cook, in order to give his genius full play, had to have so many assistants. They have often been described, but you have never heard of Headland's stuffed crabs and terrapin soup, that were unrivaled—of the callapash and callapee—of the sweet wafers and rice waffles—nor of the rendering of game and fish that was a symphony in taste. Of course Uncle Edward died of gout; just before the war, fortunately, and Aunt Mary followed him in a month—broken-hearted. Marriage was a success in those days.

There was another memorable thing at Headland—the beds. They absolutely wooed one to sleep; the linen was so fine, the pillows were so big. I preferred to lie awake and enjoy the comfort, and watch the red glow from the lightwood fire play on the white walls—on the white frill around the top of the big four-poster—on the silhouettes of my grandparents, in their funny gilt frames, that hung over the dressing table—on the dressing table itself, standing on four long, slim legs, held together at the bottom by a shelf, at the top by two shallow drawers which supported an oblong looking glass. If I had only a thousand dollars I would give it all for that old dressing table. I think I could find Ted's face in that glass.

Ted had some strange ways. He would float alone in his boat on the moonlit waters all night. He would spend nights and days in the woods and swamps, and he knew the voice and habits of every beast and bird that lived there. But the first time that Ted took shape for me, so that I had any impression at all of his looks, was once while we were at home from college.

It was a brilliant day in July, with a stiff breeze blowing, that put a cap on every ripple in Deep Haven sound—"river," we called it. So much for the wind; the sun was scorching. There was a devilfish expedition on foot among our uncles, and fathers, and cousins, and we were keen to go. Ted had his own boat and oarsmen, but that was not the point. It is dangerous sport, and Ted was not altogether well, and Aunt Mary was miserable; so Uncle Edward said a flat-footed "No" to us, although he was the leader of this very expedition. Ted, however, manned his boat, got his harpoon and lances in order, stretched his line, and asked me to go with him to see the fun. At the last moment Cousin Fred stepped into our boat, and sat down near me where I was holding the tiller ropes. cousin Fred always dressed in white in summer, with a dandy white hat and a white umbrella. The most immaculate person possible. This day, as he sat down, Uncle Edward looked at him quizzically.

"You are aiding and abetting my boys in rebellion, Frederick," he said. Cousin Fred drew his hand over his beard thoughtfully, and his eyes smiled behind his glasses.

"I understood that Ted and Robin were going as spectators," he answered, "and four oars do not promise a long cruise."

"Yet, that looks like work," and Uncle Edward pointed to Ted's harpoon and skillfully coiled line.

"So it does," Cousin Fred answered, musingly, "but perhaps those are put in for safety. Suppose a dangerous fish should attack us? These waters abound in jellyfish."

Uncle laughed. "You are always on their side," he said; "but, remember, there is your Cousin Mary to settle with."

We followed modestly behind the big boats as they made their way over to Broad Creek, drawing out a little further than the rest, which was perfectly in keeping with our part as audience. Presently a wing appeared above the water; every boat dashed forward except ours. Ted, standing in the bow, harpoon in hand, made his men back water, and Cousin Fred smiled. Very soon we heard cries and exclamations, and saw confusion in the little fleet; then we knew that the fish had gone. They had turned to come back, when a black wing swept all the oars from one side of our boat! Ted's harpoon literally hurtled through the air as he sprang backward to save himself; the next instant he was in his former place, hatless, with the line spinning through his hands! The boat righted itself, the terrified Negroes drew in the remaining oars, and we went rushing through the foaming water after the great sea monster. Cousin Fred lowered his umbrella, and taking out his handkerchief waved it to the forsaken fleet, while he said: "Be ready to cut the line, Ted; this speed is dangerous." Then I looked at Ted as he stood bare-headed at the bow of the boat, clearly outlined against the pale summer sky, and for the first time I realized him. Tall, slim, well poised; Saxon features, and fair hair that the wind pressed back as it whistled by; a jaw like a rattlesnake, and blue Celtic eyes that were gleaming and flashing! I have never forgotten it. I can hear how the wind whistled—how the water swished by us—I can see the moving panorama of the disappearing land—see how the day died down behind us—how the ocean rose up before us, and Ted standing there the incarnation of youth, and strength, and joy!

Later, when the battle was over, and we were beating our slow way back with the dead devilfish dragging in the rear, Ted sat down beside me that I might help him with his hands. His thick gloves had been torn to ribbons by the spinning line, and the skin of his palms had followed suit, and now he wanted me to pull the remains of the gloves off, and the fragments from where the dried blood held them.

"Wait till Aunt Mary can bathe them, Ted?" I pleaded.

"Dip them over the side," Cousin Fred said, coolly, from where he was amusing himself driving the sharks away from the carcass we had in tow.

I caught Ted's hands from the water; I had only just learned how much I loved him.

"It will burn you like the mischief!" I said.

"If it burns like the devil, it does not matter now," he answered. "I've won!"

II.

Isabel was our third cousin, and I do not remember any time in her life when I did not adore her. I had a great deal to do with teaching her to walk, and I taught her to read entirely. To me she was always beautiful, though every one declared that she changed wonderfully between fifteen and eighteen. Down at Far Island in the summer, where all the little children went barefooted and paddled all day on the edge of the surf, Isabel never ventured more than to wet her little toes unless I held her hand. "Wobbin," she called me; and I dug canals, built houses, picked up shells, and even humbled myself to make mud pies for her. As years advanced, I caught crabs with her; I baited her hooks; I read aloud, and helped her with her lessons. Then Ted and I went to college, and Isabel went off to school. For three years I did not see her, but we corresponded regularly. When she was eighteen she returned to Deep Haven, the loveliest vision I have ever seen. "Robin," she called me; and kissed me as she had always done, and as quietly as if I were wood or stone. She was a little taller than I, not much, but she laughed and patted me on the head, then looked up at Ted, whose eyes had never left her since she entered the room. She shook hands with him; she standing a little behind me with her left hand on my shoulder, and called him "Cousin Ted," and my heart bounded within me as I thought how much more she was mine than his! She talked to me of all the old days, how I had taught her the things she most cared for, and how she used to think that all the wisdom of the world was mine.

"And I am not sure that I was wrong, Robin," she said, "and when we get down to Far Island we will dig some canals and make some mud pies for old times' sake."

"Of course," I answered; "we will say the alphabet if you like, and go out even now and dig for doodles."

How she laughed; such a sweet, ringing laugh!

Ted sat almost silent, sometimes watching us as we talked together on the sofa—sometimes looking past us out of the window. I think it was the first and only time I ever felt that I had something apart from Ted, and was glad to have it so. The sun was setting as we walked home, and all the splendid pageant of the evening clouds was mirrored in the sound. Joy seemed to be bubbling and rushing through my veins—I felt as if walking on air—as if breathing the beautiful colors, and the stillness seemed to throb with life and happiness. Then Ted's voice fell on the silence, and a deadening power was in it that arrested everything.

"She is like a white jonquil, and they say Cousin Fred is in love with her."

In love with Isabel—*my* Isabel! A sudden fury possessed me; then the reflection came, how could he help it? and I asked quietly: "Who says so?"

"Mother."

"I don't blame him," I said.

"Who could?" Ted answered. "Cousin Fred is a man of the world," he went on slowly, "has been everywhere, is rich and handsome. What do you think, Robin?"

A moment before I had thought of Isabel as mine, and not Ted's; now I looked on him as an ally.

"Cousin Fred," I said, "is a Methuselah!"

"Thirty," Ted answered, "and girls like that sort of thing. You are only twenty-one, and I twenty-three; she may call us callow!"

"Why, man, I've brought her up!" I cried.

We went down to Far Island for July and August; most of Deep Haven did, for both Deep Haven and Far Island belonged to the Clan. It was only a collection of rough frame houses interspersed with tents, sometimes of canvas, sometimes of palmetto, where everybody marooned for the sake of the sea-bathing. It was all temporary, because Far Island was sometimes covered by the sea in the September storms.

But it was idyllic: comfortable uncles and aunts; old-fashioned, shy girls; boats of all shapes and sizes; violins, guitars, and banjos for music; surf-bathing, fishing, and boating by daylight and moonlight for fun; idleness; health; youth; good servants; what could be wanted more? The storms were brief, and the rain came seldom in that fairyland; indeed, shelter from the sun was a far greater question than protection from the rain, and for both purposes frames were run out from the houses and thatched with broad palmetto leaves, while for floor there was the white sand. We would gather sometimes at one house, sometimes at another, with cool melons and guitars, and hammocks, and smoking chairs and tools; and golden hours would pass while the fresh sea wind rustled the dry palmetto leaves, or the rain pattered and splashed on them—and the boom of the sea kept time to the thrum of the music, and the wind swept the soft songs away. Then the afternoon wanderings on the wide white beach, when the world was wrapped in the golden glow of the dying day, and the sea gulls dipped and skimmed from wave to wave.

All those days, and places, and people are ever wrapped in a golden mist for me. No words can describe the life, and no mortal eye will ever see its like again, for the civilization that made it has passed away. They are scattered to the four winds of Heaven now, those quiet gentle folk, and the world says that it is best. That they were degenerating; that like all aristocracies they were being put on the shelf by the vigorous, pushing masses. Perhaps; but in the shipwreck that overtook them, they showed themselves to be the stuff of which martyrs are made. Not many of them are left, but whenever you meet one of those exiles, you find a passionate love for that old time and place, and an unquenchable longing, looking out from tired eyes. Those of them who died on the battlefield, full of strength and of heroic purpose, had the best of it. But do not suppose that Far Island and its inhabitants was like any seaside resort of today; not at all; even the young men were a little shy. I think I was the one privileged character, and it was because, as my cousin Emma said, "Robin is poetical and musical—is everything, indeed, that a ladylike little man can be—quite fit to fetch and carry for Isabel." Nor was it all music and melons. Manly sport was the rule. Among the younger men, Ted led, and even among the veterans he was taking position. For me, I had but one thought, Isabel; and but one occupation interfering with Cousin Fred. Whenever I saw them together, I would appear on the other side of Isabel with some claim on her attention, and she never failed me.

Sometimes Cousin Fred would smile, and once he said—"What will you do, Isabel, when Robin falls in love, and carries his weal and woe to other ears?" For the moment I hated him, and looked it, but for answer his eyes only twinkled a little more as they met mine, until Isabel answering—"I will turn *you* into a brother, then, Cousin Fred"—a new possibility came to the front, and we looked away from each other. But whenever Ted took his place by Isabel's side, I felt quite safe from Cousin Fred; sorry for him, because we were two to one.

One day a heavy windstorm came up which was alarming in itself, but terrifying in the light of the fact that a large fishing expedition had gone out. By sunset all the boats but four had come in; by midnight, all but Ted's. By morning Far Island was miserably anxious, and boats went out in every direction; but as the day grew, they came back one after another without any tidings. All the men were sitting about in groups, smoking furiously; most of the feminine community were gathered about poor Aunt Mary; sitting dry-eyed and white, in her silent house. I stood on the beach with a spyglass until I was exhausted, then I went to Isabel. She was sitting alone with a book open before her.

"How *can* you read?" I asked, taking a seat.

"Ted is so brave and skillful," she said, slipping her hand in mine. "And he never fails, does he?"

"Never," I answered, "not even in his college examinations."

"He is weakest there? You are hard on him."

I turned on her sharply and began a rapid defense of my hero.

"He is a poet," I finished. "He has never written a verse, but he lives it—he feels it—feels all the beauty and pathos of the universe. Look into his eyes and you will see it—if we ever look into his eyes again!"

"Hush!" she whispered.

"How cold your hand is!" I cried.

"It is yours that is cold," and she drew hers quickly away.

Near sunset a rumor came that something had been sighted.

"Go and find out," Isabel said, and went indoors, while I took my way to the beach. My glass trembled so at first that I could see nothing, then I descried a speck that in the setting sun looked like the wing of a pink curlew; suddenly it flashed into the silver of a gull's wing. My breath came sharply—it was a sail boat, but had veered away.

"Something is wrong with her," Cousin Fred said.

"Great God!" cried Uncle Edward, "where are my lazy scoundrels? Caesar, call out the hands—have that boat ready in five minutes if you love your life! Robin, stay with your aunt; if it should not be Ted it will kill her!"

In twenty minutes every boat had left the island. I went to the house and took my seat on the steps of the piazza, for within all Aunt Mary's sisters and aunts and cousins were sitting about her. She caught sight of me and came out. I rose to meet her and she clasped my hands convulsively.

"I am sure it is Ted's boat," I said.

A shudder went over her. "But, is he in it?" she whispered. "Oh, Robin, he may have been swept overboard!"

"Not Ted," I answered.

"He might have succumbed to the heat."

"There is the shadow of the sail," I comforted, again. Then I brought her a chair, and resumed my seat on the steps, while we watched the boats as they went. If it was Ted they would fire a gun. It seemed hours that we watched. Within was the low hum of women's voices, like the voices of those in the house of the dead; without, groups of awe-stilled boys waited on the beach; the silence of death had fallen, and nothing stirred save the wind and the waves. The sun sank down a ball of red; it seemed to rest on the sea for a moment, turning it to blood, then disappeared slowly like the mechanical sun in a show. The waves bobbing up in front of it, gave it the appearance of going in jerks, as if the machinery needed greasing. In my misery I smiled at the incongruous thought and the badly managed sunset, but I have never forgotten it. Then everything turned gray. The boats were specks—the groups of boys had gathered into one—and the murmur of voices within took a lower tone. Every moment, without the sound of the gun, was a segment of hope gone. I was too anxious to be still, and I took out my watch.

"What do you think?" Aunt Mary whispered, faintly.

"It will be a half hour yet before they can distinguish the boat," I answered, at random. She took the open watch and fastened her eyes on its face.

"Five minutes," she said, presently, then—"ten minutes—fifteen minutes," she went on—"twenty."

What a fool I had been to time her!

"Twenty-five minutes—twenty-six—"

"I had no ground for timing them, Aunt Mary," I said.

"Twenty-seven—twenty-eight—"

A far, far-off reverberation! I sprang to my feet, the boys on the beach gave a cheer, the watch dropped with a smash, and all the women rushed out to Aunt Mary, who had fainted.

Everybody flocked to the beach now, and we talked about nothing, and laughed gaily in the glad reaction. The boats were growing as they neared us, and now we could hear the Negroes singing—all the boats singing the same thing—"Roll, Jordan, Roll!" It made a great volume of sound, and it was one of the grandest things I have ever heard.

Ted was landed safe and sound, and in the face of all that company I did a thing that no man or boy there would have done at the point of the bayonet—I threw my arms round Ted's neck and kissed him!

"Emma will call you *un*ladylike, now," he said, softly, while his eyes shone, and his face, that looked so pale under its bronze, turned quite red. But he kissed me in return, and I know he would rather have fainted.

That night the moon was full, and coming out from Aunt Mary's room, where I had been telling her over and over again of the scene on the beach, I looked for Ted or Isabel, but could not find them. I felt a little lonely, a little injured, and stepped into one of the boats that was beached near by. I arranged a comfortable place in the stern, and stretched myself back luxuriously. I could look out over the sweep of the ocean glittering under the moon, or down the long curve of shining beach that dwindled as it went, and far, and far away vanished to a point that seemed almost to touch the quiet stars. The tide was going out, the waves that were little more than ripples, plashed distantly; the wind had fallen.

How long I lay there I do not know. If all my dreams were waking dreams, or if I slept, I do not know; but far off up the shining pathway of the beach—far off by the quiet stars, I saw a thing that moved. Slowly it came down the broadening, silvered curve. I watched it, fascinated; a round thing—no, an oblong thing that moved on end; then two little horns appeared. Nearer down the wide white way it came; now half was floating drapery, half was still black. The horns had turned to heads—two people, a man and woman! Slow they came. Nearer; their voices, their words were with me. I could almost have touched them. They stopped and looked up to the great moon; then he bent his head between her and the light.

"I am jealous even of moonbeams," he said, and they turned away toward the house.

Aunt Mary had broken my watch, so I do not know how long it was before Ted came back alone. I rose up to meet him.

"What will Cousin Fred do?" I asked.

He turned upon me quickly. His face was all alight; his eyes gleamed like stars; he raised his arms to heaven and looked up while the moonlight made a glory in his fair, wind-blown hair—"What matter," he said, in a low vibrating voice; "I've won, and she is mine!"

I will never forget that picture, how Ted stood there radiant, with his arms stretched up to heaven.

I stayed all night in the boat. I watched the tide go down—the moon ride higher, and the silvered sea that seemed so sound asleep. There came a moment when it held its breath—not a sound—not a motion—poised at the point of rest! I held my own breath.

Something stirred somewhere, and a sigh swept by me, and out over the face of the great deep, shivering it into millions of glittering ripples. They flashed just once toward the paling moon, then rushed shoreward. The tide had turned, and a new day was pushing up from the underworld.

III.

In 1863 Ted was sent for by the General commanding the department where he was then serving as Major of Artillery, and asked if he would take charge of a ruin, called a fort, in one of the harbors. He was to have a limited garrison, and of course, hold the fort to the last gasp. I went with Ted to headquarters, but was not present at the interview. When it was over he walked in silence to his room at the hotel. Once there, he drew the one chair in the place to the window and sat down. He had not taken off his hat, and he was occupying the only chair to the exclusion of his guest; two signs of mental excitement that made me expect important revelations. I took my seat on the table, and waited. When he told me, I said quickly—"That is a forlorn hope, Ted, a useless sacrifice of you. It is sheer folly!"

"Folly—forlorn hope! It is a crown of glory!"

"Do you forget Isabel and the two boys?"

"Would you have those boys hear that I refused the position because of the risk?"

"It is only a pile of rubbish," I urged.

"I will hold it, or leave it a pile of bones."

"Suppose they overwhelm you, what will you say then?"

"When that happens I will be dead, and not in a conversational mood. I wish I could put Isabel and the boys in one of the casemates," he went on, beginning to walk up and down the room; "the little chaps have been under fire, and are not a bit gun-shy."

I got down from the table. "Good-bye," I said, "I will do my best for your widow and orphans; I suppose the Government will bury you."

He turned quickly. "I am not going to leave you out of it," he said, "I shall have you transferred."

As I was only a chaplain, I was assigned next day, and we went down to the fort together. That very afternoon Ted inspected everything, down to the last half-brick, and by night the garrison was his, body and soul. He then insisted that his promised number of men should be made up at once, as the nights were dark and good for assaults. After the company came I believe Ted prayed for an assault. It did not come that night, nor the next night; but it did come the night after.

It was awfully dark. Before us was the ink-like water, that we could only hear as it lapped against the walls; behind us, the black hole we called the fort. The sentries looked like ghosts lurking here and there; the stillness was intense. Ted kept watch himself that night, lying flat on the highest point of *debris.* The water had been his home, and he knew every sound and motion it could make. Still-hunting had been his delight, and the darkness held no shadow he did not know. I was lying close beside him, yet I could scarcely define his outline in the gloom, and his face looked an impalpable bit of whiteness.

For hours we lay there, when, shortly after midnight, my musings faded from me, and I became conscious of some disturbing change. I would have said that the atmosphere had tightened about me. I turned; Ted had drawn closer to me, and was gazing over my shoulder, almost. His face was drawn; his eyes had narrowed to points of light; he was quivering like a high-bred dog on a tense point!

"Yes—ss" he hissed softly, "yis—ss!" I looked in the direction of his gaze. There was a blacker line on the black water!

"Barges!" Ted said. "Go to your headquarters; and, Robin, bricks can kill, too!" Then he went away quickly into the darkness.

There came a silent sort of stir in the fort; a little rolling of rubbish as the men went to their positions; a few low-voiced orders, then we waited. The black line came nearer, and behind it another line that turned toward the right.

A sort of blood-thirsty excitement took possession of me, and I fingered the hand grenades impatiently. Our fire was to be held until the moment of landing, when the orders were to give them all we could. It was a breathless moment, then a line of fire darted from point to point, outlining the grim old ruin against the darkness. Cries and shouted orders; for the confusion of surprise was on the enemy; while the whole harbor blazed with shot and shell from other batteries and gunboats! And on the highest point, exposed to fire of friend and foe, full in the lurid glare, I saw Ted standing for an instant, glowing with the fierce joy of battle! When all was over, Ted sat down by me. "It was a near thing, Rob," he said; "but we won, and 'twas worth ten years of ordinary life." He held that brickpile for months; was wounded, was sick; but he never went to hospital. I did, but not by the path of glory. The magazine exploded, nobody knew how, and some fellows were caught in the passage. It was hot work getting out those burned, broken creatures from that raging fire, and I would have done better if I had been bigger. As I got the fellow I was dragging to the opening; they took him from me so suddenly that I stumbled, and a falling timber caught my leg. The enemy were shelling us like fun, but Ted let everything go and worked like a convict till I was freed. Then he took me up as if I had been a baby, with the tears rolling down his cheeks, and kissed me like the mother he had always been to me. The men who helped were sniffling, but perhaps that was the smoke.

IV.

It is not often given to a people to suffer as the Southern people have suffered, and whether the war was their own fault, or whether it was a judgment on them for their sins of omission and commission, of "negligence and ignorance," is between them and their God. But whatever was the account against them, it has been wiped out with a sponge dipped in tears and blood, and the slate is clean for the score of this new generation—this "New South." God help them! In '64 Ted was ordered to Virginia. We did a good deal of work round the "Crater" at Petersburg, where Ted lost an arm, and was made brigadier-general. We went through it all, he and I, down to Bentonville. The cause died there, and the blackness of darkness seemed to settle over us. Deep Haven had fallen in '62, and everything had been confiscated. Most of the country houses had been burned; most of the town houses were occupied by Negroes or "carpetbaggers," and all of the lands had been cut up into forty-acre lots and given to the Negroes. Some people had gone back, I don't know why, and among them, Ted. He had become possessed of the overseer's house on grandfather's plantation, and had settled there with Isabel and the boys. Late in '65 I had two parishes in the upper part of the State, with a salary of four hundred dollars a year—a fortune just after the war. In

March, '66, I determined to go down and see Ted and Deep Haven for myself, for the letters were unsatisfactory. I had no trunk, so I packed a large box full of comfortable things for Isabel's housekeeping, and putting my clothes in my old knapsack, I set forth on my journey. A railway to Deep Haven seemed as bad to me then as a railway to Jerusalem does now, and the station, and Cousin Charles Caryl's house as a hotel, was all like a nightmare. I found that I could not get a boat to go over to Ted's until next morning, so I determined to walk out to Headland that afternoon. A Federal General had made it his home, hence the ferry was kept up. It would take a book to tell all I saw and heard, and felt on that walk—and Headland itself! The house had been painted afresh, and the grand old trees had been trimmed, and the trunks whitewashed! It had a snobby, shoppy look to it that was dreadful. I hated it! But in the garden Aunt Mary's jonquils were swaying in the wind, and the same old Toby working among them. I sat down behind a hedge and cried. I stopped presently, for I was weary with my journey and the walk, and tears hurt a man—even a little man.

The hedge behind which I was sitting went up to the garden, so that I was safe from observation, and to calm myself I looked away from Toby and the jonquils, out over the water. That was unchanged, and a canoe being propelled across by one oar at the stern, looked supremely natural. As the boat neared the shore my heart rose up to my eyes, and I crept along the hedge, watching the little craft like a snake-charmed bird. A fair-haired little boy made it fast to the landing. I don't know how I saw that, for all my being was watching the tall, gaunt figure in the old gray uniform, with one empty sleeve pinned to his breast. All the gold had gone off of coat and cap; all the buttons were covered with black. His beard and hair were touched with gray; his face was thin and white and set. He walked up the old path as quietly as if he still owned it, carrying a string of fish. Old Toby met him, hat in hand.

"Huddy, Mawsa!"

"Well, Toby?"

"Yes, Mawsa; lucky, suh."

"'Here are the fish, Toby." The old man took them away to the back of the house, and, left alone, Ted stood there like a wooden image. He did not lean against anything; he did not look at anything until a lady appeared on the piazza. He did not look at her, but he took off his cap and held it until Toby came back with some money.

"Good-bye, Mawsa."

"Good-bye, Toby." Then as Ted turned away the old gray cap went on with a grace no prince could have bettered, and the old Negro, leaning on his rake, watched him wistfully, like a puzzled child.

A week after this Ted lay dying. Insufficient food, insufficient clothing, and a broken heart; the doctor called it pneumonia. Isabel and I had been watching all night, with Teddie and Robin taking turns to bring in wood for the fire. In the dark hour before the dawn, Ted opened his eyes.

"I wish I had some of mother's jonquils," he said; "I should like to take them to her."

"I will get them," I answered.

It was a long pull. The sound was as quiet as if smothered by the heavy white mist that lay on it. The stars were beginning to pale before the coming day, and the brimming tide still flowing in, was near its turning. I tied the boat and stole up the walk. All was still as death, save the long gray moss that swayed like ghostly cerements, and the white jonquils that seemed to beckon.

When I reached them I think I grew mad, a frenzy of hatred and revenge seized me, and I gathered, and gathered, and gathered, till not one was left on the stems. I had brought a rice-fanner, the only basket Isabel had, and I filled it to overflowing. The flowers secured, I pulled up the roots—pulled and pulled—then trampled and stamped the beds down—down—down! My fury was growing, and I went away quickly in the ghastly light that was neither night nor day. I was afraid of myself because of the matches in my pocket.

We put his insignia back on Ted's collar (Isabel had kept the things as women will), and took the black covers off his buttons. We put on his red sash, and his belt and sword, and the gold cross-cannon on the old gray cap that we laid down by his side with the sword; but in the hand that rested on his breast, we put the white jonquils for his mother.

Did he say any last words? Yes. He said, "It has been a hard fight to forgive my enemies, Robin, but I've won; and for reward the stranger people sent me all the jonquils."

A LONG DREAM

It was November, and a cold morning for that season of the year in the far South. The sun was resplendent, the sky so vivid a blue that it seemed to sparkle, and a strong wind was blowing that promised still colder weather. Tearing its way through one primeval pine barren, the wind that was becoming savage, swept straight across a live-oak avenue into another untouched pine wood. Long ago masters had planted the avenue, and had covered with pounded shells the straight road they had cut through the pine forest. A Southern master with his band of Negroes easily made a civilized spot in the wilderness, easily cleared fields and occupied large tracts of land, and the beams of the older plantation houses were hewn, and the nails were hand-wrought.

It was one of these old houses that stood at the end of the avenue where the wind was harrying the wide-spreading oaks, and swaying and stretching the long gray moss that draped them. By evening there would be bunches of moss on the ground, rolled up and tangled with sticks, and the little leaves would be huddled into the ruts and piled up in heaps, and the road would look swept and garnished.

The avenue was long, the white road dwindling and seeming to find a natural finish in the distance, but there was a big gate, and beyond that, running at right angles, a broad, sandy public road that went through gloomy swamps where the brown water seemed never to 'stir, through forests where the foot of man seemed never to have trod, on and on, silent and shadowy to the far off town, passing, perhaps, one or two other big gates in all its great length. Against this gate leaned a woman who was looking up and down this public road. The wind had loosened her hair a little, and the swaying boughs above her head made great play of light and shadow, causing her slight figure to seem slighter in the flickering light. There was no use in listening, for no sound of horse's hoofs could come from that deep sand. She could only look, look longingly toward the town, with now and then a careless glance in the other direction.

15

"I'm foolish," she said at last, smiling to herself. Her husband had been gone three days now, and he had said good-bye for only one. True he had sent a messenger to explain that he would be detained, but not for three days, so surely he would come this evening. There was a plenty to do on the place, however, the more so in that he was away, and the day would soon be done. Then he would come on his black horse cantering up the avenue, and she would meet him at the gate, the little gate that shut the house and garden from the wider domain. And how glad he would be—and she? She turned toward the house and ran a little. It was nice to run with the wind behind one; besides she was cold without either hat or wrap. Duke did not like her to run, however, and she came down to a walk. A tall woman should never be anything but calm and dignified, he said, and she sighed. He had trained her a good deal in the years they had been married.

Nor did he always like her meeting him at the gate. Dear old Duke, he was so stately himself, so reserved, so still, it would be impossible for her ever to attain to his perfection in such matters. She sighed again. He would have been happier if there had been any children. She looked up to the blue sky that sparkled through the tossing branches. She reached to catch a swath of moss, pulling it through her fingers, looking carefully where it branched and tangled itself, only to cast it away and gather up her skirt for another run. Duke was many miles away, and she loved to run. She felt awfully old sometimes when she counted up that her next birthday would mark her down twenty-nine, then after that came thirty! But she did not feel old today for she was happy, Duke was coming—Duke was coming! Meanwhile, she would go to the sick-house, would interview the poultry-minder, would go to the smokehouse and give out the meat for the week, and go to the house where the little Negroes were cared for while their parents were in the fields. There was much to do, and she must do it before she could meet her Duke with a clear conscience. Then a grand, glorious, gorgeous dinner must be arranged as a welcome. And Simon and his satellites had to be admonished as to the silver, and Marcus warned as to the harness and the horses. The master was coming, surely coming that night, and the servants must be found watching.

She laughed a little, her thoughts had run as fast as her feet, and now having reached the garden gate at the end of the avenue, she sat down on the horse-block to rest. In spite of all that she had to do it was going to be a very long day, and she had been very foolish to run from the gate when she could have absorbed time by walking. True, she could go to drive, but there was only the one road, and only the people on the nearest plantations whom she had seen over and over again since she had returned in October. When everybody had parties out for Christmas it would be better, but not now. If Duke would let her ride alone, she would have liked that, for on horseback one could explore, but that was not dignified for his wife, he said.

She went into the house, a simple old house, full of simple old furniture such as we collect now from "Antique" shops, a house which seemed to have habits and manners of its own, and that demanded of its inhabitants a certain probity and dignity; a house so filled with the shadows of gentlefolk gone before, that of itself it could teach deportment, could preach hospitality. Now it was very still. In the sunshiny drawing room there was only the sound of the wood fire talking to itself; in the study across the hall where there were as many guns and rods almost as books, there was no fire. One must be built instantly if the room was to be warmed by night. And the master always marched in there at once. The study was his, he said, the parlors were hers. She did not love the study. Duke stayed in there too much, and yet, he was not a student. He smoked a great deal, and rode over the fields a great deal, and wrote a great deal, but she did not know what.

The first few years it had been different. He had not seemed to have so much business then, had stayed more in the country, had been able to go away with her in the summer. He explained that now he had a better overseer than factor; an overseer who could manage the plantation better than he himself, could, but his factor in town was inadequate and had to be looked after. She had suggested that he change his man of business, or let them live in town. Her people were in town, her dear brothers. Then Duke could ride out to the plantation when it was necessary. His father's house had never been deserted, he had answered, and never should be. Never should be, and they had no son—no child!

"Simon, Simon!" she called, going out into the hall. "Simon!"

"Yes, Missis,"

"Make a fire in the study at once, Simon. Your Master'll be here tonight, and it'll never be warm, you know, if you don't make it now."

"Yes, Missis."

"And have all the silver rubbed, and all the brass."

"Yes, Missis, I meck de boys rub de silber yistiddy, m'am."

"Yesterday? Well, give it an extra rub today. You know that your Master does not like the smallest speck to be on it."

"Yes, Missis."

To the stable next, where old Marcus was smoking in a sunshiny corner.

"Your Master comes tonight, Marcus."

"Yes, Missis," stepping forward briskly.

"Is everything in order?"

"Yes, my Missis, ebery t'ing. En de horse is tired restin'."

She paused a moment. "Then I'd better take a drive this afternoon," she said interrogatively.

"I t'ink you is, Missis, kase Mawsa say de horse muss go out ebery day, en—"

"Very well, I'll be ready at two o'clock. Now send Jonas to the smokehouse."

Of course she ought to exercise the horses. It was one of the few things that Duke asked her to do. "Behave as his wife should," he had said, "and so preserve his name clean and honorable, keep the house as his mother had kept it, and exercise the horses." This had been once when she had begged him to give her something to do for him. Now she threw her head back a little as she walked across the wide yard. His mother had left most things to the servants, but she had kept the horses well exercised trotting about from one friend's house to another. Her head drooped a little. She had failed in the matter of the horses, but she had been much more exclusive socially than her mother-in-law, and Duke had commended her. The old lady had been very good to her, however, and she missed her, and she looked wistfully to where the family burying ground lay in a group of cedars. Things had been more cheerful, more natural when she was alive.

Yes, she would take the horses out this afternon, would drive in state to see old Mrs. Sincler, who declared that Duke was the handsomest man in the state—and he was.

It was colder every moment, but there would be hot bricks in the bottom of the big old carriage, and Marcus should drive fast. That would be good for the horses, and she'd like to go and hear her Duke called the handsomest man in the state. Duke who loved her, belonged to her. Long ago, before she had said yes, he had absolutely pursued her. Always still, always reserved, his eyes would flame, and his strong, slim hand would grip hers like steel even in an ordinary greeting. Yes, he loved her. His reserve was growing on him, and his solitary ways. Little children would have won him out of that, poor fellow.

It was a long drive, and it was colder than she had thought, much colder. She tapped on the front window. "Faster," she said. "Faster, Marcus."

Then Marcus stopped entirely, and bent down to speak in the window. "De horse ain't been out in three days, Missis, en I 'fraid fuh dribe too fass."

"Of course, but as fast as you can Marcus." She ought to have driven each day, she ought to like driving about to see the old friends of the family. There were four plantations within driving distance, nice people of whom she was fond, she must go more frequently. Staying at home and just waiting for Duke as he went and came was not wholesome, and besides it made her dull when he did come home. And she would persuade him to let her have people out oftener to stay with her. What would she do with the men when he was absent? Why nothing at all; she would let them take care of themselves. There was too much of "The Moated Grange" about her life, she had been foolish to fall in with such ways.

She smiled a little, sitting alone in the big old carriage. How often she had gone over all this ground; how often she had made all these resolutions, and the moment her husband looked into her eyes she was content—content to know that he was in the house, or would soon come into the house.

Colder and colder. It would be a bitter night, and suppose Simon allowed the fire to go down in the study. Duke would think of her as careless, hopelessly careless of his comfort. At last they were at the gate. She would be glad to reach a fire, and Marcus must drive round to the stable for how ever short a time they were going to stay, and it must be short on account of the fires at home. This avenue was not as handsome as Duke's, nor so old, Duke said, nor was the name so old or so important. Dear old Mrs. Sincler was at the window, had seen her. There must be visitors, every thing seemed so on the alert.

"Drive round to the stable, Marcus, but don't take the horses out; I shall not be here long enough."

"Day is horse yer from town," Marcus answered. "I see um stannin' yonder now."

"Yes, well, I won't be long, Marcus."

Just such another house as the one she had left, just the same air of repose, just the same type of furniture, and the old lady who greeted her seemed to suit it all.

"Oh, my dear Ann!" she said, kissing her visitor softly on either cheek. "I am so glad to see you, but it is so cold. Come in, come in to the fire. Peter some wine and cake for Mrs. Duvol; Minty, take Mrs. Duvol's things. You look pale, my dear Ann. Is anything the matter?"

"Only chilly, Mrs. Sincler, otherwise, well and happy. I must confess that I did not know quite how cold it was, and Marcus thinks the horses too fat to be driven out of a walk. But you, Mrs. Sincler, are you quite well?"

"Of course, my dear, why not? Just now I am a little disturbed. Mr. Weatherby has this moment arrived from town nearly frozen. Truly, my child, nearly frozen. The cold has come so suddenly, and our systems are not prepared for it, so that we feel it dreadfully. And he drove out in an open gig, think of it, an open gig all this distance in the teeth of the wind! I am afraid that he will be ill, pleurisy at the very least, a very serious thing for a man of his age."

"Dreadful! but why did he come?"

"He's gone to lie down in the library by the fire, and Minty has put hot bricks to his feet and back, and has covered him up, and now she is giving him hot coffee. He thinks that is better than mulled wine. I was shocked when I saw him. He was blue, poor gentleman, and could scarcely walk, and not one of my sons at home to receive him, dreadful!"

"Dreadful! But why did he come? I suppose you did not ask him? I hope that he won't be ill; he is so good. He was father's lawyer, and Duke pins his faith to Mr. Weatherby."

"Everybody does. He is as near a saint as a lawyer can be, I think."

Mrs. Sincler seemed full of uneasiness, but on Ann's face a brighter look came. "I wonder if he will go home with me," she said. "Duke will come out this evening, and it would be such a pleasant surprise to him to find Mr. Weatherby there; a man to talk to."

"Go home with you—"

"Yes, in the closed carriage he will be protected."

"He is—he is—I'm sure he will not be able to move for an hour yet, quite sure, even if then—can you—can you wait?"

Ann shook her head. "Duke is coming," she said, "and I must return to make ready, but I can send the carriage back for him, Mrs. Sincler, easily send it back, only I must be there to meet Duke."

Mrs. Sincler rose hastily. "Am I wanted, Minty?" she said, going into the hall, but there was no Minty, and she returned with the same nervous haste.

"Not at all, my dear child," she went on, "do not think of such a thing, I can send him on without the least trouble."

"Perhaps he will not want to come?"

"Perhaps—but—yes—but yet, I think perhaps, almost surely, that he will. You must be lonely sometimes, Ann?"

"Oh, no! Duke is never away more than two or three days, never. Tell—why how quickly Marcus has come round and how funny Negroes look when they are cold, quite gray."

"Yes, or frightened. Marcus is a good servant."

"Very. Sometimes I really feel as if he owned not only the place, but me and Duke. Old family servants are very possessive sometimes. Don't come out, Mrs. Sincler."

"Absolutely so, my child, old servants are absolutely so. I don't mind the cold. Is that Pindar on the box with Marcus? What a respectable looking Negro he has grown to be. Howdy, Marcus; well, Pindar. Drive fast out of the cold, Marcus, and get Miss Ann home quickly, be sure, Marcus." And Mrs. Duvol being safely shut into the carriage, the old lady shook her head at the servant, and laid her finger on her lips.

Marcus was not sparing the horses now, not a bit. Her visit had not been in the least satisfactory. Everything seemed to have been completely upset by Mr. Weatherby's condition. And Mrs. Sincler was usually so serene, so full of repose. Really, the horses seemed to be running away! She was not sorry, she wanted to be at home to make sure about the fires. And now a room must be warmed in case Mr. Weatherby should continue his crazy journey. How odd it was, very odd. And she turned over and over again in her mind the unusual speed of the horses, the unusual manner of Mrs. Sincler, and the most unusual visit of the family lawyer.

Presently they stopped and Pindar opened the gate. How strange he looked. His face seemed flattened, and his lips were fairly hanging down. Was he so cold as that? suffering to that point of distress? Now she lowered the glass and put her head out; she could see the house, and the windows, the small, old panes shining in the low afternoon sun; looking from under the deep piazza like friendly eyes. A dear old home and she loved it.

They stopped at the horse-block, but there was not the usual flourish in the opening of the carriage door and the letting down of the steps. Pindar usually grinned from ear to ear when he served her, but not now.

"So cold, Pindar?"

"Yes, Missis," with lowered head.

"I'm sorry, Pindar, I did not know it."

"Dat ain't nuttin', Miss Ann," Marcus spoke sharply from the box. "Please m'am, go in de house. Dese young nigger is too good fuh nuttin'. Git up yer, boy, git up, I gwine lick you sho'. Please go in de house, m'am, Miss Ann, please m'am."

"You are getting very cross, Marcus; Pindar, do you go to the kitchen and tell Mawm Amy to give you something hot. You too, Marcus."

Out in the stable Marcus shook the boy sharply. "Enty I tell unner no fuh look dat way w'en Missis kin see you? Enty I tell you so? Fust t'ing you'll cry, den you'll tell Missis. Dis t'ing is fuh w'ite people to tell. I'll kill you boy, sho. Go 'long to you mammy house, doan you go in dat kitchen. Now mine what I tell you, mine," and he pushed the boy from him.

In the house the fires were burning briskly; the low sun shot a red light in at the study windows; the wind seemed to be rising still higher, and made strange sounds in the pine woods. Ann shivered a little. How would she ever get a room properly warmed in so short a time for Mr. Weatherby. How crazy to venture so far on a day like this. The wind really sounded like a tired voice, and how it roared across the chimney tops. It was lonely with Duke away, and if he intended to go again very soon, she would tell him about it. Tell him how the wind cried, and how the house seemed to crack in the night, and how she heard tickings in the wall, and soft steps. She was sure that she heard steps tipping through the hall in the middle of the night. Yes, she would tell him now. It was beginning to wear on her nerves, for now he went so often and stayed so long. Good heavens! There was Mrs. Sincler's closed carriage coming up the avenue!

"Simon! some wine here at once; tell Mawm Amy that I want a pot of coffee quickly!" She pushed an arm chair nearer the study fire, then went out to welcome her guest. Quite out to the gate she ran.

"Oh, Mr. Weatherby!" holding out both hands. "I'm so afraid that this will make you ill. Come in, come in, you look frozen—white—worn out! Take Mr. Weatherby's coat, Simon, put another log on the fire, bring up the coffee—"

But the old gentleman waved his hand. "No coffee, Simon, nothing, just take my coat. Then you may go, Simon, and of course you will shut the door after you."

A dead silence fell, and lasted while the servant closed the door slowly and softly behind him. Ann had not moved, one hand was still extended in a little gesture of command, her lips were slightly parted, her eyes wide with astonishment.

"Sit down," Mr. Weatherby went on, "sit down, my dear young lady, I—I have—I have something to tell you—something—"

"Duke."

"Yes, sit down."

"Tell it quickly—tell it!"

"I will, but sit down."

"Sit down, sit down, why sit down!" and she stamped her foot. "Tell me at once—at once! Duke, Duke, something has happened to Duke! My heart will break just as surely sitting down." Her voice was sharpening, her words were tumbling from her lips. "Tell me—tell me! You have kept me waiting so long already, and I've built up all the fires—have put his slippers out upstairs in his room—have ordered a special dinner. How dare you keep me like this? How dared you stop at Mrs. Sincler's—how dared you let me come from there so happy—to meet him—to meet him! Poor me—poor, lonely soul. And this morning I waited a long time down at the gate, waiting and watching. And it was coming then, coming all the time down that long road, stopping on the way, stopping to warm itself! All the time preparing to kill me in a leisurely manner, yes, when it suited your convenience. You know that it will kill me."

"It will not kill you."

"Then he is not dead. Tell me, I command you! You do not answer. He is dead—I see it in your face, tell me. Thrown from his horse? No horse living could throw him. How then, how?" and she clapped her hands together sharply above her head.

"He was on his way home," and the old gentleman took both her hands in his, fastening his eyes on hers as if to keep her still. "He was on his way home, and passing through Black Swamp—he was shot—"

"Dead."

There was no answer and the man and woman stood staring at each other.

"Dead," she repeated under her breath. She pulled her hands away, moving about and wringing them together above her head. "And all these days he might have been with me, and I have been waiting, waiting and watching so lonely. Who was his enemy—who murdered him!"

"It was a fair fight."

She wheeled on her heel to face her companion, and her hands dropped at her sides.

Mr. Weatherby drew a paper from his pocket. "It has been coming longer than today," he said, "or than yesterday."

Ann had seated herself now, in a low chair near the corner of the wide fire place. Her white lips were shut closely. She shivered as with a mortal chill, and a dull glaze had come over her eyes.

"He made this will," the old gentleman went on, pointing to the paper, "made it years ago. He leaves you one half of his property."

Ann straightened up. "One half? And the other half?"

"To Mrs. Pauline Bernon and—"

"Well?"

"Her children."

"And Mr. Pauline Bernon has fought him?"

"There is no Mr. Bernon."

She was gazing at the lawyer now, her face straining and hardening. "The children?" she said slowly.

Mr. Weatherby turned his face away. The color rushed to her throat, her cheeks, her forehead, a furious crimson flood, leaving all as suddenly a deathly white. She did not move. She still looked toward the old man, but she no longer saw him. She seemed to be busy putting on a mask. She had had eyes like a too faithful dog, beautiful and pathetic. They were changing, were hardening and brightening, and the lines of her face were changing too, and when at last she spoke, her voice was quite different.

"Why did not James, my own brother, come out to tell me, or Percy?"

"James is attending to things in town—Duke was carried to his house."

"Duke is dead?"

"His body—"

"Oh!—I forgot his body."

"And Percy has left town."

"He has just come back!"

"He left town when your husband did."

She saw her companion now, and her eyes flashed. "Percy knew about Mrs. Pauline Bernon and—her—the children?"

"He discovered it by accident yesterday evening."

"And James?"

"Was told last night."

"I was listening to the wind last night, and to things ticking in the wall. The moon was full, and an owl was out in the big magnolia tree."

A look of anxiety came into Mr. Weatherby's eyes, but the next question was sane enough.

"You told Mrs. Sincler?"

"What the rest of the world has heard, that he was thrown from his horse. His horse came into town with a broken bridle,—and of course, James was the first person to find him."

"So? So much arrangement as that? Have they arranged for my mourning?"

Again the look of anxiety came into the lawyer's eyes, and he said, "It has been managed with the greatest care in order to protect both names—to protect you."

"And Mrs. Pauline Bernon?"

"The will provides for her silence."

"And she wants the money. She might have my share, too, if it were feasible. Of course he knew that I would not break the will, so he protected me to the extent of silencing the woman."

The lawyer's eyes flashed.

"You think that he did it to protect his own name?" she went on. "Probably so. And you could not have stopped it, Mr. Weatherby?"

"The will was my first knowledge of it, and it was many years too late when that was made."

She passed her hands over her eyes, then sat silent. At last she rose.

"You have been very good to me, Mr. Weatherby," she said, "and I am grateful." She paused and pushed back and forth idly for a moment the chair she had been sitting in. "Now I shall go to bed," she went on, "and stay there. That is what orthodox widows do, and of course the shock has been great and I shall be too much prostrated to attend the funeral. Mrs. Pauline Bernon will laugh if she hears that. Mrs. Sincler will wish to come to me, and that also will be the correct thing, so if you will kindly stop on your way to town and ask her in my name to come, I shall be very much obliged to you."

The old man had risen too, and now laid his hand on her shoulder. "You are overdoing it."

"On the contrary, I shall be absolutely conventional. I shall lie white and wordless, the easiest and best way, and shall be spoken of with sighs as a 'widow indeed.' I shall betray nothing. When I am gone upstairs, I'll be glad if you will call Simon and order your dinner. Also send to Marcus your directions for the carriage in the morning. In addition, please tell Simon about your breakfast, and do not let Nancy come to me tonight. Give my love to James, and say to him that Percy must come out and stay with me. This is the only possible excuse for his being absent from town at such a time. I want to see Percy very much indeed; give him my love and tell him so. Poor old Percy, always so kind and tenderhearted. This business is hard on him, but of course James being married could not run the risk. And kindly put the will through as quietly as possible. I suppose that my sister-in-law will see after my mourning. Let it be very deep; and Percy and Mrs. Sincler being with me, she need not come out. Does she know about Mrs. Pauline Bernon?"

"No one knows but your brothers and I; and Mrs. Bernon, like the rest of the world, thinks that he was thrown from his horse. I informed her myself—this morning."

"Told her first. Well—You will be sure to send Percy out. Dear old Percy, so hot-blooded. Good night."

"Good night."

At the door she paused and turned her eyes full on Mr. Weatherby.

"How old is the eldest child?"

"Seven years."

"Seven. I am twenty-nine, and I married at nineteen. A long dream. There is that owl again, and how the wind blows! There, the sun has gone; how suddenly it grows dark. And the steps will come through the halls tonight, and the house will crack—and the wind! Seven years— good night."

A SPECULATION IN FUTURES.

I.

The large tabby house, washed yellow, with its outbuildings, covered a block in the heart of the old city. On all sides a brick wall, washed the same yellow color, shut out the streets. Double wooden doors gave entrance at the back, where some roses grew, and one or two fig trees; beyond this were the stables and the outbuildings for the servants. In front, were high, wide iron gates, inside of which stood thick camellia trees that secured the privacy of the house as completely as did the wall. Not that there was anything to hide, far from it; since the building of the city the Cecils had lived there, their name honored, their friendship sought and trusted, their lives an open book to be read of all men; but it had been the fashion in the early days that people of the Cecils' standing should have large houses with surrounding gardens and enclosing walls.

A gray-haired man, erect to stiffness, clean-shaven, carefully dressed with high stock and a collar that pointed up on either side of his face: a man who looked as though he treated himself, as well as the world, with the most punctilious respect, sat now in the library of the big, yellow house, in front of a big mahogany table. On all sides of him were family portraits—some of them dating back to the mother country—and high, old-fashioned bookcases, filled with mellow-tinted fine editions. Leaning against the side of the window that looked over the front garden, was a young copy of the man at the table: the same blue eyes, the same clear-cut features, the same erect carriage. Near the door at the lower end of the room was a third man, the overseer. He was seated between the door and the broad hearth, where though it was March, all the glittering brasses shone in the light of a fire; for on the South Atlantic coast where swamps abound, the air is damp.

The overseer seemed to be rendering a report, and as he talked he played with a soft felt hat, glancing the while from the fathe, who lis-

27

tened to him with his face turned a little over the side of his collar, to the son, whose look was fixed on him with what seemed an alert watchfulness.

"No, sir," the overseer was saying. "He ain't wuth a cent 'cept to plough. Sire an' dam with pedigrees long's my arm, that colt's got ears like a buck-rabbit, an' stripes on his legs."

"Most extraordinary!"

"Yes, Mr. Cecil, but it happens some times; didn't breed true; he throwed back. Folks do, too; I've got black hair, an' my wife's got black hair, all both fam'lies, an' my little Joe's got hair like fire; he throwed back. Somehow, it will happen.'

"Yes," Mr. Cecil answered, looking up at an old, old portrait that might have been his own picture, "it does happen."

"I'd counted on that colt as a trotter," the overseer went on.

"Yes," Mr. Cecil answered again, "it is a pity. Anything else, Mr. Green?"

There was a scarcely perceptible pause, then the overseer said slowly, "Of course, sir, you know Toby's gone?"

Young Cecil straightened himself away from the window, and his watchful look changed from the overseer's to his father's face, while the father turned his chin a little more over his collar to fasten his eyes on the overseer. "Toby—gone?" he said slowly, while a pink flush stole up under his clear skin.

"To Mr. De L'Orme's; had a ticket to go—sold."

"I came to explain this, father," the son interrupted, coming forward a little, "Toby belonged to me."

"Of course, my son, but he is the best horse-breaker on any of the plantations!"

"And when Mr. Green has finished, I will tell you."

"Oh, I'm done," Green answered, rising quickly, "An' I had to report, Mr. Edward. Well, good mornin', sir," and he left the room by the lower door, closing it carefully behind him. There was silence while the man's steps died away down the back hall, then—You knew Toby's value, my son?"

"Yes, sir, and ascertained that he was willing to go to De L'Orme; his wife is there."

"I have been negotiating to buy his wife; you knew that?"

"Yes, sir." The young man walked slowly down the room, his hands in his pockets, his eyes fixed on his mother's portrait hanging above the mantelpiece. "I exchanged him."

"De L'Orme has not a Negro worth half as much as Toby."

"I have been arranging this for a long time," the son went on as if not hearing his father's words, "ever since the early days of my return home."

"It yet needs explanation?"

"For months I have been working so that when—what will seem to you a catastrophe, should arrive—it would fall on you and my mother as lightly as possible. I am afraid that educating me abroad—sending me in childhood away from Southern views—was a mistake."

"You have convincing arguments?"

"I fear so; I hate slavery."

"They are the best cared for working class in the world." A crispness had come into the father's voice and his words had a clipped precision which showed that they belonged to an old argument.

"But they are not free."

"They would not understand freedom any more than children would. The Africans have never advanced an inch until placed under white influence, even though on their northern coast they have the oldest civilization in the world."

"That does not give us the right to buy and sell them."

"They came to this country savages—many of them cannibals—we must control them, discipline them until they become civilized."

"And then do we free them?"

"The responsibility is a grave one; I hope for gradual emancipation; to free a few makes it harder for the many; to free all is to endanger our own civilization."

"I do not see that."

"The lower class of foreign emigrants might intermarry with them— never the Anglo-Saxon, thank God—and in this country, where all are free to rise, what might not the future bring to us as a nation?"

"You grant them souls?"

"I pay a missionary to teach them that they have souls."

"The unhappiest moment of my life, father, was when you wrote me that Aunt Eleanor had left me her plantation and Negroes. I had determined to ask you to leave everything to Charles—to set me free, in fact—but Aunt Eleanor's will put the problem into my own hands, compelled me to face the issue, and now—" he paused in front of the fire and leaned his arm against the high mantelpiece.

"I would give a great deal, my son, to be able to buy your Negroes and land."

"I would not allow it; it would be against my convictions. I realize your point of view, the burden, the responsibility, and have determined as soon as may be, to sell the land, to march with the Negroes to some border state and there to free them."

"To starve?"

"I can see no other solution; meanwhile..."

"My son, you take an exaggerated view—the Negroes are happy."

"But I am not, and—to seem entirely inconsistent—I have exchanged Toby."

Mr. Cecil pushed back his chair, rising and asking slowly, "For whom?"

"Madeleine."

"I do not understand."

"Marie De L'Orme's maid."

"The Octoroon?"

"She is white." Young Cecil's eyes were fixed on the fire, his voice had gone very low.

"My son—you sink to this!" Mr. Cecil's two hands rested on the table, his body leaned forward towards his son.

"You misjudge me." The young man did not raise his voice.

"Declaim against slavery and buy an octoroon woman!"

"If your suspicions were true, society would condone the situation."

"Never! You malign your own people!"

"Madeleine was brought to me an hour ago—" the young man paused a moment then went on as if speech were difficult—"humble, beautiful, defenceless, my chattel—" he stopped with a sharply drawn breath.

"Well?"

"I freed her."

"There is more behind?"

"There is." He turned quickly to face his father. "As far as the law will allow, I shall marry her!" The father still leaned forward over his writing table gazing at his son, but the blood seemed to be settling in spots about his face. His eyes seemed not to see. He swayed a little; his son sprang forward. Instantly Mr. Cecil straightened to his full height, his eyes flashing, his hand raised to ward off his son's touch. "How dare you enter this house!"

"I thought it right that I, myself, should tell you." There was a pause while they looked at each other, then the elder man sat down in his great chair slowly, as if spent.

"Your mother?"

"I have told her." He waited, then added, "She has gone to bed; old Elsie is with her."

The father covered his face with his hands and his head drooped as though his forehead would touch the table. The son walked back to the fireplace, once more resting his arm on the high mantelpiece and leaning his head against it. The clock ticked, the fire flickered and sighed, the flowers atop the camellia trees nodded in the soft wind, the few sounds from the sleepy streets beyond the closed sashes and high wall were dim and distant. Young Cecil shut his eyes. The sound of the clock seemed to grow louder and louder; time seemed to drag more slowly between each beat.

At last in a voice as dim as the street sounds—a wail—"My son, my son!"

"Father!" coming a step nearer, his voice eager—pleading—"I war against prejudice—I break down the barriers of ages—I am determined—"

"To breed a mongrel race—to drag my name in the dirt!" Mr. Cecil had lifted his head.

The son recoiled. "Your name is left you," he said, "I have changed mine—legally. I shall sell my land, free my Negroes, go to Europe, to Paris—there are no prejudices there!"

"This is fanaticism—bravado!"

"No, sir, I love her!"

Mr. Cecil leaned his elbow on the table and covered his eyes with his hand. "Do you realize," he began in a slow, carefully controlled voice, "that your own Negroes will rebel against this; that it will be impossible to take her to your own plantation? Will it not be wiser to wait until I can get the money to send you off to Europe—a day, two days—and leave your affairs to be arranged by me?"

"I object to running away."

"She is totally uneducated," the careful voice went on. "She will have vulgar tastes," clasping his hands, his voice rising, while the look that he fixed on his son was full of agony—"will day by day become a more terrible burden! Oh, my son, a sin against the laws of God—a sin against nature! I beseech you, pause before it is too late!"

"It is too late. I have taken a small house on the outskirts of the town, have hired an Irish woman."

Mr. Cecil sprang to his feet. "Impossible!" he cried, "monstrous! A cheap house, one servant, a mongrel race! God help us!"

"Father—"

"I forbid you to use that name—I—." The upper door of the room opened and shut quickly, and Charles came forward.

"You know, father?"

"More than you do," Edward answered sharply.

Charles turned his back on his brother. "I've been to the club, father, to strike his name off the books—it was your privilege or mine—but Louis De L'Orme has been before us; at the Jockey Club, too, even at the Historical Society, and we cannot resent it."

"We can resent nothing!" the father answered, "we are disgraced beyond redemption!" Turning quickly to Edward—"Leave this house, sir!"

Charles instantly took position with his back against the upper door. Edward paused a moment looking at him, then went out through the lower door. Charles dashed into the hall and braced himself against the front door, but Edward did not come. Out at the back door, out through the stables he strode, and the Negroes watching him from every crack and corner. Those whom he passed turned their backs on him insolently; if he saw, he made no sign.

II.

The year had waxed and now was waning to its close. The pitiless, long summer had breathed its last a week before, done to death by the first November frost, and the Cecils had returned for the winter to the big, yellow-washed house. A brilliant day with a crispness in the air that yet held no malice in its soft touch, a day to cheer the heart and make life seem a sweet and desirable thing.

Mrs. Cecil, looking like the ghost of a woman, half reclined in a deep chair close to the library fire. Mr. Cecil sat at his writing table with the same erectness that had always characterized him, but the writing on the page before him was tremulous and his eyes had lost their brightness.

Charles, with his hands clasped behind him, had paused in his walk to and fro in the long room, to look down on his mother.

"My dear mother," he was saying, "I think you have been unwise."

"Perhaps, my son, but I could stand the silence no longer. Since last March I have had no word, no sign from Edward, and however deep his disgrace, I love him. I told Elsie to wait near the house until she should see him, and discover if he looked well or ill. Edward has never spent a summer in this climate, and I was afraid."

"That he would die? What greater mercy could we ask for him, mother?" "If he were dying I should go to him." There was a dead silence. "And we may not have long to wait." A break came in her voice. "Elsie says that he looks wretchedly. She says that even his clothes and hat look like 'po' buckra clothes'."

"Then you sent her again, mother?"

"Of course, every day, and I have sent him—" she paused, but no one helped her, and she continued with evident effort—"little notes, and some money. He returned the money. But the child may be born at any hour, and I was afraid that he needed money and might deny himself to give to that creature! Oh, my husband, forgive me. I could not help it!" She put her handkerchief to her eyes and her soft sobs were the only sound.

Mr. Cecil turned to his son. "I wish you to find out from the overseer, he said, "all that is possible concerning Edward's financial condition; if he needs money, for the sake of your mother's health, he must have it. He has not been able to sell his land yet, and I hear that the storm in September ruined his crop."

Mrs. Cecil looked up. "He thinks that he is right," she said, "that the curse that the Negroes shall be 'the servants of servants,' means nothing, that it is all Southern prejudice; poor boy, and we do not know what he has suffered all these months, what his punishment has been. Elsie is there now, she went just after breakfast; she adores Edward, and I have told you all these things because I am afraid." She sat up straighter in her chair. "Elsie has become so excited about it, so desperately hates the woman—'dat white nigger,' she calls her, that I am afraid she will do her some bodily injury. This morning I told her that she must not go, and she was frantic; she rolled on the floor, she tore her apron to pieces, and her head hankerchief, actually pulled out her hair and threw it into the fire. You were both on this side of the house. I was afraid; I let her go." "That was all a trick, mother, to get her own way."

"Not entirely, my son. She is horribly jealous, and has never gotten over Edward's disgrace and your continuance in favor. Elsie did not nurse you. You were nursed by Susan, a woman whom Elsie hated, and in whose death, the Negroes whisper, Elsie had a hand. I do not believe that, but all these considerations enter into my fears. I wish Elsie spoken to, reasoned with a little; but do not forbid her to talk of Edward. She remembers all his baby ways—has a lock of his yellow hair— his broken toys and even some marbles he gave her when first we sent him abroad to school. It was a mistake. Elsie looks on our keeping you at home as a mark of greater love. She says, 'Ef Mass Eddie been stay wid he own people, he would know des es well es Mass Challie dat white is white, en black is black fuhrebber!' She never ceases her moan; declares that the woman has cast a hoodoo spell on Edward, and she, Elsie, must take the charm off him. She has made a little wooden image and stained the half of it black, and every night as she sits on the floor by my fire, waiting until I am asleep to put the lights out, she burns a little bit off the white side of the image. I asked her what it meant. She said she was burning 'de white outer dat nigger, and den Mass Eddie will hate um en kill um!' Oh, it is awful! While the image smoulders her eyes are like fire. She makes all sorts of signs and mutterings. She curses it under her breath, she spits on it, then carefully, with a knife she cuts of the charred part and puts away the image until the next night. I am afraid."

There was silence, and Charles walked away up the length of the room. A log on the hearth broke and the fire fell together. Mrs. Cecil started. Charles turned to look. The iron gates clanged outside, and he sprang to the window.

"Elsie—running!"

In an instant a wild voice in the hall—"Missis—Missis!" The father and mother rose to their feet, and Charles flung the door open.

"Hush! Come here!" he ordered, as a tall Negress rushed in. A second she paused, looking about her wildly, then flung herself down at her mistress's feet. "De hoodoo is gone—de hoodoo is gone!"

Mrs. Cecil stretched out a hand against the mantelpiece. "What have you done, Elsie!"

"Sit up," Charles commanded. "Stop this nonsense. Tell us!" Mr. Cecil came a step nearer. Charles stood close beside his mother. The Negress sat back on her heels, her breath coming in gasps, her eyes gleaming.

"Yes, suh, Mass Challie, I tell you." She wiped her face with her apron, and moistened her lips with her tongue. "Yes, suh," still panting a little. "When I git to Mass Eddie house, dat Irish 'oman what cook, is at de gate. She say, 'De chile is bawn,' den she laugh. I say, 'What you laugh at?' She say, 'Come en see.' I say, 'Is de mammy dead?' 'No.' 'Is de chile crooked?' 'No, he is a fine, straight chile. He gwine meck good plough man,' den she laugh 'gain. I say, 'What you laugh at?' She say, 'Come en see,' den we gone in de house. When we git in de entry she say, 'Ef I show you, you must'nt tell de mammy, de doctor say de mammy mustn't know tell she husban' come.' She husban'! Missis—" waving her arms wildly while her voice scaled high, "I want to kill dat Irish 'oman when she call Mass Eddie dat!"

"Go on!" Charles commanded.

"Yes, suh," again wiping her face with her apron, "I nebber knock dat Irish 'oman kase I hole my han' tight, en I say, 'I won't tell de mammy, show me.' She say, 'I done sen' fuh Mr. Edward, he'll come in a minute,' en she laugh 'gain. I say, 'Ef you doan stop dat laughin' I'll kill you!' Den she hole she side; 'You'll laugh when you see,' she say, 'but doan tell de mammy.' Den we gone up to de room. Missis," her voice fell and she looked up at her mistress deprecatingly, "dat room wuz like white people room, m'am, en dat gal," her voice rising again, "wuz laying' up 'ginst pillers like white ladies. Yes, m'am; en she say 'How dee do, Elsie, yo' master is comin' in a minute!' Oh, Lawd! my missis, call me, me Elsie like she wuz white people! It wuz good t'ing dat Irish 'oman ketch me."

"And the child," Charles demanded.

"Yes, suh, I gwine tell you, suh. De Irish 'oman say, 'yez de chile, Aunt Elsie,' en she drag me to de sofa up by de fire. 'He's unde dat putty little white blanket,' she say, den she gone stan' twixt me en de bed, so dat nigger cahn see me. Missis, I wuz trimlin' tell I kin scacely liff my han', m'am, en de sweat wuz stannin' on my face, m'am, but I wuz 'fraid Mass Eddie would come 'fo' I could see, en I draw back de little white blanket!" A look of ecstacy came over her face, and she began to sway back and forth, clapping her hands rhythmically, holding up the charred remnant of a rudely cut figure, and chanting as in a song of victory—
"Oh, my Missis,
Come out de Willerness, come out de Willerness!
Moses en Aaron
Come out de Willerness, come out de Willerness!
I burn de white blood out in de fire,
Come out de Willerness, come out de Willerness!
See my Master, see my Mistis,
Come out de Willerness, come out de Willerness! Oh, Mass Eddie,
Come out de Willerness. Come out de Willerness!
Yo' ole Mawmer call you, Sonny,
Come out de Willerness. Come out de Willerness!"
"Elsie, Elsie, tell me!" "Yes, my missis," said the woman, flinging her arms about her mistress's knees, then letting go and gesticulating dramatically, "yes, m'am; I pull down de little white blanket en I look—en look! Den I open de chile little gown so I kin see he breas', en de mark, you 'member, missis, de mark what is 'cross Mass Eddie breas', de red mark—it was layin' 'cross de chile breas', yes, m'am; den I yeddy Mass Eddie comin'! I pull de white piller up good behine de

chile, en I kivver um up quick, en I gone stan' by de do'; de Irish 'oman wuz stannin' by de bed. When Mass Eddie see me he say, 'All right, Elsie?' I say, 'Yes, suh, Madeleine is doin' berry well.' He stop en say, 'She is my wife, Elsie!' I say, 'No, suh, Madeleine is nigger same es me.' He raise he han'—I step back en say, 'En de baby is fine chile, suh, layin' on de sofa, suh, under de little white blanket up 'ginst de white piller, suh, en I wants to teck it home, Mass Eddie, en show my master en my Mistis what a fine chile you hab, suh!' Po' Mass Eddie; he pull down de blanket—I wuz 'fraid he gwine fall—den, quick, des like I do, he open de little gown, en he own mark look up at um—layin' 'cross de little breas'—white es milk!"

"White! How could you see it, Elsie!"

"When Mass Eddie see dat mark," the woman went on not heeding her mistress, "he tu'n roun' quick, en gone out de room, out de house! De front do' slam, de gate slam! Den Madeleine cry out, 'Way's my husban'! En I say, 'Yo' master, gal, en he'll nebber come back no mo'!' En I come runnin' fuh tell you, missis."

"But the child, Elsie?"

"De chile is black, m'am."

Mr. Cecil grasped the back of a chair, the mother swayed a little, smiling vacantly, Charles strode away to the window and the Negress sat back on her heels, her excitement spent, her look wandering from one white face above her to the other. Suddenly a step came up the back hall toward the lower door, passed, and went up the stairs. An electric shock seemed to touch the watchers in the library; Charles came from the window, treading softly, and Elsie leaned forward on her hands, listening with her ear turned to the floor. A door shut somewhere. A moment, then a sharp sound clove the stillness of the big house. Elsie rolled over with a cry, the father and mother seemed turned to stone, Charles sprang towards the door, out, and up the stairs.

Not long, and then they heard him coming back again. He stood in the doorway. His eyes were alight. Then he went straight to his father's side. "Edward," he said, "up in the old nursery—on his own little bed," and he laid a pistol down on the big shining table.

BESIDE STILL WATERS

Long ago in the far South, on the low Atlantic coast, on an arm of the sea that ran far into the land, a quiet old town lay white and sleepy. From the outside it could scarcely be seen for the fringe of live oaks that grew close to the water's edge; from the inside one could look through the greenness across the shining water to the far, dim woods on the other shore. Figs and pomegranates and oranges ripened there then,—for the sheltering woods to the north had not been cut away,—and oleanders and roses and myrtles filled the big gardens. The old houses were built of "tabby" or of wood, with deep, encircling piazzas, and whitened to a dazzling whiteness; and the shady streets were white also, and hard with pounded shells. No hotels, no railways, no stages, no touch from the outer world save a steamboat that, plying between two neighboring cities, paused twice a week for mail and passengers.

It was almost Arcadian, the life in this "ancient and secluded town," where the setting sun turned the great river into a sheet of gold that mirrored with marvelous splendor the glory of the evening clouds; where the sails of the pleasure boats gleamed like "white, flitting souls;" where the far-off thrum of a soft guitar, or the wild, low song of the Negroes, keeping time to the stroke of the oar, seemed like fairy music; where the soft wind swayed the long, gray moss, and the slow tides rose and fell.

This town of Kingshaven was the private property, almost, of a few large clans of planters, more or less nearly related. They kept their horses and dogs, their rowboats and sailboats; they owned hunting islands, and islands that were little more than sand bars, where in summer they marooned for the sake of the sea bathing, spending the winter months on their plantations. Their wine, their silver, their furniture and books and gout and church were standard, and from the mother country, sent over in exchange for the silky, long-staple "sea-island cotton." All these customs and habits and manners were of ancient date,—had been held sacred by every one of the many generations that lay asleep about the walls of the old church built of English brick,—and having been handed down intact, Kingshaven could not change.

But if the days followed each other in peaceful monotony, happy in having no history, they were not idle days. There were the seasons, with their planting and reaping. There were the overseers to be watched and the Negroes to be cared for. There were the innumerable aunts and uncles and grandparents and cousins out to the fourth and fifth degrees, dining and teaing and visiting from house to house, and keeping kindly and conscientiously abreast of each others' affairs. There were friends coming and going from the outside world, and all manner of simple, plentiful hospitality to be used toward them. There were books and flower gardens and beautiful kinds of embroidery and important kinds of sweetmeats; for there were noted housekeepers, after the prodigal Southern fashion, in this town, whose recipes for certain things were of a wide and enduring reputation, such as the making of exquisitely carved orange preserves and the various ways of preparing crab and terrapin. Then there were missions, foreign and domestic, and politics, growing darker and more lurid as the years drew toward the furnace of the War of Secession.

No, Kingshaven had no desire to change, not even when the rising generation declared it to be no more lively than average ditch water. They were young and ignorant, and did not know when they were well off. A proposition they agreed to in after years.

And in this peaceful town one place seemed more peaceful than all the rest. It was a corner room on the side of a big house that was turned away from the bay-like river which gave the town its name of Kingshaven. For old Mrs. Bullen, who was the daughter and mother and grandmother of one of the largest clans in the place, dreaded thunder storms as she dreaded nothing else in life, and as the storms generally came from the bay side of the town, her room had been selected with regard to her fears. Of the four large windows, two looked across the side yard to a narrower blue water known as "Backriver," and the other two opened down to an upper piazza that looked out over the front garden and gate, beyond which was the "Green," a large, open space owned by the Bullens, and kept vacant for the sake of privacy.

The room itself, which would have held at least two ordinary rooms, was wainscoted from floor to ceiling and painted white. The narrow, high mantelpiece, under which yawned a cavernous fireplace bricked red, was also painted white, and supported some tall silver candlesticks standing inside of tall glass shades; the fender and dogs and tongs and shovel were all very big and shiny, as indeed was everything in that airy and comfortable, but extremely simple, apartment. The floor was covered with white matting; the bedstead, the windows, the couches, and the high-backed, stuffed armchair in which Mrs. Bullen always sat, were all curtained and covered with light, flowered chintz, and trimmed with knotted fringe. A glass-fronted bookcase on legs, and with a flap for writing, and some high-shouldered, mahogany chairs, completed the furnishing.

Old Mrs. Bullen, small and fair, sat in her armchair, with her white hands folded in her lap. Her silver hair, rippling down over her temples, was covered by a white muslin, high-crowned, widow's cap tied close under her chin; a white kerchief was crossed on her breast over a plain black frock; her little feet, encased in the finest stockings, were in the lap of a Negro maid who was seated on the floor, and who rubbed them with a slow, soothing motion. At the corner of the hearth, also on the floor, was seated another Negro maid, holding in her hand a flat red brick, which from time to time she dipped into a little wooden piggin of water at her side and rubbed slowly on the hearth, the process by which it was kept smooth and red. She was resting from her labors now, however, for near a window sat Miss Sophia Bullen, reading from the Psalms for the day:

"For he commandeth, and raiseth the stormy wind, which lifteth up the waves thereof. They mount up to the heaven, they go down again to the depths; their soul is melted because of trouble."

Mrs. Bullen straightened herself in her chair. "Sophia," she interrupted, "is not this steamboat day?"

"Yes, mamma," closing the book on her finger.

"And your brother George has gone down to Poonah! Why did I not remind him that it was steamboat day? · Suppose the steamboat should run into his boat?"

"There can be no danger, mamma," Miss Sophia answered, quietly, this being, like the thunderstorms, an old and well-established anxiety, "the river is so wide, and you can see the smoke of the steamboat so long before it comes."

"Did he take any of his sons with him?" Mrs. Bullen went on.

"Yes, I think Georgie and Jack went with him."

"Sophia, please call the boy John; I cannot bear Jack. Maria Cathcart's coachman is Jack." Then to the maid: "Put on my slippers, Myra, and you go over to Miss Ellen's, and give my love and ask who Massa George took with him and when he expected to come back. And,

Myra," as the girl reached the door, "tell Caesar to send Minty's Joe down to Backriver landing, to watch for the steamboat and to look for your Massa George's boat. I am really very uneasy."

There was silence in the room after this, save for the shaking of the green Venetian blinds, which were partially closed, subduing the glare of summer light and rattling pleasantly in the south wind. Presently Mrs. Bullen shifted her position a little and shook her head.

"I am really uneasy," she said, "steamboats are such dangerous things. I shall never forget my journey on one to see Cicely when her daughter Esther was born; it was most disagreeable. I never approved of public conveyances for ladies, never! You meet so many strangers—really common people! I did not lift my veil once during the journey, except when I was in my stateroom, when my maid, your Mawm Rose, brought me my food. And I could not bring myself to eat anything but eggs and potatoes, things protected by skins and shells. It was most trying."

The old lady rose and walked to one of the windows that looked toward Backriver, as if to recover from the thought of the iniquity of public conveyances. She stood there for a moment, then began to walk slowly up and down the room, with her hands clasped behind her.

"You must finish my reading later," she went on, to her daughter. "I am too much agitated to listen farther; and you may go on with the hearth, Judy; the sound is not unpleasant. And Phoebe, I wonder where she is?"

"The flat came from Broadoak plantation this morning," Miss Sophia answered, "and she is seeing to the things being put away."

"To be sure; I had forgotten that," and the old lady continued to walk up and down slowly, while Miss Sophia, taking up some hemstitching, worked diligently.

There was silence again for a little while, save for the monotonous scraping of Judy's brick and the rattling of the blinds in the wind.

"It was what you read about the storm in the Psalms, Sophia; it made me nervous," Mrs. Bullen said at last. "Forgive my stopping you. Will you go on now, my dear, and read something soothing? The ninety-first Psalm always quiets me; my life has been so sheltered and so blessed that it makes me afraid! And that really seems a lack of faith. Stop rubbing, Judy, and listen. These are beautiful and true words that Miss Sophia is going to read; try to understand them, girl. Read slowly, my daughter."

She paused by a window while Miss Sophia read, and as she finished, Mrs. Bullen repeated: "'He shall give his angels charge over thee.' Think of that, Judy,"—to the Negro girl,—"angels to have charge over you, that is, if you love God. Do you love God, Judy?"

"I dunno, missis."

"Do you obey, Judy—do all you are told to do?"

"I dunno, missis, ef I do all, but I try fuh do all, 'ceppen w'en Aunt Aggie bodder me."

"Then you love God, Judy, for to obey is to love, and God will bless you, girl."

"T'enky, missis."

Here Myra reappeared. "Miss Ellen say, 'e say Massa George is to git back 'fo' sundown; en' 'e sen' 'e love, en' say Massa George en' Massa Jack is gone 'longer Massa George."

"Very well; but you must say Massa John, Myra, not Massa Jack; I don't like it. Now take your sewing. Miss Phoebe wants those wristbands finished today." And Myra retired to a low chair near a window where there was a basket and some work.

After the early dinner Mrs. Bullen's anxiety as to the return of her son increased to the extent of putting her to bed. It was a needless anxiety, but an habitual one, so much so that no one ever argued with it, and Mrs. Bullen felt no compunction in succumbing to it. Miss Sophia stood at one of the side windows that commanded Backriver, watching and listening for her brother's boat, while Mrs. Bullen, looking more fragile than ever among the folds and frills of white linen that encompassed her in the great bed, waited anxiously. There was a song that Philip, the stroke, always made the oarsmen sing as they neared the town:

"To my mawsa en' my missis,
Goin' home, goin' home.
To my wife en' my chillun,
Goin home, goin' home.
To my sleep en' my res',
Goin home, goin' home.
To my Lawd en' my Master,
Goin' home, goin' home."

One voice scaling high, the deep refrain booming in between each line, the rhythmic stroke of the oars, and the dash of the waves filling out the measure. It would sound clearly a long way across the water, and it was for this that Miss Sophia listened.

"Don't you hear the singing yet, Sophia?" Mrs. Bullen asked from the midst of her frills and pillows. "They will be singing old Anthony's song, 'Going Home.' It seems to sound so far! They sang it when my father died. Anthony rowed stroke for my father, and he always called 'Going Home' his town song; and Philip rows stroke now, and he is old Anthony's son. Anthony was my father's favorite servant; Caesar was another. Caesar will not live much longer now, he is so old. Do you give Caesar his brandy every day, Sophia?"

"Yes, mamma, with my own hands, and I read his Bible to him every day. I see to it that he is thoroughly comfortable."

"I know, my dear, only I like to make sure; he has been a faithful servant, he and Anthony, dead so long ago! Ah me, how far away it all seems! When my father was dying, he sent for his drivers from his plantations and gave them their orders. He would never have overseers; he did not trust them, and he had to pay a fine for each place every year because of it; but he preferred to select his most trustworthy Negroes for drivers, and to overlook them himself. And your father has never changed the custom; he has never put an overseer on one of the Tremelstoun places, nor has your brother George; but Georgie, I'm afraid, will be different. Well, I shall be gone by that time. Do you hear the old song yet, Sophia?"

"No, mamma, not yet."

"In his last illness my father was brought up from Poonah in the *Big Sally* his twelve-oared boat, and he made the hands sing that song—that very song. In the middle of it, Anthony drew in his oar, and knelt, crying, at the foot of the mattress where my father lay: 'Oh, me mawsa, doan' go an' lef' Antinny—doan' go, doan' go!'"

"I think that was the first thing that made my father realize his condition. Only the day before he had flown into a fury with the doctor because he had warned him of his extreme danger. My father had a tremendous voice, and he roared at the doctor: 'What do you mean by saying such a thing as that, sir? Send your bill to my factor, and don't let me see your face again!' The doctor was an old friend, and of course did not heed him, and he persuaded father to come up to town the next day.

"I was young then, my dear, and I was inexperienced, and consequently very brave,—life has taught me better,—but when Anthony fell down at my father's feet like that, I saw a tremor go over his whole body. He lay quite still for a moment; then he held out his hand to Anthony. 'God's time must be our time, Anthony,' he said. 'I'm going home now, where all have gone before me but your little Miss Polly,' and he laid his hand on mine as I sat on the mattress beside him, 'and I expect and charge you—every one of you—to be faithful to her as long as she lives.' Then Anthony held up his hands as he knelt in the boat. 'I answer fuh all, mawsa,' he said, 'en' 'fo' Gawd, we'll stan' by little missy—'fo' Gawd!'

"And they have, most faithfully. Philip and Scipio were in that boat, and Sam and Will, mere boys they were; and old Caesar—he will not live much longer.

"My father died a few days after that, just at sunrise. Anthony had brought his blanket in and was lying on the floor near the door. Caesar was father's body-servant, but Anthony crept in and stayed there all night. At dawn father asked him, 'When will the tide turn, Anthony?'

"'At daylight, mawsa.'

"'Is it a full tide, Anthony?'

"'A big spring-tide, mawsa, clean ober de landin'.'

"'A full tide,' my father said, and raised himself to look out of the window. 'A brimming tide, and my soul will go out with it.'

"Then Anthony called up the hands, and in the dawn they stood outside, under the windows, and sang, 'Going Home.' Father ordered them all in, and all the other servants came in, too—into this very room. He said good-bye to them all; then his mind seemed to wander a little, for he began talking to his mother, and repeated the fifty-first Psalm all through, just as his mother had done when dying. And when he said 'Amen' he held up his hands like this, and all the Negroes said 'Amen!' It made a great sound, and all the hounds in the yard began to bay. He listened, then smiled to himself. After a moment he looked up at his brother, standing there. 'We've swum Broadriver together, Bob,' he said; 'we need not fear the river of death. No, daughter,' I had caught his hand in mine, 'I'm not afraid. I have not been all good, but I have loved the Lord, and I've been a gentleman.' The sun flashed in, a wind swept by me, and his soul was gone! My father, my dear father!"

Miss Sophia stood quite still by the window. She so loved the old story and the teller—and now she listened for the same old song. The sun was setting, and a red glow was spreading itself over the silent, flat land; the water was turned to the color of blood, and every leaf to the semblance of gold.

The silence was unbroken save for the occasional sound of the soft, flat voices of the Negroes in the yard or the stamping of the horses in the stables.

Then, faint and far away, there came a throb in the air, scarcely more than a sob or a sigh, but Miss Sophia bent her head to listen. Was it old, dead Anthony's song?

Presently, on a wave of wind came the ghost of a sound, surely the refrain of a boat-song, but was it the one for which she was listening? It faded away entirely; a bend in the river or a denser growth of woods had shut it off. Again there swept by on the wind a vibration that might have been anything; then suddenly, faint and far off, but distinct, she heard the booming refrain: "Going home, going home!" She did not speak to her mother at once; she waited a little while; now she could distinguish the words—now a black line shot out from behind the last bend into the wide sweep of the river.

"I see Brother George's boat, mamma," she said. "If you listen, you can hear them singing," and coming to the bedside, she smoothed the perfectly smooth pillows on which her mother rested. "They are quite near now."

"Yes," and Mrs. Bullen raised herself a little, "yes, thank God! the same old song. I can hear the oars in the rowlocks. Now—there, they are landing—hear the hounds! And George's voice—dear fellow, how like he is to my father! Not so tall; my father stood six foot three. George is only six foot two. God bless him and spare him, my boy, my only boy!"

MISS MARIA'S REVIVAL

Religion sat easily in Kingshaven, but was by no means neglected. The old church had been added to more than once, until at last it partially covered the grave of the first John Tremelstoun, who might have been called the founder of the town. But it could scarcely be said that religious enthusiasm had caused the building to be enlarged; it had to grow a little in order to accommodate the population, which, though it increased only naturally, yet did increase, and there being no rival house of worship in the place, the old church had to be added to.

In the thirties, however, there was a revival; it could be called nothing else, even though extremely quiet; for the people waked up spiritually, and in a way that went against all the teachings of the past, against all the training and customs, and that amounted almost to a scandal. Indeed, the extremely conservative people said, in so many words, that it " *was* scandalous to let a stranger and a Baptist turn the town topsy-turvy." Nevertheless it was done, and many who went to scoff remained to pray. The meetings were held in the Sunday-school room day after day for a week, and at the end of that time Kingshaven was a new place, and a Baptist church was projected.

This awakening was epoch-making, and superseded, once for all, the war of 1812 as the thing to date from. Indeed, the war of 1812 was scarcely ever mentioned again, and the effects of the revival were not only numerous, but apparently everlasting. Among other things, the marriage of one of the youngest and loveliest of Kingshaven's daughters to a missionary was thought to be due entirely to the arousing visit of the Baptist preacher. Not that this marriage followed immediately on the stranger's visit; far from it; the young woman had scarcely finished teething when the revival took place; but in a town as conservative as Kingshaven even so ephemeral a thing as a revival remained new for a long time. So this marriage was looked on as one of the most decided results of the revival; because, unless the environment of everybody had been spiritually changed, no one could possibly have married a missionary and have gone to live in China.

45

When all was done and said, and the girl gone, it was found that a great fillip had been given to the cause of foreign missions, and the religious papers were read far more diligently than ever before; and when letters began to appear in their columns signed by Margaret St. Clair, the papers became fashionable, and those persons who had believed in the revival and in Margaret St. Clair's marriage became more important, and assumed an "I-told-you-so" air that was to some people extremely irritating. It was thus it affected Miss Maria Cathcart, one of the aunts of the town. She remembered the days when the diocesan convention, which was the spiritual event of the year, and the races, which were the secular event of the year, were always arranged to fall together, and were most harmoniously mingled, and she had never been brought to say that it was even incongruous, much less wrong. She had disapproved entirely of the revival, and had declared that those who had announced themselves as "converted" had cast a slur on their forefathers. She, for one, required no change in her religion; those who were gone had been good people, and nobody could ever have changed *them* .

Meanwhile Miss Maria prayed very earnestly for her niece Margaret, and wrote to her regularly and lovingly; but she did not give to China; for she could not divert her charity fund from the channels in which it had always flowed, and she was not able to give more; for long division makes short provision, and if the division of the family property for generations had not in her case made short provision, it had at least made limited provision. She was not poor, for she had her comfortable house and servants, and a regular, if small, income from the family estate; she had her little carriage and her fat little horse; she could not have less; for in Kingshaven the ladies lived in almost Eastern seclusion, and never walked—except to afternoon service on Sundays, when the overfed horses and servants were supposed to need rest.

It was a pretty sight to see the whole town walking across the wide greens and down the shady streets to the old church in the middle of the churchyard, where all their dead lay under the great live oaks and swaying moss. It was not a very tidy graveyard, but it was solemn and beautiful, and it gave one a reverential feeling. Time, and the genuine faith and love of those buried there, and of those who had buried them, transformed the place, maybe, and hallowed it. People lowered their voices when they came inside the high walls, and ceased talking altogether by the time they reached the church door; and the young men who waited for the young women after service—for even in Kingshaven this thing was done—waited for them outside the big gates.

It was a pleasant day in May when Miss Maria ordered her little carriage, and told her maid Kizzy to put her cap into a covered basket and her knitting into her reticule, and had herself driven to see her cousin, old Mrs. George Bullen. To "spend the morning" was one of the habits of Kingshaven, and this was what Miss Maria purposed doing. She was very fond of her cousin Bullen; and then, Miss Sophia having a large correspondence with the outside world, and Miss Phoebe being thoroughly practical and interested in everything, Miss Maria found a morning spent there a very pleasant thing, and always came away feeling herself fully abreast of the times.

Old Mrs. Bullen sat in her armchair; Miss Sophia, in her low sewing chair, was reading aloud; and Miss Phoebe, in a higher, straighter chair, near a window, was making a cap for her mother.

"I see C..sin Maria's carriage coming across the green," she said, interrupting her sister.

"She must have a letter from Margaret."

"Possibly she has heard of this Mr. Bowers who has come," Miss Sophia answered.

"I doubt that," and Miss Phoebe rose. "I'll go down and meet her." So she did, giving orders on the way for cake and wine to be brought up to Mrs. Bullen's room; then she waited in the wide shaded doorway until Miss Maria arrived. "So glad to see you, cousin Maria," she said. "Mamma is quite well today."

"I have come to hear all the news," Miss Maria answered, as she slowly mounted the stairs. "Living alone as I do, one hears nothing. Ah, Polly, how well you are looking!" she went on, as she entered Mrs. Bullen's room. "Your daughters take such good care of you!"

"You are looking well yourself, Maria," Mrs. Bullen answered. "Take off your bonnet, my dear, and sit near me here out of the wind. What is the news?"

"Asking *me* for news! Indeed, I have come here for that very thing. Sophia has more letters than anybody in the town, and Phoebe is such a grand manager! Why, even at the sewing school her Negroes do better than any others. Heard from Cicely yet?"

"Yes; she is to send Dick and the two little girls to us very soon. And what do you hear from Margaret?"

"Nothing since I was here last; she might be dead and buried for *weeks* before *we* could hear. I never thought that I should live to see one of *my* family a missionary. You need not remonstrate, Sophia," shaking her head; "I shall *never* approve of it—*never!*"

"Have you heard of Mr. Bowers?" Miss Sophia asked.

"Bowers?"—putting down her knitting and looking over the top of her spectacles—"who is Bowers?"

"He is staying at Eliza Tremelstoun's; he has just come over from China, and is begging through the country for money; he is going to preach tomorrow morning. He came yesterday evening on the boat. No one expected him, and Cousin James *happened* to be on the *Bay,* and, seeing that he was a clergyman, he spoke to him. He had brought letters from Cousin Richard Denny, so Cousin James took him to his house."

"Of course if he had letters from Richard Denny he must be a person of some distinction," Mrs. Bullen said. "Richard is very careful in such matters."

"But a clergyman, mamma," Miss Sophia remonstrated, "would have a *right* to hospitality."

"Not without proper letters;" and Miss Maria reared her head back with much dignity. "You got that from that Baptist man, Sophia. You have never been the same since that disagreeable time when everything was upset. I have never given in to those teachings, and I *never* shall. But for that revival—and until that time I had never heard of revivals except among Negroes—my niece Margaret would never have gone gallivanting off to China on any such wild-goose chase; and I don't intend to encourage *this* man, for the first thing we know we shall have another revival on our hands, and I *do not* approve of such things."

"But you will surely go to church, Maria," Mrs. Bullen said. "If it were in the week you might stay away, but to stay away on Sunday would cause a great many remarks—it would be very disagreeable."

" *I* am anxious to meet him," Miss Sophia put in, looking out of the window with something like longing in her eyes. "I think it múst be glorious to go out and work—to spend one's life in elevating one's fellow creatures, as Margaret is doing. I—"

"Sophia!" and Miss Maria turned on her sharply. "Don't *you,* a sensible woman, get any such nonsense into *your* head. There are plenty of ordinary people to go out and save Chinese souls; ladies and gentlemen are not meant for such work."

"There is no caste in souls, Cousin Maria," Miss Sophia answered, laughing; "and there is no danger of my ever accomplishing anything. Even if I could leave mamma and Phoebe, I have no strength."

"The 'Lord's mercies are ever sure,'" Miss Maria said, decidedly; "and even your delicate constitution, Sophia, is a mercy. Polly," turning to Mrs. Bullen, "you should let this make you resigned to Sophia's delicacy. Think, if she were strong, what might happen!"

"I hope I have never rebelled, Maria," Mrs. Bullen answered, "and I hope that I should not rebel even if Sophia should go away as a missionary—but I think it would kill me."

"Of *course* it would kill you," Miss Maria assented, promptly. "If I, a maiden aunt, was almost killed when Margaret went, you, a mother, would die immediately—*immediately* . But I am sorry this man has come, and he would never have *thought* of coming to Kingshaven but for that revival, and Margaret's going out as a missionary. I wish we could have been left in peace; and perhaps the Chinese wish so, too. I am *quite* sure we should not like any one to come here and worry *us* about a new religion—I am *sure* we should not."

Miss Sophia laughed. "Cousin Maria, we have the *truth* ," she said.

"That Baptist minister did not think so," Miss Maria retorted. "It is twenty years ago now, but I remember it as if it had been yesterday how he roared out, 'Ye are dead in your sins!' And I got up immediately and left the room; that a person no one knew anything about should speak to me in that way was *insolent* . But the Chinese—what worse can Margaret say to the Chinese than that? Only I hope she has been too well brought up to roar as that man roared."

"That may all be so, Maria," Mrs. Bullen answered, gently, "but that revival did great good in the town. Think of three of our gayest young men being turned to the ministry—*think* of it! That was a great blessing."

"You can't be sure of that, Polly," Miss Maria returned; "even though they are now middleaged men, you can't be sure it was a blessing until they are dead; and, blessing or not, I did not think it was dignified to be converted by a man outside of the Church."

"But you will go to church tomorrow, Cousin Maria," Miss Sophia urged. "There can be nothing against Mr. Bowers; he is a regularly ordained clergyman."

"Well, if I go to church, it will be because it is Sunday, and I always go to church on Sunday, and not because I am the least interested in this man or his mission; I have suffered enough in that way. I never was more shocked in my life than when Margaret told me what she intended to do; but in these days people do not seem to realize what is due to their birth and position."

"Won't you have a glass of wine, Cousin Maria," Miss Phoebe asked, "and a bit of cake?"

"Yes, my dear—thank you! And, Sophia, you may right my knitting; I always drop stitches when I am excited, and I always become excited when I speak of missionaries and revivals. There, my dear, take it."

Sunday morning saw Miss Maria in her usual place in church. But there was no humility in her bearing; rather a lofty toleration and a resigned pity—presumably for those who had departed, or who might now depart, from the ways of their forefathers. She went through the service with an air of aloofness, and did not sing the hymns; and when the tall, thin stranger, with a worn, lined face, got up to preach, she turned her head aside to look out of the window—to the graves of those who had lived and died conservatively.

"Wist ye not that I must be about my Father's business?" was the text, and presently Miss Maria's eyes came in from the conservative dead and fastened themselves on a tablet to a former rector; a little later they moved on as far as the chancel railing, then gradually up the steps to the figure in the high old pulpit. Nobody saw her, for nobody's eyes seemed able to wander that day. She had brought her usual Sunday offering, which she deposited in the plate, and she spoke very little on her way from the church to the carriage, and Miss Sophia smiled to herself as she saw Miss Maria's preoccupied manner.

It was a very fine sermon, Miss Maria thought, as she ate her dinner—a really fine sermon; and a preacher like that should not be wasted on Chinese—certainly not; but of course Richard Denny would not have given him letters unless he had been a worthy person—of *course* not. She spoke to Kizzy, the girl who waited on table, and told her how thankful she should be that she was a Christian in a Christian land, and not still a poor deluded heathen, as her people were in Africa. And after dinner she went into her cool chamber and walked about with her hands behind her, thinking still of the sermon and of the blessings of Christianity. It might be very disagreeable to the Chinese to be disturbed, as she had said to Sophia Bullen the day before, but still it was good for them; it was a necessary thing—yes, quite a necessary thing; that man had shown it to be so. And that had been an uncommon sermon; the more she thought of it, the more impressed she was. How blessed to be able to preach in such a way, and how blessed to hear such preaching; how blessed she had been in all her life; how comfortable she was, and how good God had been to her; and how sure a Christian's hope was! Poor heathen! Poor Chinese! How sorry she felt for them!

She extended her walk to the front piazza, which was on the shady side of the house. How quiet and peaceful it all was, and a nice breeze from the water! Her lot had fallen in a fair place, and all who had gone before had lived in this same delightful town, and had died in this same sure faith. Up and down she walked, with her hands clasped behind her and her face filled with peace; then, in a quavering voice that was not at all true, she began to sing, "How firm a foundation." She sang it all through, rendering the last verse with much vigor, her voice quivering with excitement; then she walked hastily into her room and went down on her knees. Fervently she prayed, then rose up. Alms and prayers went together—of course they did; so, taking a key from a drawer, she opened her wardrobe, and inside of that unlocked a money-box. There was her supply in two neat piles, and she took out five dollars. Yes, she could give that much; she would take it to Sophia Bullen at afternoon service, and ask her to put it with the fund she was collecting for foreign missions. Perhaps she had been wrong in her views of missions; but of course the revival was another affair entirely, and she could never change her views of that. But the poor heathen! And again she began walking up and down the piazza in the pleasant summer weather. Poor Chinese, they had a bad climate; and Margaret had always been so good—not very sprightly, though. Perhaps she *would* help the deluded things. Poor child, she must be lonely sometimes; but God would reward her. Yes, "His mercy was ever sure." Once more she lifted up her thin, old voice, this time beginning, "When streaming from the eastern skies." There were no passers-by to hear and be amused and astonished; and if there had been, they would have said, "Only Miss Maria." So on she sang, wiping her eyes over the last verse; for, in spite of all her comforts and friends and relatives, she was very lonely sometimes. But she finished the hymn triumphantly—"To see Thy face and sing Thy praise," and at the last word she retired to her room and knelt down once more. This time her prayers were almost audible, and longer than before; then the money-box was opened and another five dollars was laid aside to be sent to Miss Sophia Bullen. Of course she could give ten dollars—a small tithe from all that God had given her.

"Praise God! praise God!" she said, aloud, and broke forth into the doxology before she reached the piazza. This time she sang quite loud and long, beginning with, "There is a fountain filled with blood." How *good* God was!—how His blessings surrounded her on every side! And she sang another hymn. How joyful she felt! She must pray again. She prayed aloud—for all her friends and relatives; for all God's children— then laid ten dollars more on the pile for Miss Sophia Bullen. What better could any one do than push forward the glorious work of converting the world, of bringing all men to her state of happiness? Think, if every one were as happy as she was this beautiful afternoon!

"Forth in Thy name, O Lord, I go"—she sang at the top of her voice, that rang through the still evening air. That was what the missionaries did; aye, all good people could do it. She was old, past sixty, but she could praise and pray and give—yes, give of her substance. Pray once more; yes, and again she went down on her knees, and afterwards laid another bill aside for missions.

"Fain would I still for Thee employ
Whate'er Thy bounteous grace has given—"
She stopped abruptly, and looked at the pile of bills—
"Good gracious!" she cried, "if I don't stop singing and praying, I shall give *all* my money!" and she pulled the bell rope violently; then, locking up the money-box and the enclosing drawer hastily, she stood still in the middle of the room, holding the key in her hand.

Presently her maid, Kizzy, appeared.

"Is you ring de bell, Miss 'Ria?" she asked.

"Yes, Kizzy, I rang. Here—I want you to take this key and keep it until tomorrow; never mind if I ask for it, you keep it. Now put out my bonnet and mantilla; it must be almost time for church."

"Ki! is you gwine chu'ch, Miss 'Ria?" the Negro asked, as she opened the wardrobe doors, which Miss Maria had closed a few moments before. "I been yeddy you sing summuch, I t'ink say you is hab chu'ch up yer—'e soun' same liker 'vival."

Miss Maria started.

"A 'revival'!" she cried. "You are foolish, Kizzy—an extremely foolish girl. A 'revival'!" She walked up and down nervously for a moment, then stopped, while the maid took off her cap and put it away and brought her bonnet. She put it on quickly, then her mantilla and gloves. Then Kizzy caught sight of the money. She looked at it a moment.

"Is you gwine leff dat money dey, Miss 'Ria?" she asked.

"No, *no*," Miss Maria answered, decidedly; "give it to me; that is to go to the heathen, Kizzy," and Miss Maria folded the bills together and slipped them into her prayer book, that went into her silk reticule. "The poor heathen. I am going to take it to Miss Sophia to send off; it is to pay the preachers to preach to them, Kizzy."

"Yes, m'am; is dat what you been singin 'bout, Miss 'Ria, gittin' yo' sperret up to gie dat money? Dat's de way, Miss 'Ria; singin' 'll sho git de sperret up; w'en we niggers gits to singin' en shoutin', we ent know what we do, but I ent t'ink say white people do dat."

Miss Maria hurried away, Kizzy's words ringing in her ears. A revival! What nonsense! Miss Sophia Bullen was trying on her spotted lace veil, that fell full over her face, when Miss Maria appeared.

"I stopped to give you this money, Sophia," she said, "for missions."

"Oh, cousin!" Miss Sophia cried, " *can* you give as much as this?" holding the bills a little away from her. "Is it not too much?"

"I don't know, Sophia," Miss Maria answered, almost indignantly, while a little color crept up her face; "but I *do* know this, that I sang and prayed until I had to lock my money-box and give Kizzy the key to keep for me. It was a most ridiculous proceeding; but that is the money, the result, and I hope it will help your cause."

Miss Sophia smiled.

"A little private revival, cousin!" she said, and kissed the old lady gently.

BALDY

Before the war, before Miss Maria left her home as a refugee, Baldy was one of the delights of Kingshaven. He was very fat and sleek and slow, and was nicknamed "Baldy" because of the absence of hair on his tail. This horse was the property of Miss Maria Cathcart, and from having been the pride of her life, he had, in consequence of this vexatious affliction, become a source of the deepest mortification.

His real name was "Prince"; then, because of his slowness, the young people dubbed him "Jog," for they declared that though Miss Maria thought he was going, because she saw Daddy Jack holding the reins and because she saw the horse moving, Prince was in reality only quietly jumping up and down in the same place.

Miss Maria was indignant, and old Jack was insulted, and looked the other way whenever he drove past the houses or carriages of these revilers. But Jog the horse was called until the hair began to drop out of his tail; then Baldy became his universal appellation.

This horse was one of the loves of old Jack's life, so to him the. misfortune that was overtaking Baldy's tail was a deep grief, and he tried every known and many unknown remedies on the offending member. To make one infallible salve he even went so far as to go to the old churchyard alone at twelve o'clock on a Friday night in the dark of the moon to gather "rabbit tobacco," which was a chief ingredient. But nothing seemed to stop the awful devastation, and at last Baldy became such a mirth-provoking spectacle that Miss Maria felt that he must be replaced. But how was she to tell Jack this?

Her nephew, who was looking for a safe horse for her, roared with laughter at the thought of her hesitation.

"Why, what can Jack say or do, Aunt Maria?"

"Of course *nothing* Miss Maria answered.

"But it will be a dreadful blow to him, Charles, a *dreadful* blow!"

"I'll call him and tell him at once," Mr. St. Clair said.

"No, oh no!" and Miss Maria raised both hands and shook her head. "Don't tell him suddenly. Poor Jack! he still hopes to cure the affliction."

After Mr. St. Clair had gone, Miss Maria began walking up and down her long, deep piazza, with her hands clasped behind her. It would have been better, perhaps, to have let Charles tell Jack, she thought; even trusted servants like Jack could sometimes be very disagreeable, and Jack *was* obstinate, very obstinate indeed. Her cousin Polly Bullen said that she spoiled her servants. The idea of Polly Bullen saying such a thing, Polly, whose Negroes were notoriously lazy and pampered, as Tremelstoune Negroes had always been! No, on reflection she was glad that she had not allowed Charles to tell the news to Jack; that would have looked as if what her cousin Polly Bullen said was true; she would tell Jack herself; she would call him in at once.

She walked briskly through the house to the back piazza, but she paused there. Under the big live oak tree that shaded the whole stableyard she saw Baldy tied, and behind him stood old Jack, platting carefully the few hairs that remained of his tail. The old man was completely absorbed in his task; his big fingers moved as carefully as if handling spun glass, and at each movement of the horse, if it were only a twitching of the skin, he paused, so fearful was he lest any sudden motion should loosen even one hair! When all was done, Jack stood off with his head a little on one side, and looked at the spindling braid contemplatively. Was it less than yesterday? He raised it once more and looked at the ends; again he let it go out of his hands slowly, almost reverently. Would it be better to leave it hanging, he pondered, or should he wrap it up again? A fly buzzed by. Jack started; Baldy might use it on flies! Might try to *switch* flies with it, and *all* might go! The thought made him almost reckless in his movements as he began rapidly to fold up the thin queue and to wrap it in a bandage of red flannel. When it was safe he stood looking at it with an "I've-done-my-best" air, that was little short of tragic.

Miss Maria turned away in silence, and went back to the front piazza.

It was a pleasant day, with the wind rippling the broad expanse of water in front, and touching into motion the waves of silver hair on Miss Maria's peaceful brow, and the tiny frills of white muslin that, lying one upon another, formed a soft, close border around her face. She looked out at the water, then down on the garden, where under the hot sun the flowers were giving out sweet odors. It was indeed a pleasant day, and one that she could have enjoyed thoroughly and peacefully, save for the annoyance caused by Jack and that poor horse's tail. It was ridiculous the feeling Jack had, perfectly ridiculous, and she could not stand it any longer. The horse looked too droll for anything; of course people would laugh—they could not help it; that barrel body on four legs, with no tail to balance the head, was ludicrous and undignified, and she could not be made the laughingstock of the town. She had not betrayed that she minded it, but she did, and this very afternoon while out driving she would tell Jack that it was for the last time. Yes, she would tell him this very afternoon; it would be a better time than now, when he was so intent on the very thing in question.

When the hour for driving came, she gave the order for the carriage more sternly than usual, and when she said to Kizzy, "Take off my cap, and bring my bonnet and mantilla," there was such determination in both voice and eye that Kizzy wondered a little, and moved more quickly than usual. Old Jack did not look happy when he drove round to the front door, for even though Baldy's tail was streaming in the wind, it made no show at all, and gave no sign of the care bestowed on it.

"Wey you gwine, missis?" he asked, when, having shut Miss Maria into the little carriage, he had taken his own seat. "Muss I dribe roun' Pigeon P'int, m'am?"

"No," Miss Maria answered, firmly; "drive round the bay and out on the shell road."

There was a moment's pause, and as the front windows of the carriage were open, Miss Maria, who was on the same level with Jack, could see that he had not gathered up the reins.

"Round the bay and out on the shell road, Jack, to the Cottage," she repeated. "Don't you hear me?"

"Yes, missis."

"Well?"

"Miss 'Ria, if we go roun' de bay, m'am," Jack answered, slowly, "enty you know say we gwine pass Mass John house wey awl dem chillun gwine laugh at we; en we gwine pass Mass George Bullen house, en awl dem is gwine laugh at we; en awl dem turrer house, same fashi'n; en I know say unner ain't gwine like *dat.*"

"Jack, your business is to *obey!*" Miss Maria commanded. "I am *shocked* that you should speak in this way! Drive on!"

Slowly, and with protest in every movement, Jack gathered up the reins; then drawing his infinite lips into a knot, he made a sound that caused Baldy to move off.

Miss Maria sat very erect in the carriage, with the expression of determination which had quickened Kizzy's steps grown strong on her face. Jack had now given her a very good opportunity for telling him of her intentions with regard to the horse. She could scold him for speaking to her in such a disrespectful way, and show him how his bad behavior was the cause of her ordering another animal. A *very* good opportunity. And alone as she was, Miss Maria shook her head, and reared it back to emphasize her thoughts. For the present moment, however, she was herself too deeply interested in watching the effect of her own progress through the town to begin her sermon; there would be a plenty of time for that once they were beyond the limits.

First they would pass the St. Clairs', her sister's family; yes, there they were, and of course laughing! A faint color came on her faded cheeks, and a light that was not faint came into her bright blue eyes. She sat very straight indeed, but no one got the benefit of her dignity, because it was a close little square carriage with glasses only over the doors and in front between her and the coachman, and though they were now all open, an outsider could have no view of any one on the back seat. Miss Maria, however, had a full view of Jack's profile, for he turned his head away from the houses, and looked out across the river. His expression was extremely sullen, and Miss Maria began to feel provoked with him. It was high time she got a new horse, if only to teach Jack a lesson; he really behaved as if *he* owned the horse!

Now they were passing George Bullen's house; yes, here again she saw all the young people laughing! And even if she had gone round Pigeon Point she would have had to pass her cousin Polly Bullen's, and all Cicely Selwyn's children would have been *there* laughing. Really, the manners of the the rising generation needed mending; *nothing* was safe from their ridicule. A misfortune such as had befallen her horse ought not to make her a laughingstock; they should remember that it *was* a misfortune.

Yes, and the William Caryls were just getting into *their* carriage, and they were smiling; it was intolerable—really intolerable! Of course if she had gone by Pigeon Point she would have escaped much of this, but she could not have respected herself.

They would soon be through the town now, and then by tomorrow afternoon she would have a new horse. She would almost have consented to a prancing steed, if by such a risk she could have changed the laughter of her friends and relatives into admiration, tinctured with a little mild envy!

The James St. Clairs' was the last house on the bay, and soon they would have passed it. They tried not to show themselves, but she knew they were peeping.

Now it was all done with; and how sweet the air was, and the great river looked so blue, and the sunlight came so red from the low western sky. Kingshaven was surely blessed—blessed in every way. So secluded, so religious, so cultivated and educated, so different from the outside world with its dreadful vulgar progress and new inventions. Richard Denny always said that after a visit to Kingshaven, he regretted the duty that kept him away from it. Yes, the quiet and the seclusion were the pleasantest things; even the steamboat twice a week was more than was desirable; it was bringing occasional excursions of very common people—very *rough* people. For one, she preferred the old days when the gentlemen used their own rowboats to go to Williamstown and Everglade; or their own wagons and carriages for traveling inland.

The thought of this inland travel brought her mind back to Baldy. They were quite out of the town now, with the shining water on one side and groves of oaks or reaches of pine on the other; the warm air was full of the smell of pines, with sometimes quite strong whiffs from the salt mud, which Miss Maria liked just as well, having grown up to it. Jack was looking straight ahead now, so that she could not see his face; but there was a droop to his high hat and a curve to his blue-coated shoulders that made Miss Maria more than suspect that he was asleep. "How careless!" she said, aloud, glad of an opening for her projected sermon, which was to end with the solemn announcement of Baldy's approaching deposition. "Suppose something should frighten the horse? Jack!"—raising her voice—"Jack, is it *possible* that you are *asleep?* Asleep, and I, your *mistress,* alone in this carriage, and entirely unprotected? I am *astonished* at you—at a man of *your* age being so reckless! Really, Jack—really, I am *shocked!*"

"No, m'am—no, missis, I ain't 'sleep, m'am," Jack protested; his head was well up now, and his shoulders straightened. "No, m'am; I 'clay I 'ain't been 'sleep; I des been steddyin'—yes, m'am."

"You *were* asleep, Jack," Miss Maria pursued, relentlessly. "You were almost nodding—yes, actually *nodding!* and at *any* moment the horse might have run away! Because he has no tail, that is no reason why he should be trusted *implicitly;* he still has four legs, and I dare say can run very briskly—*very* briskly, indeed. And I am surprised, Jack, that a person with such Christian teaching as you have had should attempt such bold deceit; I am *shocked!* And the harness, Jack, looks quite dingy. I am sure that you have not paid it the slightest attention for a long time; it needs a good rubbing—a most thorough cleaning; I am ashamed of it. It is much worse than the horse's tail, for that we cannot help, while the harness shows great carelessness and neglect. And I observed this morning that the stableyard had not been raked or swept in some time; and the cellar, too, needs cleaning out. Really, you seem to be neglecting everything, and in addition trying to deceive me, as you did just now."

"Miss 'Ria, I 'clay, Miss 'Ria, I 'ain't been 'sleep," Jack reiterated; "no, m'am, I 'ain't; en I rub de hahness good dis *berry* day—yes, m'am, dis *berry* day. En fuh de ya'd, dem boy Mingo en Moses, is fuh *dem* to rake *awl* de ya'd; I too ole fuh rake ya'd; en who *ebber* yeddy say coachman rake ya'd? None o' *my* ole Mawsa fambly 'ain't say nuttin like *dat*—no, m'am. Miss 'Ria, you know say yo' Pah 'ain't *nebber* meck no coachman rake ya'd."

"It is for *you* to make Moses and Mingo do their work," Miss Maria went on, sternly. "You have only *one* horse to take care of, and two boys to help you, and it is *shocking* that things are not in better order. Your old master would be surprised to see your carelessness, Jack, for he told me that in giving you to be my coachman he was giving me a fine boy and a faithful servant. Forty years ago that was, Jack—think of it, *forty years ago*—and then see how horrid that harness looks! Why, the overseer's harness would look as well. Forty years ago, Jack, my father gave you to be my coachman, and all that time you have been cared for, and your first wife and children, and now Kizzy and this other baby—*think* of it!"

"Yes, m'am, en I is awl w'at my Mawsa say I is—yes, m'am; en fuh de ya'd en dem boy, dey 'mos' meck me loss awl my 'ligion. I lick um, en you stop me, 'kase you say I gwine hot um, en you know say if nigger ain't lick, nigger ain't no 'count; en I cahn' meck dem boy wuck, ceppen I lick um."

"You can order them, Jack, and see that they do not stop; and besides, you do not whip them, you *beat* them, and I cannot have it. But, besides the yards, there is the cellar."

"En w'at ail de cellar, Miss 'Ria?"

"Why, it's dirty, *very* dirty. I was very much ashamed yesterday when your Mass John went in to see what I needed from the plantation; it looked horrid. Now *that* is your work, and not the boys', and you *must* see to it."

"Yes, m'am; you 'ain't say nuttin' befo' now 'bout de cellar, en I 'ain't know say 'e been dutty."

A silence ensued, while Baldy jogged along the white road, and Jack flapped the reins on his back by way of encouragement. There was no other ground for faultfinding that Miss Maria could think of, and she felt somewhat at a loss, seeing that she had not yet driven Jack into making an excuse of Baldy's tail, as she wished to do in order to break the dreadful news to him with a plain reason behind it.

Thimp, thump; thamp, thump, Baldy pounded along, and old Jack, looking straight ahead, moved his lips as if speaking to himself. Presently he made a little grunting sound, and immediately Miss Maria began again.

"You need not grumble, Jack," she said, at a venture, and yet decidedly; "you *are* neglecting your work, neglecting it *shamefully.* Now *why* is this? You have no more to do than usual; *why* should you not do it properly?"

"I t'ink say I been doin' prop'ly, Miss 'Ria; t'ings looks des de same like dey always looks to me; en I rub de hahness dis *berry* day—yes, m'am."

"And what else have you done today?" Miss Maria pursued. "Now tell me exactly what has been your day's work."

"Well, m'am, I git up dis mawnin'," Jack began, literally, "en fus t'ing I do I milk de cow fuh Sis Lucy, 'kase she han' hot she; den I 'tend to de horse, en eat me breakfuss; den I rake in de gahden, en trim de rosebush what is runnin' roun' de muttlebush—"

"The myrtlebush?" Miss Maria interrupted. "I don't remember any rose that touches the myrtlebush."

"Yes, m'am, dat yaller-white rose is for*ebber* gittin' to de muttle bush—yes, m'am; den I rake de gahden wey I trim de rosebush, en teck of trash 'way; den I gone to de stable 'gen, to de horse—"

"What for?" Miss Maria struck in, quickly.

"Fuh gie um some water, Miss 'Ria," was answered, disarmingly; "co'se horse muss drink—yes, m'am; den I gone to de kitchen fuh light me pipe, en Sis Lucy say please fuh shell de pease, 'kase she han' hot she 'gen; den Kizzy git bex, en say if I gwine wuck, I muss wuck fuh she; den I come 'way, 'kase I know say if I wuck fuh Kizzy one time, I ain't *nebber* gwine git done, en I gone to de stable 'gen—"

"What for?" Miss Maria demanded, with increased eagerness.

"To git 'way from Kizzy, m'am," Jack returned, with unmistakable earnestness. "Miss 'Ria, you ain't know dat nigger like I know um; heaper time I sorry say I married Kizzy, 'kase Kizzy bodder me to de't'—yes, m'am. Miss 'Ria, Kizzy is a tarryfyin' gal, en I gone to de stable kase I know say Kizzy ain't gwine come dey, 'kase I done tell um say if 'e come to de stable I gwine teck dat carriage whip en lick um, so 'e 'fraid."

"And what did you do in the stable?"

"Dat is de time I rub de hahness, m'am."

"And after that?"

Jack paused a moment; as long as he had served his mistress he had never seen her in this inquisitorial mood, and it puzzled him; besides, his dignity was hurt that at his time of life he should be taken to task like a boy, and into his next answer there crept a note of impatience.

"Den I gone to me dinner, Miss 'Ria—please Gawd, I hab to eat!"

"Of course," Miss Maria assented; "and you know quite well, Jack, that I never grudge my servants anything that they need—I am a good mistress, Jack, and you know it; but I must find how it is that you do not get time to keep things in good order. Now, what did you do after dinner?"

"I res' a minute, Miss 'Ria, tell I smoke me pipe; den I gone to see what Moses en Mingo is doin', m'am, en meck um clean de stable; den I gie de horse some mo' water; den I unwrop 'e tail—"

"Ah!" cried Miss Maria, with a long breath of relief, as at last she caught the excuse she had been pursuing. *"That* is it, Jack, that is the root of *everything* ! At last you acknowledge it—the horse's tail. You spend *so* much time on the horse's tail, Jack, that *everything* in the yard and garden and cellar looks *wretchedly,* and I am continually mortified; and I tell you *plainly* , Jack, that I cannot put up with it any longer. Then this afternoon you were quite disrespectful about driving down the bay, and quite in a bad temper about it; it has really reached a point beyond my patience."

"Miss 'Ria," poor Jack cried, "I 'ain't plait dis horse tail but two time today—"

"I watched you myself, Jack, and saw you spend quite a half-hour on it; then you are sullen and disagreeable if people laugh—"

"Yes, m'am," Jack struck in, "it do hot my feelin's, Miss 'Ria, when de people laugh at we; you Pah wouldn't like it, Miss 'Ria; en you ain't to say like it, nurrer; en I ain't usen to see *my* Mawsa fambly laugh at—no, m'am, I *ain't.*"

"Of *course* not!" Miss Maria cried, with a ring of triumph in her voice—" of course not, and so I must get another horse."

To Miss Maria's excited mind the universe seemed to pause for a moment—even Baldy's stolid trot seemed "far away on alien shores," and the wind and the water had ceased to sound—one moment, then Jack laid the reins down on the dashboard and folded his hands. Miss Maria's eyes grew big with astonishment.

"Jack," she demanded, *"what* do you mean?"

"Miss 'Ria," was answered, solemnly, "I cahn' stan' it—no, m'am, I cahn' stan' it if you say dat 'gen. No, m'am, Miss 'Ria, if you say dat ting 'gen, I gwine git out dis carriage en walk home, en leff you right yer in de broad road. I cahn' stan' it, Miss 'Ria, fuh sell dis horse."

"Miss Maria clasped her hands and looked about her as if the sky had fallen. To be left alone in the carriage—alone with a horse—so far from home! She raised her eyes to the top of the vehicle. "Lord, I am oppressed!" she said, solemnly. There was silence for a moment; then Jack, with mingled feelings of awe for Miss Maria's invocation and of satisfaction for having carried his point, took up the reins once more, and they proceeded on their way.

Reaching the usual end of the drive, they turned and drove back to the town in absolute silence, Miss Maria not speaking even when Jack chose to go home by secluded back streets. But she was angry, and her thoughts were busy. Something must be done to punish Jack; such behavior could not be overlooked—but what? If she told her brother John, or her brother-in-law, or her nephew Charles, it would be looked on as a joke, and there would be the laugh against her through the whole connection. That must not be—she must manage this thing herself. She thought about it a great deal that afternoon, and when her sister came in that evening to say that Charles had secured a very fine horse for her, Miss Maria felt as if Jack's punishment had come thus quickly in answer to her prayer. Besides this divine judgment, however, she must find some way of showing her displeasure to Jack, distinctly and personally—some pointed way.

The next morning she was still undecided when Jack came to ask for the key in order to clean the cellar; then an idea came to her. She preceded him to the cellar, and opening the door, showed him what was to be done, telling him to call her when he had finished; then, going up once more to the back piazza, she began to walk up and down with her hands clasped behind her, humming to herself. Up and down, up and down, shaking her head when she was not singing, and rehearsing the words she would presently say to Jack. Sometimes her eyes would flash as she remembered the provocation; then she would smile to think what a severe lesson she would teach him. Up and down, until Jack came to say that the work was finished; then she followed him once more to the cellar. She almost relented when she saw how carefully he had done his work; evidently he was trying to please her, but it would not be right to allow his behavior to pass unrebuked.

"It looks *very* well," she said, heartily—"very well indeed; it should always look so," she went on, while Jack rearranged some jars on one of the shelves; "and you should never behave nor speak to me as you did yesterday, Jack, *never* ; and now I shall give you a little time to think it over," and stepping out briskly, she shut the door, locking Jack into the cellar.

"Miss 'Ria!" he called.

"No, Jack; you deserve it."

"Lemme out, missis."

"No, Jack."

"Miss 'Ria, I is ole man, m'am."

"And should know better, Jack."

"Miss 'Ria, how long is you gwine to keep me yer?"

"Until you are in a better mind, Jack."

"Miss 'Ria, is you gwine tell Kizzy? Miss 'Ria, if you tell Kizzy, m'am, I gwine to lick um, sho. I'll be 'bleeged to lick dat gal if you tell um dis t'ing." His voice was rising.

"I shall not tell Kizzy," Miss Maria promised. Then she went upstairs, and resumed her walk up and down the piazza.

Jack meanwhile, sitting on a box in the cellar, pondered the situation. That his mistress had outwitted him was very clear, and he rubbed his head in wonder.

"Miss 'Ria is sma't," he said, at length. "I nebber know say Miss 'Ria is sma't es dis. She ketch me in dis trap same liker fox. I nebber t'ink say Miss 'Ria would do sicher t'ing. White people is sma't, dat is de Lawd's trute. En awl my Mawsa chilluns is sma't, but I nebber know say Miss 'Ria is *dis* tricky—nebber. En if dat nigger Kizzy ebber know dis t'ing, I'll be 'bleeged to lick um, en no mistake. She'll know what she laugh at when I done wid um. Please Gawd dat gal 'll laugh out de turrer side she mout'. I dun'no what I married dat gal fuh anyhow. 'Lizer wuz a settled 'oman, en she nebber hab no swonger way, en I 'ain't good bury um 'fo' dis gal Kizzy fool me. But if she show she teet' 'bout *dis* t'ing, I'll bruck Miss 'Ria carriage whip on she back—*dat* I will—yes."

The cellar was dark and cool, and presently Jack's head went back against the wall, and a snore resounded through the room, so that he did not hear the little tumult that arose in the yard.

Miss Maria, however, held her breath for a moment. What was it the washerwoman was crying out? Fire! Good heavens! And there were the flames leaping out of the washhouse chimney.

"Kizzy!" she called. "Mingo! Moses! Lucy! Look! the washhouse is on fire! Bring water! Come and help Julia!"

Down flew Kizzy; out rushed the cook; Moses and Mingo and half a dozen smaller darkies tumbled out of the stable.

"My Lawd! it's ironin' day," cried Kizzy, "en dey ain't no water in de tubs. Wey is dat ole nigger Jack?"

"Uncle Jack in de cellar," cried the boys. Then all the Negroes rushed to the cellar.

"Come out dey, you ole tarrypin!" Kizzy called. "Enty you know say missis house is bunnin' down? Come out, come out!"

Jack was dazed with sleep, and he realized only that his young wife was rattling the door.

"You wait till I git dat carriage whip ober yo' back," he retorted.

Kizzy rushed away. "Missis," she cried, breathlessly, "Jack in de cellar, m'am, en woan come out—no, m'am."

"Bring all the water down out of the house," Miss Maria commanded. "I will see to Jack." And trembling in every limb she went down to the cellar and unlocked the door. "Jack, Jack, come quickly, the washhouse is on fire! Quickly! Kizzy is upstairs."

Jack needed no second bidding, but ran out instantly to the scene of the catastrophe. In a few moments, before Jack got there almost, it was all over, and Kizzy, rushing out breathlessly with two pitchers of water, found herself too late for anything but Jack's lofty sneers.

"Hollerin' en hollerin' 'bout one ole chimbly," he said, "scarin' Miss 'Ria to de't' for nuttin. I know say Kizzy ain't hab nuttin but mout', but I t'ink say Sis Julia en Sis Lucy is hab eye—hab eye 'nough fuh see house from chimbly." He wondered how much they knew, these women.

"I yeddy you holler so loud I t'ink say de chu'ch is bunnin'," he went on, "en come to see des one ole chimbly."

"Talk," Kizzy retorted—"talk. Dat's awl you kin do. Sleepin' in de cellar wid de do' lock. I gwine meck missis onderstan' 'bout dat—you wait."

"That will do, Kizzy," Miss Maria commanded.

"Jack, some one is rattling at the stableyard gate."

"Hullo, Jack! open this confounded gate."

"Dat's Mass Chahlie," and Jack ran to undo the fastenings.

All stood silent as Charles St. Clair rode in sitting sidewise on a bare-backed horse.

"Here he is, Aunt 'Ria," he called, "as gentle as a lamb and as strong as an ox, and with a beautiful tail warranted to last. See?"

Jack's eyes were like saucers.

"Bring out Baldy, Jack," Mr. St. Clair went on, "and let Moses ride him over home. We'll send him out to the plantation until his tail grows out again."

Somehow it was not so hard to let Baldy go as Jack had imagined, and that afternoon as he drove Miss Maria down the bay behind the fine new horse he sat up very straight, looking proudly from side to side, while Miss Maria nodded gayly to the congratulations waved in handkerchiefs and hands, and given in "nods and becks and wreathed smiles."

FAITH AND FAITHFULNESS

Early in the sixties the town of Kingshaven was surrendered and abandoned, and, on entering, the Federal army found the place deserted save for the Negroes. The people had only a few hours' notice, for they had felt quite secure behind the one small battery of light artillery at the mouth of the river. They knew nothing whatever of the warships that were approaching; but they did know that the battery was manned by the gentlemen of the town, and commanded by George Bullen, and what more could be needed?

George Bullen had warned them, and had warned the government, that the little battery would scarcely be heard by the warships; was, indeed, little more than a joke; but the government either agreed with the ladies, or was careless whether Kingshaven fell or not. So the battery retreated, and the war-vessels only waited for the tide to steam up to the town. It was during this short delay that the hegira took place, the inhabitants moving in a body, driving away in their wagons and carriages, taking with them what they could, and accompanied by many of their Negroes. By night and by torchlight they marched up to the ferry, across which they were taken in flatboats to the mainland, then, some following one road and some following another, these people, who had lived and loved and disputed, who had wept and prayed and rejoiced together for generations, bade each other farewell, and went away into a wellnigh unknown world.

Miss Maria Cathcart cast in her lot with her nephew, Charles St. Clair, as being her nearest of kin; and her little carriage and a wagon drawn by one mule brought away for her and her servants all that they could transport. In the front of the carriage, under the feet of Jack the coachman, was a basket of silver; on the seat beside him, a box of Miss Maria's caps, and another basket of ancestral candlesticks. Inside, piled all about Miss Maria, were her clothes and house linen, and in either hand she carried a cut-glass decanter. The wagon behind was driven by Kizzy, Miss Maria's maid, who was the wife of the coachman, and in it were Kizzy's little children and the children of other servants, and all that could be saved of household stuff. Behind came other carriages and wagons, and many Negroes walking with their bundles on their backs—a patriarchal procession; but Jack and Miss Maria were in the lead, because, Mr. St. Clair having to go with his company to join the army, Jack, as the oldest and most responsible Negro, had the care of the party as they journeyed to the nearest town within the Southern lines, from whence they were transported by rail to the interior.

Miss Maria and the St. Clairs took a house together, and Jack hired out the Negroes and collected the wages, and took care of the place they had rented, and things were more comfortable than could have been expected.

"Indeed, we get along famously," Miss Maria asserted; "we have everything quite decent, and Jack is a very good servant—butler, coachman, overseer, and several other things rolled into one; and Kizzy is doing admirably; yes, we are surprisingly comfortable, and I am most thankful."

One day the news came of her nephew's death—killed in Virginia. It was a dreadful blow, and the results which followed were most disastrous to Miss Maria, for her nephew's widow took her many children and went to her own parents. Jack and Kizzy declared that it was "berry ha'd fuh Miss 'Ria to be leff wid nuttin' but niggers"; but Miss Maria, who had no idea of being under obligations or of being a burden, bore it very quietly.

So the niece and the children went away, the children very reluctantly and with many tears, and Miss Maria moved into two rooms on the sunniest corner of the ramshackle old house, the owner agreeing to let her have them for a nominal rent, seeing that in the town houses were going begging.

The neighbors seemed to feel with old Jack and Kizzy that Miss Maria had been hardly treated, and became more friendly.

But worse times came: old Jack died. Kizzy and Miss Maria did everything possible, and also the doctor and the neighbors, but nothing could save him. After this Miss Maria began to feel the want of money. She sold the mule and wagon, and later her little horse and carriage; but she did it quite pleasantly, not alluding to her needs. She and Kizzy consulted as to ways and means, and Kizzy took in washing, and her little daughter Milly became Miss Maria's maid.

The surrender came, and with it came absolute demoralization. This was a black period—a blackness that involved the whole country—and

Kizzy spent much of it leaning over the back gate abusing the refugee Negroes she knew, as one after another they came to ask if she were going home. "Goin' back home!" she repeated, scornfully. "What you got down dey to go to? Who is gwine gie you bittle en close? You foolish; you t'ink say 'kase you free dese t'ings is gwine grow on de tree. No, I ain't goin'; I gwine stay right yer wid Miss 'Ria. Enty I done promise Jack say I would stay? Enty I got house yer fuh me en my chillun; enty I got fire, en close, en bittle? No, I ain't goin'. En I ain't t'ink say you would leff missis like dis; 'fo' Gawd, I ain't t'ink it!"

"Sis Kizzy, I 'bleeged to go," was the usual answer; "I cahn stay in dis po' red-clay country no longer. I des wants to smell de ma'sh one mo' time, en tas'e dem fish, en crab, en 'yster, des *one* mo' time; en I wants to feel dat good lightwood fire 'gen. I 'clay, Sis Kizzy, I des 'bleeged to go; but I cahn tell missis good-bye; dat I cahn do."

And they did not, but disappeared one by one during the week, until Kizzy alone was left. She did not tell Miss Maria all at once, but when the last one was gone she opened up the subject gradually, when, one morning, she was putting Miss Maria's breakfast on the table.

"I des wish I had a good fish fuh you, Miss 'Ria," she began—Miss Maria's breakfast was bacon and hominy. "I done yeddy Mingo say turrer day dat 'e was hongry en trusty fuh dem crab en fish, en I ain't shum f'om dat day to dis, en I spec' say 'e gone home. Mingo ain't no 'count nohow, 'ceppen somebody stan' by um awl de time en meck um wuck."

Miss Maria looked up. "You think that he has really gone home?" she asked.

"Yes, missis, I spec' 'e is, 'kase I ain't shum fuh dese t'ree day."

"Perhaps they will all go, Kizzy," the old lady said, making no motion to touch her breakfast.

"I spec' so, missis," Kizzy answered, pushing the little dish of hominy nearer to her mistress; "'kase since Jack daid, en Mass' Cha'lie is kill, de nigger ain't feel like dey's got no mawsa; en now when people tell um dey is free, den dey awl t'ink say if dey kin git back home t'ings is gwine be des like dey is always be."

Miss Maria was silent for a moment, then the light kindled in her bright old eyes, and she drew herself up. "They are very ungrateful, Kizzy," she said, "and forget that I have cared for them all their lives, and that now they ought to care for me. I hope that *you*, Kizzy, will be better behaved, for you must remember that you have lived in the house since you were two years old—indeed, your mother died *before* you were two years old—and that for more than thirty years I have had you cared for and have provided for you. But perhaps," she went on, her voice softening—"perhaps the poor things *were* homesick—perhaps they were; I am homesick myself sometimes; and, oh, my country—my poor country!"

And Miss Maria put her handkerchief, a piece of old linen, to her eyes and wept; and Kizzy, throwing her apron over her head, knelt down by her mistress's chair and sobbed too, begging pardon all the time for crying in Miss Maria's presence. But it was not long that Miss Maria wept—the tears of old age are hard, but they are few—and presently she wiped her eyes and blew her nose, which seemed to recall Kizzy's self-control, and rising, she took the dishes of bacon and hominy off the table.

"Dis is done git cole, Miss 'Ria," she said; "dis will do fuh me en de chillun; I'll git you some hot."

So the old lady ate her breakfast, and when she had finished, Kizzy beat up the cushions in the chair by the fire and brought Miss Maria her books for daily reading, then went away to her washing.

After this it seemed to Miss Maria that the whole country had dissolved, and her cheerfulness wavered a little. If she could have written to any one to ask for news, or have known where her kinsmen were—whether in prison, or killed in the last battles, or gone with the despairing to Mexico—if any one had sent her a line or a word, it would have been a great help; but there was such confusion that no one seemed to know anything certainly, and she knew nothing at all. For a few days she was depressed, then she took herself in hand and gave herself a good scolding. Where was the faith of her youth? Why should it fail now, "when the bread she had cast on the water in Kizzy's direction was returning to her in such substantial fashion"? This thought made her laugh a little, and she began to walk up and down her two bare rooms and to sing her hymns as bravely and as badly as in her old Kingshaven home; and Kizzy, hearing the quavering voice, paused over her washtub to wipe her eyes.

Money became more scarce, so Kizzy began to work for barter—milking for a share of milk, cooking for food, and washing for a return in wood. Meanwhile Miss Maria got one or two notes, which told of nothing but death and disaster, of privation to the extent of need, and of great mortality among the uncared-for Negroes. Again Kizzy came in and knelt by her mistress's chair to weep.

"We's better off wey we is, Miss 'Ria," she comforted; "en I tell dem nigger dey is foolish. Mingo is des been gone 'bout t'ree munts, en now 'e daid—po' Mingo!"

"And just think," Miss Maria said, "Mass George Bullen has just got home; he has been so ill; and Miss Phoebe has been *cooking*. Yes, Kizzy, God has been very good to us, for at least we have enough to eat and are in good health. And, Kizzy, think of your Mass Tom St. Clair ploughing in his field barefooted! Think of it—educated in Europe, and owning three plantations! Poor fellow! poor fellow! And his wife cooking and washing. Kizzy, it is *awful*!"

"Yes, missis, it's berry bad, m'am," Kizzy answered; "en we's better off right wey we is; en ef dem triflin' niggers had stay wid *we*, dey is been better off too; 'kaze who know wey dey is gone now dey is daid? Nobody kin say, 'kaze dey ain't do right in leffin' we up yer by we seff. No, dat ain't been right, en I tell 'em so 'fo' dey gone; en Gawd ain't want 'em ef dey ain't do right—no, m'am, 'e ain't. Please Gawd, somebody will come en git we bime-by—please Gawd."

So Miss Maria and Kizzy set themselves to wait patiently for this "bime-by"; but again for several days Miss Maria could not sing.

Cold weather came. Cracks were everywhere in the old house, and curtains and carpets nowhere. The big chimneys took a vast quantity of wood even to heat them so that they would draw, and Kizzy was dismayed. At length she and Miss Maria came to the conclusion that all the furniture had better be moved into the warmest room; then, by having a fire always, Miss Maria might keep comfortable.

"If you ketch a cole, missis, it'll be berry bad, m'am," Kizzy agreed; "en now ebbrybody is so po' dat nobody ain't gwine t'ink nuttin' 'bout yo' baid bein' in de pahlor."

It was dreadful to live in one room, Miss Maria thought; but how much better than Tom St. Clair ploughing barefooted! And when the move was made she declared that the parlor looked much nicer for having everything in it, and it was much more sociable to have things closer to her—even poor sticks of furniture.

But Kizzy found less and less work, and she did not know what to do unless she hired out by the month. A place was offered to her by a new family who had just come to town—a clergyman and his wife. Kizzy had been scouring for them, and from her present standpoint they seemed to her to be very rich. They offered her good wages if she would come and do all the work, and she might spend the nights at her own home. She had a week in which to decide; but how could she do

it—how could she leave Miss Maria and her own little children all day?
She could take the youngest with her, but that would leave two besides
Milly at home, and how would they keep warm?

The day before Kizzy's answer was due was cold, and Kizzy had no
work at all. She thought a long time while she mended various articles,
sitting on the floor by the fire in Miss Maria's room. At last she said:

"Is you glad fuh simme settin' yer en sewin', missis?"

"Yes," Miss Maria answered, looking up from her book; "it seems
quite proper, Kizzy; but how is it you are not working today?"

Kizzy waited a moment, then said, slowly, "I 'ain't got no wuck, Miss
'Ria, en I cahn git none."

"No work!" Miss Maria repeated; then, after a pause, she sat up
straighter in her chair and looked down on Kizzy. "Why, girl," she
said, "what does this mean?"

"Miss 'Ria—I'clay, Miss 'Ria, dat is de trute," Kizzy asserted, so
mournfully that she showed all the whites of her eyes. "De trute is de
light, Miss 'Ria, en dat is de trute; I try en I try, en I cahn fine nuttin'
to do; no, m'am, 'ceppen—" But here Kizzy broke down, and threw
her apron over her head, crying.

"Well," Miss Maria said, "excepting where?"

"Scuge me, missis; I know 'tain't no manners to cry, but I cahn he'p
it, Miss 'Ria."

"Of course I'll excuse you," Miss Maria answered, rather sternly, for
she did not know what to expect; "but what does it all mean?"

Kizzy wiped her eyes: Miss Maria's sternness quieted her.

"I mean, Miss 'Ria, dat I kin git wuck, but I hafter go 'way from
home to do it, m'am. I kin come yer to sleep at night, but I muss go
by daylight in de mawnin', en come home after da'k—yes, m'am."

"Well?" said Miss Maria.

"Well, m'am, dey won't be nobody yer but Milly, Miss 'Ria, en de
two nex' chilluns—I'll teck de younges' one wid me."

"Well?" Miss Maria said again.

"En who's gwine teck care o' you, Miss 'Ria, en git yo' dinner hot,
m'am?"

"Milly," Miss Maria answered.

"En who's gwine teck care o' de chillun, m'am?"

"Milly."

"En how is dey gwine keep wa'm?"

Kizzy's voice was low, and her eyes were fixed on her mistress's face
like the eyes of a dumb creature, and Miss Maria looked at Kizzy. This
was the critical point. To have a fire out in Kizzy's room for these two

children would be dangerous as well as expensive; to send them to the house of another Negro would be expensive also, and not altogether safe; yet to expect that they should sit on the floor in Miss Maria's room was to Kizzy far more presumptuous than to expect that they should sit on the floor of heaven. A dozen little Negroes might come into her mistress's room to be taught if Miss Maria pleased, or to serve Miss Maria, but for her to *ask* Miss Maria to let her children stay there all day while she was gone seemed to her to be preposterous—to be reversing things and asking Miss Maria to serve her! It had somewhat this look to Miss Maria too for a moment, then she saw an escape from the dilemma. In Kingshaven she had taught all the little Negroes who lived in her yard, every day, hymns and such things; so to teach these children would be only to keep up old customs. It might entertain her, would surely do them good, and at the same time save appearances and embarrassment both for her and for Kizzy. Still looking in Kizzy's eyes, she said:

"They may stay in here, Kizzy, and I will teach them; Milly shall give them their dinner in the kitchen. It can be easily managed, I think."

And so it was. Kizzy cooked food for the day, and left that for the children in the kitchen, and that for Miss Maria in the cupboard; and the children, spotlessly clean, waited in the back room until Miss Maria had dressed and breakfasted; then Milly, with stern disciplinary whispers, brought them into Miss Maria's room, and put them into a warm corner, from which coigne of vantage they, sitting cross-legged like little black idols, stared at their mistress, who was a part of their faith; or, with eyes that turned so far round in their sockets as to seem all white, they watched Milly as she pattered about putting things to rights. And Milly developed so wonderfully under their admiring gaze, and skipped about so nimbly and assuredly on her batter-cake feet and slim little legs, that Miss Maria, looking at her over the top of her spectacles, told her she would equal her mother some day. Whereupon Milly fizzed into mirth, like a siphon of Vichy, and the little black idols in the corner rolled their eyes from Milly round again to their mistress, and fastened them there.

The weather grew colder; the big chimney in Miss Maria's room "eat wood," and Kizzy's wages made very scant provision. One thing after another Miss Maria said that she could do without. Butter was not at all necessary, nor coffee, nor sugar; milk was quite enough for her to drink. Then lights were not necessary; Miss Maria could do her reading in the day, so that for the evening the firelight would do. Fuel, too, must not be burned with any view to a special blaze for the sake of light. Sitting alone in the dusk seemed to double the desolation, and putting on two shawls and her rubbers for warmth seemed to deepen the poverty; but it could not be helped; and every evening, as Kizzy came in to make Miss Maria comfortable for the night, to bank up the precious fire and to take the children away, she seemed to bring a little freshness in, a little cheer; and as she rubbed her mistress—in an old-fashioned way, it is true, but soothingly—Miss Maria would say:

"We are one day nearer to going home, Kizzy; for somebody will surely come to fetch us."

"Yes, missis," Kizzy would answer, "somebody will come en git we bime-by."

Then with a sigh and a smile Miss Maria would go to sleep as quietly as a child, and Kizzy would steal away.

One day, in going his rounds, the new clergyman heard of Miss Maria—of her age, her loneliness, her poverty, and her cheerfulness. It made a moving story, and impressed the good man; but in the faithful, humble servant "Kizzy" he did not for one moment recognize his wife's dignified treasure, who had introduced herself as Mrs. Kezia Adams. He was full of the story, and at supper he retailed it to his wife, who was also deeply moved. They did not observe that Kizzy left the room hastily, nor that they had to ring twice before she returned, nor that when she did come her eyes were flashing, and her head was held unusually high. Indeed, they were so busy planning relief for Miss Maria that they did not observe Kizzy at all; but very little escaped Kizzy of the plans they made to send the stores they would buy to Miss Maria before they called, so that she would not trace the gift to them. The things should be sent in the morning, and they would call in the evening.

"Think of her having so little wood, and no lights at all, not even one candle!" Mrs. Jarvis said. "How pitiful to sit alone in the dark! I wonder if she would use a stove; but these Southern people are so devoted to their open fireplaces that I doubt if she would; yet these big chimneys are dreadfully wasteful."

Mr. Jarvis shook is head. "To send a stove," he said, "would be to tell her who sent the things, and she might not accept them. Feeling runs high, you know; I meet it at every turn—poor people!"

Kizzy almost dropped a dish at this juncture. *Her* white people *poor*! No deeper insult could be offered to ex-slaves than the suggestion that their former owners had not been born in the purple and with the wealth of Croesus, and Mr. Jarvis unwittingly had offered this insult. Kizzy was in a fury.

That night she took an armful of wood. "If he t'inks I is po' buckra nigger," she muttered, vindictively, "I'll do like po' buckra nigger; en if he is so rich, Gawd knows *I* ain't gwine let *my* missis look po' 'fo' *him*—not *me.* Any nigger 'll hab better manners en *dat.*" But Kizzy kept the secret of the coming stores to herself, for she had caught the idea that Miss Maria might refuse them.

The next morning there was the most marked change in Miss Maria's room; there were extra touches everywhere, a much large fire than usual, and the two little black idols had disappeared.

Gone to help their mother, Milly said.

Just as Miss Maria finished her reading, the front door was heard to open and steps sounded in the hall. Miss Maria waited, thinking some friend had come in; then hearing the door close again, she sent Milly to investigate; then following herself, found a large basket and an uncovered box filled with all sorts of bags and bundles, addressed to Miss Maria Cathcart.

Miss Maria and Milly stared; then Miss Maria said:

"It is a present. How kind!" Her face lighted up like a child's. "You can't move the basket or the box, Milly," she went on, "but you can bring in the packages." And forthwith Milly began work; and sometimes running and sometimes staggering, and at all times puffing with excitement and delight, she transported bundle after bundle to the table in the back room, Miss Maria walking back and forth with her, touching and pinching each thing to guess what it might be.

"A very handsome present indeed," Miss Maria said, when everything was at last on the table—"a *very* handsome present. Crackers; very good. Here, Milly. Coffee—butter—grits—rice—gingersnaps. Her, Milly. Tea—flour—candles—pickles—nuts. Here, Milly. Sugar—lump-sugar. Here, Milly. Cheese. Here, Milly. Bacon—lard—raisins. Here, Milly." By this time Milly was holding her apron. "And wine," Miss Maria finished. "A very handsome present. I shall put some in the de-canters at once. Two bottles of wine. Suppose I had not saved the de-canters! A glass of wine and a cracker will be very comfortable at twelve o'clock—*very* comfortable indeed; quite like old times. Get the scissors, Milly."

So the cork was poked out of one bottle, and the contents divided between the two decanters, which had stood on the high mantelpiece for safety. Miss Maria placed them on the table, with a plate of raisins, a plate of nuts, a plate of crackers, and a plate of gingersnaps, and her

only wineglasses, three in number and three in shape; then she stood
off and surveyed it; and Milly, standing on one foot in her excitement,
surveyed it too, and smiled an ear-to-ear smile.

"Very comfortable," Miss Maria repeated, nodding her head at the
table. "Put on more wood, Milly."

"Missis!" Milly cried, returning with a log in her arms, "dey is a big
new pile o'wood in de back ya'd—yes, m'am."

Miss Maria stepped briskly to the window. There it was, a *very* large
pile—the biggest pile she had seen since leaving home. The old lady's
face beamed as she folded her hands together.

"God is good," she said, softly, "*very* good. Now Kizzy can return to
her proper duties. Yes, with all that has been provided, we can live decently once more. Praise the Lord!" She felt like sending Milly off immediately to call her mother home, but her eyes falling on the boxes of
candles, she thought of something she wished to do at once. The candles must be put into the candlesticks—for what else had she saved
them? So from the mantelpiece and the closet all the candlesticks were
taken; and Milly, seated on the floor, rubbed them with a woollen rag,
munching the while from her store of confections piled away in the corner; and Miss Maria, hunting up a piece of white paper from around
one of the packages, cut little frills with which to make the candles
stand firm in the sticks.

It was a very busy day indeed, Miss Maria scarcely wishing to stop
for dinner; but by the afternoon the candles were all put into the sticks,
with the jaunty little frills about the base of each, and were arranged—
and every few moments rearranged—about the room.

The big branches were on the table, where the wine and other re-
freshments still stood; the smaller branches were on the mantelpiece,
flanked by two straight candlesticks; the others were put about in various places, for Miss Maria had decided that she would have a plenty of
light. The candles had been sent to give her light and comfort and
pleasure, and as soon as it was dark she would gain all this by lighting
them. Things had been very bad, but they had taken a turn for the better, and she was weary of darkness and loneliness. In the back room she
had stuck the candles into bottles, and Milly had made a fire in there
too, so that her mistress could go in and out without fear of taking
cold. Miss Maria felt as if she had been keeping house once more; and
all being arranged to her satisfaction, she waited anxiously for the evening and the illumination. By five o'clock she and Milly were in a glow
of light. Fine fires were blazing on both hearths, and Miss Maria was
walking up and down singing, when a knock came at the outer door.

Not a remarkably loud knock, but one that made Milly spring to her feet and Miss Maria stop in her walk. The neighbors usually came to the inner door, and this knock, being on the outer door, was a stranger's, and being loud, was a man's.

"Put another log on the fire, Milly," Miss Maria said, as she stepped over to the glass to see if her cap and kerchief were straight. "It must be the new clergyman. And sweep up the hearth, quickly, before you go to the door." Then Miss Maria took from a box filled with dead rose leaves one of the squares of old linen which she had hemmed for pocket handkerchiefs, and holding it by the middle, resumed her seat, while Milly put away in the corner the bunch of feathers that served as a hearth broom.

To Milly and to Miss Maria the room looked very fine and cheerful, while to the strangers entering it seemed inexpressibly incongruous and pathetic.

Miss Maria rose and stepped forward to meet them, bowing graciously, and extending her delicate hand as they introduced themselves as Mr. and Mrs. Jarvis. There was wonder in their eyes, and putting it down to the brightness of her apartment, Miss Maria was pleased that they should be surprised.

"It has been such a cloudy day," she said, cheerfully, when they were seated, "that I lighted the candles early, and lighted them all. I enjoy light and warmth, and am so thankful to have it; of late it has not been plentiful"—and she smiled a little to herself at the mild way in which she had stated her case.

"It looks very cheerful indeed," Mr. Jarvis answered, slowly, while Mrs. Jarvis, suffering "pain and grief" for the wild waste she saw, looked on the solidity of the candlesticks and not on the candles, and on the sparkle of the old decanters rather than on the wine. "A kind friend has sent me quite a batch of nice things," Miss Maria went on "Won't you try a glass of wine and a cake?" She rose and filled the glasses; but Mrs. Jarvis declining, the ceremony was between Mr. Jarvis and herself.

"Your very good health, sir," she said, with a bow.

"Your very good health, madam," Mr. Jarvis returned, and felt as if he had suddenly reverted into his own grandfather.

"Things have been very bad for everybody," Miss Maria continued as she sipped her wine; "but I knew that they would get better, and they have. I have always been of a very hopeful and cheerful disposition. I had begun to think too much so"—nodding gayly—"and that was being chastened for it; but now you see how little good the cha tening has done"—making a gesture that took in all the flaring candles—"for at the first opportunity I have an illumination, and change my mind."

After this the conversation ran on smoothly, but chiefly between Mr. Jarvis and his hostess; and to Milly, standing at attention between the strangers and her prog in the corner, Miss Maria seemed a new being—so quick and ready of speech, laughing so gayly, and gesticulating so vivaciously, but with no mention whatever of woes or wants, save as they were the woes and wants of the country.

And Mrs. Jarvis felt defrauded. As they closed the gate she said, "Those candles should have lasted her all winter."

And her husband answered, "I feel like spending my whole salary on candles."

Kizzy was enchanted, especially at the illogical command to come home. Her eyes and teeth reflected all the lights; she looked over the stores, felt the height and length of the woodpile, deposited the three little black idols in safety, then ran back to Mrs. Jarvis.

"I cahn come yer no mo'," she said, breathlessly, to that astounded lady; "I got to stay home. Miss 'Ria Cat'cart, wey you sen' de t'ings, is my missis."

"Is she sick?"

"No, ma'am; but we hab plenty now, en I cahn stay yer no mo'."

"Miss Cathcart ought not to take you."

"Ki! I b'longs to um."

"But you said you'd stay—"

"I say dat when we 'ain't hab nuttin'."

"You *promised.*"

"Kaze we 'ain't hab nuttin'."

"You *must* keep a promise." "Who gwine meck me? nigger do what 'e wants to do, en what'e meck to do. Who gwine meck me?"

"I won't pay you."

"You 'bleeged to pay me fuh what I done do, 'kaze it is done do."

"Not if you go without warning."

"I muss go."

"Why?"

"'Kaze I wants to, en 'kaze my missis wants me, en I tired. If you doan pay me, well—you doan pay me; I cahn he'p dat; but I gwine. I'll sen' somebody fuh cook you breakfuss."

All the way home Kizzy chuckled.

"Dey call me po' buckra nigger; I'll do like po' buckra nigger!" and she clapped her hands and laughed aloud as she ran through the darkness, and remembered the stores only as a further revenge on Mrs. Jarvis for the imagined insult.

Of course Mrs. Jarvis sent Kizzy's money, but she prophesied dire want for Miss Maria and her *menage*; poetical justice must take account of such childish improvidence. But no harm came to Miss Maria; Mrs. Jarvis herself would not have permitted it; still, it did not even threaten, for before the stores were exhausted, Mr. George Bullen came to bring Miss Maria and her retinue home to her own people.

So the remaining supplies were given away with much generosity, and, to Kizzy's proud delight, she was sent with a pair of the silver candlesticks as a parting present to Mrs. Jarvis. For, as Miss Maria said to a neighbor, she had not been able to pay anything towards Mr. Jarvis's salary, which had mortified her very much.

JIM'S VICTORY

Late in the spring of 1865, in the hill country of Georgia, the night was damp and cool, and very dark. Through the mist that was heavy enough to be called unarticulated rain, a house loomed dimly, visible only because it stood on a hill with the sky for background. At either end of the house the black shadows of two trees stood up like the head and footboard of a grave, the level line of the roof bridging the distance from tree to tree. The upper windows were shut and dark, and the house door and lower windows could not be descried in the denser gloom of the deep piazza.

No glimmer of light was visible, and if any smoke came from the chimneys the mist weighed it down to the wet roof.

In the road, about twenty yards away, a horseman was gazing intently at the house. His military cap was drawn low over his eyes; a heavy cape enveloped him down to his knees, partially covering rolls, as of blankets and clothing, which were strapped before and behind him on the saddle, and in one hand he carried his sabre, which else would have rattled.

Steadfastly he looked at the house, while his horse's head drooped, and the mist gathered into drops that rolled slowly down his back and shoulders.

"Good-bye," he whispered at last, and there seemed a catch in his voice. "Good-bye," he said again, but he did not ride away, instead he bent his body a little more toward the shadowy house.

"Good-bye," he whispered the third time, then dismounting as if against his will, he opened the gate and led his horse in softly. Quickly he threw his heavy cape over the saddle and blankets, then, tying the bridle fast to a post, he walked rapidly toward the house, avoiding the gravel paths and mounting the steps with extreme caution. Once on the piazza he tapped gently on the closed blinds of a window; again he tapped, then turned the slats, and rapped lightly on the windowpane with his knife.

This sharper sound seemed to be heard, for presently an upstairs window was opened, and a voice asked: "Who is there?"

"Jim," was answered.

There was an exclamation, then hurried movements, and in a little while steps coming rapidly toward the door that opening showed a tall, gray-haired gentleman carrying an old-fashioned silver candlestick, in which an attenuated home-made "dip" burned dimly.

"My son!" he said, and the soldier put his arms about the old man's neck. Then they paused and looked into each other's eyes as if they could never look enough.

"We have heard nothing of you since Bentonville," the father said.

"And I've had no rest and little food since Bentonville," the son answered. "And, father, don't waken any one but mother."

She met them at the head of the stairs trembling with excitement. "We had almost given you up," she whispered brokenly; "so many are missing."

Once in the big bedroom, furnished with odd-pieces of furniture which would never have been introduced to each other save for the exigencies of refugee life, she closed the door, and taking from a large closet some lightwood, brightened up the fire, then deftly, though with slim white hands, she put a kettle to boil.

The soldier sank into a deep armchair as if completely exhausted, dropping his grimly stained old haversack on the floor beside him.

"There's some whiskey in my haversack," he said, then his voice seemed to fail him. The mother moved about rapidly with dilated, pitiful eyes, while the father took off the soldier's stiff cap and unbuttoned the heavy coat.

"He is almost starved," he said brokenly, slipping his hand in over the young man's ribs, and the mother drew a sobbing sigh as she went away to get some food. It was a strange meal she set before her son at last; cold cornbread, cold sweetpotatoes, and cold bacon.

"The only thing I have that is good," she said, "is coffee. I have managed always to have a little of that for your father; in a moment it will be made."

But the soldier did not wait, he did not seem to hear her, so steadily and quietly was he consuming what was there before him, pausing only to look wonderingly at the empty plates. The coffee he drank thirstily, quickly holding out his cup for more.

"I'll get more food," the mother said, but her son caught her arm.

"Don't go again," he begged, "you might rouse some one. I've stopped only to tell you and father good-bye; and, mother," looking about him. "are you so very poor?"

" *Good-bye* !" the mother repeated.

"I'm escaping to the army of the Mississippi," Jim answered, "if Kirby Smith surrenders, I'll go to Mexico. I've not surrendered, and I'll never surrender—*never!*"

The father standing, tall and a little bent, with his elbow on the mantelpiece, looked down on his son sadly. "God has decided against us, my son," he said slowly, and with some effort, even though his coat was black and clerical, "and we must submit."

"Never!" the young man answered sharply; "I'll never submit— never!"

"Wait," the father urged, "wait with us a week and see how things fall out."

"And be caught?" the young fellow interrupted.

But the father went on. "We are all here now," he said; "all who are left, and every day some poor fellow we know stops on his march home for food and shelter, and news of other refugees. We who live here put each into the common store what is possible, and so we manage to live. Stay with us?"

"I've nothing to contribute," the young man said sullenly.

"My son!"

He sprang to his feet. "I didn't mean it!" he cried, with his hand on his father's shoulder; "but don't keep me! Don't keep me here until I'm captured and have to take the oath! Father, I'd rather die."

"There is no longer any question of capture," the father answered, "and few have had to take the oath."

"I had to avoid troops on my way here," the son said.

"They patrol the country to keep order. They have not disturbed us refugees, nor any of the soldiers with us. My son," and there came a break in the old man's voice, "we are not worth disturbing now."

The soldier covered his face with his hands and a groan broke from his lips.

"It's the best way to make money, and I'll do it."

The speaker was a wan, thin boy, who in spite of his worn gray uniform, seemed not to be beyond the growing age, for his hands and feet had left his coatsleeves and trouser legs far behind. "And now that Jim is going to wait here a week," he went on, "I'll borrow his horse."

"It's a splendid plan," answered a girl who was sitting on the window sill, swinging her feet, "and I'll sew my fingers off for it."

"I don't understand," Jim said. He was looking haggard and worn, and a sombre light burned in his eyes. His detention by his father was a bitter thing to him, for his hot young heart was consumed by the sense of defeat, and he longed to get away from the sight of the consequences that to him were the depths of humiliation. His plan was to go down into Mexico as soon as his father would let him, and to settle there, and in time, perhaps, persuade his father and brothers to join him in making a new home. Meanwhile he kept himself out of sight, lest by accident he should be arrested and compelled to take the oath of allegiance.

In vain his father said, "This is your country, your duty is here, and good or evil, we must abide the consequences of this war." Jim's answer was always, "I cannot; I will not. I will leave the country; I will not take the oath." And now as his younger sister and brother talked, they seemed to him to be frivolous and foolish as well as sordid, and almost traitorously happy as they planned their pathetically small ventures for the making of money.

"I don't understand," he said and he looked down on the young schemers severely.

"It's just this," the thin boy went on, looking up at Jim with deprecating determination; "a fellow paid Charlie a debt in tobacco, and an old fellow sent father a present of some sole leather. Very little, still, it is sole leather, and plug tobacco for which we have no earthly use. Nan, here, has made some millinery efforts and is willing to manufacture more by tomorrow. My plan is to take the small spring wagon and your horse, some tobacco, the leather, and Nan's stuff, and turn peddler."

There was a dead silence, then Jim walked away.

"May I have the horse?" the boy called after him insistently; "father and mother are willing."

"Yes."

The boy watched his brother rather sadly until he was out of sight, then he turned to the girl.

"Dear old Jim is so magnificent," he said; "he does not see where we are at all. Peddling's a wretched thing to do, but it's better than starving," and he looked at his thin hands reflectively.

The thin boy, Tom by name, and his wagon, stopped at the gate of a farmhouse. It was dusk, and he made his presence known by calling— "Hello!"

"Hello!" was answered. "Come in."

Tom had left home that morning early, and having no permit he had traveled by a circuitous route, and had avoided stopping anywhere. Long ago he had finished the lunch his mother had packed for him, and now being once more dreadfully hungry, visions of something hot to eat and drink danced before his eyes.

"You look tired," the farmer said; "have you come fur?"

"From Sandville, but not as the crow flies. I've been dodging the patrol; they are all around the town."

"Would they want your load?"

"Perhaps," Tom answered; "I'm a peddler."

"Not for long," and the farmer touched Tom's gray coat, then his own gray trousers. "I've been back to farming one week; how long have you been peddling?"

Tom laughed. "Just twelve hours," he said.

"What you got?"

"Wait 'till after supper."

"That's so; but fetch in your horse and cart and put up for the night. I'll tell the old woman."

The supper was plentiful, such as it was, and Tom went to work on it with a soldier's earnestness.

"I've been traveling all day," he said.

"Eat, eat!" the farmer's wife answered, "you don't look like you'd been filled right full for many a long day. Pete there come home empty, down to his toes."

"I've had chills and fever for six months," Tom went on, "and I had a chill yesterday."

"Pete's chillin', too, tomorrow's his chill day; but eatin's good to git up your strength 'ginst nex' time. Sherman did'nt tech us, so thar's lots mo' bacon in the smokehouse, an' meal, an' lard, an' butter a plenty; an' the gals here ain't got nothin' to do but cook."

Tom cast a glance at the three girls opposite him, who every now and then went back and forth to the big fireplace for fresh relays of food.

Perhaps they would like some of the things Nan had put into the wagon? "Things imported especially for our country custom" Nan had declared, when displaying to the family her stock of wonderful looking lace collars and fancy aprons, and really terrible bonnets and hats made from all the odds and ends of silk, and lace, and old finery that had done duty for the four years of the war. "I have always longed to keep a shop," Nan had continued to the amusement of her family, "and if Tom succeeds now, I see no reason why we should not go into business together just as soon as we go home again. I think I should enjoy it very much indeed."

Now, Tom was wondering how in the world he would have the audacity to ask his entertainers to buy anything. He felt as if he ought to give them all they wanted in return for their hospitality. He did not wonder long, however, for as soon as supper was cleared away the demand was made to see his stock. First he brought in the tobacco and leather, then returned for Nan's big basket and hatbox; immediately matters were taken out of his hands by the young women and their mother, and the table and chairs were soon covered with an extraordinary assortment of things.

"Them's surely pretty," the girls said; but did not know how to put some of them on, and Tom, who had been carefully instructed, had now to come to the front.

"This fancy apron is worn in this way," he said, half tying the apron about himself, "and these things go over the shoulders, see?"

The girls were giggling, huddled together, but Tom stood firm, very red, but smiling, with his head a little on one side, and his thin fingers holding up the lapels to his shoulders.

The mother joined in the laugh now, then took the apron from him.

"I see how it goes, an' it's pretty," she said. "Janey-Lou, you kin hev thet, an' Mary-Lizer, you an' Julie-Ann kin choose somethin' else. What's them lace things—they looks tastey?"

"Collars," Tom answered, grown bolder, "very becoming collars," and he put one of the huge things about the neck of the farmer. This provoked a shout of laughter, but two collars were laid aside for Mary-Lizer and her sister. By this time Tom had risen to the occasion and drew out an enormous scoop-shaped bonnet, such as one sees in the mournful old photographs of the sixties, constructed of pale pink silk that had been washed and ironed, and surmounted by a pyramid of artificial flowers which looked as if they might have been washed and ironed, too; but such a structure had never before met Mrs. Dobs' eyes, and she stood open-mouthed under its shadow. "That beats all!" she said slowly.

Then Tom put it on his own head, holding the strings together under his chin, while his pale, thin face, still smiling, looked paler and thinner, and infinitely pathetic in the depths of the pink silk tunnel.

The girls giggled, the farmer chuckled, but to Mrs. Dobs it was a serious matter. At last she said, "Thet'll make the Meetin' house surprised, sure! Yes, I'll take thet." Then in a rigorous, yet longing way, she began to fold away the things, putting them carefully into the basket. The farmer laid aside some tobacco; then they began to cast up accounts.

"We'll have to pay in truck," he said, "'caus 'bout money, it's like in the spring 'bout chicken; hens are out, an' chickens ain't in—confederate money's out an' greenbacks ain't in—there ain't no money."

"All right," Tom answered.

"Bacon, lard, meal, butter, flour, chickens—" the farmer enumerated; "What'll you have, or will you have some of all?"

"I may be out several days," Tom answered, "and I have no place for chickens, and the butter may spoil."

"If you an' Pete 'll say what it's wuth in dollars," Mrs. Dobs struck in, "I'll pack it all safe enough, an' the nex' time you come, Mr. Selwyn, you kin fetch back the buckets an' things—jest tell me the dollars."

"'Bout a thousand dollars in confederate money," Pete answered. Mrs. Dobs nodded. "Then I know jest what to give you," she said, "An' it'll be ready in the marnin'." "You must take out my board." Tom suggested, blushing very red.

"I never do charge folks fur vittles," Mrs. Dobs answered promptly, "an' your sleepin' in one o' my beds don't cost me nothin' nuther; an' you don't look fitten to be projeckin' aroun' no how; you go over to Mill Creek, five miles over yander, an' sell out quick, an' go home to your mammy."

"Sure enough, you can sell your leather over to Mill Creek," the farmer said. "There's a shoemaker over there will take it."

"Yes, an' he hes money, too," Mrs. Dobs struck in sharply. "Born an' raised a Southoner, he ain't fought a lick—said he didn't care which side beat, an' he's been at home makin' money all the war, says he could'nt see! But he could see to sew shoes an' to charge prices, an' not to take no confederate money nuther; everybody had to pay him in truck, or cloth, or yarn, an' when he heard Sherman was a-comin', his wife an' his ugly daughter—she ought to be killed she's so ugly—drove two wagons loaded down with vittles, an' shirts, an' knitted socks, thirty miles cross country to sell to Sherman's army; an' he went over with his tools to do mendin', an' they took different names, an' didn't seem to know each other; an' they cut under each other in prices, an' they sold out every thing an' came home with lots o' greenbacks; so when you go to him you sell yo' things high, an' fur money, nothin' but green-backs money. They do say they're goin' to burn his house down."

"Now, wife!" the farmer expostulated.

"Yes, they do, Pete, an' you knows it." "Course I do," Pete answered calmly; "I'm only 'fraid that if you go on talkin' McKorkle'll know it, too. Mr. Selwyn ain't agone' to tell; boy as he is, he's been fightin' tell he's lookin' most dead with starvin' an' chillin.' How long have you been fightin' anyhow, honey?"

"A year and a half."

"An' how'd yo' mammy ever let you go?"

Tom laughed a little, while a faint color stole up his cheeks; "I cried," he said. "Then mother begged father to let me leave school and go."

"Did—you—ever!" the woman said, standing still with her arm akimbo, and looking at Tom reflectively, "cried to go an' fight—po' chile—God bless you!" Then wiping her eyes with the corner of her apron, she went on, her voice grown sharper. "Well, McKorkle didn' cry to fight, an' I'd ruther shoot him than any Yankee that come to fight us fa'r an' squa'r."

"So should I," Tom answered, "only shooting's too good for a coward like that."

"That's right!" Mrs. Dobs cried, nodding her head emphatically, "an you sell all you kin to McKorkle on this trip, 'cause he'll be gone West when you come agin'. Ha, ha! we mighter beat the war if he'd helped us! ha, ha! now we'll lick *him* , you bet. We've just been awaitin' fu theh men to come home to do it rale nicely—the good-fur- nothin'—consarned—cur-dawg!"

"See here, Molly," her husband began.

"You let-me 'lone, Pete," she retorted, "you've hed your fight out an' I hevn't, I've jest been stayin' home here an' bilin' over, an' now I'm goin' to bile over on to McKorkle, drat 'im!"

The next day Mr. Dobs went to Mill Creek with Tom, and himself drove the bargains with McKorkle; indeed, he rather got the better of the fellow, as, having a number of the villagers for audience, McKorkle was at a great disadvantage. Tom, however, because filled with contempt for the man who was afraid to fight on either side, gave over generous measure and weight, and added one or two things to the bargains made by the wife and daughter, then drove away, wondering what punishment the irate neighbors would mete out to the family.

In the next two days Tom had disposed of his little stock and had turned his horse's head homeward. He was elated with his success, while yet a little ashamed of his elation, for now the success seemed so slight. He had brought home some provisions it was true, but the money in his pocket amounted to a very small sum. Toward evening he found himself on the road leading into Sandville, on the outskirts of which town was his temporary, refugee home. It was a poor makeshift place, but his mother was there, and that made any place a home for Tom; and now he longed for his mother's care and for shelter most especially, for he felt creeping over him all the horrid sensations of an approaching chill.

The memory of all that he had suffered while marching with a chill on him—the fence-corners where he had tumbled down, half hoping to die; the hospitals, worse than fence-corners; the jolting of ambulances, or the baking sun as he lay on top a caisson—all this came back to him now, as he drove through the lonely woods. And all had been suffered for nothing! Ruined and sick, and nothing to look forward to but poverty! And his father was old, and his mother; and the little ones younger than he to be cared for, and nothing to do it with!

He put his hands over his face and bowed his head. His boyish heart was hopeless, as only inexperienced youth can be hopeless, and tears filled his reluctant eyes.

The horse was trotting along smartly, seeming to know that he was nearing the end of his journey, and in the deep sand of the country road Tom did not hear the sounds of hoofs coming up behind him until an authoritative voice called, "Halt!"

The army trained horse stopped so suddenly that Tom was pitched forward against the dashboard, and instantly anger took the place of despair as he saw a Federal officer coming up alongside of him, followed by a country man.

"What do you want?" he asked defiantly, forgetting the signs of tears on his face and in his eyes.

"Have you a permit to travel?" the officer asked.

"I know him!" the countryman interrupted, "he's a peddler named Selwyn; he came to my house t'other day."

"And you're McKorkle," Tom answered, looking at the countryman while his mind was filled with anxiety for his load of provisions, as well as for his wagon, for he had no permit. What should he do!

"Did you have any hand in that disgraceful outrage?" the officer went on.

"Did they worry you?" Tom asked, still looking at McKorkle, trying to gain time to plan.

"Worry me!" the man repeated, "they drove us out, put all our things in the road, and burned the house down. *Worry me?"*

"Was that all?" Tom asked with a sort of wondering simplicity, touching his horse with the whip, and smiling vacantly.

"All!" the man screamed, "An' you a'laughin'!"

"Look here, young man," the officer said, keeping up with the wagon which was now moving briskly, "you have not answered my questions."

"I may be deaf," Tom answered slowly.

"You may be put in the guardhouse before night and your wagon confiscated."

"That's very true," Tom answered, meditatively and shaking his head slowly.

"Then keep a decent tongue in your head."

Tom poked his tongue out as far as he could and tried to look at it, then again shook his head slowly, once more touching up his horse.

"Are you sane?" the officer went on.

"Seine? you mean am I a fishing net?"

"An idiot!" the officer said sharply.

"Am I?" Tom asked, turning to McKorkle. McKorkle looked at him thoughtfully. "Dobs *did* come along with him," he said slowly, "and traded fur him, too."

"Yes, he did," Tom granted.

"Did you have any hand in the outrage?" the officer repeated.

Tom shook his head. "Nor foot either," he said.

The officer looked at him curiously. "Did you have any permit for traveling?" he went on, his voice grown less sharp.

Again Tom shook head. "Nothing but a horse and wagon," he answered.

"Have you a permit to keep a horse?" the officer continued.

"I have no horse."

"You are driving one."

"It's borrowed."

"Have you been in the army?"

"Yes."

"What did you do there?"

"I shot guns at men in blue coats who were shooting guns at me."

"He's a naytral sure!" McKorkle said.

"You did it, too," Tom asserted.

"*That* I didn't!"

"I had lots of fun," and Tom laughed, but he happened to look up just then, and the officer caught his eye.

"Young man," he said, "you are a fraud."

"On what grounds?" and Tom whipped up his willing horse.

"You are pretending to be an idiot, and you shall answer for it."

"Fight you any time you like," Tom cried excitedly. They were going very fast now, and their voices were raised to a very high pitch.

"Fight *you*—you baby!" and the officer reaching over tipped Tom's cap back. "Your teeth are chattering now with fright."

"Confound you!" Tom shrieked, turning his ashy face with its blue lips and flashing eyes on his pursuer, "Oh, confound you! Trembling. I'm having a chill!" He tried to rise as if to strike with his whip, but the jolting of the wagon, and the weakness from the violent ague that was shaking him, was too much, and he fell back again.

Mr. Selwyn and Jim, standing on the piazza, paused, as on the still evening air sharp, high, angry voices came to them above the rattle of wheels and the dull thud of horses' hoofs.

"That's Tom's voice!" Jim said, "cursing and swearing! He's in trouble!" He ran down the steps toward the front gate, his father following. He flung the gate open. The only voice that could be heard now was Tom's, that scaling high and higher, in its boyish uncertainty seemed as if it must in a moment break into tears like a woman's.

On they came; Tom driving regardless of his load, which, fortunately, held nothing breakable, and too excited to wonder why the gate should be so opportunely open.

The officer, too, not knowing where Tom's journey would end, and secure in the fact that the road they were following led to headquarters, scarcely saw the open gate, but the horse did, and increased his speed; and McKorkle did, and cried out: "He's gwine to turn in! He's gwine to turn in!"

Whereupon the officer cried: "Halt!" and in the sudden stoppage Tom found himself on top of the horse, holding on for dear life. In an instant Jim cried: "Forward!" and with a whinney of delight the horse dashed through the gate, which Jim closed promptly, while poor Tom dropped off onto the grass.

The officer on the other side of the gate looked at the group angrily, yet curiously.

"It is your horse," he said at last, looking straight at Jim.

"It is." Jim answered.

"And that impertinent boy—"

"Is my brother, and I hold myself responsible for all that he has said."

"Very good."

"My name is Selwyn;" Jim went on, "I am your equal in rank," pointing to the insignia on his own collar. "You will find me here whenever you want me, and I agree now to any weapons, and any terms."

"Are you a parolled prisoner?"

"I am not."

"Have you surrendered?"

"I have not. I am still a Confederate officer with unimpeached rank; you need not hesitate about that."

"Very good," and the officer turned his horse's head toward the town, followed by McKorkle.

During the short, curt interview, the family who were at home had collected on the piazza. Tom had picked himself up and was leaning against the horse, listening with intense delight to Jim's rash words, while the father with his hands clasped behind him, and the wind blowing about his silver hair, had on his face a look of infinite tenderness and trouble.

"You have made a great mistake, my son," he said.

"I'll be delighted to fight him," Jim answered quickly, glad of anything to ease the soreness of his feelings.

"He will not fight you; of course he will not, it would be foolish. Do you suppose he will risk his life under *these* circumstances? He has you now completely in his power, and who knows what may follow?"

"He ought to feel more bound to fight me, to give me a fair showing, *because* I am in his power, even if he got into trouble about it."

Mr. Selwyn shook his head.

That night Tom burned hot with fever; the week's exposure to the sun, winding up with the excitement of his home-coming, when the chill was on him, was too much for his weakened condition, and the attack was far worse than usual.

All night he talked wildly, sometimes cursing the officers; sometimes laughing at McKorkle; sometimes imploring his mother to hide the money, and always with a tone of anxiety as to his next journey into the country.

"Mother, the officer said he would confiscate the wagon and all in it; but the money—the money—take it out and hide it—hide it mother, it will help you for a little while. Take it out, mother, will you—*will* you?"

"I have it, my son."

"Oh! and the bacon and the lard, some of it will have to be sold, and Jim and father will hate that, but I couldn't do any better. Old McKorkle is a dog—a cur dog! and the officer—he said—mother, he said that I was trembling because I was afraid—afraid. Oh, father, can't you kill him? I tried to beat him with my whip. I was shaking so— shaking so, and my head—oh, my head! Mother, mother, I'm burning up. And if Jim's horse is taken—if Jim goes to Mexico—how can I make any more money? How can I take the cans and basket back? She was so good to me. I was so tired and hungry. I'm always tired. Old McKorkle—Dobs worried him so—all the people stood about and worried him, miserable wretch! But I gave him good measure, father, and I gave his daughter an extra bow of ribbon. By George, she was ugly! And Nan's terrible bonnets! *I* tried them on—ha, ha! *I* tried them on— you see, I look like mother. If only Charlie were here to help father and Jim fight; but if they take the horse—I am too weak to work in any other way now. What shall I do? Charlie and Jim ought not to work— ought not to work, 'twould kill them to work; but I don't mind—no, mother, I don't—work is good enough for me; I don't mind. We must hide the money, mother, and the horse. Please, father, save the horse, *please.* Selling things is no harm—I've thought about it—*please.* Think of walking all the way to Mrs. Dobs' with the basket? I should die, father; please save the horse?"

"I will, my son, you try to sleep now. In the morning I shall go to town and see about it myself.

"And will you kill the fellow that called me a coward? Kill him, and tell him that I had a chill. Oh, mother, I was so tired! I am so tired! Mother, hold my hand, please, mother. Next week I shall go again."

And so through the night, until at dawn he fell asleep; and Jim, watching the haggard boyish face upon the pillow, wondered if any of them were as brave, or as true, or as self-sacrificing as this boy who so humbly held himself as only good enough to work.

The next morning an officer, not the one whom Jim had challenged, came with a file of soldiers and a requisition for Jim and his horse.

The excitement in the house was kept under, but it was very intense, for war measures were an unknown quantity, and Jim in his full uniform, with his sword clanking at his side, angry and uncertain, but declining the company of any of his friends, rode away. Arrived at headquarters, his name was registered, an officer received his sword, and he was told that unless he took the oath, his horse also would be confiscated.

In an instant Tom's fevered pleadings were ringing in his ears—Tom's pathetic venture was knocking at his heart—Tom's haggard, boyish face came before him as in a vision! His father—his mother—his duty!

He had been on many bloody fields—he had led forlorn hopes—he had fought desperate odds—he had seen those he loved fall dead beside him—but this was worse than all!

All day he struggled, sitting dumb and still—walking about restlessly. His father—his mother—his duty? No, it was Tom, Tom who had weakened him—Tom's pathetic scheme—Tom's pitiful pleading; but for that what would the horse matter! Tom, poor Tom, was he sleeping now? So weak, so sick, so brave! curly headed, obstinate little Tom had suddenly sprung into a power. He had made the first venture under the new order of things—had made the first success. What right had he to let his pride cripple Tom's efforts however small, however obnoxious? All day long he struggled with himself—all day; the longest day he had ever lived, but at last, with a drawn white face, and with set lips that scarcely moved, he swore allegiance to the government against which he had fought for four long years, and riding his horse home again in the gathering dusk he gave it to Tom.

From the depths of defeat he had risen to the heights of victory.

PROGRESS

Mr. Sam Long stood in the doorway of his shop, with a troubled look on his face: a lengthening, line-drawing look that was a ridiculous misfit, for his face had been planned and prepared for the lines of laughter and kindly friendliness; his voice had a ring of hospitality all through it, and his laugh made one think of spareribs and sweet potatoes and "midnight 'possums" and Christmas turkeys—not to speak of hot apple-toddies by a big wood fire, and of other things on the shady front piazza. There was not a commercial line about Mr. Long, and the shop background seemed to be as unsuited to him as the look of trouble on his face. "Things have changed," he said to himself impatiently, and rubbed his chin. After a moment, he drove his hands down into his pockets, and took a turn up and down the empty shop; then coming back to his stand in the doorway, he sighed profoundly.

Of course, when the war was ended and the Negroes were freed, there had been a change. But that was not what had caused Mr. Long's trouble; his difficulties had begun much later, when a railway had worked its way through the country, skirting the old farm and putting a station at the fence corner. He had been paid what he thought a good price for the land where the station and, later, the post office had been built, and felt quite rich when a young physician came, and buying another slip of the "big field," built a small shop, where he dispensed drugs. It had all looked very cheerful and prosperous at first; and Mr. Long had liked it, for he necessarily posed as the great man of "Longville." Presently the post office and the doctor's office caused Longville to become the lounging place for the surrounding country, and a Negro blacksmith building a shed to cover his anvil, it became, as if by magic, a swarming-place for Negroes. After this, a traveling man suggested that a shop for general merchandise was needed, and why did not Mr. Sam Long build and keep one?

But all these changes had come about so naturally, the sequence had been so logical, that it took some time for the Longs to see what had happened. From the very first, the old people had bemoaned them-

"Now we'll have to go and tell her," Betsy answered.

selves for the lost peace and quiet of their days, and because of the dirt and hideousness that were encroaching on the old household. But, then, they were old. After a while, however, Mr. Sam Long's wife began to be troubled about many things, and, later, Mr. Long himself. And now, as he stood in his shop door, waiting for his friend, Mr. Hicks, who was coming to advise with him concerning his financial condition, he remembered that all these changes had begun just ten years ago.

Ten years ago this very month the engineers who were surveying the line had come, and had made his house their headquarters. They had stayed with him a month; then had gone away leaving him feeling that the whole South was making tremendous strides; that a grand new era of prosperity was dawning; that progress, with an enormous capital P, was pushing and pulling every creature in the poor, old, belated South into a financial paradise. And he remembered, too, that he had never thought of the South as being poor or old or belated until that time.

"My gracious!" he sighed, "I wish we'd stayed poor and old and belated. Progress!" and there was enough scorn in his voice, as he said this last word, to have withered that relentless blessing to its very root.

He sighed again as he looked up and down the horrid little thoroughfare, where pigs were wandering, and where old tins and papers and dusty weeds filled all the crooked turns and odd abutments. This very thoroughfare had been a part of his best field. He had plowed it many a time, and had picked good cotton off it, too. And just over yonder, where the post office now stood, the fence had run, and blackberries and wild white morning-glories had grown all over it, and goldenrod in every corner. And the children used to go there and fill their little buckets with berries and their hands with flowers. How peaceful and green it had been! And he sighed again.

Then down the road he saw his friend coming, jogging along on a rough country horse. "Progress ain't helped Abe Hicks much neither," he said to himself, and his greeting of his friend was without spirit.

Lawyer Hicks hitched his horse to the rack in front of the shop, and mounted the one step to the door.

"What is it, Sam?" he asked.

"Everything," Mr. Long answered, as he dropped into a hide-bottomed chair and pointed Mr. Hicks to another. "I'm afraid I'm ruined, Abe; but I can't agree to it till somebody proves it." Then he tipped his chair back against the counter, and put a fresh piece of tobacco into his mouth; and Mr. Hicks, tilting his chair back against the side of the door, so that he faced his friend, treated himself to the same luxury.

"I thought this railroad was going to make me rich," Mr. Long went on, "and it did look so at first; but I've been getting poorer and poorer ever since it came. I've just been counting up, and it's been just ten years since those fellows came, buying up land and laying off the road. They stayed a month, and when they went away they left me thinking that the whole South was going to enter on the millennium. That's what I thought."

"I did too," the lawyer agreed.

"And that was the first time," Mr. Long continued, with a note of indignation creeping into his voice, "that I ever heard the South called poor or old or belated. Why, they made me feel fifty years behind time and that I'd have to canter to catch up. And, my gracious! I've been cantering ever since, till now I'm foundered, and am further behind than ever I was before. I wish they'd never come."

"Well, I don't know about that," Mr. Hicks demurred. "A railroad is bound to be a gain to a country."

"I used to think so," Mr. Long admitted; "but now I can't see why. We'd always had enough to live on and enough to wear, and what more does a Christian want?"

"Well, there's trade—"

Mr. Long held up his hand. "Don't mention that," he said.

"And newspapers," Mr. Hicks went on, "and a knowledge of what the world's a-doing."

"Maybe; but *we* didn't want any of that. We didn't know about it, and ruin's a mighty high price to pay for newspapers. But I'm not to blame, please God," and Mr. Long sighed. "I didn't go out hunting for any of these things. They came and shoved 'em on me, and called 'em progress. Jerusha! I hate that word so I wish there wasn't a P in the alphabet."

The lawyer smiled. "You're a born farmer, Sam," he said. Then more earnestly, "But I don't see how you lost, Sam. How was it?"

"I can't say rightly myself," Mr. Long answered with a puzzled look. "I can't add it up to save my life; but I'll tell you the best I can. Me and Betsy thought we were losing because everybody stopped with us as they passed by, and because we had to buy so many things we'd never bought before, like canned things, and cloth, and poor cloth at that, Betsy not having time, because of the people, to spin or to weave. So we took the advice of a traveling fellow, and turned the old home into a boarding- house, and I opened this store. But, I tell you, Abe, there's some funny things about keeping a store or a boardinghouse, some right funny things. Sometimes we felt like we was bewitched, we or the money, one. Now there was that young Dr. Jinkins. Just as soon as I opened this store, he said, 'Mr. Long, it'll be better for both of us if I move into your store, for then the people who come to buy my things will see yours; and the people who come to buy your things'll see mine. There's nothing like concentration.' And it looked so, Abe? Well, sir, he rented out his little shop, and I didn't charge him anything for coming into mine, because it didn't cost me anything. But, Abe, when that fellow slipped off leaving his debts unpaid, it seemed a big loss, and to save me I couldn't see where I'd lost. He didn't come for meals to our house 'cept when I took him there, and he didn't owe for any dry goods, for he sent to town for such as that. All he owed for was for hams and potatoes and firewood and things that came off the farm and didn't cost me nothing; but yet I seemed to lose a heap by that fellow. Betsy 'llowed it was the confidence I'd lost."

"Maybe it was the confidence," Mr. Hicks said thoughtfully; "but it strikes me he was a mighty sharp rascal."

"Well, it did look mean," Mr. Long admitted, "mean enough to make me feel sorry for him; but the actual money loss wasn't much. I've often given away lots more than he owed for, and it never seemed to count."

"Maybe," Mr. Hicks said again, "but you weren't trying to make money then, Sam. You know we never tried to make no money till this railroad came; all the time before that we just lived along comfortable and easy, and nothing seemed to count much. But just you try to make things pay, and every blessed feeling and person and thing looks different, and in no time you feel poor enough to beg."

Mr. Long sat silent for a moment. "That sounds like the truth," he said at last; "I'll think about that."

"Well, how else did you lose?" Mr. Hicks went on.

"Why, Betsy," Mr. Long resumed sadly—"Betsy felt like things ought to be heaps nicer, and heaps more of it, when folks were paying board; and of course we couldn't charge old neighbors, and between us, Abe, just as many of them stopped in for meals as boarders, and of course Betsy gave all alike. She couldn't have a poor table for old friends, and a good table for strangers, just because they paid; of course not. Then my being always in the shop and the boys over at the station, the farm sorter got away from us. But Simon's learned to telegraph, and Jimmy's learned right smart about the express business, and they don't like to plow any more. It *is* right hard work, Abe."

"But it's honest, healthy, happy work, Sam."

"Yes," Mr. Long rejoined sadly, "and God knows I'd give a heap to be back to the old times. I used to like to plow along with daddy. The fresh earth used to smell so good, and I used to be so tired when the day was done."

There was a few moments' silence, as if some dream of straight furrows and cornshuckings and the like had fallen on the two men, until at last Mr. Long broke the spell with: "Bad accounts, Abe, accounts I can't realize a cent on, they're the worst of all. The people haven't got anything even if I'd sell them out; and I couldn't do that, you know—not old friends. Then the truck business lost me a heap; and coal oil, too, I've lost a lot on that. The fellow who sold it to me told me I'd have to charge for wash and evaporation. He was right kind about that; but all the same, charging for evaporation didn't seem honest to me. Charging for what couldn't be seen, or felt, and for what nothing got the good of 'ceppen your nose, and then 'twas bad"—laughing a little. "I sure don't feel like laughing, Abe, but that did seem funny, too funny to charge for, and so I lost."

"Well, Sam, and then?"

"Well, then, when I found that I was losing on every blessed thing and raised my prices, why, bless my soul, didn't the whole country turn against me? Yes, sir, they did! Said there was no competition, and so I was squeezing 'em, and in a way stealing from 'em. My gracious! and I being ruined—plumb ruined. I swear it, Abe; come look at my books."

Down the long, narrow shop the two men walked, to the high desk at the end, where the books were—thumbed, greasy, dog-eared books, kept after the simplest fashion, for Mr. Long knew nothing of bookkeeping. For some time Mr. Hicks worked diligently, unraveling the cramped figures, crossing out the bad debts, listening to explanations of leakage, of generous weight and measure, of out-and-out gifts, of failure to collect, and, long before his task was finished, realizing the disastrous results that must follow his summing up.

"It's bad," he said at last, "very bad. You haven't treated people in a businesslike way, Sam."

"Businesslike?" Mr. Long repeated slowly, looking at his friend wistfully. "I don't know about that; but I've tried to be honest and friendly, and to do as I'd be done by; I *have* tried that."

"Of course," Mr. Hicks answered gently, "everybody knows you're honest and friendly, Sam."

"Yes," Mr. Long struck in, his voice scaling high and thin with despair; "yes, always friendly, and yet when I had to raise my prices to cover handling; when I tried to collect promptly to save myself, the folks I've known all my life won't speak to me and have taken all their trade to the next station."

Mr. Hicks shook his head. "I know," he said, "and it all looks, and is, mighty unjust; but people are like that. And being friendly, and doing as you'd be done by, takes a heap of capital; and, Sam, that ain't what they call business."

Mr. Long leaned his head down on the high desk. "What'll I do, Abe?" he asked.

"Sell."

Then a silence fell, so tense, so all-pervading, so heavy with this little, everyday, crossroads tragedy, that a rat gnawing in the wall seemed to cry ruin, and the oil that dripped from the oilpump into a tin cup seemed to ring a knell. Mr. Hicks could not bear it long, and he slapped his friend on the back. "Bear up, old man," he cried, "bear up. Your land is good, rich land, and in prime condition. Maybe you can sell for enough to pay the mortgage and your debts, too, and have a little over."

"Sell the old place?" Mr. Long said, raising his head and looking about him in a dazed way. "Sell the old place? What'll my mother do— and Betsy? Oh, Abe, it'll kill 'em!" and the face he turned toward his friend was drawn and aged and changed. All the ruddiness had faded from it, and the round cheeks hung down in flabby creases.

Mr. Hicks did not like the sight, and turned away. "It's pretty bad," he acknowledged huskily, looking down the length of the shop, "pretty bad; but I'll tell you, Sam," his voice growing firmer, "that when it comes to trouble, women bear up better than we do. They'll fret themselves to death if you clean your gun in the wrong end of the house or track up a floor, but when it comes to a great big thing that knocks a man all to flinders, they'll not turn a hair. I'm a lawyer, you know, and have lots of experience with ruin."

"Betsy'll bear up," Mr. Long moaned, "she's prepared; but my mother, oh, my mother! She's so old," and again Mr. Long's head dropped on his arms, that were crossed on the high desk.

Mr. Hicks walked down to the shop door, and stood looking out. Presently a young fellow came from the telegraph office, and he called him. "Come here, Simon," he said; and when the boy had reached his side, he went on, "I want you to keep the shop a while; I want your father to go over to the house with me."

Then he took Mr. Long out of the back door and across the fields to the old homestead. It was a friendly looking old house, low and rambling, the oldest part being of logs, and with no beauty but its friendliness, and Mr. Hicks found himself looking away from the old house, as he had looked away from the face of his friend. The two men entered slowly, Mr. Long's step dragging. He had had one last hope that his friend would be able to help him to some solution of his difficulties, and over in the shop this hope had died.

Mrs. Long met them in the hall, and went with them into the empty dining room, where the table was laid for supper and where places were arranged for many more than the family. For some time now these places had been unused, but Mrs. Long had hoped that, when once their old friends had realized that the shop at the next station was charging the same prices as the prices to which her husband had advanced, they would bring their trade back to Longville, and prosperity would come with them. But this afternoon, as she looked from the window and saw the two men coming across the field, she realized that it had been folly to arrange these extra places. "I knew we'd have to sell, Sam," she said at once, slipping her hand into her husband's, "though I did hope that Abe could show us a way out." Her voice trembled a little, and the hand that held her husband's was very cold, but the eyes that looked up into the lawyer's eyes were steady and dry.

The lawyer shook his head. "No," he said, "I'm most as broke up about it as Sam is; but there's nothing to do but to sell."

"Everything?" and Mrs. Long's voice had grown quiet.

The lawyer nodded. Then after a moment's silence he asked, "How much does the mother know?"

Mr. Long almost wrung his hands. "We've tried to keep it all from her, me and Betsy. She's never liked the new ways, so she took the old weaving room, at the far end of the house, and she moved in there, she and daddy. I thought she'd move out when he died, but she didn't, and she's there now. And living out of the way like that, we've tried to keep all the troubles from her, and now," looking at his wife and possessing himself once more of her work-hardened hand, "and now, Betsy?"

"Now we'll have to go and tell her," Betsy answered. "I can't save you this, Sam. She's your own mother, and she'd take it hard, and rightly, if you didn't go to her yourself. And Abe must come, too, for the respect of the thing. She'd think that we mistrusted her if we treated her like she couldn't bear it as well as we bear it. No, we must all go and make it plain to her, though I don't reckon you'll surprise her as much as you think you will, for Sam ain't much of a hand for keeping things outer his face. Come on; the longer you look at bad things, the bigger they grows. Come on."

After several turnings and following of piazzas, they entered a large, low room, ceiled with unpainted wood and lighted by four windows. A piece of rag carpet was before the big fireplace; on the mantelpiece there were some old-fashioned china ornaments and brass candlesticks; a large bedstead occupied one corner, and all other wall-space was filled with frames for weaving and wheels for spinning. A quilting frame was in the middle of the room, balanced on the backs of chairs, and an old woman, small and spare and straight, dressed in a homespun frock, with great silver-rimmed spectacles over her still bright eyes, was quilting a patchwork quilt.

She stopped working as her daughter-in-law entered, followed by the two men, and busied herself placing chairs for her visitors. It was an unusual influx, but she evinced no surprise.

"We've come with some bad news, mother," Mrs. Sam Long began just as soon as she had seated herself, "some very bad news."

The old woman looked from one to the other, then fastening her eyes on Mr. Hicks, she said: "If it'd been death, you'd have brought a preacher; as you've brought a lawyer, it must be money."

Mr. Hicks looked at Mr. Sam Long, and both men nodded; then Mr. Hicks answered, "Yes, ma'am, Aunt Nancy, it's money."

"Well," she said, "go on."

So the story was gone over carefully from the very beginning: all the reasons for loss, down to the fact that custom of all kinds had been transferred to the next station. There Sam Long and his wife paused; their words failed them before the enormous fact of the necessary sale. The old mother had listened quietly, and when they ceased speaking, she once more fastened her eyes on the lawyer. "Is there any mortgage?" she asked.

Mr. Hicks nodded.

"Any credit?"

Mr. Hicks shook his head.

"My husband mortgaged this place once," she said slowly; "just after the war, for enough to start on when the niggers went; but we had good credit then, and by the time Sam was married it was all cleared off. Now it's different."

Again Mr. Hicks nodded.

"A mortgage and no credit means ruin." She took off her spectacles. Perhaps she did not wish to see too clearly the faces before her; perhaps she was afraid of dimmed glasses that would need to be wiped. Nobody spoke. Her son sat with his hands clasped and his head drooped on his breast. His wife watched him with eyes full of care, and Mr. Hicks, standing with one hand resting on the quilting-frame, was studying the toes of his big, dusty boots. "We're ruined," the old woman repeated. "But," she went on, "I've been expecting it. I've been shut away back here; but Sam's my child, and a mother's got eyes and ears in her heart as well as in her head. I scuffled through the war, and a scuffle like that don't leave folks without some experience; and my experience is that changes is mighty bad, or mighty good, one. If you're getting along with enough to eat and enough to cover you and good health, then don't go out hunting for a change, for it's mighty apt to be a bad one. For even the faithful God Almighty promises only enough."

Mr. Sam Long looked up quickly. "I didn't go out hunting for no change, mammy," he interrupted reproachfully.

"No, boy, you didn't," the old mother answered. "The changes come and hunted for us, but we took to 'em too quick. If we'd sold the corner of the big field, then have left a broad road 'twixt us and that corner, and have put up a high fence—ten rails and a rider—'twixt us and that road, we'd have lost land, but we'd have done better."

Mr. Hicks nodded. "You're right," he said.

"But these is hindsights," the old woman went on quickly, as if not to take too much credit, "and we all know the old saying about hindsights and foresights. Sam couldn't see, nor Betsy couldn't see, and both done their best. And anyhow, it's the new times has done it. It takes new people to fight new times."

Then rising, she went to a large chest that stood in a corner, and unlocked it with a key which she took from her bosom. The group she had left watched her curiously as, stooping over the chest, she laid one after another on the floor, quilts, and weaves of cloth, both cotton and wool, and hanks of yarn.

"I've been making and saving, too," she went on, "and I've laid all this by. It'll clothe us for a long time, Betsy. And I've sold a good deal in all these years, and I've got a little money;" and drawing from the depths of the chest an old deerskin wallet, she returned to her seat, and quickly emptied the contents of the wallet into her lap.

"There's not enough to save the place," she said, "but there's enough to buy in some things to start us off fresh. I've got a piece of land—my daddy gave it to me—ten miles back in the hills, and we can go there. It's never been cleared, and a log house is easy built where there's timber. And things go so cruel cheap at a sale, Abe, that maybe this money'll buy us back a yoke o' steers, and a little bedding and furniture, and things for cooking, and maybe a cow. But you'll know what to buy, Abe; you'll know," crowding the money back into the wallet and thrusting it into Mr. Hicks's hands, "you'll know; and maybe, Abe," her voice breaking a little at last, "maybe you'll let us come to your house while the sale is going on?"

Mr. Long was down on his knees with his arms around his mother and his head on her breast; his wife was sobbing quietly where she sat, and Mr. Hicks was looking steadfastly on the face of the old woman turned up so bravely to meet his own, while her tremulous, wrinkled hand smoothed tenderly the gray head of her "boy."

"You'll do it, Abe? You'll manage it all?"

"God bless you, Aunt Nancy," he stammered. "I'd sell myself to help you; but I'll do better than that"—his voice gaining in steadiness,—"I'll stave off this sale till Sam gets that house built; then we'll take you all to my place till the sale is over and your things is moved. That's what I'll do, Aunt Nancy. And Sam," looking down tenderly on his friend, "all will come out right. And it ain't your fault, old man; it's all these new ways that's creeping in. And soon your old friends'll be mighty sorry for the way they've done you, and, Sam, you must forgive 'em, for they don't know no more about business than you do."

There was a moment's pause; then Mr. Hicks added, while he lifted his eyes to the window and looked out over the woods and fields he knew so well: "I reckon things is bound to progress, bound to; but what you say, Aunt Nancy," he went on sadly, "is true; it takes new people to fight new times. Maybe we'll see the good of all these changes some day, and maybe—God help us—maybe the next generation will forget old times and old ways, and be knowing enough and hard enough to wrestle with this progress!"

"Maybe," Mr. Sam Long echoed, "maybe, and God help us!"

WITHOUT THE COURTS

It was a wide marsh, with a dim blue shore on the other side. Away down to the right the horizon was clear, for there was the sea into which the tidewater river emptied itself. To the left the river showed more definitely and in longer reaches, though still shored by the marsh. The low sand bluff that bounded the marsh on the south was fringed with saw palmettoes and bunches of wild myrtle, with here and there a solemn pine rising to lonely heights, and here and there wide-spreading, moss-draped oaks making dense shadows.

Where the trees were thickest a plantation house, built very much on the plan of the oaks, low and wide-spreading, stood looking out through its old-fashioned, small-paned windows, as it had looked for many, many changing years over the desolate marsh and sinuous river. So many had lived and loved, had come and gone, in that plain, heavily timbered old house, that at last it seemed almost to have acquired personality and the cheerful expression of a serene old age, which could look back on a simple, honorable, kindly past, and forward to a safe future. Today its outlook was misty, for a fine white film was stretched across the sky that dimmed the sunshine a little, and blurred the outline of the far horizon. A mild, gray day, which, while demanding fires, yet permitted the master of the house to bring his book to the front piazza. His feet were on the banisters, his chair was tilted back, and a soft hat was drawn a little over his eyes. Some pipes and a box of tobacco were on another chair beside him, and at a little distance a red setter lay, with his head on his front paws, watching his master wistfully, with now and then a nervous start and a tremulous long breath that was almost a whimper. Out on the bluff, under the trees, a Negro woman sat sewing, and a little child, with long fair curls creeping out from under the deep frill of her white sunbonnet, played beside her.

It was very still—so still that as far away as she was the words of the child would now and then reach her father where he sat, and hearing, he would lift his head and look towards the little group. It was a dull-looking book that he held, bound in brown leather, and heavy; for

104

when wheels were heard driving up to the side door, and he dropped it on the floor, it jarred loudly, so that the sound reached the child under the trees. She focussed her long bonnet on her father as he moved quickly down the piazza and cut across the corner to the side steps, where an open vehicle had stopped; then catching sight of the traveller who had arrived, she ran towards him as fast as her little legs could move, crying,

"Tad! Tad!"

The two men shook hands; a servant, coming round from the back, took a valise from the wagon; and Tad going to meet the child, the master turned to the coachman.

"Did your mistress give you any orders last night?" he asked.

"Yes, suh," the Negro answered; "Miss Lise say fuh me to come to de P'int fuh her dis mawnin' des es soon es I bring Mass Tad from de station."

"Then go at once," and Mr. Beverley pulled out his watch.

"Yes, and be in a hurry." When once more he had reached his chair, Beverley pushed the heavy book aside with his foot, then, as if on second thought, he turned it up so that the title would show.

Before he took his seat he drew another big chair forward, then filling his pipe he lighted it slowly while he watched his friend, who, having returned the child to her nurse, was coming towards the house, stooping and patting the dog as he came. "Poor old doggie," he said, "who's been trampling on you? What ails him, George?" he went on, when he reached the piazza. "He's trembling as if he had a chill, and winces as if he were sore."

"I had to thrash him this morning," Beverley answered, and a gleam came into his eyes that seemed to stop the poor dog in his tracks, and he lay down as before, tremulous and watchful.

Tad's own eyes took on a watchful look. "Where's Lise?" he asked.

"Over at Aunt Bowman's."

Then, as sitting down Tad's foot struck the big book, he said, "Reading law, and beating old Dash, and writing me that extraordinary letter yesterday, something must be very wrong, George—by Jove! infernally wrong."

Beverley handed him the tobacco box and pipes. "Light up," he said.

Tad obeyed, and for a little while they smoked in silence; then Tad, still with the watchful look in his eyes, went on:

"Your letter bothered me—bothered me because I could not come out yesterday."

"Yes," Beverley answered, "I meant you to come yesterday."

"I've wanted to come all winter," Tad went on, "but I've been away attending court, you know."

"Yes, I wish you had come," and Beverley blew out clouds of smoke. "That letter should have been written long ago. Well, I sent for you as my lawyer, Tad, and as you did not come yesterday, I reduced everything to writing."

"Reduced *what* to writing?"

"My instructions;" then Beverley turned his head away, and added, "I've decided to sell."

Tad's chair came down on its front legs with a bang; his pipe, jarred from its stem, fell on the floor, and the dog sprang up with a nervous yelp.

Beverley nodded as if he had expected this outbreak, and taking his pipe from his lips he began to stir the tobacco in the bowl with his knife-blade, watching his own motions attentively. "I know all that you want to say," he went on, "but there's no use in saying it. I know that no creature has ever owned this land but Beverleys; I know that I belong to the soil as that tree does; I know that it would have broken my mother's heart, and my father's"—his voice shook a little. "Well, never mind; if he knew, he would commend what I have done."

Tad was still leaning forward, with the pipestem forgotten between his fingers, gazing at the pipe-bowl forgotten on the floor. Beverley was looking out across the marsh.

"That club has offered me a fancy price," he continued, his voice growing more and more monotonous, as if he had rehearsed his speech, "and I mean to take it. They want this house just as it stands, the high lands, and the fields down to the barn; in short, all of the original Beverley tract, which will give them the best shooting and fishing. I want you to begin at once to look up the deeds, and to get everything in readiness; but I do not want the bargain concluded, nor the transfer made, until next autumn, and I shall put everything into your hands, as I do not wish to enter into any of the details. I shall keep all the up-river tract and continue to plant it, living in the overseer's house—"

"And Lise and the child?" Tad interrupted; and now he raised his eyes from the fallen pipe and fixed them on his friend's averted face.

"They will go to Europe—and live there." There was a moment's pause, then Beverley went on: "The money I get for this place, together with what I make planting, will enable me to keep them there—the child always under the supervision of a careful English governess, to whom I myself will give instructions, for I shall take them over. In case of my death, there is yourself, and my life insurance made out to the child—"

Tad grasped his arm. "George!"—and he shook him as if to waken him—"George, for God's sake, tell me all!"

"I am telling you all."

"But Lise has learned to love the place!"

"Yes, she has learned to love the place."

"And your aunt Bowman, and Jack, and Sandy, like your own brothers! George, you'll pull up the growth of generations!"

There was no answer, and the look across the marsh became more set.

"George!"—again shaking his arm—"George, for God's sake, tell me all!"

"I *am* telling you all. Aunt Bowman? Yes, it will hurt her; this was her father's house—"

"And Sandy!" Tad struck in, leaning a little more forward, trying to get a better view of his friend's face.

Beverley glanced round at the dog. "Get away from here!" he cried, springing to his feet, his eyes flashing. The dog fled down the steps, and the men's eyes met.

"I *am* telling you all!" Beverley repeated, harshly. "And it will be better for the child." He sat down again, while a deathly, spent look came over his face, and the dog once more crept up the steps.

"Better—best," he went on, as if to himself. *"Best*—yes. And as I have no son—thank God!—no son, what does it matter? Traditions? memories? all marred and blotted—*stained.* And the place must not be called Beverley any more; the name must vanish. You hear, Tad?" lifting his head quickly. "You must stipulate about the name."

Tad put down the pipestem at last, put it into the tobacco box with an exaggerated carefulness as if it were spun glass, and began to walk up and down the piazza. After a turn or two he saw Beverley bend his head to one side as if listening.

"You think you hear the carriage," he said. "I wish Lise *would* come; I don't think she should stay away when you are so worried."

"It was my arrangement," Beverley answered, coldly; "and I do not need a keeper, Tad."

There was silence while Tad walked the length of the piazza and back, then he paused behind Beverley's chair. "George," he said, "I love you as I love myself, but as surely as my name is Thaddeus Marvin, I'll throw up your business, and even your friendship, before I'll help you to do this thing."

Beverley shook his head slowly. "No," he said—"no you won't," and again silence fell between them.

Somewhere within the house a clock ticked; a bird fluttered down to a rosebush in front, and the laughter of the little child came clear and sweet from the river bank. Presently the dog lifted its head sidewise and grew rigid, and Beverley, putting his pipe slowly into the tobacco box, laid his two hands on the arms of his chair. Tad looked quickly from one to the other. The dog heard something that the master expected to hear! Then coming nearer on the still air was the thud of a horse's hoofs, and a mad rattle of wheels. The dog rushed out, barking wildly; the Negro woman gathered the child up into her arms; Tad ran to the side steps, and Beverley rose slowly to his feet.

On the horse came; but now Tad could see that the driver was urging him, and that the lady on the back seat was leaning forward urging the driver. What was she fleeing from! It was scarcely a moment before they reached the steps, and Tad sprang forward.

"What is it, Lise?" he cried, and almost lifted her from the wagon.

Her forget-me-not-blue eyes looked as if they had seen some dreadful vision, which they would forever see; her fair hair, blown out here and there by the wind, crisped and curled about a pallid face; her colorless lips were drawn back squarely, as in a mask of tragedy, and her breath seemed hard to get.

"What is it?" Tad repeated.

She clutched his shoulder. "Sandy," she whispered—"brought home dead!" She drew a long, sobbing breath—"shot!"

In Tad's honest eyes that looked into hers there dawned a growing horror of knowledge: and slowly, as if directed by some stronger power, he loosened her hand from off his shoulder and laid it on the railing of the steps.

"Call the carriage back," Beverley said, looking down on them from above, "I must be needed at the Point."

A rigidity crept over the trembling woman; she drew her lips together, catching the lower one with her teeth, and began to mount the steps as a blind person might. At the top, her husband stood aside out of her way; their eyes met—it was not long—then she passed on slowly into the house.

It was very still at the Point when they arrived. Mrs. Bowman sent at once for her nephew to come to her where she had shut herself into her room, while Tad took his seat on the front piazza with others who were waiting about, and watching, and talking in hushed voices.

"It is so dreadful!" said the distant cousin, who took her seat next to Tad. "Sandy was *so* handsome! and his mother's darling—me! me! it is always the dearest who is taken," wiping her eyes. "And last night he was the gayest of the gay—he and Lise Beverley. George went home early, just as soon as they began to dance. He is so quiet, you know, so deadly still. I always feel a little bit sorry for Lise; poor, pretty, gay Lise. But George left her here last night, and she was in a gale of spirits, she and Sandy, dancing like mad, and keeping us in roars of laughter. Cousin Bowman was so pleased to see the young ones so gay, and to think!—oh, me! to think!"—and again she wiped away her tears. "Have you heard the particulars?" she went on, turning squarely on her silent companion.

Tad shook his head. "Only the bare fact," he answered.

"How strange!" Then she began eagerly: "Sandy went out very early this morning to shoot—he often does, you know—and told the boatmen to meet him at nine o'clock at the long bend below the far swamp—you know it?"

"Yes," Tad answered

"And they found him lying there dead! Accident, of course, for both barrels of his gun were empty, and just by the trunk of a fallen tree; he must have tripped in stepping over it, don't you think so?"

"Yes," Tad answered again.

"They brought him home; we were all late at breakfast, laughing and talking, and those stupid Negroes brought him to the front landing! Lise saw the boat coming. 'There's Sandy!' she said, and ran out. Oh, it was awful! Cousin Bowman and Jack were nearly frantic!" This time she sobbed a little, and others near wiped their eyes.

"Jack has gone out to walk by himself, poor fellow," she went on, recovering herself, "and I'm *so* glad George has come over; he'll be a comfort to Cousin Bowman. He and Sandy have always been so devoted; he's like another son to Cousin Bowman; she depends on him greatly, as the head of her family. Poor George! he adored Sandy."

"Yes," Tad answered, "he did. He did most of Sandy's work at school, and took many of Sandy's whippings."

"Poor George!" she repeated, "it will break his heart. And Lise—Lise stood there like a dead woman while they brought him, lying on an old door, straight up to her—past her! Oh, it was awful!"

Tad rose hurriedly, "Take this chair," he said, and gave his place to a newcomer. After this he kept himself as far from his late companion and as near to the hall door as was possible, and waited patiently through all the long, lagging hours, while people came to make inquiries and to offer help; and food was served in the dining room and eaten between whispered sentences that told the story of the unfortunate accident over and over again, and so sent it away through all the countryside, and into the town newspapers.

At last, as evening fell, Jack Bowman came in at the back door, and down the hall. Beverley came out quickly from his aunt's room, and Tad stepped in from the piazza. The three men paused a moment, then Bowman led the way into the parlor where, on a couch in the middle of the room, the dead man lay. He shut the door and turned to Beverley. "It was buckshot," he said.

Beverley nodded. "For our good names' sake there could be no scandal," he answered.

Bowman bent his head.

"He agreed in this," Beverley went on, "and arranged it all himself so that no living soul, and especially his mother , need ever know."

Again Bowman bent his head.

"And at the last"—Beverley's voice broke a little—"at the last he fired both barrels into the air."

Bowman laid his hand on the folded hands of his brother, and Beverley turned towards the door with shudders as of mortal agony going over him.

Tad took the reins himself, leaving the coachman to walk, and he and his friend drove through the lonely night together. Through all the distance Beverley sat silent, bent over like an old, decrepit man, but as they turned in at the big gate, he laid his hand on Tad's arm.

"You must take the old dog with you," he said, "out of my sight. This morning I had to beat him to make him come away, and at the last he ran back and licked his face."

THE HEART OF IT.

It was a dark night and raining, and the level, sandy road could be distinguished only because of the greater dark of the wilderness on either side. A broad, white road it was, that led by swamp, and river, and pine barren, and now was greatly under water, not only because of rain, but because of a spring freshet that had swelled the great river that was an arm of the sea. Along this road a large blur was moving, with creakings and splashings; gradually emerging as a cart with a canvas cover and one horse, going at a leisurely gait. It was heavy traveling and slow, and reaching a little upward incline, the horse stopped.

"Mos' dead, is you Job?" said the man sitting just under the cover; "an' yo' travelin' ain't half done."

"Are we there?" a woman's voice asked from the recesses of the cart.

"In jest about five yards of it."

"You mean..."

"The railroad track; my horse is restin' a min'it; it ain't rainin' now, if you're sure goin' to git out."

"Yes, thank you, I must get this next train that passes."

"Well, if you git out here, you've got fo' miles to walk down the track; but I kin drive you three miles fu'ther on to Mr. Percy Lasston's place an' you might hire a horse there an' drive down to the nex' station."

"No, thank you, I'll get out here and walk."

"Fo' miles on the crossties."

"Yes."

"An' you ain't skeered?"

"No."

"Well, I'm right sorry, but I can't drive down the crossties."

"No, and I thank you for bringing me so far. You mentioned a name just now."

"Mr. Percy Lasston."

"Do you know the people about here?"

111

"No, I don't. I'm only a peddler sellin' to the niggers; but I knows the names of the planters. I've stopped tradin' round here though, its too po'. I never stops to sell nothin' this side o' Jonesborough, an' that's nigh to thirty miles fu'ther on; an' frum there I goes on to Greensborough. This is Friday night, an' I muss git to Jonesborough by Sat'day night, for then the man's gits paid off an' comes to town, an' that's my chance."

"Do you expect to travel all night?"

"I do; an' I hate to leave a white woman in the road 'leven o'clock of a rainy night; I certainly do."

"It doesn't matter. No, you need not bother to help me out. Good-bye."

"Good-bye, an' good luck to you, Lady; you're travelin' back to yo' own people, you say? They ought to be mightly proud you'd take sicher journey, an' I hopes you gits there safe; good-bye. You ain't skeered?"

"No, good-bye," and the woman stood still in the mist and the darkness, watching the wagon toil up the incline to the railway.

Not long, then the wagon became a blur, then the sounds faded. Still she stood there poised attentive as if one more "Git up" of the kindly voice; one more grind of wheel, or splash of hoof might reach her; waited in the silence where, gradually, there intruded a soft sound as of whispering rain, or sweeping wings; a sound that as she listened seemed to grow on her awakening senses into a tremulous terror! She caught the stem of a young tree; what was coming? People with panting dogs? A train with glaring lights that would reveal her?

The river! Only the old river; brimful, rushing, swirling, deep and strong; the river that went by home! The young tree swayed a little for she sobbed against it. Dogs, people, would they search for her? Would they bring the dogs? To the pond, to the swamp, to the river? The dogs could not tell, no, at the junction of the three ways the wagon had come. How kind the man had been, a stranger, and white, how fortunate.

Fortunate? The pond, the swamp, the river would have been better. Search for her? Never! As that morning—was it only that morning—? In the awful light that had searched her heart, her life; that had seemed to scorch her physical eyeballs as she had read the letter thrust under her door, so now, she went over slowly, but with the bitterness of death, all the things of her life that had hurt her. From her orphaned babyhood there had been a lack of love, a lack that Alan partly filled, and yet, she had never told him of the lack because he was her Aunt Alicia's only child. But Percy—the leaves of the young tree shivered as in a sudden gust of wind.

That was all past, and now—now it was only a few steps to the railway; here it was; now, four miles on the crossties to the station. The night train passed at two o'clock. The man had said it was eleven now; yes, she had time. Once at the station, she would look up a schedule and decide where she would go. Fifteen dollars she would spend on traveling; this would leave her ten dollars for expenses until she found work. Meanwhile, she would slip off her frock skirt and fold it under her coat where, for the sake of dryness, her thick veil now was. Just before she reached the station, she would put them on. The thick veil would hide her face. Besides, the man at the station would be too sleepy to observe much.

Tired—tired, too tired! The river was just beyond that bank? They'd find her body beaten up against one of the rice dams; or swept aside, entangled in brush and logs; and they would realize. But it did not matter what they realized. They had done what they thought was their duty by her. Better, less cruel, it seemed, to have drowned her as they did the worthless puppies, far better.

Yes, she had told Percy. Percy was her third cousin; lived on his own plantation, and was the head of the family. How he laughed at that; land-poor, tax-ridden, poverty-stricken. And talk of 'The Head of the Family'! But she had been so proud of it; it was fine, she declared, and it was. She—she was still a Lasston! She must go on; must think of something else.

Yes, Percy was older than Alan, and Alan older than she, and on the fateful day when she had been driven to the conclusion that her aunt did not love her—a day in February when the fires were still necessary—those great fires, how sweet they smelled—her despair had demanded outlet and she had told Percy; had poured out all the longings of her life, all the pain of loneliness that had been with her day and night, had told it all clinging to his arm. And he?

The rushing river was nearer now! The friendly river that would lodge her somewhere near the old place. And, yes, she had not hauled her boat up! She stopped a moment, they might think she'd gone out in the boat. Why had she not thought of that? Out on that wild, sweeping tide in her little boat; out with the wind and the rain beating in her face! And she could have fought for her life then; have had the battle that would have dulled her fear of death, and with all her fighting, not have saved her life.

Again she sobbed a little, a tearless sob with a catch in it, and plodded on in the darkness. She knew she would never have entered the
boat. She had courage only to endure; endure life a little longer, a little
longer until her vision cleared. Had she not endured—endured
herself—her life, since—since when? How long was it? The morning
before this night, the morning which she could only remember in fragments as she moved along the dark railway track.

She had been about to do something that morning. What was it? She
was on her way out the door of the big old house which had always
been home to her and Aunt Alicia—taking breakfast to old George. It
was old George who had kept the place running after Aunt Alicia was
left a widow, until Alan had become old enough to begin to look after
things. All this had been her knowledge for all her life. Old George,
good old George, the special care of the family—all who were left, her
Aunt Alicia, Alan and—not herself now—no. And old Mawm Sue,
George's daughter, she was good too, was cook and general servant at
the big house, and his great-grand daughter, little Juno, black little
Juno, down at the cabin to wait on the old man. All her life they had
been about her, and it was this morning she had gone down carrying
George's breakfast in a basket, and with it a pitcher of hot coffee. This
morning!

She must not hasten; she could not run away, not escape; this thing,
no, it would be with her forever—forever. And it was too dark to run;
she would fall, would injure herself, perhaps be unable to get even to
the river! She must walk quietly, steadily.

The woolly little dog, dirty, but with a ribbon about its neck, had
rushed out at her, had stopped her, not its small bark, but the surprise
of such an anomally. Instantly, old George had stood in the door,
blocking the entrance. She could hear his—"Mawnin, Li'l Missy Hagar,
mawnin' ma'm," and his call—"Juno, come teck dese t'ings! Come
quick, gal!" And Juno had dodged under his arm that to steady him,
was against the door frame, and had taken the basket and pitcher.

"But the dog," she had insisted. If she had not; if she had gone
away, her curiosity unsatisfied, would it all have happened?

He said, "Lou's dawg, Li'l Missy Hagar; Lou come las' night." Then
behind the old man, lolling in a rocking chair, she saw a figure in
white. Old George had been careful to block the door, but she, she
had moved forward. Her own fault. The old man had made way for
her, but the figure in white had not moved from the rocking chair. Instead, she had said, "How do you do, Miss Lasston?"

Her face burned now, remembering. She had paused and had stood looking down on the girl who as a child had been a runner of messages up at the big house; a clever, light-footed little creature whom her Aunt Alicia had sent to a mission school in the city. The little thing had cried, had begged not to go, and all her own child sympathy had gone out to the black child. And that had been ten years ago; Lou must be twenty now.

Yes, even now her face burned as she remembered the interview; but then, she had said quietly, "How are you, Lou," How careful the girl's pronunciation had been, how emphasized the "Grandpar-par", how slowly and carelessly she had rocked, old George's great-granddaughter, Lou, yes, all these things she must remember, and the old man leaning on his stick with his old wrinkled face so full of pain. But he was not well, he said, and Lou explained, "I told him all my plans, Miss Lasston, not wise at night; but I wished him to share my joy. I am engaged to be married, Miss Lasston, to a gentleman at the school, one of the teachers." Then old George's sharp interpolation; "A yaller nigger, Miss Hagar!"

"And Grandpar-par," Lou had gone on smoothly; "and Aunt Susan, and Juno must come to live with me. My family must not be servants any longer." But Old George would have none of it. His dim eyes flashed.

"No, ma'm, Miss Hagar!" he had cried quite loud, striking his stick on the floor; "no, ma'm en ef Missis'll lemme stay, I ent gwine; no, ma'm; en Sue ent gwine, en Juno ent gwine nurrer, no, ma'm! En we is berry mad, Miss Hagar; en we ent to say been want you fuh see Lou, no, ma'm!" They had been wise, these old people; but she had pushed in.

Then Lou had talked of the unholy slavery to which her race had been subjected. And she had turned on the Negro girl. "Slavery raised your race," she had said sharply; "you came to this country, savages!" She seemed to hear her own voice now as she announced that; it was true; and once more she sobbed a little as she plodded on in the darkness. Then Lou's retort—"You mean that we are an inferior race," she cried; "made lower than the whites!" And old George's—"Cose, gal!" and he raised his stick as if to strike the girl. Quickly she had saved Lou from the stick, and pushing on, ever pushing on, she had asked, "What do you think, Lou?"

"That we are a little backward," had come glibly, then her voice sharpening; "it is a great tragedy; an awful tragedy! Yes, and you don't care! But there is an outlet, yes, an outlet to this terrible tragedy, yes, we cross over to you whites!" How the words seemed to echo about her out here in the darkness, and the cry, "We cross over and you don't know it, ah ha!"

It had been as a physical blow and she had caught her breath while all the teachings of her life as to the awfulness of amalgamation; the hopelessness of the hybrid; the horrors of the "Return to Race" had swept over her. Her aunt had taught her all this—how carefully it had been done—it had sickened her at the time, and the assertion of the Negro girl was as a sword thrust!

"Impossible!" she had faltered, and at last had turned toward the open door, while through the horrid confusion old George had cried, "En who wants ter be er yaller-white nigger! Ole Mawsa always drown dem half-breed puppy." And she, weakly, "You could never be pure white, Lou, never!"

"But if nobody knows the black blood is in us?"

"Somebody always knows!" She had been taught that too.

"But I know better!" Lou had cried; "wait! Last night I found that my own family had crossed over! That I have white cousins; as white as you! Wait!" and she had run out of the room. Then old George had wailed, the tears running down his face. "Oh, Miss Hagar, Miss Hagar! Please ma'm scuze Lou? Please ma'm? Dee school is done meck she foolish, ma'm? She ent hab no manners, ma'm; en dat letter what she is gittin', Miss Hagar, she done git out she Mah trunk w'at is lef' yer w'en she Mah daid, yes, ma'm; en I ent know say she Mah is keep dat letter, no, ma'm, I ent know it. Dat letter hot my feelin's w'en I fust git it, Miss Hagar, en it hots my feelin's now, ma'm; hots my feelin's des dee same dis berry min'it. Oh, Lawd!"

It was almost a cry as Lou had rushed in. "Read that!" she ordered. Race instinct, race experience, all had then risen up within her, all were with her now as she remembered, even now! And would she ever forget the grime and dirt of the letter, the worn age of it! Written in the thirties, and to old George from his aunt, telling him that after she had gone North, her Negro husband had left her to return South, and that then she had married a 'very white man', so she had expressed it; a German carpenter; that George's first cousin, her daughter by this German, had also married a white man and had gone west, where she was considered a white woman, and her name was 'Mrs. Henry Smithers'. That her advice to George was to run away from slavery and to do as she had done, so as to give his children a better place in life; and the letter was signed "Lualamba Siegers." And during the reading old

George had sat with covered eyes, but Lou's eyes had watched her as she read. She had paused a second before looking up, then all that she could find to say was, "What a curious name."

"Her African name!" Lou cried.

Then at last she had stepped out of the open door which she had better never have entered, and in a maze of confusion had returned to the house, to her sewing with her aunt in the study. And for once she had felt that she must talk, must say all that was in her to say as to what she had been through, and her aunt had listened, quiet, unanswering, until she reached the letter, then, without one sign of interest she had said, "I have read the letter." And then had explained the story, how Lualamba and her brother, old George's father, had been bought by the Lasstons out of pity for their condition, as they seemed of a better tribe. "There was a great difference in the tribes," her aunt had added. How strange that seemed. Superior tribe. Lualamba had married a Negro! How foolish to shut her eyes. Of course a Negro, and on the Howard plantation. Then Lualamba had been sold to the Howards, that was the custom, so that she would not be separated from her husband. Then old Mr. Howard dying, Mrs. Howard, having no children, and being a Northern woman, had sold to Mr. Howard's nephew, everything except Lualamba and her husband; she had taken them with her to the North. "When the letter came," her aunt had finished, "old George could not read it, and brought it to my mother. At her death I found it, read it to see what I should do with it. I returned it to George. He would not let me read it to him this second time; said it was a wicked, sinful letter."

And she had cried—"It is, Aunt Alicia, it is!" "Yes," her aunt had answered in a toneless voice. "And what good does it do them to 'Cross Over'," she had pushed on. "It is forever in the blood; they are always Negro, always, forever!" "Forever," her aunt had agreed. "I'd kill myself," she had cried! There had been a second's pause, and then, "Perhaps," was all the answer, but in the voice there had been a strange tone and her aunt had added, "But the Negroes would not feel it as you do; they have not been trained—" and she had interrupted sharply—"They have not my blood! My blood that goes back and back!"

"Nor your prejudices," came the quiet reply.

"Race instinct!" her aunt had cried. "Prejudices," was repeated.

"The world calls it prejudice; and the Negro does not mind," her aunt had gone on; "and ambitious, they do not tell their secret, and many, many people do not know the marks," then she had added slowly—"all the marks."

"Do you know them?" and now she had leaned forward, and—"tell me?" she had whispered, had slipped from off her low chair to her knees close beside her aunt. Then like a physical blow came a low, fierce "No!" and a quick movement away from her as if she were a repulsive thing—"the subject is abborrent to me! Hush!"

She felt the hot tears in her eyes, tears for the poor girl who was herself, kneeling there. She had got up slowly, had tried to go on with her sewing. Her heart had seemed wrung, somehow; she longed that her aunt should talk to her of this dreadful question; should say something, something pitiful for the poor Negroes. Never until that moment had she thought of them as having any feeling on the subject of being black. That they were black and were servants, had seemed to her a foregone conclusion. But that they had this hopeless desire—wicked, horrible desire, she had called it—to be white, to mingle their blood with the blood of the white race, was too appalling, it seemed almost to suffocate her! Poor things, poor things! They could not escape their fate; they were blacks just as birds were birds. "Cross Over!" Unendurable! Better raise themselves as a black race, as a black nation, so she had thought; had wondered why some leader did not rise to tell them this; to preach a hegira; to take them quickly back to their own country, such a rich country, before the white nations took it all; rouse their self-respect, their ambition as blacks! "Poor things, poor things!" and in her absorption she had said this last aloud, and started, looking up, "I meant the Negroes, Aunt Alicia," she had explained; "the poor things who long to be white and cannot. I wonder if they know about the 'Return to Race'," Then she had caught sight of the clock. "Already eleven," she said.

She stopped in her walk. Twelve hours ago! Twelve years—twelve centuries! All time had swept over her, had blighted her! What remained? She must not think, no, just walk. Her life lay all before her in which to think; now she must walk, step from crosstie to crosstie until she reached the station.

Twelve hours ago when her aunt had said, "You cannot go to walk, the dogs are out with Alan." Then she had got her hat and a small pistol that Percy had given her; she did not know it was an expensive one; "Just down the Avenue," she had explained.

"How could Percy afford it?" was demanded; and—" Is he in the habit of giving you things?" And the look! One moment it held her, then, "You may go." And she had gone.

That look burned and seared her still! Down the avenue she had sped, under the live oaks, that draped in the long gray moss did what was possible to keep out the brilliant sunlight. On either side, beyond the avenue, had stretched the level pine woods, and wherever there was a hillock or any support for a vine, there grew the yellow jessamine, filling the air with an ineffable sweetness. She could see it all, this dear home of all her life, could smell the jessamine; out here in the darkness as she walked, the picture seemed to shine about her, and yonder, at the end; there, by the big gate—Percy!

She had a right to dream—to remember? How fair and tall he was, how blue his eyes with ever a laugh in them. How strong the clasp of his hand, how rich his voice.

"And what are you running from?" he had demanded. But she had not told.

The haste had given her a color, it made her beautiful, he said, quite gave him "indigestion of the heart!" And she was so "Fizzy, always driving the cork out; not at all a Lasston; a changeling, with red-black eyes." His "Blossom" for whose love he was "hungry and thirsty".

And she—"I give you all! My life, my soul!"

"Hagar!" was all he said; her name that she hated, that she had not understood; why—why name her Hagar?

Then, "We must tell Aunt Alicia," she had declared; "She murdered me with a look!"

"And so you ran—of course we'll tell; I've always wanted to tell, but you, little coward, would not. But now I've sold the pine lands, and we can be married at once."

For a little moment she had looked within the gates of Paradise, at least she had done that; then again fear had cowed her. "But that look!" she had whispered; "that look about the pistol; I felt burned up! Now that you love me perhaps she will love me." And to his assertions she had answered, "Never, and yet she adored my father; he was 'The Head of the Family' and if I had been a boy—"

She paused a moment. If she had been a boy? It was a new line of thought and she followed it as she tramped; if she had been a boy. She must think that out in the days to come.

Then Percy had untied his horse and had gone with her to the house. "It's unlucky touching perfect happiness," he said.

Then she—"I am not happy."

Once more he called her 'little coward' as they walked together. From the garden gate where he tied his horse, she could see her aunt standing at the study window that was a door, and upstairs, in the sunshine by an open window, her cousin Sabina Lasston, sewing. How her

fair hair glittered in the sunshine; and all the connection had wanted
Percy to marry Sabina. A choking came in her throat. He would, in
time.

He had laughed at her when they reached the gate. "I'll kiss you
here where they can see," he said; "such an easy way to tell them. Why
so terrified? You really are a coward." He had held her hand as they
went around the big tea olive bush, how sweet it smelled! Then her
aunt had called them in at the study window. How gay and debonair
he had been about it all.

"Cousin Alicia wants us to go in there," he whispered; "trap us as it
were; don't worry, I'll protect you. Here goes! Hullo, 'Bina!", and he
waved his hand to the upstairs window. "Good morning, Cousin Alicia,
how are you? Shall we come in there? I love this dear old study. Too
cool? Let me close that window; the wind has still a little nip in it, only
we've been walking.

Then—"You went to meet him, Hagar?"

"We are engaged, Cousin Alicia," he had struck in; "third cousins,
no harm, and I've come to ask you to the wedding. Why—why, are
you not well!

"Yes, yes, I—I think so; I had, I have had, no suspicion of this;
Hagar—"

Then for once she had been brave. "My fault," she had cried; "my
fault, I would not let him tell you."

Then the order—"Leave the room." And she had gone despite
Percy's order to stay, despite his clasp of her arm.

That was the end. She was glad she had got to the end; had it all
clear of confusion in her mind even though she could not remember
how she had got up the stairs.

Lying face downwards on her bed was the next clear thing she could
remember; then to the window; and he had not turned his head, had
gone slowly away from the house, as if suddenly crippled. In silence she
had endured this, endured, yes.

She had eaten the food put down outside her door for the sake of
the strength to endure. She had not died, no, she had endured the horrors of the letter thrust under her door, the hideous anticlimax of its
ending: "I have said that you have a nervous headache and must not be
distrubed"! All this she had endured; but not yet had she dared. She
had not dared even to think, not dared to realize, not dared to feel—to
die! Not yet. Recalling and arranging memories, scenes, that was all.
"Afraid?" the man had asked. Yesterday, this walk would have been a
terrifying impossibility. Now? Well, now, if anything further happened

to her, perhaps, perhaps she would have the courage for the river; no, she was not afraid of this.

The day was still as death; a fine rain was falling noiselessly; the bright jessamine of the day before now were hanging heavy with moisture, the long moss showed a pale, dim green because of the wetness. Near one of the windows stood Mrs. Jarnigan, still and gray as the day. She seemed to be watching, listening. She walked from window to window, then out to the front door, standing for a moment to look down the avenue. Something sent a shiver through her, perhaps the rain, or the wind that now and then came in little gusts, and she went in again.

She was cold, colder than the rain or the wind could have made her. For twenty-four hours she had not rested, had not slept; had again and again gone over the scenes of the day before. How radiant Percy had looked; had come to ask her to his wedding—wedding with Hagar!

Great God! Blind! How blind she had been, how foolish; had she not eyes to see that the girl was beautiful? How his fair, level brows had drawn together when Hagar at her order had left the room, closing the door, how his blue eyes had flashed! What avail that she had pleaded to him, "Before God, I had no thought of this! I have kept the girl so secluded." How he had stared.

"What!" he had whispered it. Then her own voice answering, low, intense, that seemed to still the universe.

"It killed my brother," she had said; "it crucified me!" Then dimly, through the closed windows she had heard a mockingbird singing.

"Think," she had gone on, and she had come closer, peering into his face; "think had there ever before been a brunette Lasston?" A white line had settled about Percy's lips.

"Sit down, sit down," she had ordered; "it is a long story;" but he would not. Then with her hand on his shoulder, she had told him the story.

"My brother, so young, that when he finished his part in the war went to college, and there met his wife, older than he, but very beautiful. We opposed this stranger; he was infatuated. He brought her here a bride. Just before the child was born, an old German came on a visit, a scientific man. He stayed here for two days. The German said to me, "You do not mind the Negro blood, then?"

In telling the terrible story to Percy she had given the German's very words that for years had been burned into her heart, her memory.

"She has one mark of Negro blood," the German had said, "that may fade in her child; but she lacks, she has not the mark of the pure white. The hair, the modeling of the nose—one drop of Negro blood eliminated that delicate modelling."

The words seemed even now actually to sound in her ears; she shivered and went to the fire. How cold she was. She put on a fresh log, made it blaze cheerfully, then stood there warming herself. Why could she not forget; would she be always seeing Percy's face gone so gray, so drawn? And beyond that seeing again, as she had seemed to see the day before, the face of her young brother, dead all these years? He had overheard the German telling her! He had come in at the door—the door there behind Percy—and his fair young face had gone gray and drawn just as Percy's had; and yesterday he had come and stood behind Percy—she had had a vision of him and of his dead wife standing there!

And the wife had known that she had black blood; after the German left them, the whole story had been told. She had known that the Lasstons had owned her ancestors, but not that in old George and old Sue she had black cousins left there. That had been a terrible shock to her; unknowing, they had bowed down before her as their master's wife—before Hagar as their master's daughter! They had been as an awful nightmare to the young wife and she had died when her child was born. Hagar, the father had named the child; Hagar, "'An alien', he said; 'an outcast'."

The story told, Percy had turned his dead eyes, his ashen face to her; "Thank you," he had said. "Thank you—may I go this way?" and had put his hand on the window latch. How loud the mockingbird had sounded as the window opened, singing its heart out! Still singing as when he and Hagar had come inside. The sun was still shining. Then he had crossed the broad piazza to the steps, down to the garden path, round the olive bushes to where his horse stood at the gate. He did not once turn, not once look back.

She drew a sobbing breath; how still the house was. Not a footstep, not a voice, no sound anywhere, just the wind outside, the drip of the rain from the roof. She started away from the cheerful fire so suddenly that she overturned a small screen; the sound seemed to echo, to come, to go. Hastily she went from the window to the door and back again; up and down; out to the piazza. And old George had hobbled up to the kitchen this morning, hearing the awful news that his young mistress was missing, and she was waiting there in the kitchen now for some word. His kinswoman. He had a right to know it all? Never!

She wrung her hands together; she must stop thinking. Would this terrible waiting never end—would no one ever come! Once more she went from window to door and back again; up and down the piazza. At last she bent her head, stopped, went quickly to the door. Yes, there, she could see her son now, and coming alone!

A horseman dismounted at the gate and tied his horse, slowly he came as if neither rain nor shelter meant anything to him. She met him at the step.

"No sign," he said, going into the study; "We've dragged the pond, have searched the swamp out to the river; the freshet makes the river impossible; but the dogs did not go to the river—"

"Where?" It was a whisper.

"They lost scent in the middle of the public road, and I found this." In his extended palm there lay a gray button.

Her whole being seemed to relax. "Her gray frock," she said; "that tells nothing; she had that on yesterday, too."

"You say that so quietly, mother," laying his hands on her two shoulders. "Mother," swaying her slightly; "why did you let her live here as our equal?"

"A girl, I could not cast her off; poverty-stricken, I had no money to place her elsewhere; I could not bring myself to explain, the disgrace would have killed me! The disgrace, the horror of it, killed my brother. But, where's Sabina?"

"She and the Doctor have ridden again to the river; she will not give up the search."

"She does not know our secret; and Percy?"

"Percy? Good God!"

"What?"

"Says, God has been merciful!"

"He has; and Hagar has been well trained."

"Mother!" Staring into Mrs. Jarnigan's eyes; "your niece, your—"

"Hush!"

"Your only brother's only child; trained by you; beautiful, gentle! Mother, did you not love her?"

"Love her? God! My life has been torture! When she touched me my blood turned backward in my veins! Eating at my table; sitting near you; treating you as a brother! The unspeakable misery! Her black hair, coarse, curly! Could you not see, boy? And I, I cut myself off from my people; I could not take her into their homes any more than I would take a disease there. Lonely, wretched, I've lived here with that calamity, turning over and over in my mind what to do for her—with her. A boy, I would have sent away, but a girl? A little black-eyed, black-haired baby, she killed her father. He died within the year. 'My blood!' he cried; 'My race! "

"And now, mother, she has vanished; that is noble, mother."

"She has Lasston blood in her; she has been well trained."

"She might not have lived up to it."

"She may not yet."

"She may not be alive, mother."

"In all my training of her I looked forward to this day, and now, in the first trial, she has done the right thing."

"I say, she may not be alive."

"She is afraid; she would not kill herself. She loves the soft things; she was not direct; was hard to train. I taught her daily the 'Noblesse Oblige' of the Lasstons; it became her creed; it is guiding her now; pray God it will continue. Her father named her 'Hagar Black'; if I should go out into the world to hunt for her, I should hunt for Hagar Black. Thank God, Percy needed no arguments! Your attitude, Alan, shames me."

"Suppose Sabina find trace of her?"

"I should send Percy to lose it."

"Oh, mother!"

"What would you have? Bring her back as our equal? Place her in old George's cabin? You have no answer. There is no answer. To lose herself to us; to make her own place in life, that is the only thing. Pray God she may remain true to her training and not marry a white man—"

"How dare you, mother!"

"Not marry at all; her children might—"

"Here is Sabina."

"We have ridden miles and miles, cousin, down the river. It is over the banks; the current is terrific!"

"Thank you, dear Sabina, you must be wet."

"No, the clouds are breaking."

"And Doctor Bruce?"

"He left me at the gate, cousin," she paused, "cousin, he has no hope."

"Yes, Sabina."

"She must have gone out early this morning in her boat; old George said she often did—she did not mind weather."

"Perhaps."

"And, cousin, if you do not mind, will you let Alan ride home with me now? And bring the buggy back for you? Won't you come too? A little change, cousin?"

"Oh, Sabina, yes! Thank you dear."

"And Alan, too?"

"Thank you, dear;" her voice faltering a little; "thank you."

"Poor cousin," putting her arm about the elder woman; "Mama will be so glad to see you; the first time in all my life that you have come to us; you'd never bring Hagar, too many, you said; but now?"

"Yes, now I can come; I shall be ready when Alan returns."

"You've led such a hermit life; you seemed to need no one but dear Hagar; but now you must come out to us."

"I shall be glad; but none of you must be pitiful, sorrowful; it would kill me! Good-bye, dear Sabina; I shall be ready; yes, close the door."

She stood quite still until the door was fast, then she went to the window. "In her boat on the river; that story will do; and old George suggested it." She raised her arms above her head. "Free!" she said, looking up, while a great light broke over her face; "once more, once more myself—free among my own kind, once more!" Her voice broke and the sobs came, deep, heart-rending, almost cries, that shook her from head to foot. Down on her knees she prayed, "God have mercy! If I have failed, have mercy!"

And out in the olive bushes a bird was singing—singing.

Morris, standing over his fallen foe, looked about him as if dazed.

AN INCIDENT

It was an ordinary frame house standing on brick legs, and situated on a barren knoll, which, because of the dead level of marsh and swamp and deserted fields from which it rose, seemed to achieve the loneliness of a real height. The south and west sides of the house looked out on marsh and swamp; the north and east sides on a wide stretch of old fields grown up in broomgrass. Beyond the marsh rolled a river, now quite beyond its banks with a freshet; beyond the swamp, which was a cypress swamp, rose a railway embankment leading to a bridge that crossed the river. On the other two sides the old fields ended in a solid black wall of pine barren. A roadway led from the house through the broomgrass to the barren, and at the beginning of this road stood an outhouse, also on brick legs, which, save for a small stable, was the sole outbuilding. One end of this house was a kitchen, the other was divided into two rooms for servants. There were some shattered remnants of oak trees out in the field, and some chimneys overgrown with vines, showing where in happier times the real homestead had stood.

It was towards the end of February; a clear afternoon drawing towards sunset; and all the flat, sad country was covered with a drifting red glow that turned the field of broomgrass into a sea of gold; that lighted up the black wall of pine barren, and shot, here and there, long shafts of light into the sombre depths of the cypress swamp. There was no sign of life about the dwelling house, though the doors and windows stood open; but every now and then a Negro woman came out of the kitchen and looked about, while within a dog whined.

Shading her eyes with her hand, this woman would gaze across the field towards the ruin; then down the road; then, descending the steps, she would walk a little way towards the swamp and look along the dam that, ending the yard on this side, led out between the marsh and the swamp to the river. The over-full river had backed up into the yard, however, and the line of the dam could now only be guessed by the wall of solemn cypress trees that edged the swamp. Still, the woman looked in this direction many times, and also towards the railway embankment, from which a path led towards the house, crossing the head of the swamp by a bridge made of two felled trees.

But look as she would, she evidently did not find what she sought, and muttering "Lawd! Lawd!" she returned to the kitchen, shook the tied dog into silence, and seating herself near the fire gazed sombrely into its depths. A covered pot hung from the crane over the blaze, making a thick bubbling noise, as if what it contained had boiled itself almost dry, and a coffeepot on the hearth gave forth a pleasant smell. The woman from time to time turned the spit of a tin kitchen wherein a fowl was roasting, and moved about the coals on the top of a Dutch oven at one side. She had made preparation for a comfortable supper, and evidently for others than herself.

She went again to the open door and looked about, the dog springing up and following to the end of his cord. The sun was nearer the horizon now, and the red glow was brighter. She looked towards the ruin; looked along the road; came down the steps and looked towards the swamp and the railway path. This time she took a few steps in the direction of the house; looked up at its open windows, at the front door standing ajar, at a pair of gloves and a branch from the vine at the ruin, that lay on the top step of the piazza, as if in passing one had put them there, intending to return in a moment. While she looked the distant whistle of a locomotive was heard echoing back and forth about the empty land, and the rumble of an approaching train. She turned a little to listen, then went hurriedly back to the kitchen.

The rumbling sound increased, although the speed was lessened as the river was neared. Very slowly the train was moving, and the woman, peeping from the window, watched a gentleman get off and begin the descent of the path.

"Mass Johnnie!" she said. "Lawd! Lawd!" and again seated herself by the fire until the rapid, firm footstep having passed, she went to the door, and standing well in the shadow, watched.

Up the steps the gentleman ran, pausing to pick up the gloves and the bit of vine. The Negro groaned. Then in at the open door, "Nellie!" he called, "Nellie!"

The woman heard the call, and going back quickly to her seat by the fire, threw her apron over her head.

"Abram!" was the next call; then, "Aggie!"

She sat quite still, and the master, running up the kitchen steps and coming in at the door, found her so.

"Aggie?"

"Yes, suh."

"Why didn't you answer me?"

The veiled figure rocked a little from side to side.

"What the mischief is the matter?" walking up to the woman and pulling the apron from over her face. "Where is your Miss Nellie?"

"I dun'no', suh; but yo' supper is ready, Mass Johnnie."

"Has your mistress driven anywhere?"

"De horse in de stable, suh." The woman now rose as if to meet a climax, but her eyes were still on the fire.

"Did she go out walking?"

"Dis mawnin', suh."

"This morning!" he repeated, slowly, wonderingly, "and has not come back yet?"

The woman began to tremble, and her eyes, shining and terrified, glanced furtively at her master.

"Where is Abram?"

"I dun'no', suh!" It was a gasping whisper.

The master gripped her shoulder, and with a maddened roar he cried her name—"Aggie!"

The woman sank down. Perhaps his grasp forced her down. "Fo' Gawd!" she cried—"'fo' Gawd, Mass Johnnie, I dun'no'!" holding up beseeching hands between herself and the awful glare of his eyes. "I'll tell you, suh, Mass Johnnie, I'll tell you!" crouching away from him. "Miss Nellie gimme out dinner en supper, den she put on she hat en gone to de ole chimbly en git some de brier what grow dey. Den she come back en tell Abram fuh git a bresh broom en sweep de ya'd. Lemme go, Mass Johnnie, please, suh, en I tell you better, suh. En Abram teck de hatchet en gone to'des de railroad fuh cut de bresh. 'Fo' Gawd, Mass Johnnie, it's de trute, suh! Den I tell Miss Nellie say de chicken is all git out de coop, en she say I muss ketch one fuh unner supper, suh; en I teck de dawg en gone in de fiel' fuh look fuh de chicken. En I see Miss Nellie put'e glub en de brier on de step, en walk to'des de swamp, like'e was goin' on de dam—'kase de water ent rise ober de dam den—en den I gone in de broom grass en I run de chicken, en I ent ketch one tay I git clean ober to de woods. En when I come back de glub is layin' on de step, en de brier, des like Miss Nellie leff um—" She stopped and her master straightened himself.

"Well," he said, and his voice was strained and weak.

The servant once more flung her apron over her head, and broke into violent crying. "Dat's all, Mass Johnnie! dat's all! I dun'no' wey

Abram is gone; I dun'no' what Abram is do! Nobody ent been on de place dis day—dis day but me—but me! Oh, Lawd! oh, Lawd en Gawd!"

The master stood as if dazed. His face was drawn and gray, and his breath came in awful gasps. A moment he stood so, then he strode out of the house. With a howl the dog sprang forward, snapping the cord, and rushed after his master.

The woman's cries ceased, and without moving from her crouching position she listened with straining ears to the sounds that reached her from the stable. In a moment the clatter of horses' hoofs going at a furious pace swept by, then a dead silence fell. The intense quiet seemed to rouse her, and going to the door, she looked out. The glow had faded, and the gray mist was gathering in distinct strata above the marsh and the river. She went out and looked about her as she had done so many times during that long day. She gazed at the water that was still rising; she peered cautiously behind the stable and under the houses; she approached the woodpile as if under protest, gathered some logs into her arms and an axe that was lying there; then turning towards the kitchen, she hastened her steps, looking back over her shoulder now and again, as if fearing pursuit. Once in the kitchen she threw down the wood and barred the door; she shut the boarded window shutter, fastening it with an iron hook; then leaning the axe against the chimney, she sat down by the fire, muttering, "If dat nigger come sneakin' back yer now, I'll split 'e haid open, *sho* ."

Recovering a little from her panic, she was once more a cook, and swung the crane from over the fire, brushed the coals from the top of the Dutch- oven, and pushed the tin kitchen farther from the blaze. "Mass Johnnie 'll want sump'h'n to eat some time dis night," she said; then, after a pause, "en I gwine eat *now* ." She got a plate and cup, and helped herself to hominy out of the pot, and to a roll out of the oven; but though she looked at the fowl she did not touch it, helping herself instead to a goodly cup of coffee. So she ate and drank with the axe close beside her, now and then pausing to groan and mutter—"Po' Mass Johnnie!—po' Mass Johnnie!—Lawd! Lawd!—if Miss Nellie had er sen' Abram atter dat chicken—like I tell um—Lawd!" shaking her head the while.

Through the gathering dusk John Morris galloped at the top speed of his horse. Reaching the little railway station, he sprang off, throwing the reins over a post, and strode in.

"Write this telegram for me, Green," he said; "my hand trembles." "*To* Sam Partin, *Sheriff, Pineville:*

"My wife missing since morning. Negro, Abram Washington, disappeared. Bring men and dogs. Get off night train this side of bridge. Will be fire on the path to mark the place. John Morris."

"Great God!" the operator said, in a low voice. "I'll come too, Mr. Morris."

"Thank you," John Morris answered. "I am going to get the Wilson boys, and Rountree and Mitchell," and for the first time the men's eyes met. Determined, deadly, sombre, was the look exchanged; then Morris went away.

None of the men whom Morris summoned said much, nor did they take long to arm themselves, saddle, and mount, and by nine o'clock Aggie heard them come galloping across the field; then her master's voice calling her. There was little time in which to make the signal fire on the railroad embankment, and to cut lightwood into torches, even though there were many hands to do the work. John Morris's dog followed him a part of the way to the woodpile, then turned aside to where the water had crept up from the swamp into the yard. Aggie saw the dog, and spoke to Mr. Morris.

"Dat's de way dat dawg do dis mawnin', Mass Johnnie, an' when I gone to ketch de chicken, Miss Nellie was walkin' to 'des dat berry place."

An irresistible shudder went over John Morris, and one of the gentlemen standing near asked if he had a boat.

"The bateau was tied to that stake this morning," Mr. Morris answered, pointing to a stake some distance out in the water; "but I have another boat in the top of the stable." Every man turned to go for it, showing the direction of their fears, and launched it where the log bridge crossed the head of the swamp, and where now the water was quite deep.

The whistle was heard at the station, and the rumble of the oncoming train. The fire flared high, lighting up the group of men standing about it, booted and belted with ammunition belts, quiet, and white, and determined.

Many curious heads looked out as the sheriff and his men—six men besides Green from the station—got off; then the train rumbled away in the darkness towards the surging, turbulent river, and the crowd moved towards the house.

Mr. Morris told of his absence in town on business. That Abram had been hired first as a field hand; and that later, after his marriage, he had taken Abram from the field to look after his horse and to do the heavier work about the house and yard.

"And the woman Aggie is trustworthy?"

"I am sure of it; she used to belong to us."

"Abram is a strange Negro?"

"Yes."

Then Aggie was called in to tell her story. Abram had taken the hatchet and had gone towards the railroad for brush to make a broom. She had taken the dog and gone into the broom grass to catch a fowl, and the last she had seen of her mistress she was walking towards the dam, which was then above the water.

"How long were you gone after the chicken?"

"I dun'no', suh; but I run um clean to the woods 'fo' I ketch um, en I walked back slow 'kase I tired."

"Were you gone an hour?"

"I spec so, suh, 'kase when I done ketch de chicken I stop fuh pick up some lightwood I see wey Abram been cuttin' wood yistiddy."

"And your mistress was not here when you came back—nor Abram?"

"No, suh, nobody; en 'e wuz so lonesome I come en look in dis house fuh Miss Nellie, but 'e ent deyyer; en I look in de bush fuh Abram, but I ent see um nudder. En de dawg run to de water en howl en ba'k en ba'k tay I tie um up in de kitchen."

"And was the boat tied to the stake this morning?"

"Yes, suh; en when I been home long time en git scare, den I look en see de boat gone."

"You don't think that your mistress got in the boat and drifted away by accident?"

"No, suh, nebber, suh; Miss Nellie 'fraid de water lessen Mass Johnnie is wid um."

"Is Abram a good boy?"

"I dun'no', suh; I dun'no' nuttin' 'tall 'bout Abram, suh; Abram is strange nigger to we."

"Did he take his things out of his room?"

"Abram t'ings? Ki! Abram ent hab nuttin' ceppen what Miss Nellie en Mass Johnnie gi'um. No, suh, dat nigger ent hab nuttin' but de close on 'e back when 'e come to we."

The sheriff paused a moment. "I think, Mr. Morris," he said, at last, "that we'd better separate. You, with Mr. Mitchell and Mr. Rountree, had better take your boat and hunt in the swamp and marsh, and along the river bank. Let Mr. Wilson, his brothers, and Green take your dog and search in the pine barren. I'll take my men and my dogs and cross the railroad. The signal of any discovery will be three shots fired in quick succession. The gathering place 'll be this house, where a member of the discovering party 'll meet the other parties and bring 'em to the discovery. And I beg that you'll refrain from violence, at least until we can reach each other. We've no proof of anything—"

"Damn proof!"

"An' our only clew," the sheriff went on, "the missing boat, points to Mrs. Morris's safety." A little consultation ensued; then agreeing to the sheriff's distribution of forces, they left the house.

The sheriff's dogs—the lean, small hounds used on such occasions—were tied and he held the ropes. There was an anxious look on his face, and he kept his dogs near the house until the party for the barren had mounted and ridden away, and the party in the boat had pushed off into the blackness of the swamp, a torch fastened at the prow casting weird, uncertain shadows. Then ordering his six men to mount and to lead his horse, he went to the room of the Negro Abram and got an old shirt. The two lean little dogs were restless, but they made no sound as he led them across the railway. Once on the other side, he let them smell the shirt, and loosed them, and was about to mount, when, in the flash of a torch, he saw something in the grass.

"A hatchet!" he said to his companions, picking it up; "and clean, thank God!"

The men looked at each other, then one said, slowly, "He coulder drowned her?"

The sheriff did not answer, but followed the dogs that had trotted away with their noses to the ground.

"I'm sure the nigger came this way," the sheriff said, after a while. "Those others may find the poor young lady, but I feel sure of the nigger."

One of the men stopped short. "That nigger's got to die," he said.

"Of course," the sheriff answered, "but not by Judge Lynch's court. This circuit's got a judge that'll hang him lawfully."

"I b'lieve Judge More will," the recalcitrant admitted, and rode on. "But," he added, "if I know Mr. John Morris, that nigger's safe to die one way or another."

They rode more rapidly now, as the dogs had quickened their pace. The moon had risen, and the riding, for men who hunted recklessly, was not bad. Through woods and across fields, over fences and streams, down by-paths and old roads, they followed the little dogs.

"We're makin' straight for the next county," the sheriff said.

"We're makin' straight for the old Powis settlement," was answered. "Nothin' but niggers have lived there since the war, an' that nigger's there, I'll bet."

"That's so," the sheriff said. "About how many niggers live there?"

"There ain't more than half a dozen cabins left now. We can easy manage that many."

It was a long rough ride, and in spite of their rapid pace it was some time after midnight before they saw the clearing where clustered the few cabins left of the plantation quarters of a well-known place, which in its day had yielded wealth to its owners. The moon was very bright, and, save for the sound of the horses' feet, the silence was intense.

"Look sharp," the sheriff said; "that nigger ain't sleepin' much if he's here, and he might try to slip off."

The dogs were going faster now, and yelping a little.

"Keep up, boys!" and the sheriff spurred his horse.

In a few minutes they thundered into the little settlement, where the dogs were already barking and leaping against a close-shut door. Frightened black faces began to peer out. Low exclamations and guttural ejaculations were heard as the armed men scattered, one to each cabin, while the sheriff hammered at the door where the dogs were jumping.

"It's the sheriff!" he called, "come to get Abram Washington. Bring him out and you kin go back to your beds. We're all armed, and nobody need to try runnin'."

The door opened cautiously, and an old Negro looked out. "Abram's my son, Mr. Partin," he said, "an''fo' Gawd he ent yer."

"No lyin', old man; the dogs brought us straight here. Don't make me burn the house down; open the door."

The door was closing when the sheriff, springing from his horse, forced it steadily back. A shot came from within, but it ranged wild, and in an instant the sheriff's pistol covered the one room, where a smouldering fire gave light. Two of the men followed him, and one, making for the fire, pushed it into a blaze, which revealed a group of Negroes—an old man, a young woman, some children, and a young man crouching behind with a gun in his hand. The sheriff walked straight up to the young man, whose teeth were chattering.

"I arrest you," he said; "come on." "That's the feller," confirmed one of the guard; "I've seen him at Mr. Morris's place."

"Tie him," the sheriff ordered, "while I get that gun. Give it to me, old man, or I'll take you to jail, too." It was yielded up—an old-time rifle—and the sheriff smashed it against the side of the chimney, throwing the remnants into the fire. "Lead on," he said, and the young Negro was taken outside. Quickly he was lifted on to a horse and tied there, while the former rider mounted behind one of his companions, and they rode out of the settlement into the woods. "Git into the shadows," one said; "they might be fools enough to shoot."

Once in the road, the sheriff called a halt. "One of you must ride back to Mr. Morris's place and collect the other search parties, while we make for Pineville jail. Now, Abram, come on."

"I ent done nuttin', Mr. Partin, suh," the Negro urged. "I ent hot Mis' Morris."

"Who said anything 'bout Mrs. Morris?" was asked, sharply.

The Negro groaned.

"You're hanging yourself, boy," the sheriff said; "but since you know, where *is* Mrs. Morris?"

"I dun'no', suh."

"Why did you run away?"

"Kase I 'fraid Mr. Morris."

"What were you 'fraid of?"

"Kase Mis' Morris gone." They were riding rapidly now, and the talk was jolted out.

"Where?"

"I dun'no', suh, but I ent tech um."

"You're a damned liar."

"No, suh, I ent tech um; I des look at um."

"I'd like to gouge your eyes out!" cried one of the men, and struck him.

"None o' that!" ordered the sheriff. "And you keep your mouth shut, Abram; you'll have time to talk on your trial."

"Blast a trial!" growled the crowd.

"The rope's round his neck now," suggested one, "and I see good trees at every step."

"Please, suh, gentlemen," pleaded the shaking Negro, "I ent done nuttin'."

"Shut your mouth!" ordered the sheriff again, "and ride faster. Day'll soon break."

"You're 'fraid Mr. Morris 'll ketch us 'fore we reach the jail," laughed one of the guard. And the sheriff did not answer.

The eastern sky was gray when the party rode into Pineville, a small, straggling country town, and clattered through its one street to the jail. To the Negro, at least, it was a welcome moment, for, with his feet tied under the horse, his hands tied behind his back, and a rope with a slip knot round his neck, he had not found the ride a pleasant one. A misstep of his horse would surely have precipitated his hanging, and he knew well that such an accident would have given much satisfaction to his captors. So he uttered a fervent "Teng Gawd!" as he was hustled into the jail gate and heard it close behind him.

Early as it was, most of the town was up and excited. Betting had been high as to whether the sheriff would get the prisoner safe into the jail, and even the winners seemed disappointed that he had accomplished this feat, although they praised his skillful management. But the sheriff knew that if the lady's body was found, that if Mr. Morris could find any proof against the Negro, that if Mr. Morris even expressed a wish that the Negro should hang, the whole town would side with him instantly; and the sheriff knew, further, that in such an emergency he would be the Negro's only defender and that the jail could easily be carried by the mob.

All these thoughts had been with him during the long night, and though he himself was quite willing to hang the Negro, being fully persuaded of his guilt, he was determined to do his official duty, and to save the prisoner's life until sentence was lawfully passed on him. But how? If he could quiet the town before the day brightened, he had a plan, but to accomplish this seemed wellnigh impossible.

He handcuffed the prisoner and locked him into a cell, then advised his escort to go and get food, as before the day was done—indeed, just as soon as Mr. Morris should reach the town—he would probably need them to help him defend the jail.

They nodded among themselves, and winked, and laughed a little, and one said, "Right good play-actin'"; and watching, the sheriff knew that he could depend on only one man, his own brother, to help him. But he sent him off along with the others, and was glad to see that the crowd of townspeople went with his guard, listening eagerly to the details of the suspected tragedy and the subsequent hunt. This was his only chance, and he went at once to the Negro's cell.

"Now, Abram," he said, "if you don't want to be a dead man in an hour's time, you'd better do exactly what I tell you."

"Yes, suh, please Gawd."

"Put on this old hat," handing him one, "and pull it down over your eyes, and follow me. When we get outside, you walk along with me like any ordinary nigger going to his work; and remember, if you stir hand or foot more than to walk, you are a dead man. Come on."

There was a back way out of the jail, and to this the sheriff went. Once outside, he walked briskly, the Negro keeping step with him diligently. They did not meet any one, and before very long they reached the sheriff's house, which stood on the outskirts of the town. Being a widower, he knocked peremptorily on the door, and when it was opened by his son, he marched his prisoner in without explanation.

"Shut the door, Willie," he said, "and load the Winchester."

"Please, suh—" interjected the Negro.

For answer, the sheriff took a key from the shelf, and led him out of the back door to where, down a few steps, there was another door leading into an underground cellar.

"Now, Abram," he said, "you're to keep quiet in here till I can take you to the city jail. There is no use your trying to escape, because my two boys 'll be about here all day with their repeating rifles, and they can shoot."

"Yes, suh."

"And whoever unlocks this door and tells you to come out, you do it, and do it quick."

"Yes, suh."

Locking the door, the sheriff turned to his son. "You and Charlie must watch that door all day, Willie," he said; "but you mustn't seem to watch it; and keep your guns handy, and if that nigger tries to get away, kill him; don't hesitate. I must go back to the jail and make out like he's there. And tell Charlie to feed the horse and hitch him to the buggy, and let him stand ready in the stable, for when I'll want him I'll want him quick. Above all things, don't let anybody know that the nigger's here. But keep the cellar key in your pocket, and shoot if he tries to run. If your uncle Jim comes, do whatever he tells you, but nobody else, lessen they bring a note from me. Now remember. I'm trusting you, boy; and don't you make any mistake about killing the nigger if he tries to escape."

"All right," the boy answered, cheerfully, and the father went away. He almost ran to the jail, and, entering once more by the back door, found things undisturbed. Presently his brother called to him, and the gates and doors being opened, came in, bringing a waiter of hot food and coffee.

"I told Jinnie you'd not like to leave the jail," he said, "an' she fixed this up."

"Jinnie's mighty good," the sheriff answered, "and sometimes a woman's mighty handy to have about—sometimes; but I'd not leave one out in the country like Mr. Morris did; no, sir, not in these days. We could do it before the war and during the war, but not now. The old niggers were taught some decency; but these young ones! God help us, for I don't see any safety for this country 'cept Judge Lynch. And I'll tell you this is my first an' last term as sheriff. The work's too dirty."

"Buck Thomas was a boss sheriff," his brother answered; "he found the niggers all right, but the niggers never found the jail, and the niggers were 'fraid to death of him."

"Maybe Buck was right," the sheriff said, "and 'twas heap the easiest way; but here comes the town."

The two men went to the window and saw a crowd of people advancing down the road, led by Mr. Morris and his friends on horseback.

"I b'lieve you're the only man in this town that 'll stand by me, Jim," the sheriff said. "I swore in six last night, and I see 'em all in that crowd. Poor Mr. Morris! in his place I'd do just what he's doin'. Blest if yonder ain't Doty Buxton comin' to help me! I'll let him in; but see here, Jim, I'm going to send Doty to telegraph to the city for Judge More, and I want you to slip out the back way right now, and run to my house, and tell Willie to give you the buggy and the nigger, and you drive that nigger into the city. Of course you'll kill him if he tries to escape."

"The nigger ain't here!"

"I'm no fool, Jim. And I'll hold this jail, me and Doty, as long as possible, and you drive like hell! You see?"

"I didn't know you really *wanted* to save the nigger," his brother remonstrated; "nobody b'lieves that."

"I don't, as a nigger. But you go on now, and I'll send Doty with the telegram, and make time by talkin' to Mr. Morris. I don't think they've found anything; if they had, they'd have come a-galloping, and the devil himself couldn't have stopped 'em. Gosh, but its awful! Who knows what that nigger's done! When I look at Mr. Morris, I wish you fellers had overpowered me last night, and had fixed things."

He let his brother out at the back, then went round to the front gate, where he met the man whom he had called Doty Buxton.

"Go telegraph Judge More the facts of the case," he said, "an' ask him to come. I don't believe I'll need any men if he'll come; and besides, he and Mr. Morris are friends."

As the man turned away, one of the horsemen rode up to the sheriff.

"We demand that Negro," he said.

"I supposed that was what you'd come for, Mr. Mitchell," the sheriff answered; "but you know, sir, that as much as I'd like to oblige you, I'm bound to protect the man. He swears that he's never touched Mrs. Morris."

"Great God, sheriff! how can you mention the thing quietly? You know—"

"Yes, I know; and I know that I'll never do the dirty work of a sheriff a day after my term's up. But we haven't any proof against this nigger except that he ran away—"

"Isn't that enough when the lady can't be found, nor a trace of her?"

"I found the hatchet."

"And—!"

"It was clean, thank God!"

Mr. Mitchell jerked the reins so violently that his horse, tired as he was, reared and plunged.

"Mr. Morris declines to speak with you," he went on, when the horse had quieted down, "but he's determined that the Negro shall not escape, and the whole county'll back him."

"I know that," the sheriff answered, patiently, "and in his place I'd do the same thing; but in my place I must do my official duty. I'll not let the nigger escape, you may be sure of that, and I've telegraphed for Judge More to come out here. I've telegraphed the whole case. Surely Mr. Morris'll trust Judge More?"

Mitchell dragged at his mustache. "Poor Morris is nearly dead," he said.

"Of course; won't he go and eat and rest till Judge More comes? Every house in the town'll be open to him."

"No, he'll not wait nor rest; and we're determined to hang that Negro."

"It'll be mighty hard to shed our blood—friends and neighbors," remonstrated the sheriff—"and all over a worthless nigger."

"That's your lookout," Mr. Mitchell answered. "A trial and a big funeral is glory for a Negro, and the penitentiary means nothing to them but free board and clothes. I tell you, sheriff, lynching is the only thing that affects them."

"You won't wait even until I get an answer from Judge More?"

"Well, to please you, I'll ask." And Mitchell rode back to his companions.

The conference between the leaders was longer than the sheriff had hoped, and before he was again approached Doty Buxton had returned, saying that Judge More's answer would be sent to the jail just as soon as it came.

"You'll stand by me, Doty?" the sheriff asked.

"Cause I like you, Mr. Partin," Doty answered, slowly; "not 'cause I want to save the nigger. I b'lieve in my soul he's done drownded the po' lady's body."

"All right; you go inside and be ready to chain the gate if I am run in." Then he waited for the return of the envoy.

John Morris sat on his horse quite apart even from his own friends, and after a few words with him, Mitchell had gone to the group of horsemen about whom the townsmen were gathered. The sheriff did not know what this portended, but he waited patiently, leaning against the wall of the jail and whittling a stick. He knew quite well that all these men were friendly to him; that they understood his position perfectly, and that they expected him to pretend to do his duty to a reasonable extent, and so far their good nature would last; but he knew equally well that in their eyes the Negro had put himself beyond the pale of the law; that they were determined to hang him, and would do it at any cost; and that the only mercy which the culprit could expect from this upper class to which Mr. Morris belonged was that his death would be quick and quiet. He knew also that if they found out that he was in earnest in defending the prisoner he himself would be in danger, not only from Mr. Morris and his friends, but from the townsmen as well. Of course all this could be avoided by showing them that the jail was empty; but to do this would be at this stage to insure the fugitive's capture and death. To save the Negro he must hold the jail as long as possible, and if he had to shoot, shoot into the ground. All this was quite clear to him; what was not clear was what these men would do when they found that he had saved the Negro and they had stormed an empty jail.

He was an old soldier, and had been in many battles; he had fought hardest when he knew that things were most hopeless; he had risked his life recklessly, and death had been as nothing to him when he had thought that he would die for his country. But now—now to risk his life for a Negro, for a worthless creature whom he thought deserved hanging—was this his duty? Why not say, "I have sent the Negro to the city"? How quickly those fierce horsemen would dash away down the road! Well, why not? He drew himself up. He was not going t turn coward at this late day. His duty lay very plain before him, and he would not flinch. And he fixed his eyes once more on the little stick he was cutting, and waited.

Presently he saw a movement in the crowd, and the thought flashed across him that they might capture him suddenly while he stood there alone and unarmed. He stepped quickly to the gate, where Doty Buxton waited, and standing in the opening, asked the crowd to stand back and to send Mr. Mitchell to tell him what the decision was. There was a moment's pause; then Mitchell rode forward.

"Mr. Morris says that Judge More cannot help matters. The Negro must die, and at once. We don't want to hurt you, and we don't want to destroy public property, but we are going to have that wretch if we have to burn the jail down. Will you stop all this by delivering the prisoner to us?"

The sheriff shook his head. "I can't do that, sir. But one thing I do ask, that you'll give me warning before you set fire to the jail."

"If that 'll make you give up, we'll set fire now."

"I didn't say it 'd make me surrender, but only that I'd like to throw a few things out—like Doty Buxton, for instance," smiling a little.

"All right; when we stop trying to break in, we'll be making ready to smoke you out. The jail's empty but for this Negro, I hear."

"Yes, the jail's empty; but don't you think you oughter give me a little time to weigh matters?"

"Is there any chance of your surrendering?"

"To be perfectly honest," the sheriff answered, "there isn't." Then, seeing the crowd approaching, he slipped inside the heavy gate, and Doty Buxton chained it. "Now, Doty," he said, "we'll peep through these auger holes and watch 'em; and when you see 'em coming near, you must shoot through these lower holes. Shoot into the ground just in front of 'em. It's nasty to have the dirt jumpin' up right where you've got to walk. I know how it feels. I always wanted to hold up both feet at once. I reckon they've gone to get a log to batter down the gate. They can do it, but I'll make 'em take as long as I can. We mustn't hurt anybody, Doty, but we must protect the State property as far as we're able. Here they come! Keep the dirt dancin', Doty. See that? They don't like it. I told you they'd want to take up both feet at once. When bullets are flying round your head, you can't help yourself, but it's hard to put your feet down right where the nasty little things are peckin' about. Here they come again! Keep it up, Doty. See that? They've stopped again. They ain't real mad with me yet, the boys ain't; only Mr. Morris and his friends are mad. The boys think I'm just pretending to do my duty for the looks of it; but I ain't. Gosh! Now they've fixed it! With Mr. Morris at the front end of that log, there's no hope of scare. He'd walk over dynamite to get that nigger. Poor feller! Here they come at a run! Don't hurt anybody, Doty. Bang! Wait; I'll call a halt by knocking on the gate; it 'll gain us a little more time."

"What do you want?" came in answer to the sheriff's taps.

"I'll arrest every man of you for destroying State property," the sheriff answered.

"All right; come do it quick," was the response. "We're waitin', but we won't wait long."

"I reckon we'll have to go inside, Doty," the sheriff said; then to the attacking party, "If you'll wait till Judge More comes, I promise you the nigger 'll hang."

For answer there was another blow on the gate.

"Remember, I've warned you!" the sheriff called.

"Hush that rot!" was the answer, followed by a third blow.

The sheriff and Doty retreated to the jail, and the attack went on. It was a two-story building of wood, but very strongly built, and unless they tried fire the sheriff hoped to keep the besiegers at bay for a little while yet. He stationed Doty at one window, and himself took position at another, each with loaded pistols, which were only to be used as before—to make "the dirt jump."

"To tell you the truth, Doty," the sheriff said, "if you boys had had any sense you'd have overpowered me last night, and we'd not have had all this trouble."

"We wanted to," Doty answered, "but you're new at the business, an' you talked so big we didn't like to make you feel little."

"Here they come!" the sheriff went on, as the stout gate swayed inward. "One more good lick an' it's down. That's it. Now keep the dirt dancin', Doty, but don't hurt anybody."

Mr. Morris was in the lead, and apparently did not see the "dancin' dirt," for he approached the jail at a run.

"It's no use, Doty," the sheriff said; "all we can do is to wait till they get in, for I'm not going to shoot anybody. It may be wrong to lynch, but in a case like this it's the rightest wrong that ever was." So the sheriff sat there thinking, while Doty watched the attack from the window.

According to his calculations of time and distance, the sheriff thought that the prisoner was now so far on his way as to be almost out of danger by pursuit, and his mind was busy with the other question as to what would happen when the jail was found to be empty. He had not heard from Judge More, but the answer could not have reached him after the attack began. He felt sure that the judge would come, and come by the earliest train, which was now nearly due.

"The old man 'll come if he can," he said to himself, "and he'll help me if he comes; and I wish the train would hurry."

He felt glad when he remembered that he had given the keys of the cells to his brother, for though he would try to save further destruction of property by telling the mob that the jail was empty, he felt quite sure that they would not believe him, and in default of keys, would break open every door in the building; which obstinacy would grant him more time in which to hope for Judge More and arbitration. That it was possible for him to slip out once the besiegers had broken in never occurred to him; his only thought was to stay where he was until the end came, whatever that might be. They were taking longer than he had expected, and every moment was a gain.

Doty Buxton came in from the hall, where he had gone to watch operations. "The do' is givin'," he said; "what'll you do?"

"Nothin'," the sheriff answered, slowly.

"Won't you give 'em the keys?"

"I haven't got 'em."

"Gosh!" and Doty's eyes got big as saucers.

Very soon the outer door was down, and the crowd came trooping in, all save John Morris who stopped in the hallway. He seemed to be unable even to look at the sheriff, and the sheriff felt the averted face more than he would have felt a blow.

"We want the keys," Mitchell said.

The sheriff, who had risen, stood with his hands in his pockets, and his eyes, filled with sympathy; fastened on Mr. Morris, standing looking blankly down the empty hall.

"I haven't got the keys, Mr. Mitchell," he answered.

"Oh, come off!" cried one of the townsmen. "Rocky!" cried another. "Yo' granny's hat!" came from a third; while Doty Buxton said, gravely, "Give up, Partin; we've humored this duty business long enough."

"Do I understand you to say that you won't give up the keys?" Mitchell demanded, scornfully.

"No," the sheriff retorted, a little hotly, "you don't understand anything of the kind. I said that I didn't have the keys; and further," he added, after a moment's pause, "I say that this jail is empty."

There was silence for a moment, while the men looked at each other incredulously; then the jeering began again.

"There is nothing to do but to break open the cells," Morris said, sharply, but without turning his head. "We trusted the sheriff last night, and he outwitted us; we must not trust him again."

The sheriff's eyes flashed, and the blood sprang to his face. The crowd stood eagerly silent; but after a second the sheriff answered, quietly:

"You may say what you please to me, Mr. Morris, and I'll not resent it under these circumstances, but I'll swear the jail's empty."

For answer Morris drove an axe furiously against the nearest cell door, and the crowd followed suit. There were not many cells, and as he looked from a window the sheriff counted the doors as they fell in, and listened for the whistle of the train that he hoped would bring Judge More. The doors were going down rapidly, and as each yielded the sheriff could hear cries and demonstrations. What would they do when the last one fell?

Presently Doty Buxton, who had been making observations, came in, pale and excited. "You'd better git yo' pistols," he said, "an' I'll git mine, for they're gittin' madder an' madder every time he ain't there."

"Well," the sheriff answered, "I want you to witness that I ain't armed. My pistols are over there on the table, unloaded. Thank the good Lord!" he exclaimed, suddenly; "there's the train, an' Judge More! I hope he'll come right along."

"An' there goes the last do'!" said Doty, as, after a crash and a momentary silence, oaths and ejaculations filled the air. He drew near the sheriff, but the sheriff moved away.

"Stand back," he said; "you've got little children."

In an instant the crowd rushed in, headed by Morris, whose burning eyes seemed to be starting from his drawn white face. Like a flash Doty sprang forward and wrenched an axe from the infuriated man, crying out, "Partin ain't armed!"

For answer a blow from Morris's fist dropped the sheriff like a dead man. A sudden silence fell, and Morris, standing over his fallen foe, looked about him as if dazed. For an instant he stood so, then with a violent movement he pushed back the crowding men, and lifting the sheriff, dragged him towards the open window.

"Give him air," he ordered, "and go for the doctor, and for cold water!" He laid Partin flat and dragged open his collar. "He's no dead—see there; I struck him on the temple; under the ear would have killed him, but not this, not this! Give me that water, and plenty of it and move back. He's not dead, no; and I didn't mean to kill him; but he has worked against me all night, and I didn't think a white man would do it."

"He's comin' round, Mr. Morris," said Doty, who knelt on the other side of the sheriff; "an' he didn't bear no malice against you—don't fret; but it's a good thing I jerked that axe outer yo' hand! See, he's ketchin' his breath; it's all right," as Partin opened his eyes slowly and looked about him.

A sound like a sigh came from the crowd; then a voice said, "Here comes Judge More."

Morris was still holding his wet handkerchief on the sheriff's head when the old judge came in. "My dear boy," he said, laying his hand on John Morris's shoulder. But Morris shook his head.

"Let's talk business, Judge More," he said, "and let's get Partin into a chair, where he can rest; I've just knocked him over."

Then Morris left the room, and Mitchell with him, going to the far side of the jail yard, where they walked up and down in silence. It was not long before Judge More and the sheriff joined them.

"The evidence was too slight for lynching," the judge said, looking straight into John Morris's eyes.

"Great God!" Morris cried, and struck his hands together.

"What more do you want?" Mitchell demanded, angrily. "His wife has disappeared, and the Negro ran away."

"True, and I'll see to the case myself; but I'm glad that you did not hang the Negro."

A boy came up with a telegram.

"From Jim, I reckon," the sheriff said, taking it. "No; it's for you, Mr. Morris."

It was torn open hastily; then Morris looked from one to the other with a blank, scared face, while the paper fluttered from his hold.

Mitchell caught it and read aloud slowly, as if he did not believe his eyes:

"'*Am safe. Will be out on the ten-o'clock train.* 'Eleanor'."

Morris stood there, shaking, and sobbing hard, dry sobs.

"It'll kill him!" the sheriff said. "Quick, some whiskey!"

A flask was forced between the blue, trembling lips.

"Drink, old fellow;" and Mitchell put his arm about Morris's shoulders. "It's all right now, thank God!"

Morris was leaning against his friend, sobbing like a woman. The sheriff drew his coatsleeve across his eyes, and shook his head.

"What made the nigger run away?" he said, slowly—adding, as if to himself, "God help us!"

A vehicle was borrowed, and the judge and the sheriff drove with John Morris over to the station to meet the ten-o'clock train. The sheriff and the judge remained in the little carriage, and the station agent did his best to leave the whole platform to John Morris. As the moments went by the look of anxious agony grew deeper on the face of the waiting man. The sheriff's ominous words, falling like a pall over the first flash of his happiness, had filled his mind with wordless terrors. He could scarcely breathe or move, and could not speak when his wife stepped off and put her hands in his. She looked up, and without a query, without a word of explanation, answered the anguished questioning of his eyes, whispering,

"He did not touch me."

Morris staggered a little, then drawing her hand through his arm, he led her to the carriage. She shrank back when she saw the judge and the sheriff on the front seat; but Morris saying, "They must hear your story, dear," she stepped in.

"We are very thankful to see you, Mrs. Morris," the judge said, without turning his head, when the sheriff had touched up the horse and they moved away; "and if you feel able to tell us how it all happened, it'll save time and ease your mind. This is Mr. Partin, the sheriff."

Mrs. Morris looked at the backs of the men in front of her; at their heads that were so studiously held in position that they could not even have glanced at each other; then up at her husband, appealingly.

"Tell it," he said, quietly, and laid his hand on hers that were wrung together in her lap. "You sent Aggie to catch the chickens, and the dog went with her?"

"Yes," fixing her eyes on his; "and I sent"—she stopped with a shiver, and her husband said, "Abram"—"to cut some bushes to make a broom," she went on. "I had been for a walk to the old house, and as I came back I laid my gloves and a bit of vine on the steps, intending to return at once; but I wished to see if the boat was safe, for the water was rising so rapidly." She paused, as if to catch her breath, then, with her eyes still fixed on her husband, she went on, "I did not think that it was safe, and I untied the rope and picked up the paddle that was lying on the dam, intending to drag the boat farther up and tie it to a tree." She stopped again. Her husband put his arm about her.

"And then?" he said.

"And then—something, I don't know what; not a sound, but something—something made me turn, and I saw him—saw him coming—saw him stealing up behind me—with the hatchet in his hand, and a look—a look"—closing her eyes as if in horror—"such an awful, awful look! And everybody gone. Oh, John!" she gasped, and clinging to her husband, she broke into hysterical sobs, while the judge gripped his walking stick and cleared his throat, and the sheriff swore fiercely under his breath.

"I was paralyzed," she went on, recovering herself, "and when he saw me looking he stopped. The next moment he threw the hatchet at me, and began to run towards me. The hatchet struck my foot, and the blow roused me, and I sprang into the boat. There were no trees just there, and jumping in, I pushed the boat off into the deep water. He picked up the hatchet and shook it at me, but the water was too deep for him to reach me, and he ran back along the dam and turned towards the railroad embankment. I was so terrified I could scarcely breathe; I pushed frantically in and out between the trees, farther and farther into the swamp. I was afraid that he would go round to the bridge and come down the bank to where the outlet from the swamp is and catch me there, but in a little while I saw where the rising water had broken the dam, and the current was rushing through and out to the river. The current caught the boat and swept it through the break. Oh, I was so glad! I am so afraid of water, but not then. I used the paddle as a rudder, and to push floating timber away. My foot was hurting me, and I looked at last and saw that it was cut."

A groan came from the judge, and the sheriff's head drooped.

"All day I drifted, and all night. I was so thirsty, and I grew so weak. At daylight this morning I found myself in a wide sheet of water, with marshes all round, and I saw a steamboat coming. I tied my handkerchief to the paddle and waved it, and they picked me up. And, John, I did not tell them anything except that the freshet had swept me away. They were kind to me, and a friendly woman bound up my foot. We got to town this morning early, and the captain lent me five dollars, John—Captain Meakin—so I telegraphed you, and took a carriage to the station and came out. Have—have you caught him? And, oh—but I am afraid—afraid!" And again she broke into hysterical sobs.

She asked no explanation. The Negro's guilt was so burned in on her mind that she was sure that all knew it as well as she.

"You need have no further fears," her husband comforted. And the judge shook his head, and the sheriff swore again.

A white-haired woman in rusty black stood talking to a Negro convict. It was in a stockade prison camp in the hill country. She had been a slave owner once, long ago, and now for her mission work taught on Sundays in the stockade, trying to better the Negroes penned there.

This was a new prisoner, and she was asking him of himself.

"How long are you in for?" she asked.

"Fuhrebber, ma'am; fuh des es long es I lib," the Negro answered, looking down to where he was making marks on the ground with his toes.

"And how did you get such a dreadful sentence?"

"I ent do much, ma'm; I des scare a white lady."

A wave of revulsion swept over the teacher, and involuntarily she stepped back. The Negro looked up and grinned.

"De hatchet des cut 'e foot little bit; but I trow de hatchet. I ent tech um; no, ma'm. Den atterwards 'e baby daid; den dey say I muss stay yer fuhrebber. I ent sorry, 'kase I know say I hab to wuck anywheys I is; if I stay yer, if I go 'way, I hab to wuck. En I know say if I git outer dis place Mr. Morris 'll kill me sho—des sho. So I like fuh stay yer berry well."

And the teacher went away, wondering if her work—if *any* work—would avail; and what answer the future would have for this awful problem.

OLD TIES

Back in the Seventies, before Louisiana began to put a cheap rice on the market; before the tariff had been taken off rice, permitting Rangoon rice to come into competition with the fine rice of South Carolina and Georgia, all which spelled ruin to the Atlantic Coast planters; before the masters had fully realized the great gulf set between them and their former slaves, the old plantations on the South Eastern coast retained many of their old-time customs, and the bonds between master and man were still tinctured with responsibility on the one hand and dependence on the other, and through all there ran a thread of affection. It is in those days that this story was lived.

On a bluff, shadowy with live oak trees draped in the long gray moss, and with a black background of solemn pine barren, there stood an old plantation house. It was low, and was encircled with deep piazzas, which looked out over a silent marsh and a winding river. On the front piazza, a gentleman sat in a long smoking chair, reading. The season was early Spring; the time was high noon.

Away off in the fields the Negroes could be heard faintly crying to their beasts as they worked, but nearer, it was so still that a bird fluttering down to the rosevine climbing up the piazza post, seemed almost afraid of the sound of its own wings and flew away swiftly when the dog lying at its master's feet, stirred in its sleep. Some flies buzzed back and forth aimlessly, and a hen and her brood, wandering round from the back of the house, scratching contentedly as she came, made little sounds of clucking and cheeping that seemed to accentuate the stillness.

Presently, a step was heard coming from the same direction that the hen had come; a slow step with something of a drag in it. The dog lifted its head sidewise, the hen called her chickens together hurriedly, and the gentleman looked up.

It was a woman, who if she had been white, might have been pronounced to be about sixty, but as she was black, she might, with equal assurance, have been pronounced either forty or eighty; as it was, she at this moment walked with the step of very advanced age. She was tall and spare, and was decently clothed in a black skirt and sack and a blue checked apron. Her head was tied up in a bandanna handkerchief, which was surmounted by a black straw hat guiltless of trimming, and her steps were supported by a hickory stick, that from the whiteness of the spots from which the twigs had been cut, was manifestly a most recent acquisition.

The gentleman turned his book down on his lap, and watched her with a waiting expression as she came along the path parallel with the piazza, toward the steps, at the top of which he was seated. He evidently knew that he would not be able to read for sometime to come. Whether the woman realized that she was being watched could not have been told by any motion made by her. She seemed to be entirely self-absorbed, each step becoming a little more labored as she neared her goal, and the hand which she reached out to the bannisters, trembled very visibly.

"Huddy, Mass Tommy!" she said enthusiastically as she paused.

"Well, Mawm Myra," the gentleman answered quietly.

"Enty you glad fuh see me, Mass Tommy," she went on, "unner gran'pah po' ole nigger?"

The gentleman leaned over, and taking from the floor an old cigar box full of tobacco, and a brierroot pipe, proceeded to fill the pipe, while the woman, mounting four of the six steps leading to the piazza, took her seat facing him, with her back against the bannisters. She laid her stick on the piazza floor with a little ostentatious clatter, and her hat beside it. Then smoothing her apron over her knees, she rubbed them, grooming a little.

"Gawd knows I tired," she said. "I dat tired I mos' dead; yes, suh, Mass Tommy, I gittin' ole, suh, I gittin' berry ole."

Mr. Selwyn lighted his pipe with slow deliberation, and began to smoke. For a few moments the woman, though seeming to be entirely occupied with her knees and her weariness, watched him furtively with her glancing black eyes, and presently, while she looked, she began to fumble busily among the folds of her dress. Then Mr. Selwyn turned his head in her direction. "Get your pipe," he said.

"Yes, suh, Mass Tommy, yes, suh;" and with hands that forgot to tremble, she took quickly the box of tobacco which Mr. Selwyn was holding towards her. "Yes, suh, Mass Tommy, en I berry glad fuh git little bacca; tenky suh. En I dis been t'inking say hummuch you look like unner gran'pah, my ole Mawsa! Po' Myra ole Mawsa. Tenky, Mass Tommy, tenky, suh." Her corncob pipe was filled by this time, and picking a loose match from out the tobacco box, she lighted it and began to smoke with much satisfaction, while her face seemed to grow smoother, and her back to straighten, and to throw off many years. Mr. Selwyn watched quietly for a moment or two the transformation which was going on in the woman, then he broke the silence asking, "How'd you come?"

"Who, me?" taking her pipe from her lips. "How kin I come, Mass Tommy, lessen I walk? Yes, suh, ole es I is, I walk ebbry step out yer; yes, suh." She laid her hand on her stick and rattled it a little. "En Mass Tommy, nobody ent know 'bout my knee, no suh! My two knee is dat bad I kin scasely drag 'long. Enty you see say I got stick?"

"How long have you been using a stick?"

"Who, me? Ki! Mass Tommy, enty you know say I hab de bad leg dis t'ree year? Yes, suh, dis t'ree year."

"Your stick looks pretty new."

"Yes, suh, dat's new stick, I cut dat stick dis mawnin' kase my ole stick bruck. Yes, suh."

"What have you come for?" Mr. Selwyn pursued.

"I come fuh ax you fuh help me, Mass Tommy. I dat po' en sick tay I hab to baig, yes, suh; unner gran'pah po' ole nigger hab to baig. Po' me!" She was rubbing her knees once more now, and once more her back was bent.

"You've been free some ten years now," Mr. Selwyn suggested, "you ought to be doing pretty well."

"Yes, suh, I free, but I ent do well; no, suh, I ent."

"Where's Ben?"

"Who, my little Ben, Mass Tommy? Ki! Enty you know say Ben is run 'way en leff me? 'E wife daid, en 'e chillun daid, en Ben run 'way; yes, suh."

"And June?"

"Who, my son June, Mass Tommy? Ki! Enty you know say June wife is debbil? Enty you know say June wife is keep dog fuh bite me? Yes, suh, June wife is debbil."

"And your daughter Nancy?"

"Lawd, Mass Tommy! Enty you know say Nancy husban' is teck Nancy en gone? Yes, suh, Nancy been gone dis t'ree munt; yes, suh; en I leff yer awl by mese'f, en I t'ink say, Mass Tommy'll 'member say Myra is 'e gran'pah ole nigger; so I come yer fuh baig you fuh he'p me."

"But you belonged to Uncle James, not to father."

"Yes, suh, I know dat—"

"And if you deserved help he would give it to you."

"'Zerve he'p, Mass Tommy!" her eyes flashing. "Who say I ent 'zerve he'p, Mass Jeemes? If Mass Jeemes say dat, 'e say um kase 'e ent nebber like Myra, no, suh. When ole Mawsa gie my husban' Caesar to Mass Jeemes, 'e gie me 'long o' Caesar, but Mass Jeemes ent like me, en Mass Jeemes wife ent like me nurrer."

"Why not, Myra?"

"Ki! Mass Tommy, how I know dat?"

"Weren't you a field hand?" Mr. Selwyn went on.

"Yes, suh, en I wuz good fiel' hand; I done my tas' ebbry day 'fo dem turrer nigger. Yes, suh, I wuz good fiel' hand."

"And they had to take you out of the field because you sold as much rice, as Uncle James did, wasn't that it?" Mr. Selwyn's voice was so kindly inquiring, that the woman looked puzzled for a moment, then she turned her shifty eyes up until nothing but the whites showed.

"Lawd—Lawd!" she whispered as if on close and confidential terms with the Almighty; "blessed Lawd, yeddy dat chile wuh 'e say! My ole Mawsa gran'chile; yeddy um what 'e say, Mass Tommy," her eyes flashing round on him, and her voice changing sharply," Mass Tommy, who tell you dat? Who ebber tell you dat? You cahn 'member dat, en who tell you? No, suh, dey teck me out de fiel' so I kin go in de sickhouse; de plantation sick-house en teck care de people what is sick; yes, suh, dat what I teck out de fiel' fuh. Who ebber say Myra steal, who ebber yeddy sicher t'ing!"

"And the people in the sick-house never had enough to eat while you were there," Mr. Selwyn went on quietly, "and when they got well they could never find their clothes."

"Mass Tommy," and Myra's voice had a world of reproach in it, "enty you know say nigger will tell lie 'bout nigger? Enty you know say dem nigger tell Mass Jeemes lie 'bout me? 'bout po' ole Myra; enty you know dat, Mass Tommy?"

"And after that, they put you to take care of the children whose mothers were in the fields;" Mr. Selwyn resumed, without answering her.

"Yes, suh!" She struck in glibly, "yes, suh; kase I hab sicher good han' wid chillun! Yes, suh."

"Yes," Mr. Selwyn answered, "and you whipped the children so, that Uncle James had to stop your doing that."

"Lick dem chillun!" she cried scornfully, "co'se I lick dem chillun; chillun is 'bleeged to be lick. Enty unner mah lick you, Mass Tommy? Co'se I lick dem chillun, kase chillun is tarrifyin' tings."

"But you nearly killed them," Mr. Selwyn amended. "Then Uncle James made you poultry-minder."

"Yes, suh; dat's de trute, en I hab a lucky han' wid chicken, en aig, en—"

"And Uncle James," Mr. Selwyn interrupted, "could never get a hen or a chicken, or an egg while you had the poultry yard."

"Mass Tommy—Mass Tommy—Mass Tommy!" she cried as if in despair over his lack of reason, "Who ebber yeddy sicher talkin' to unner gran'pah ole nigger? All dese t'ings is done do 'fo' you is bawn, Mass Tommy; all dese t'ng you talk 'bout is done pass; clean done pass, en who ebber yeddy 'bout diggin' up t'ings what is done bury fuh de Jedgement day? Ki! all dese t'ing is done fuhgit."

"And people won't give you their washing," Mr. Selwyn added suggestively, "because you lose their clothes."

"Mass Tommy," her voice changing from tragic reproach to patient explanation, "dat 'oman what I wash fuh is too 'tickler; too 'tickler fuh deal wid nigger," and she looked up pleadingly as if really she had a defense. "Enty you know say nigger ent know 'bout sich 'ticklerness? En w'en dat 'oman meck sicher quar'l 'bout ebbry t'ing, den I t'ink say dat 'oman is been po' buckra, en I cahn stan' po' buckra; no, suh, I cahn stan' um, en I tell um so. I tell um say I been b'long to rich people what ent 'bleeged to count ebbry t'ing so 'tickler; den 'e call me t'ief, en I laugh en I come 'way. Enty you see, Mass Tommy, say 'e too 'tickler?"

"Yes," Mr. Selwyn assented, that is just the way you treated Aunt Mary, until she lost nearly everything."

"No, Mass Tommy," the old woman objected, shaking her head as at an unreasonable child, "no, suh; but you know say Miss Mary ent we own people; Miss Mary is stranger what Mass Jeemes is marry, en she is 'tickler des de same like dat turrer strange 'oman; enty you know dat?"

"No, Myra," and taking his pipe from his lips. Mr. Selwyn turned slowly to look at her. "No, I don't know anything of the kind."

The woman shifted her position uneasily under his look, then she said persuasively, "I'se tell you de trute, Mass Tommy, de Lawd's trute."

Mr. Selwyn shook his head. "No," he said quietly, "you don't know what truth means; you don't ever tell the truth; that is why Uncle James has ceased to help you; that is why your children have all left you; that is why I do not think that I shall help you today. I know too much about you."

The woman's face had grown lowering and sullen while Mr. Selwyn was speaking, and her eyes were shining with rage. She sat still for a moment, then picking up her stick she hurled it as far as she could throw it. "Go 'way!" she cried, "I done tote you a whole mile des fuh nuttin!"

"Go 'way!" and her eyes glared on the harmless stick as it struck against a tree and bounded back almost to her feet. The dog roused up at this, looking at Myra suspiciously, while an amused gleam came into Mr. Selwyn's eyes, but he said nothing, waiting to see what she would do next. After a moment's thought she knocked the ashes out of her pipe, then refilling it slowly, she began once more to smoke.

The buzzing flies could once more be heard, and the cautious old hen came stepping slowly back, turning her head from side to side watchfully, and eyeing Myra as if in her she recognized a hereditary enemy. It was all as still now as before the woman's advent, and after a little the silence and the peacefulness seemed to restore her equilibrium, for taking her pipe out of her mouth, she said reproachfully, "I ent t'ink say my ole Mawsa gran'chile gwine say de t'ings to me what you is say dis day, Mass Tommy; en when you is baby, I hole you in dese same two han's," holding out her hands and looking at them as if they were a new discovery. "Dese same two han's, yes, suh; en dese same two han's is wuck fuh unner gran'pah; is wuck fuh unner Uncle Jeemes; is wuck fuh unner Mawm Lucy."

Mr. Selwyn turned his head quickly. "Mawm Lucy?" he repeated, with an alert tone in his voice. But Myra was looking out over the marsh and river with an expression of resigned mournfulness on her face. Mr. Selwyn fixed his eyes on her. "Well?" he said.

"En I t'ink," she went on in the same forsaken voice, "I t'ink say if you ent help me, you'll help unner Mawm Lucy,—unner Mawmer what mine you when you is baby; my husban's po' ole sister Lucy."

"What do you mean?" Mr. Selwyn asked sharply; "I *do* help Mawm Lucy, and you know it. What in the mischief do you mean, talking in this way?" An expression of malicious satisfaction began to dawn on Myra's countenance, but she still looked out over the marsh.

"I mean des what I say," she answered with a ring of impertinence in every word, that made Mr. Selwyn look longingly at the stick which the woman had cast away. "Yes, suh, en Sis Lucy is ole, Mass Tommy, en ole people eat heaper bittle; Sis Lucy is ole, Mass Tommy, en ole people bu'ns heaper wood 'fo' dey gits good en warm."

"Well?" Mr. Selwyn repeated sharply.

"En Sis Lucy is hongry, Mass Tommy; en Sis Lucy is cole, Mass Tommy; en I sell all 'e blanket ceppen one, fuh git mo' bittle; en I sell all 'e chair en table fuh git mo' wood. En Sis Lucy is cole, Mass Tommy, cole dis minute; en Sis Lucy is hongry, Mass Tommy, hongry dis minute."

Mr. Selwyn sprang up. The dog started aside. The hen and her chickens fled away. "What in the devil do you mean!" he cried angrily.

Myra rose, stepping down one step. "Des w'at I say, Mass Tommy," she answered, with the joy of battle in her eyes. "When June debbil wife dribe me 'way, den I gone to Sis Lucy, kase I say Sis Lucy is my husban' sister, en I gwine teck care um. En I sen Lil' Lucy 'way kase dey ent no nuse fuh hab two dey fuh eat, en fuh cook."

"Confound you" Mr. Selwyn cried, "How dare you—you—"

"Mass Tommy!" raising her arm tragically, "My ole Mawsa, ner Mass Jeemes ent nebber cuss Myra, no suh; en I cahn stan' it, no, suh!"

"You'll stand whatever I choose to say!" Mr. Selwyn shouted. "I'll have you put in jail. I hire that house for Mawm Lucy; I hire Little Lucy to stay there; I provide everything that is necessary, therefore it is all mine; how dare you go there and sell my things!"

Myra's arm dropped. "Unner Gran'pah po' ole nigger in jail, Mass Tommy?"

"Damn it! how did June dare let you meddle with my property!"

Myra smiled scornfully. "June!" she said contemptuously, "June? Lawd, Mass Tommy, t'nk say unner know nigger, but you ent know nigger; no w'ite people kin know nigger kase nigger ent nuttin like w'ite people. En ebbry nigger is fraid o' me; yes, suh; I kin *witch* um, yes, suh," watching Mr. Selwyn furtively; "I kin witch people."

"Dublin!" Mr. Selwyn called, "Dublin!"

Myra stepped down one more step, an alert look on her face. "Wuh you gwine do, Mass Tommy?" she asked. "Wuh you gwine do?"

"Stop the wagon that's going to town," Mr. Selwyn said to the black man who answered his call.

"Yes, suh; I des gwine dribe out de gate, suh."

"Stop then and saddle my horse;" then turning to the woman, "You are to go to town on that wagon," he said.

"To town, Mass Tommy? To jail?" looking at him doubtfully.

"You are to go," was his answer, and meeting his eyes, she seemed to agree with him, for she walked off briskly without another word.

It was not long before Mr. Selwyn, riding rapidly, overtook in the sandy, shady road the leisurely wagon, from which Myra, seated beside the driver, greeted him in an unabashed voice. "Dat's a nice horse,

Mass Tommy," she called, then, Mr. Selwyn not answering, she added, "But 'e ent gwine lib long." As she spoke the horse stumbled a little, and Mr. Selwyn heard an amused laugh echoing behind him.

Riding at once to the country suburb of the town that was given up to Negroes, Mr. Selwyn made his way to a small house that looked in a little better repair than the others. He knocked, and receiving no answer, he tried the door, only to find it locked; he listened but could hear no sound. By this time every door and window in the little street, that was no more than a narrow roadway, was occupied by one or more Negroes watching him, but no one approached him, nor was any word of explanation vouchsafed. He paused a moment, then called to a woman who stood in the door of the next house.

"Where's June?"

"June gone to 'e wuck, suh."

"Where's Little Lucy?"

"She's in yer, suh."

Mr. Selwyn walked over to the house, and entering, found a young girl ironing with suspicious diligence. "Haven't I paid you to stay with Mawm Lucy?" he asked sternly, standing by the table.

"Yes, suh," the sweat dropping from her forehead on to her work.

"Why did you leave her?" There was a dead silence.

"Where is the key of the house?" No answer. He waited a moment, then turned to the woman. "Are you afraid of Myra?" he asked. "Didn't June send her away from this house?"

"Yes, suh."

"Did any thing happen to him or you?"

The woman moved uneasily.

"Has anything happened?" he repeated. The girl paused in her ironing, and the outside Negroes began to creep in the door. "Has anything happened?" Mr. Selwyn asked for the third time. Then the woman looked up desperately.

"Doan ax me, Mass Tommy," she pleaded, "doan ax me! I cahn say, suh; I cahn say, kase if I say no, den somet'ing'll happen sho; en if I say yes, den de t'ing what happen'll git wuss, yes, suh. Doan ax me Mass Tom, doan ax me."

"Is Mawm Lucy in the house?" Mr. Selwyn went on. Again there was no answer; he waited patiently, then asked, "Who has the key of the house?" A woman near the door, big, brawny, and bold looking, held up a hatchet.

"Dis is de onliest key, Mass Tom," she said. Mr. Selwyn turned.

"Ah, big Minty, you know then? Come with me."

But big Minty shook her head. "No, suh," she answered, "I big, I kin lick Aunt Myra, but Aunt Myra kin kill me; Aunt Myra kin look de't, yes, suh. Mr. Selwyn knew that to combat the fear of the "evil eye" was useless, and in impatient despair of further information, he took the hatchet and strode over to the house, the door of which he had found locked. He paused a moment and listened, but he could hear nothing. Had Myra ill-used his old nurse? Was the old woman dying— dead? The old creature who stood as a background to all his childhood; who for years had looked to him for care and support? He was angry, and he swore a little bit under his breath; but he was anxious, too, and he made as little noise as possible. In a few moments he had forced the lock, then putting the hatchet down, he pushed the door open slowly, and stepped in.

Everything was shut up tight; it was dark; there was not a movement anywhere; not a spark of fire, and it felt damp and close. He paused a moment until he could see, then he went to the one window of the room and opened it; the room was absolutely bare. He looked about in astonishment. He had furnished it decently, and now all was gone. Not even a pot, or a pan, or a cup was left! There were only two rooms, and going into the next he was met by the same cold, empty darkness. He opened the second window, and there on a mattress in a corner, covered with a piece of blanket, he discovered the object of his search. Was she dead? He kneeled down on the floor by her, "Mawmer?" he said softly, laying his hand on her shoulder.

"Mawmer?" The eyes opened slowly, then closed again. "Are you sick, Mawmer?" he went on.

The old woman lying on the scant pallet made a motion of assent, and he thought that he heard the word "hongry". He felt her pulse, it was faint and flickering. Quickly he went back to the door, and looked out to where the Negroes were standing about in groups, watching for him. He knew that neither fear nor favor, neither threats nor offers of reward would for a moment overcome their superstitious fear of Myra, whom they regarded as having the evil eye; his only course would be to tell them that she should never come back.

"You need not be afraid of Myra," he said. "She came out to the plantation this morning, and I told her that I would have her put in jail; so you can come and help me without being afraid."

They hesitated a moment, then big Minty came forward, followed by June's wife and Little Lucy.

"Go and get some milk," he said, putting some money into the girl's hand. "And Minty, you bring some wood and make a fire; and Peggy, you come and see what you can do for Mawm Lucy."

He asked no further questions as to Myra's actions, because he knew that he would get no answers; besides, the case was as clear to him as if he had seen the house emptied, and the things sold. He had not been to see old Lucy for several weeks; thinking of her as well provided for and safe; cared for by her niece, and surrounded by acquaintances from various plantations, whom she had known all her life; he had felt no anxiety, and if Myra had not betrayed herself—he paused a moment in his thinking. Had she betrayed herself? Had she not rather, come to tell him? She had sold everything possible; there was nothing more to be made by staying with her old sister-in-law, and so she had come out to the plantation to persuade some money from him first, and then to give him a warning hint! Having found him more informed and obdurate than she had expected, she had tried to soothe her own defeat by making him angry, and thus had revealed more than she had at first intended. How clear it all was, and of course she would not come to town in the wagon, of course not. And he laughed a little at himself.

Old Lucy had revived somewhat by this time; the fire, and food, and more than all the presence of Mr. Selwyn, seemed to give her strength. Her dim eyes followed his every movement with the look of a frightened animal, and whenever he left the room she closed them as if shutting out some unbearable terror. At last he explained to her that he would buy her another bedstead; that he would refurnish the little house; that both big Minty and Little Lucy would stay with her, and that Myra was gone. She clung to his hand, shaking her head, the tears running down her withered cheeks.

"Doan—leff me—?" she pleaded, "doan leff me!" and she tried to draw him nearer. He bent his head to listen. "I fraid," she whispered,

"I fraid o' black people. Black people doan like ole people like me. Doan leff me 'gen, Mass Tommy; doan leff unner ole Mawmer!" Just then a wagon was heard to stop outside. Old Lucy's grip on his hand tightened, and her eyes grew wide with terror. "It's only Dublin," Mr. Selwyn said reassuringly. "He has driven in from the plantation. Do you want to go out there and stay as long as I do, and move into town when I do?"

The old woman gave a hysterical sob. "Please, Mawsa; please my chile," she whispered, clasping her hands; "teck me wid you, please, suh. I kin go right now in Dublin wagon, "and she tried to rise.

"No, no, Mawmer, lie still," Mr. Selwyn whispered in return, "lie still, and you shall go."

Outside, the Negroes were crowding about Dublin and the wagon, standing a little back when Mr. Selwyn appeared. "Where's Myra?" he asked. Dublin turned his hat over in his hands once or twice. "She gone, suh," he answered.

"Where?" There was a breathless silence, and the crowd drew nearer.

"W'en we gat to de railroad," Dublin began slowly, "she meck me stop en go wid um fuh buy ticket, yes, suh; den she git in de cah en gone."

"Where?" Mr. Selwyn asked again.

"She gone to Ben, 'e son Ben, yes, suh."

"Gone to Ben," the woman Peggy said reflectively. "Po' Ben!"

"Ben'll run 'way gen," another suggested, and for the first time a laugh was heard.

"She mos' ober dey by dis time," said a third.

"Yes," Dublin answered, fumbling his hat as if he had further revelations to make, "yes, suh, Mass Tom," he went on, "en w'en I done buy Aunt Myra ticket, en put um in de cah, en de cah gone, den I come back to de wagon en I cahn fine my coat."

A shout of derisive laughter went up at this, Myra being safely away.

"No, suh," Dublin resumed dolefully, "I cahn fine my coat. I put my coat fuh Aunt Myra fuh sit on, en w'en she gone, my coat gone too!"

"The old villain!" Mr. Selwyn said, "she ought to be in jail."

"Yes, suh," Dublin answered, "en she say fuh tell you say you done dribe unner gran'pah po' ole nigger 'way; yes, suh, dat w'at she say, unner gran'pah po' ole nigger."

"Po' ole nigger!" big Minty repeated scornfully; "Aunt Myra ent po', dat she ent; Aunt Myra steal ebbry t'ing she kin see, en sell ebbry t'ing she steal. Aunt Myra had plenty money. But please, Mass Tom, teck Aunt Lucy wid you, suh, kase she'll dead if she stay yer. She so 'fraid Aunt Myra, en ebbry body so 'fraid Aunt Myra, dat she'll dead sho. So when the wagon had accomplished its errands, the old woman and her niece were put in and driven away to the safe haven of the old plantation.

AN EX-BRIGADIER

"Know General Stamper?" and the speaker looked at me with an expression of wonder in his eyes that amused me; then he smiled. "Know General Stamper—'old General Billy'? Of co'se I do. Where were you raised?"

"Not in Alabama," I answered.

"I thought as much," came with a ring of pity in the voice. "There's nobody in *this* State has to ask who is General Stamper."

We were standing outside the door of the only thing in Booker City that could be called a building—Booker City, that might have been described as a "wide place in the road."

Over the door of this building was the sign, *"G. W. S. Booker, General Merchant";* a little lower down came a smaller sign, "Post office." On either side the shop, and out behind it, stretched the unbroken pine barren; in front the trees had been cut away, and the wheel tracks between the ragged stumps showed dimly the street of the future. Beyond the stumps came a ditch that cut through the sandy soil and deep into the red clay; across this ditch two old "crossties" made a bridge to the railway.

Across the railway there was a blacksmith's shed, and one or two shanties where some bloodless looking people, with straight, clay-colored hair and vacant eyes, made shift to live. And this was Booker City.

The train had left me there ten minutes before this true story opens; my valise stood just inside the door of the shop; my overcoat was buttoned against the chill February wind. I had come straight through from New York, sent out by a great railway syndicate as a sort of private detective to look into the merits of Booker City. By profession I am a civil engineer.

"We send you because you are a Southern man," my chief had said, "and will therefore understand the people and win their confidence. I want you go down to this 'Booker City,' and see this 'General William Stamper.' Look the whole thing up incog; be anything you like, and draw for anything you may want. Here is a map of the city."

So I packed my valise and started for Booker City. Arriving, I asked the only man I saw as to General Stamper, with the results given above.

"Where does General Stamper live?" I went on.

"'Cross the railroad 'bout a mile. He owns moster this county; I own some, though. I own this store and down the railroad 'bout a mile; but our fam'lies were always friends, and me and General Stamper persuaded the railroad to have a station here. I've got Stamper in my name." This last was said proudly. "And you got the station in order to make your land more valuable, I suppose?" in a mild tone.

My companion turned on me slowly.

"Not exactly," he answered; "for it couldn't be made much more valuable. We've got coal and iron right back here in the hills, and a big syndicate behind us; we'll have five thousand people here by next month."

"Roosting on stumps," I asked, "and feeding on pine knots?"

"Maybe, and maybe not," he answered, quietly; and maybe by that time you'll have money enough to come back and see."

"If not, will you have money enough to lend me a dollar or two?"

"I'll have it, you bet; but whether I'll lend it to *you* or not, that's another question; and yonder comes General Billy."

I looked in the direction indicated, and coming through the pines I saw a muddy old buggy, very much bent down on one side, and drawn by a gray mule; of course the harness was helped out with pieces of rope, and the slim, rascally looking Negro boy who drove was ragged; so natural were these things to that kind of vehicle that I scarcely observed them; but the man pointed out as "General Billy" caught my attention instantly and firmly. When the buggy stopped I saw that his left arm and right leg were missing, but, in spite of that, he leaped out quite nimbly. He was a large, ruddy man dressed in a baggy suit of gray jeans, with a soft black hat drawn well down on his head, and from under it some fine gray hair curled over his coat collar. His eyes were bright and deep set, and twinkled as merrily as if a third of him were not in the grave. He swung himself along with great agility, and had a cherry voice.

"And how is the father of my country today?" he cried, as he hopped into the shop. Then balancing himself skilfully, he hit my friend Booker a pretty solid blow with his crutch. "George Washington Stamper Booker! By gad, man! if your name had done its duty it would have destroyed you long ago; every day I am expecting to hear that it has struck in and killed you. And your name?"—leaning on his crutches and eying me keenly. "You look very familiar somehow."

"Willoughby is my name," I answered.

"Willoughby? The devil! Kemper Willoughby?"

"John Kemper Willoughby," I amended, in some suprise.

"Oh, blast the John! Here, shake!" extending his one hand, that seemed to me to be marvellously small. "What kin are you to old Kemper Willoughby of Chilhowie?"

"Grandson."

"Bless my eyes, my *dear boy!*" and he wrung my hand painfully almost. "I wouldn't take a thousand dollars for this meeting; no, sir, not five thousand; no, not Booker City itself," throwing back his head with a ringing laugh.

It was a sweet laugh, and his voice had a tone in it that made me think of my father; his face was clean-shaven, too, like my father's, and his mouth and teeth and laugh reminded me of Joseph Jefferson.

"There was something in the cut of you," he went on, "and in the setting of your eyes, that took me back to some fig trees in your grandfather's back yard. You looked as your father Kemper used to look when we were stealing figs—it was not really stealing, you know; only Mrs. Willoughby was saving the figs for something. God knows what women save things for, but they are always doing it. But you looked just like him—surprised and amused, and a little disgusted with yourself. All the Willoughbys look alike—all cut out of the same piece of cloth. See here, General Washington Booker, look alive, and hand out the mail. I want to take the boy home," rattling on without drawing a breath. "Fifty years ago we were in those fig trees. And your father?"

"I am the only one of the name left," I answered briefly.

"Good heavens!"—taking up the one letter that Booker laid on the counter—"only one, and there used to be such lots of them—Willoughbys world without end; only one left—only one!" and, leaning on his crutch, he looked at me sadly. "The war, I suppose?" he said.

"Yes."

"And at the last we went under, all for nothing; and now we must be patient, and say we were wrong, or, at the least, unwise, and forget those who lie under the sod! Never! And, by gad, sir, I'll make something out of them—something! Forget, sir? No, sir. There's too much of me under the sod—me, myself. I'll not forget. But come, my boy, we'll have some supper and a talk, and maybe some 'condensed corn,' ha! ha!—will you have sugar in yourn?'—and I'll tell you about those figs your dear grandmother did not save. Ah, we had ladies and gentlemen in those days—ladies from afar. I have a little girl at home, God bless her! She keeps house for me. Come on; where are your traps? Here, look alive, you young imp!"—to the Negro. "Get out, sir, and put this gentleman's bag in, and you hang on behind; and don't you dare to drop off, or to get hurt. Get in, my boy"—to me. Then, calling back: "Don't answer any telegrams without consulting me, Booker; not about your own land even. Do you hear?"

"All right, General."

"Now we are off," as with wonderful ease he got into the buggy. "you can drive, of course, and will not be afraid of a runaway," laughing. "Booker City has not made my fortune yet, so I drive a mule; but just wait a little bit—just wait. I will sell every stump and tree before long, and come out on top. Have you anything to invest?"

"No," I answered, leaning forward to thrash the old mule, and for the first time realizing my position—almost a spy! Well, I need not be; but how to get out of it? Write that I preferred not to report? That would kill Booker City as dead as Hector. Write what had come to me from the general's talk? Die the thought and the thinker! Besides, *what* had come to my knowledge? Nothing really; but one thing was certain—I *could not* be his guest, and at the same time hold my present position. I thrashed the mule again, but a wave of the ears was the only answer; then the general turned to the back of the buggy.

"Get down, there, you miserable rascal!" he cried. "How dare you ride at ease, and let a gentleman exhaust himself on this beast! Get down, sir; yes, and be in a hurry." The riding at ease meant that Jupiter was hanging on to the back of the seat with his hands, while his feet were clinging to the springs of the vehicle.

He dropped off now as nimbly as a monkey, and picking up a stick as he ran, came abreast of the jogging mule very easily.

"Hi! hi! Git up, you w'ite debbil; git up!" he cried, prodding the mule as he ran. "Hi! hi! I'll make you know; I'll make you go; I'll poke you troo an' troo—hi! hi!"

"That's you, Jupiter," cried the general, "poke him lively! You'll be President of these United States yet—ha! ha! Get up now, quick, you lazy dog," as, with a grin that seemed to meet at the back of his head, Jupiter made a dash at the buggy, and swung himself into place once more. It was a wild race we were having then. The mule was cantering, with his ears backed, and his tail going round and round like a windmill.

"Negroes and mules were made for each other," the general said, as he pulled his hat on more firmly. "They understand each other in a way that can be explained only by affinity; and to see a Negro on a mule is like hearing a mockingbird sing on a moonlight night in summer—the 'eternal fitness' is satisfied."

While he talked we had come at a rattling pace through the pine woods, and now were moving more slowly along a red clay road, that, fringed with blackberry briers, ran narrow and deep between rail fences. Presently we began a long ascent, still between rail fences, and the mule settled down into a walk once more.

"We are nearing home now," the general went on, "and soon we'll see the ancestral rooftree, which will be turned into a foundry shortly, I hope. I used to have some sentiment, sir, but poverty unscrews the spinal column of sentiment. I'll be hanged if I can stand living from hand to mouth here, where once I lived on the fat of the land. No, sir. I'll sell every stick of timber, and every foot of land, and throw in the malaria for nothing. I've starved long enough on 'befo'-de-wah' memories. I'm sick of it, and it is not wholesome. I want to take my child away from this African atmosphere. Her blood and breeding will show anywhere, sir; and with a few shekels to put a halo around her head, why, she can do and be what she likes—God bless her! And I'll make those shekels; I have a few already. But just after the war, I'll give you my word, sir, I was an absolute beggar. I borrowed money, and went to Mexico—well, that is a story."

We had reached the brow of the hill by this, and halfway down the other side I saw an oasis in the red fields and a glimpse of a white house. A square white house it proved to be, with deep piazzas, and a long wing running back, and an old garden in front, with cedar trees and flags, and woodbine on trellises; there were some oak trees and locust trees, all bare of leaves; and the fence and gate were on their last legs. I had seen innumerable places like it in the inland South, felt familiar with the gullied gravel walk and the "corn shucks" door mat, even with the red clay footmarks that extended into the hall, and felt that I knew quite well the slim, fair-haired girl who greeted us with "How are you, Pappy darling?" Then she stopped, looking at me frankly from a pair of handsome brown eyes.

"A friend of my youth, Agnes, my dear; a Willoughby of Chilhowie, where my happiest holidays were spent. Kemper Willoughby, his father, was my boyhood friend, and this afternoon I found him stranded in

Booker City. I knew him by his eyes—good eyes. Shake hands; both hands, if you like. If he is true to his blood, you'll never find an honester gentleman."

So we shook hands, smiling the while, and I was glad of my blood when I looked in her eyes, and hated, without reason, my good chief in faraway New York.

A Willoughby of Chilhowie—poor old Chilhowie, lost in the war, and now a great phosphate works. The old name had a goodly sound to it, and the brown eyes took a reverent expression almost. Evidently she had heard stories of the old place and people. The rooms were carpetless—desolate expanses rather—but the fires were grand, and the few homely chairs were most comfortable. After a while we had a good country supper, then Agnes brought some tumblers and sugar, and Jupiter appeared with a kettle, that soon was singing on the fire, and the general hopped over to a cupboard in the wall and brought out a black bottle. My case was full of cigars, but the general preferred his pipe.

"I got that pipe in Mexico," he said—"a long story."

"A disgraceful story, Pappy," his daughter added, bringing her work basket from a far table—" a story that will shock Mr. Willoughby." She was seated now, with the firelight playing on her delicate features and fair hair, and as her little hands filled the battered old pipe, she looked up lovingly at the old man. "You must give Mr. Willoughby your pedigree before you tell that story."

"Oh, confound the pedigree! Willoughby *is* a gentleman, therefore he knows one under any disguise. Will you 'have sugar in yourn,' my dear boy, and the story of the pipe, or rather of the time when I got the pipe? It is the joy of my life—that time; it was life! And that old pipe was the beginning of the first comfort I had after the war. I had fought for four years in the cavalry, part of the time with Forrest. We were not what you would call a godly set, Agnes; but good fellows, who would die, or worse, would come near to lying, for a friend—brave fellows: God bless every man of them! We were a reckless set, and death meant nothing to us; but we lived, ye gods! Life since has seemed a faded rag. Well, I lost my leg first. I had a hand-to-hand scuffle for it, and I will not say how many I sent to their long homes—it hurts Agnes—but—well, my leg went; and not a year after, my arm. I killed the rascal who shot me in the arm. Then came the surrender"—his voice losing its cheery ring—"and I was fit to murder right and left. I could not stand it, or I thought I could not, and trundled off to Mexico. Beautiful country, my dear fellow, lovely, but the lowest down nation on the face of the earth to call themselves Christians, not morals enough in the whole nation to satisfy one respectable old-time darky. I could not stand it, and determined to come home, no matter what was the state of the country. But how to get here. I had the whole kingdom of Texas to cross, and no money and no railways, and only half rations in the way of legs. I worked my way to the Rio Grande on a broken-down old mustang. About ten miles from the river I came to a Mexican jacal, and hesitated about going in, they are such treacherous villains. But I was hungry, and pausing outside the door I heard a groan. Somebody in distress, I thought, and, cocking my pistol, I pushed my way in. An Englishman lay there; he had passed me two days before, traveling across country with a party of Mexicans, but I had caught him up again, and at the last gasp. The place was empty, save for him, and a pot of tamalis steaming near the fire. I looked at the Englishman first, but he was dead. I had heard his last groan probably, and his murderers had been run off by my approach. His pockets were rifled of everything save this pipe—a good pipe in its day; meerschaum, you see, and had a fancy stem; but I prefer a joint or two of cane. I was glad of the tamalis; but I did not think it safe to linger, as I did not know the number of the Mexicans. My clothes and shoe were too ragged, however, to leave a dead man as well clothed as that Englishman was, so I helped myself to a part of his wardrobe. I had not been so well dressed in years, and I laughed a little at myself. 'You look as nice as a preacher,' I said. Then folding up my old clothes, I left them near the dead man, and taking some extra tamalis, I left the house. 'As nice as a preacher,' the words came to me again: it had been a phrase in the army when a fellow was specially well dressed. 'As nice as a preacher?' Why not? Who had a better time than preachers? Why not be a preacher? I could not help chuckling a little at the thought. Why not be a preacher for the time? And visions of fried chicken and hot biscuit came over my mind, and fiery steeds furnished by adoring flocks—why not? I laughed out loud as I jogged on in the darkness. A preacher? What kind? What kind? Out on the border that did not matter. As far as my experience in that country went, all one had to do was to swear one had had a call; then preach and eat. That was more than twenty years ago, you see. So I did not come to any decision, but left it all to chance.

"I was so much entertained by my thoughts that I was surprised when I found myself at the river. It was day-dawn, and, as luck would have it, I found some Mexicans with a boat just where I reached the bank. I seemed to strike terror into most of the party, and I shrewdly suspected that it was the Englishman's clothes that did it; most probably they had been among his murderers. Some ran away, but two remained, and agreed to put me across. Of course they thought I had money, but I kept my pistol lined on them, and when we reached the other bank, my pay was to jump ashore, and tell them in their own language that I was to meet a party of Americans there, and that they had better skip with my blessing and the old mustang. They did.

"I shall never forget my first day as a preacher. I thought of the character so much that at last I began to imagine myself one. I arranged sermons with the utmost facility, and all that I had ever learned of catechism and hymns and prayers came back to me. The day passed swiftly enough, although hopping along on crutches was such weary work that I began to think longingly of even my old mustang.

"About sundown I reached a settlement—a cattle ranch—but evidently not of the highest character. Yes, they would take me in. The woman of the house had a pathetic face, and looked at me searchingly, almost suspiciously.

"'I am a man of peace,' I said, in answer to her look, 'and I have lost my way.'

"'You look like a preacher,' one of the men said.

"I bowed my head.

"'I thought as much,' he went on, turning to the woman, whose face had brightened up.

"'I 'ain't seen a preacher in five years,' she said. 'Ain't you hungry?'

"'I am, indeed, my sister,' I said; 'as hungry as your spirit must be.'

"'Now you're shoutin'!' the man cried, slapping his leg. 'That's the way to talk it. I've heard 'em a hund'ed times; an' mammy would always come to me an' say, sof'ly, "Go kill fo' chickens, Billy." I'd know that talk anywhere. Golly! go kill something, 'Liza—a horse—the baby—anythin', an call in all the fellers; bound to have somethin' to eat. Gosh! your stomach thinks your throat's cut, don't it, mister?'

"I was wild to laugh, by gad, sir! the rascal hit the nail so squarely on the head; but I answered quietly enough, 'I *would* like a little food,' adding, meekly, 'if you have anything to spare.'

"The man went out roaring with laughter, and the woman came close to me.

"'Did you ever marry anybody?' she asked.

"It gave me a sort of chill for a minute.

"'No,' I answered; 'I am not married.'

"'That ain't what I mean,' she said. 'Me an' Billy have changed rings, an' promised befo' the boys, an' mean it, too; but we ain't had no minister nor no magistrate, an' somehow I'd ruther have some words said. It's been three years gone now sence we changed rings.'

"'And you wish me to say a few words?' I asked, my compunctions fading as the woman's story went on.

"'Yes, if Billy's willin', but he don't like preachers much. He don't believe in 'em; but I do. I'll ask him,' and she went out.

"This was a position I had not counted on, for the official acts of the clergy had not occured to me, and for a few moments I wished myself well out of the dilemma; but I must go on now, for to show these men that I was deceiving them might mean death. So while I waited I trumped up, or tried to trump up, the Episcopal marriage service; but something else would come instead, and looking into the matter afterwards, I discovered it to be the catechism; but then I knew only that it would not serve my purposes, and I was still at sea when the woman returned.

"This time she was followed by several men, among them 'Billy.'

"'Come in, boys,' he cried, 'we're goin' to have a weddin', me an' 'Liza, an' that means a supper; don't it, 'Liza? An' tomorrer we'll have to loan Brother—What's your name, mister?'

"'Stiggins,' I answered, with a back glance at Mr. Weller.

"'Stiggins,' Billy repeated. "We'll have to loan Brother Stiggins a horse. I tell you , boys, it's a good thing we've got somethin' to drink tonight, an' me an' 'Liza'll change rings again.'

"It was a trying moment. To save my life I could not remember anything to begin with, and as the couple took their places in front of me I felt puzzled to death; but I *could* not fail, and I made a mad dash.

"'What is your name?' I asked, solemnly.

"'Billy Sprowle,' was answered, promptly.

"'What is your name?'—to the woman.

"''Liza Dobbs.'

"'Who gave you that name?' was the thing that seemed to come next, somehow, but I realized at once that it would not do, so determined on a common-sense question, and asked: 'Are you both of one mind in this matter? Answer as you shall answer at the last great day!' and I let my voice fall into profound depths.

"'Yes,' came from the couple; and from the subdued expression of the company I saw that my voice had impressed them. This encouraged me, and I made another grab among my memories.

"'William, will you have this woman to be thy wedded wife, to have and to hold until death us do part?' And the words tumbled out so glibly, once I got started, that I left the 'us' unchanged, and recklessly plighted my troth along with them. But they did not notice this, and Billy's 'Yes, sir,' came like a shot. 'Eliza, will you have this man to be thy wedded husband, to have and to hold until death us do part?' I said once more.

"'Yes.'

"'Change rings,' I went on, 'and both of you say-"With this ring I thee wed, from this day forth for evermore."' They obeyed, Billy looking meeker and meeker as the service went on; then joining their hands, I looked at the company sternly, saying, 'I prounounce William and Eliza Sprowle to be man and wife.'

"By this time lots more of the service had come to me, but somehow I could not bring myself to say it; it seemed to stick in my throat. But what I *had* said had made an immense impression. Every man there looked at me with something of awe in his eyes, and I heard one whisper, 'A rale sho-'nuff preacher'; and the answer, 'You bet; he crawls me.'

"The ceremony over, I sat down by the fire to wait for further developments, and the men stood about awkwardly. By this time, however, I felt quite in character, and said, in a mild tone, 'Have you much of a settlement here?'

"'Not much,' the oldest man of the group answered, 'an' the nearest neighbors is ten miles off. It's a right lonesome country.'

"'Yes,' I answered, 'but good grass.'

"'That's so, an' free. Billy Sprowle has made a right good thing of comin' out here, him an' these boys; I 'ain't been here long.'

"'Do the Mexicans trouble you much?' I went on.

"'Not as much as they'd like to.' Then with an effort, 'Do you think killin' a Mexican is any harm?'

"'No', I answered, promptly, then clearing my throat slowly—'no, not if they molest your property.'

"The man passed his hand over his face, looking at me curiously, while I gazed sadly into the fire. After a moment's reflective scanning of me he drew nearer, and, putting his hands in his pockets, stood looking down on me.

"'You've got common sense, mister,' he said, 'if you *are* a preacher, an' you answered mighty lively at first 'bout killin' Mexicans; you know they oughter be wiped off the face of the earth?'

"I gave him look for look. 'My brother,' I said, 'I fought for four years in the war, and, as you see, half of me is in the grave. I don't stand back on killing or on being killed when it is necessary. And I like hunting too,' I went on, 'but I don't like to hunt buzzards.'

"'Shake!' he cried, holding out his hand; 'that's good 'bout buzzards; Mexicans an' buzzards *is* one. Sakes-er-mussy!'—turning to the rest— 'that's sense, boys, preacher or no preacher.'

"They all drew up after this, and sat down near the fire: they had fought, too, and war stories were plenty, and before supper was over we were the firmest friends.

"Next morning, however, after the night's reflection, Billy came to me, confidentially.

"'Are you a sho-'nuff preacher?' he said; 'or did you jest put it up on the old girl? It won't make no diffrunce to us boys, you know, an' 'Liza's done eased off 'bout bein' married, an' we won't make her on-ressless by tellin' her no better—but *are* you a preacher?'

"'Why not?' I asked, drawing myself up. 'What have I done that a preacher should not do?'

"'Oh, nothin'—nothin'!' rather hurriedly; 'only you've got so much horse sense, an' preachers, you know—'

"'My brother,' I said, gravely, and I laid my hand on his shoulder in a way that would have done credit to an archbishop, 'you don't understand; I got my sense before I was called to be a preacher; I was a man first, and then a preacher. Do you see?'

"'You bet; an' you'll *always* be a man?'

"'Always.'

"'Thet's good,' heartily. 'I'd like to hear you preach.'

"Well, those fellows could not do enough for me; they lent me a horse that was to be left at the next town; they rode a long way with me, and Billy gave me a Mexican dollar as a marriage fee. But poor 'Liza, her gratitude was pathetic, and she brought her little child for me to bless. That got me, rather, but I gave him the best I had; it was the last blessing my dear old mother gave me; 'The Lord bless and keep you, my boy, and bring you home at last,' she had said. I gave it to the little fellow, and the mother cried. And I did not feel mean a bit for deceiving them, for I had done good. I had made that woman happy, and had raised the clergy in the estimation of these men. To tell you the truth, I felt myself a missionary.

"About sundown I reached a little town, a very small affair, and stopped at the largest house I could find, and the hardest-looking case I had ever seen came to the door. I asked if I could stop there; he said he would see, and went back into the house. Then a woman came— harder-looking than the man, if that were possible. I told her I was a man of peace, and wanted to spend the night; that I made a point of going to the houses of the best people in a town, because they would have the most influence, and could help me in my work. That woman's face was like a flint when I began, but before the end of my speech the whole expression had changed.

"'I ain't no 'Piscopal,' she said, the defiance that had left her face still lingering in her voice.

"'Of course not,' I answered, glibly. 'I take you to be a Wash-foot Baptist.'

"'How'd you know that?' she cried.

"'There's a look in your face,' I said.

"'My soul an' body! Come in,' and she flung the door wide. She put me in a very decent room, and presently I heard wild shouting and a cannonade of sticks and stones. As I had distrusted both the man and the woman, I was startled for a second, but the screech of a chicken restored my equilibrium. 'Fried chicken for the preacher,' I said to myself, and determined that I must become accustomed to that side of the ministerial life—and a very good side too. In a marvellously short time I was called to supper. "'I s'pose you don't mind havin' a bite,' the woman said; 'so I jest killed a chicken, and knocked up a few biscuit.'

"I did have a little feeling that the chicken was scarcely dead, and that the biscuit had rather a jaundiced look; but I had been intimate with starvation too long to be fastidious, and I ate with a will; and as I remember it now, the coffee was not bad.

"'Is you goin' to have a meetin'?' was the woman's first question as I took my seat at table. 'I 'member you said somethin' 'bout your work, an' we 'ain't had nothin' but 'Piscopal religion here for a long time.'

"'And you don't like it?' I parried.

"'No, I don't; there ain't no grit to it; I want my religion to have some sperrit; I'd ruther have a revival now than money; and the 'Piscopals jest keep right along quiet an' easy, an' I 'ain't got no mo' patience with 'em. I'm tired.'

"'Is there a clergyman here?'

"'No; he's dead. He come for his health, an' worked an' died 'bout a month ago; we 'ain't had nothin' sence; but if you're a Baptist preacher, there's nothin' henders why you can't have a meetin'.'

"'If you think so—'

"'Yes, I do think so: you look like you kin preach.'

"'Yes, I think I can.'

"'Then I'll send John out. John! I say, John!'

"The man who had opened the door for me came in.

"'I want you to go round this town, John,' she began, 'an' tell the folks that Brother—What's your name?'

"'Stiggins.'

"'That Brother Stiggins will have a meetin' to-morrer, startin' right early.'

"John looked at me slowly, then said the one word, "'Piscopal?'

"'No!' and the woman looked as amiable as a sitting hen. "'Ain't you got *no* sense, John Blye? Did you *ever* see a 'Piscopal look like him? He looks like he's got grit. Go 'long an' tell Brother Williams to come over an' help 'range 'bout it; go 'long.'

"I must confess I felt rather queer as the combat thickened round me. After all, suppose I could not preach? And I said, mildly, 'Is Brother Williams a good preacher?'

"'No, he ain't'—frankly; 'but he's a mighty good prayer. I've heard him pray right along for a hour, an' it never seemed like he drawed a breath. Yes, he's a mighty upliftin' prayer; he'll help you, don't you fret. Jest you preach, an' hit hard too, an' Brother Williams he'll raise all the hymns an' do the prayin'; an' he does line out hymns beautiful.'

"This made me more comfortable, and it was easy enough to arrange matters with Brother Williams, a small, red-headed man—a druggist— with a long red nose that he used as a speaking trumpet. Very soon he and Sister Blye had arranged all the details; even the hymns were chosen, and nine o'clock the hour fixed on. I was awfully tired; but I chose my text, and dreamed out my sermon, for by morning the whole thing was in my mind—a grand thing, with enough fire and brimstone in it to destroy the universe. 'Where the worm dieth not, and the fire is not quenched'—that was my text. I tell you, Willoughby, I have often thought that I missed my vocation in not being a preacher. If you could hear me once, I believe you would be converted yourself. By Jove, sir! all the town was there the next morning, in a big place like a barn, which all creeds used in common. Brother Williams was there, and his nose looked longer and redder than before.

"We started them off with a hymn; then Brother Williams prayed such a prayer! It was ridiculous, sir! I was dying to laugh. If you could have heard his instructions to the Almighty, and his faultfinding too: it was awful. But Sister Blye—the way in which she groaned and grunted over Brother Williams's presentation of the shortcomings of the Lord was edifying in the extreme. Then we had another hymn—a regular dynamite fuse; but nobody showed any signs of religion except Sister Blye. Then I began. I began quietly, but in the deepest voice I could muster. First, I gave a picture of heaven, quoting Milton copiously; but my audience was quiet under that, and I realized that they were in a coolly critical frame of mind. Further, I realized that I had no idea o heaven, or eternal bliss, or anything eternal for that matter. I could not conceive of heavenly bliss, for the happiest moments of my life had been passed in battle. I tell you there's nothing like the rush and madness of a charge, and you know that is no vision of heaven. I think I failed in my description of heaven; so, according to my plan, I came down to this life. I knew that through and through, and I flayed humanity alive and rubbed salt in. Then they began to prick up their ears, and Sister Blye looked uneasy. I liked to see it, and a determination came over me to do a little good, if possible. And I believe I did. I gave them the devil for a good half-hour, straight from the shoulder. Then I dropped down to hell, and *then* I made the fur fly! I knew sin and remorse;" and the general's face grew grave, and he laid his hand on his daughter's shoulder. "Yes, I knew hell better than heaven; it came easy, and I drew it strong. In twenty minutes that place was like Bedlam. I have never heard or seen anything like it, and never want to again. Such howls and screams and shouting! I did not know what to do exactly, for nobody could hear me, so I stopped and sat down. Well, sir, little Williams, who had been lying flat on the floor, howling, hopped up as spry as a cricket, and lined out a hymn. It was the best thing he could have done; it served as a vent for the excitement, and they sang with a will. Then he prayed, and exhorted people to come up and be prayed for; in fact, he got up a first-class revival on top of my sermon; then he took up a collection, to pay my expenses, he said. I don't know how much was given him, but I think he and Sister Blye got a very good return for their labors; they gave me five dollars. I refused to preach any more that day, and told them I must go on. Well, sir, people followed me to the next town—followed to hear me preach again, they said. There was a real Baptist preacher there, a very good fellow, who kept a shoe shop. He was delighted with the thought of a revival; and he and Sister Blye and little Williams arranged the programme. I had caught on to their methods by this time, and determined to take up my own collections. I did the work, and was determined to get my pay. We were in that town three days, and every one of them field days. You never saw the like; such a raging, tearing time I have never conceived of. But the funny part was that when the collecting time came, and I started out on my own hook, Sister Blye and Williams and the other preacher all dashed after me full tilt, and it was simply a race; but many refused to give to any one but me, which made me have fewer compunctions about taking the money, for it showed me that they understood each other.

"By Jove, sir, at the end of three days everybody wanted to be baptized, and I nearly exploded when their own preacher told them that there was not enough water anywhere short of the Gulf to wash away their sins, but that he would do the best he could for them in the waterhole outside the town.

"I did not take any hand in that: the official acts I did not touch, nor did I ever pray in public; but I did not see any harm in telling them their sins, and in making them wish they had never been born because of the fright I put them in. It was pitiful. But I did good; I know I did good; and I made money. By this time I had learned all the tricks of the trade, and my brother preacher proposed that we should agree to work Texas for three months, I doing the preaching, and he doing everything else; that we should dismiss Sister Blye and Williams immediately, and divide the proceeds into two parts instead of four. That fellow—Stallings was his name—was something of a wag, and he told Williams and Sister Blye that we had entered into a partnership, and did not want them any more; that we had concluded to stop the circus business and teach religion.

"It was astonishing how much money we made after that, and how wonderfully successful we were. The papers took us up: 'Stallings and Stiggins,' and their grand revivals; their preaching and praying and singing, and the rest of it. We went from town to town in style, lived on the fat of the land, and had as many horses as we wanted. And I added a postscript to my sermons that any people who changed their creed under stress of excitement were renegades and fools. I wish you could have seen Stallings's face the first time I tacked that on; but it took like wildfire. All the preachers in that town came to hear me, and thanked me for my sermons; and after that Stallings and I gave something always to every Protestant church in every town, with always the proviso that it was to go to the preacher's salary—that much extra. Well, that got out, and the effect was miraculous: money flowed in. Don't you see that I did good? Then the scoldings I gave! By gad, sir, they should have taken the skin off. Bless your heart, how I went for the people for not doing their duty by the ministry! Why, Dante's lowest round was nothing to what I promised them if they did not do better.

"But the end of it all was wonderful. We were at a little town not far from the Louisiana line, and I was preaching fire and brimstone for dear life, when a face in the congregation caught my eye. It was the saddest face I had ever seen: past middle age, with sunken cheeks and silver hair. But it was the eyes that took hold of me—big, pitiful brown eyes that looked hunted and starved.

"After I had seen that face I could not preach anything but comfort and hope: I could not say anything hard to that woman. When I came out she was waiting at the door.

"'I want to speak to you,' she said, and took hold of my arm. 'You come from my part of the country—I know it by your voice—and you are a gentleman, if you are—' And she paused.

"'If I *am* an itinerant preacher,' I put in.

"'Yes; it does seem strange to me,' she answered, frankly; 'but you *are* a gentleman, and you come from the South Atlantic coast.'

"'Yes,' I admitted, beginning to feel thoroughly ashamed of my position; 'and is there anything I can do for you?'

"'I have come to you for help,' she answered, tremulously, 'because I seemed to recognize you in some way; and yet your name is not a coast name—Stiggins—I have never heard it.'

"'Outside of *Pickwick,*' I amended. 'But where do you live? Can I go home with you and talk to you?'

"'Just around the corner: we have one room. Yes, you can come: my daughter is there.'

"In five minutes we reached the room—a poor, miserable little place, but absolutely clean—and sitting there sewing, a young girl, not more than eighteen. She looked up in surprise.

"'Mamma!' she said, and I seemed to hear my own little sister speaking, so familiar were the accents.

"'This is Mr. Stiggins, dear, the preacher; he comes from home, and will help us.' Then motioning me to a seat, she went on: 'My name is Vernon—one of the South Carolina Vernons, you know.'

"'And your maiden name?' I asked, rising in astonishment.

"'Asheburton?'

"'Marion Asheburton?'

"'Yes,' her eyes dilating with wonder.

"'And a long time ago, when I was a little boy, you were engaged to Jack Stamper, and he died?'

"'Yes—oh yes! Who are you?'

"'Willie,' I said—'Willie Stamper, the little brother: don't you remember?'

"'How, then, is your name Stiggins?' said the daughter, severly. But the mother asked no questions, needed no proofs; she simply fell on my neck, and cried as if her heart would break. You see she had gone back to her first love, and her first sorrow—had gone back to days when prosperity and luxury were the rule. Poor thing! poor thing! Then our stories came out—hers pitiful beyond compare; mine, that seemed to grow more vulgar and disgraceful as I told it. The telling of that story was an awful grind until the girl laughed—the sweetest laugh I had ever heard. God bless her! They were destitute—these Vernons—had moved to Texas, and the father had died, leaving the mother and child to struggle alone, poor things! When I met them they had not tasted food for twenty-four hours. I took charge of them at once, and sent them over to New Orleans to wait for me. I had a good deal of money by that time, but could not break my engagement with Stallings, and it lacked a month of being out. But I preached for all I was worth that last month, and tears and dollars came like rain; and at the last I had literally to run away from Stallings. He said we would make our fortunes if we stayed together; but I explained to him that I was not so anxious about making money as I was about looking up some heathen I knew across the Mississippi. So we parted, and I left Texas with two hundred dollars in my pocket, besides what I had sent Mrs. Vernon. "Well, we were married—the girl and I—and came home here to Alabama, where I have managed to live ever since. But I have never been as rich as I was when I was a preacher, for all my expenses were paid, I had horses to ride, I lived on the fat of the land, and had more clothes made for me by adoring sisters than ever since. It was a wonderful time. Agnes here thinks it was disgraceful, but she laughs sometimes when I tell the old story, just as her mother did. They are forgotten now, those happy-go-lucky old days, and my little wife lived only a year—only a year."

The fire seemed to burn low as the old gentleman paused, and the girl laid her head on his shoulder.

"But I *have* lived," and he drew a long sigh. "Yea, verily, life was worth living when I first set out; and the war"—shaking his head—"I would not take anything for those years of excitement; by gad, sir, that was life, sure enough! And just after the war it was not so very bad; there was some novelty in being poor, just at first, before we learned to strive and grind; but now the grind is awful—perfectly awful! For everybody is grinding now, rich and poor, old and young. Rich people do not stop to enjoy, because they want more, and poor people cannot stop to enjoy, because they have nothing. We have lost the art of being satisfied—an art the South used to possess to a ruinous extent. We are losing the art of having fun, the art of enjoying simple things. We are learning to be avaricious, for now in the South position is coming to depend on money; so all grind along together; and I hate it."

"But when you sell Booker City, papa," suggested the daughter, with an earnest faith in word and look, "then you will have enough?"

The twinkle came back to the general's eye, and he tossed off the last of his toddy with a wave of the hand.

"That is true, little girl—when I sell Booker City."

But I did not want to talk of Booker City, and the keen old fellow noticed it, and cocking his head on one side, he said:

"You don't believe in Booker City?"

"I don't know anything about it," I answered; "but I believe in *you.*"

"And so you *may,* my boy"—heartily; "and I tell you Booker City has a grand future."

I lifted my hand. "Don't tell me," I said, "until I tell you." Then I blurted out my story.

"Of course I will resign," I finished, "and they may send another man." The general rubbed his chin. "Don't be rash," he said. "Write your chief the whole story; let him recall you; let him come out himself if he likes. To resign because I happen to be a friend of your father is a 'befo'-de-wah' sensitiveness which we cannot afford now. That fine old sensitiveness! It was silly sometimes, but exquisite. We cannot afford it now, however; and by the time we can afford it we will have been made so tough in the grind for money that we will have lost the cuticle necessary to it. That is the reason it takes three generations to make a gentleman. For myself, I don't think he can be made under five or six. However, accepting the proposition, the first generation cannot afford to be a gentleman; the second generation might be able to afford it, but don't know how; the third generation can afford it, and maybe has learned the outward semblance, and so the saying has come. But to have all the 'earmarks,' to have the thing come naturally, to have it so bred in the bone that a man can't help being a gentleman, and has hands and feet and ears all to match—that kind of thing takes five or six generations. And even after six generations I have seen the 'old Adam' crop out in broad thumbs or big ears.

"Now you have all the points, Willoughby, but you cannot afford that 'befo'-de-wah' sensitiveness. Don't resign, but tell your story, and give your honest impressions; for the first generation cannot afford even a comfortable lie; it requires 'a hundred earls' to let a man lie with impunity. Humanity is still too crude—all except the French and Africans—to put up with a lie, except under very extraordinary circumstances of success or position. So after you have seen Booker City, and have heard all my plans, then write; but don't resign because you happen to find a friend in me, and so may be suspected of collusion. If you have no idea of collusion, don't be afraid of suspicion. Tell him that I am your friend; then, if he suspects you, he will send another fellow down; but if he has any sense he will not send to supersede *you*. If he does, why you come over to my party—me and George Washington Stamper Booker"—laughing—"and by gad, sir, we'll work those fellows for all they are worth; we'll never let them rest until our fortunes are made, and Booker City is the London and Paris and New York and Chicago and Rome and Athens and everything else of the South all rolled into one, not to leave out Pittsburgh and Boston—yes, sir; and we'll invite your chief down, and we'll take him to drive with Jupiter and the mule, and tell him about those palmy days in Texas over a good hot toddy, and by Jove, sir, he'll be one of us in twenty-four hours! We'll make him build a memorial for Sister Blye, and save a corner lot for Stallings. Just let him dare to supersede you, and so help me over the fence if I am not such a friend to him as will make him wish he'd never been born. I have not forgotten how to preach, and I'll make that old Dives think he's reached an infinite prairie on an infinite August day and not a water hole in sight; but don't you resign."

I took the general's advice; but it was a hard letter to write, and I am afraid it was a little stiff. Nevertheless the general was right; I was not superseded, and in time my chief did take a drive with Jupiter and the mule, and heard the story of the Texas days told as no pen on earth can write it.

READJUSTMENTS

He sat with his forehead down on his arms, that were crossed on the table, and from under his crossed arms a half-sheet of paper—typewritten—protruded. For a long time he had been very still, now he lifted his head and looked at the paper; only a moment, then again bent down, hiding his eyes on his arms. Something must be done, and he had not a friend to turn to. He was as lonely as when a child he was left to the servants, who did with him as they pleased,—his old nurse Chloe, and the one-time coachman, Wash, now cook and man of all work. Chloe could not understand, and old Wash—he cleaned his master's guns and pistols as regularly as if hunting parties were a constant thing and duels an everyday occurrence. The old Negroes had been good to him and had taught him "manners." "wearin' yo' hat in de house ent no manners," Wash would say; and Chloe's admonition—"Playin' wid dat ball on a Sunday, dat ent to say manners ner 'ligion, nuther; Lawd, chile, ef you coulder seen yo' mah!"

"En de kerridges en de hawses!" Wash would add, dreamily; "en brer Jack wuz de butler, en Minty wuz de maid fuh de wisitin' ladies, en Clarinder wuz de maid fuh lil Missy, unner mah; en I wuz de coachman, en dey wuz t'ree cook."

"En you sho muss bab manners," Chloe would finish.

He had thought much about his mother. He had discovered that her husband had been three times her age when she married him. Had she loved this old man, he wondered, when first the romance of youth budded in him—three times her age! And one day, hesitatingly, he asked "Was my father handsome, Wash, when he married my mother?"

"Han'some! Des liker picter! Des es tall en es straight es dat young tree w'at you is leanin' 'ginst; en 'e hair des like de chimney back. Han'some!" the old man had grumbled on. "My Mass Dan! Han'some—Lawd!"

"And my mother?"

179

"My son—my only son—is a coward."

"Lil Missy? Lil Missy ent good done growin' w'en she married Mass Dan, en she eye ent nebber leff Mass Dan face; en she tu'n red—tu'n white—en trimmle; den she laff sorter low-like, tell Mass Dan look at um, den she stop, en tu'n red—en tu'n w'ite, en look out de winder."

"Was she afraid?"

"'Fraid? Cose lil Missy wuz 'fraid; 'omans is always 'fraider mens; en ebbryt'ing on dis place, in dis county, in de town, wuz 'fraider Mass Dan; in cose she wuz 'fraid. W'en you is bawn Mass Dan say: 'Hooray—a boy—hooray! By ten yays he'll be a fine shot; by fifteen, he'll know all dey is to know—he'll be a man—he's my boy!' Den lil Missy cry. She ent lib long atter dat, des two mont's; en w'en she is dyin'—Mass Dan wuz in town—she say, 'Chloe, please, Chloe, stay wid my son please, Chloe, en meck him a good man, Chloe.' En I promise, en I stay; dat I is."

"And the carriages and the horses?" he had pushed on, taking oath to be a good man the while he swallowed the lump in his throat.

"Wuh Wash talk 'bout? Lawd! Kerridge en hawse! en dey ent been nuttin' yer w'en we come ceppen one ole rock'-way en two hawse! En my mawsa, my lil Missy pah, is hab stable full, fo' de wah; dat's de trute. En w'en de wah is done, en Mass Rob is meck mo' money, den 'e married 'e wife en yo' mah is bawn; en den Mass Rob daid en yo' mah is teck by she gahdeen. I gone wid um, en Clarinder, my chile, en we ent like it, en lil Missy ent do nuttin' but cry. Den Mass Dan come long en cote um, en she say yes, en dey wuz married, en we come yer. Lawd! den de trouble git wuss, fuh de gahdeen say lil Missy ent had no money, no prop'ty ent hab nuttin'; dat de plantation wuz he plantation fuh de money Mass Rob owe him; ef'e coulder do it, I spec' say 'e woulder claim me en Clarinder; but I tell um, say, 'I'se free, Mr. Kreener, en you cahn do nuttin' to me; en I kin 'member w'en yo' gran'pah is po' buckra, is obersay fuh my ole mawsa niggers; en you done teck awl de prop'ty, en I knows it.' En 'e order me outer de house, en I laff in 'e face! Lawd! dem wuz bad times; Mass Dan ent say nuttin' but 'Damn-damn!' Kase ebbrybody is t'ink say my lil Missy is rich young lady, en ebberybody is s'prised w'en dat po' buckra, Kreener, say she ent hab nuttin'. En 'e nebber say it tay lil Missy is done married, den 'e sen' awl de bill fuh she close to Mass Dan, en Mass Dan gone dey en t'row um back in 'e face, en say 'e gwine lick um wid 'e hawse-w'ip. Lawd! yes, chile, I'se glad w'en my lil Missy is gone to she ress; en fuh you—"

Years ago he had heard all this, and he had turned it over in his mind until the story seemed clear to him.

As a very small boy he had had a tutor. He learned rapidly, and was in the seventh heaven when his father, taking him on his knee, would praise his reading. At last one day he said, "Now you must learn to shoot," and had produced a light gun bought especially. His father loaded and fired it.

He had refused to touch the gun. For a long time after this his father took no notice of him, and almost he fell ill of grief. Then old Wash taught him to ride, and once more his father seemed to see him. Alas! On his pony he had gone out with his father and friends: old Wash had charge of him, and when by short cuts they had come in at the death of the deer, he had burst into tears—had screamed with terror when, he having been in at the death, they put blood on his forehead as if he had killed his first deer. The look on his father's face was with him still, and the few low oaths, the intensity of which could not be mistaken. Nor did he ever forget the looks of the men who stood there.

It was about this time that the tutor had been dismissed, and he was left entirely to the servants. Later, Wash took him to the county free school, warning him carefully that though the teacher was a fine man and could teach, the boys there were not to be treated as friends, and must never be brought to the house. So he had learned; and from that and the old library in the house he had won his education.

He had been a terrible disappointment to his father, he knew that, for no sports appealed to him; but old Wash's banjo had been a joy. One evening in the dusk his father had found him playing on the old piano—had come on him unawares. Something, not a sound, but something had made him turn to where the old man towered behind him in the shadows. "Tinkling on the piano," had been his greeting; "why not wear petticoats and do embroidery!"

All these things had hurt him, but he had not understood until a visitor had opened his eyes, a man older than his father, who had lived abroad ever since the war. He, himself, had been caught reading on the front piazza clothed in Chloe's creations. Trousers and coat that had fitted his father, Chloe having shortened only sleeves and legs; and shoes that his father had discarded. And when a carriage came smartly round the weed-grown circle, he had risen involuntarily; had come down the steps. The visitor had paused, looking at him, and he, returning the look, felt compelled to draw himself up and to introduce himself. "I am Archibald Sorel Wilding," he had said.

"Indeed!" the old man had answered. "And I, my boy, knew both your grandfathers. My name is Featherstone." Then they shook hands and mounted the steps together. Into the faded drawing- room they had gone, while the boy's diffidence again overwhelmed him, and he had slipped away to call his father and to tell Chloe.

"The devil! Hugh Featherstone! And you, sir, what did he take you for?"

"I told him my name."

"The last straw!"

Chloe had been wild with excitement; she rushed Wash in to make a fire and to open the windows, then set herself to make coffee. "I'll meck some good cawfee, en w'en I teck um in Mass Hugh 'll 'member ole Chloe, you'll see."

For himself, he had taken his seat by the kitchen fire, with his book closed over his finger. His father did not look like this man, whose whole appearance was so astonishing. Did men out in the world look always like this? The men who came out with his father looked quite different. They wore no cuffs, their trousers were held in place with belts, like workmen; their cravats were careless. He never felt ashamed of his clothes before them, but this man?

"Is he very rich?" he asked.

"How I know, chile?"

Then Wash came running in. "Mass Ahchie, yo' pah call you."

It was now Chloe's turn to have her eyes opened, and she cried: "En dem is yo' bess clo'es! Lawd-a-mussy!"

He stood for a moment looking down at himself. "Father knows," he said. But he was trembling. He dreaded more the look in his father's eyes than the stranger's scrutiny; and the look was there, but also a shadow of pity, of tenderness, that drew him like a magnet! "Mr. Featherstone—" the words halted him where he stood; the tenderness was gone.

"Come to me," the stranger had said, and had drawn a chair near to his own.

"He looks like the place, you see," and his father laughed a little, "gone to seed. He's not like either family; he's gunshy and never even wished for a horse."

"What is your book?" the old gentleman had asked, and to this day he remembered the kindness in his voice, just as he remembered the throbbing in his head and the burning in his face while the book was taken from him. "Rawlinson's *Herodotus*," the stranger read; "your father's copy, Dan. Is the old library still here? Let me see it." Then giving him his book again, he had put his arm about his shoulders, and together they had followed his father.

"Nobody uses it now," his father was saying, "unless this boy does; he seems to be always mooning about with books, or strumming on the piano like a girl."

The old gentleman laughed. "There spoke the old South," he said; "any man 'born in the purple,' who had a turn for anything except riding, shooting, and telling the truth, was a 'mollycoddle'; even writing must not be done for money; even money-making was beneath contempt, and only God knows how much genius was trampled to death among us. But a musician, an actor, a painter—heavens! If they were men, were almost pariahs; if they were women, it must not show beyond the home!"

"And we were right!" his father shouted, standing still in the hall. "When I found this boy playing the piano I felt like thrashing him, like cutting his fingers off! When a gentleman wants music, hire it; a man should be about manlier things."

There was much more talk like this while they drank Chloe's coffee, that was much praised, and at the last the stranger had said:

"Whenever you play the piano, my boy, think of me and be sorry for all the Southern boys whose music was killed in them; and remember that all honest work is good. Now, Dan, shoot me for heresy; but one thing, your boy speaks English; you have looked to that."

"Not I; I have taught him nothing since he cried to see a deer killed. Damn it all!"

The old gentleman laughed. "The old story, dear fellow, of the hen and the duck eggs, that's all; he may be great in his own way. God bless you, boy!"

How long ago all this was, and yet every word had stayed with him. One result was that he became ashamed of his clothes, and all honest work being good, he drove himself to work for the neighboring farmers. Chloe and Wash were greatly scandalized, until one day he went to town and returned with a new suit of clothes and a hat, and no more was said; but he was careful always to put on the old clothes when his father came, just as he was careful never to touch the piano when his father was in the house. His working for the farmers would hurt his father quite as much as his being musical.

Meanwhile he had read much criticism on his section and on his class; books about the old South by Southerners, and about the new South by outsiders, and had heard his father swear at both, declaring that the South was misrepresented all round. All this he had pondered while he, "Archibald Wilding, Gentleman," had milked cows, cut wood, ploughed for "Hill Billies," as his father called them, at a dollar a day, until a few weeks before this, when a check had come to him from a magazine in payment for a short story. A great amount of money, it had seemed to him, and for a little his head was turned.

What would his father say? Perhaps be glad—perhaps be very angry! He would not tell him now; he would wait until he had taken up the mortgages; then he would reveal his secret, and perhaps once more in his father's eyes would be the love that as a child he clearly remembered.

So he had dreamed, and now? He turned his head wearily on his folded arms. Was he really a physical coward? At this moment he was afraid, horribly afraid. Would his father remain quiet under this vulgar innuendo? Public feeling had changed on certain points and murder was murder now, never mind who did it, and his father did not realize! His father in jail—his father hanged! What should he do—what could he do?

The front door slammed and he sprang to his feet! From the day of the battle over the gun he had been afraid of his father; the memory of that struggle coming to him in the night could still make him shiver, could still bring out on him a cold sweat; his hand would tremble as his little hands had done then; he would still feel the bruised pain in his fingers' ends that had been forced to hold the gun, that with all his puny strength and gigantic terror he had dragged away, tearing the tender skin; he could hear Chloe's shrill scream, "Gimme meh chile— you'll kill um—you'll kill um!" The momentary pause as the woman seized him, then her tears on his face, the haven of her bosom, the sudden blotting out of the universe! It seemed to be her sobs that recalled him to life in the kitchen where she had barred the door. But she need not have feared; his father seemed never to see him again until the episode of the deer, and after that he did not seem to exist for his father. But the fear had never left him, and he knew what was suffered when he read of the horrors of a nervous shock. But now he'd have to play a man's part; would have to face his father and try to keep the peace.

There was a shout for Wash, then the door was flung open. The old man's face was white as death, his eyes were burning as he dashed his hat on the table. "Well, sir," he cried, pointing to the paper, "you also seem to have received that damned villain's letter; and yet you can stand there quiet!" Infinite scorn coming into his voice.

"Yes, sir, but very sorry."

"How lady-like!"

"It is not true, father."

"And therefore—?" his voice breaking and scaling high in anger.

"I should pay no attention to it." The old man raised his two hands as if deprived of speech. "No one will believe it," the son went on, his voice gaining in firmness; "your character is too well known."

"To brook an insult like that!" the old man thundered.

"There are certain people, father, who cannot insult us. From a person who does not sign his name such insinuations are simply vulgarity. You could not stoop to touch the slander of a day laborer, a Negro; how can you stoop to this creature, of whom nothing is sure save that he is beneath your notice?"

The old man stood silent, looking at his son.

"You know," the young fellow went on, beginning to quiver under the steady gaze, which, though he did not meet, he felt through all his being—"you know that what I say is true—you cannot attack a person on suspicion."

"I know perfectly well," was answered with deliberate slowness, "that my son—my only son—is a coward."

It was as if he had been struck physically, and a deep stain of red sprang to the young fellow's face.

The fire simmered, the evening shadows gathered, the old clock ticked; then at last the son asked, slowly:

"What am I afraid of, father?"

"Everything!" the old man shouted, the words seeming to leap from his lips in relief; "for all I know, you may be afraid of the dark! This damned Kreener," he hurried on, "cheated your mother out of all her property, but I could not shoot a man about money; now, thank God, he gives me my chance; he has sent this vile stuff all over the town! Do you understand what it is he insinuates?"

"I think so."

"Do you understand, sir, that he involves a woman's name?"

"Not her name, father."

"By my soul, sir, I could thrash you for that quibble! Thrash you because you do not seem to realize that nothing but blood can wipe out an insult like this!"

"You would kill him?"

"As a dog!"

"And you will?" the son cried, his voice breaking; "and be hanged?"

"Hanged, sir; a gentleman! I, hanged? Hanged for defending a woman's name and my own honor! No, sir; no jury in the South would ever return that verdict!"

"The feeling of the people toward such actions, father, has changed."

"Not here, thank God. You'd have me sue for libel, perhaps; let money pay for deathless insults! How did I beget such a heart—such a soul!"

There was a moment's pause; the young fellow was locking and unlocking his fingers, that burned at the tips; was still looking into the fire; the silence was tense.

"Well, sir?" the father demanded.

Then the son looked up; his hands were quiet now, his face was calm, his eyes were as the eyes of an accusing angel. "Was not my mother afraid—always afraid of you?" The words fell like lead. "Was not fear my portion from the first? Through my mother, did not you deal it out to me? Was she not neglected, lonely, and sorrowful? These things come home, father, and they have come home to you through me. If I had been malformed in body, it would have been your fault; but if, to you, I am malformed in spirit, if violence and bloodshed are terrible to me, if, instead of bold, I am timid—a coward, you called me—it is because I was made so by my mother, who was always afraid." He paused, and again his eyes sought the fire, while the old man, with his hands grasping the back of a chair, stood silent. Then, as if to himself, he went on, "I often wonder if I would fight; I should not be afraid to die, I think; but to hurt another—pain—cruelty—all this is so hideous." Suddenly, as out of a dream, he added quickly, "Believe me, father, I am sorry for your disappointment in me," he turned his eyes from the fire to his father's face. "All my life almost I've known that you were disappointed—all—my—" his voice faltered, ceased.

Out of the house, across the ragged garden, through underbrush and briers. What had he done; what an awful expression! What had he done—such an old man! Was he still standing there? Would Chloe find him when she went in—would not know, not see in the dim firelight! What awful words he had said! He must go back.

He groaned and turned; he must go home and see; he might yet save him; lift him from the floor, minister to him, devote his whole life to him; tell him all his hopes, his little success; open his own nature and perhaps the old man would enter in, would understand, would love him. He caught his breath in a sob. "Love," he whispered; "love me!" In his life there had been no love. Perhaps now it would be changed; his father might grow to love him, even him!

As rapidly as he had come, he returned, but in the garden he paused There was only one light, and that in the kitchen. Had nothing happened? Must he himself discover—what? He shook his head. Poor, weak creature, he could scarcely stand! At least he could go to the kitchen. Chloe and Wash would be there by the fire, waiting the call for supper.

"You have not lighted the lamps," he said, standing in the doorway.

"Mass Dan say he'll light um w'en 'e ready."

His heart missed a beat; his father was alive! "You'd better light the dining room lamp," he went on, "and take supper in." Then, "Who told you to clean those pistols?"

"Mass Dan say fuh clean um, en load um, en put um on de she'f."

He went across the yard and into the house. Out of the hearing of the Negroes, his step slackened. The sight of the pistols had doubled his fears. He had resolved to go to his father, to tell him all, to plead with him—and he was slipping in the back way! Nevertheless he would go on; to begin, he would put on his best clothes, and if his father asked, he would tell him.

When he came down he went to the dining room. A smouldering fire threw a red glow up against the ceiling and on the supper table that was carelessly set with indifferently clean things. He could have bettered all this; was he lazy as well as timid? He lighted the lamp and began to put things in order. Tomorrow Wash should clean the silver; Chloe should do the linen better, should always have a clean tablecloth. And why not flowers on the table? The honeysuckle was still in bloom. What would his father say? He had on his best clothes; the flowers would be another help to his character. Which of the old vases should he fill? He went to the mantelpiece and found a letter. His hand shook; had the magazine sent for the money back? He must open it quickly; Chloe would come with supper, then his father. Out of the long envelope fell two enclosures addressed to the care of the magazine.

He opened one, trembling still, and read:

"*Dear Mr. Dingwill,—Your story, 'A Buried Heart,' has touched me more than anything I have read in years. Is it true? Do you really know a 'Louis'? Please write another as soon as possible.*

Your great admirer,

Alice Wiles."

He read it twice, feeling a little strange; his story was succeeding! This was the other:

"*My Dear Mr. Dingwill,—Your story, 'A Buried Heart,' is too sombre, but its strength redeems it. I must thank you for it, however, and hope that a new and wholesome writer has risen on the horizon.*

Yours very sincerely,

John Weeden."

His heart was beating as never before, his blood racing furiously; for the first time in all his life he longed to shout with joy! Of course he would gather flowers; would show his father these letters! The world was behind him; success was in his grasp; he would reveal his name and at once take his place in his home community, and his father would be congratulated on his son! The present had vanished.

Chloe—! he thrust the letters into his pocket and stood looking down into the fire. The old woman paused as she rested her tray on the corner of the table.

"Who been fixin' dis table?"

"I," her young master answered. "And, Mawmer, I wish you'd tell Wash to clean the silver."

"Wuh dat you say—me tell Wash fuh clean silber? Me? Nebber; Mass Dan muss do dat."

"And the linen is very dark, too." The old woman nearly dropped the tray; then she said, slowly:

"Wuh is come to you, chile? You got on you' good clo'es—wuh is happen?"

"Nothing, Mawmer, but I am tired of things as they are; you and Wash know how things ought to be, and it seems to me that for old times' sake you'd do better."

The old woman put the last dish in its place and turned away in silence.

"Tell father," came in the new tone of her young master; she paused as if about to speak, but went on without remonstrance, and the young fellow smiled a little. Now for his father! As all his life he had trembled at his father's coming; as he had said to himself, "Pre-natal," and still had trembled, so now as he busied himself with the tea things they rattled a little. He had for a long time made the tea because his father had sworn at Chloe's methods, nevertheless he had from the first felt his father's disapproval. The old man would have liked better if he too had sworn at Chloe and had gone to town for better fare. His father could have understood that, but not a man doing woman's work.

Now, in spite of his resolutions, he made the tea in silence—a silence he tried in vain to break; at last it was his father began.

"I want to talk business with you," he said, abruptly. Then clearing his throat: "Your half-sisters have no share in this property. I bought them off just as soon as you—a son—were born; thus this valuable estate, mortgaged up to the hilt, is your proud possession."

"Thank you, sir."

"If you can bear the sound of fire- arms, you can rent the shooting; it is very good. The game laws are decently strict now, and, thanks to what most people would call my laziness, the place is mostly cover. You were pleased to arraign me this afternoon—"

"Forgive me, father—"

"You were quite right, only that view of the case had never occured to me—I see it now. If I had realized it sooner, I might have done some things differently. As it is—was—I am speaking frankly—I did not think it worth while to hold things together for you; hence the mortgages. I was wrong—I am sorry."

"It was all a misunderstanding, father; I began to know that when Mr. Featherstone was here—"

"Humph! Shiny-hatted, soft-headed, begloved chump. But that's nothing now; I simply wanted to tell you about the debts and to say that I am sorry that I did not understand sooner. I am going to town early tomorrow, and I might not see you again."

"Going away?" the son interrupted. "Then, father, let me tell you something before you go. I have—I have—"

"Married a wife?"

"Oh no—no! I have written a story—"

"Good Lord!"

"And been paid for it!"

"The devil!"

"And just now I have received these letters—" turning his pocket inside out in his eagerness. "I did not take your name; I was afraid you'd not like it. I wrote the name backwards—see?"

"Heavens and earth!" reading the letters; "and been paid—you!"

"I hope some day, father, to make you proud of me—do you mind?"

The old man folded the letters carefully, and as carefully returned them to their envelopes, while the son watched and waited.

"Mind?"

"It is an honorable calling."

"Yes."

"And in time I can pay all the debts."

"You may."

"And when I am famous will—will you—"

"Famous?" the old man interrupted, then lifted his eyes to scan his son. "Famous?" he repeated. "He has my mother's eyes—and she was always scribbling, always. I have never seen the likeness—"

"Have you ever looked at me, father, except when you were angry and I frightened?"

"For God's sake, boy—" and rising hastily, he shoved his chair away; "don't arraign me again; let us part in peace."

"Part—?"

"If your view of public feeling is correct, by this time tomorrow night I shall be in jail or dead. Don't faint; I am here now only because today that dog was out of town at a camp meeting—confounded hypocrite! But he returns to town tonight, and I shall see him tomorrow."

"And—"

"Kill him—yes, unless he kills me first. I've sent him word that I was going to shoot on sight. Don't begin over again your arguments of this afternoon; they had no effect then, they will have none now. I leave you an honorable name and all my debts; I hope you will be successful and not be weighed down by what is to you the disgrace of my taking the defence of my honor into my own hands. God only knows to whom a man could leave such a thing. The law would be in my eyes the depths of dishonor. With you it seems to be different. If any one attacks my memory, I give you my permission to sue for libel. I promise not to haunt you for such action, not even to turn in my grave. I don't know but that my 'Hant' may watch the case with amusement. You may dress up like Featherstone—hat shiny—gloves shiny, and drive to town in a most neat little carriage, and step daintily into your lawyer's office and begin suit; you may even hold your pocket handkerchief by the middle and wipe your eyes when you speak of your 'dear, mistaken father!' Good-bye. I haven't been a good father, I haven't been even decently polite; forgive me if you can. I was not kind to your mother; you ought not to forgive that; I don't ask it. Good-bye; don't say anything, it's no use, and don't cry." He swung out of the room, slamming the door behind him.

It was a gray autumn morning, the moisture was heavy on the grass and briers; the blue mists hung over all the lowlands; the sun was veiled in something like smoke when Colonel Wilding stepped into his road cart and drove away. He looked older and more bent, and he did not drive rapidly; why need he? He had all day before him; besides, he was pondering many things; first, a loss he had just discovered. One of his pistols was missing, and Wash could not account for it.

If both had been missing, he would have suspected his son of making away with them; he was innocent enough for anything; but one? It puzzled him. He would stop at Sidney's and borrow a second pistol; it might develop into a street duel; the dog might dodge or hide; but if his hand had not lost its cunning, one shot would do. Still he'd stop at Jack Sidney's office and get a second pistol.

And yet death would not be unwelcome; no, not unwelcome. The boy had given him a mortal wound; the boy who, after all, was to be worth something. A writer. He cleared his throat. His young face had been beautiful, when he turned on him about his mother, and his words had been true. His timidity was pre-natal; he could not help it.

"And I, I have been a brute," he said, aloud, to the empty road and sky.

He lifted his head as if calling down judgment on himself. "Quick death will be too good for me, too good."

The day did not seem to grow any brighter even though the sun was ascending the sky. A strange gray day, the old man thought; a suitable day on which to end his failure of a life. Yes, he'd been a failure; his class had been a failure since the war. The world had changed; he and his kind were no longer needed, were survivals! Featherstone, the old saphead, was right. He had laughed at him, at his hat, his gloves, but only because he himself had let such things go; had gone down to the commoners. And the boy? Why not go back and take the boy's advice? Sue for libel and get the rascal's money? It would hurt him more, he believed, than to give up his life. To be shot by a gentleman was far too noble a death for the beast. Good heavens! He, Alexander Wilding, sue for libel when a man had insulted him, and through him a woman! His friends would think, and with reason, that he was demented! He was surely getting old. And that boy had yesterday struck him a blow that had broken his spirit.

He heard a vehicle coming behind him and he straightened up, whipped the horse. Rapidly he sped along, the speed and the fresh air seeming to give him new strength. He had been morbid; he'd kill that creature, then go home and beg the boy's pardon; leave the country if need be. The town was soon reached, and the brisk movement there helped him back to his normal condition. He was driving rapidly now, and scattered one or two groups of people.

"They suspect what I've come for," he said, seeing that the people turned to look at him; "and soon they'll know better what they've always known, that I'm not to be trifled with."

At the door of his friend's office he found the street almost blocked with people, but they opened a wide way for him. Young Sidney, standing in the doorway, started back, then without any greeting to him rushed up the stairs, while the men around took off their hats.

The old man looked about in wonder. "What is it, friends?" he asked, standing still on the pavement.

"You don't know, Colonel Wilding?"

"Know what!" A formless terror taking all the color out of his face.

"Wilding!" a voice called sharply from within the building; "come up—come!" He went quickly, mounting the stairway as a young man would have done, and his friend met him half-way. "Your boy," he said.

"Is at home—" then the old man leaned against the wall; "is at home," he repeated.

"Is here!" was answered. "You did not know?"

"Know? Know?"

"Your boy shot Kreener."

"Archie?"

"And Kreener shot your boy, and—"

"Yes," straightening up; "the boy knew I was coming—yes, God bless him! He loved me"—fiercely—"he did!"

"Of course."

"Yes, and did this for me; he was afraid they'd hang me, his old father; or put me in the pen. Where is he—where is he?"

Then turning to face the crowd, he cried, "Who arrests him does it over my dead body!" The crowd swayed, pressed back over one another from the fierce old man behind the levelled pistol, and the police allowed themselves to be pushed down the stairs.

"Plucky to the end," Jack Sidney said, in telling the story, "but that was his last stand. When he reached my office door I had to say, 'There is no hope, you know.' I think the paralysis hit him then, for he dropped his pistol, and at the sound of the shot the fellows rushed up the stairs and the doctors came out the door. But he straightened up, like the big spirit he was, and said: 'No harm, gentlemen. I dropped my pistol—by accident—excuse me.' The crowd could not stop because of the pushing from behind, so I opened the office door and took him in. The boy lay on the table, his face turned to one side, smiling a little. Lord! When that old man stood there—when I saw the look on his face! There's no use, we've got to change our code, fellows; it's pretty deep in the blood of those who have any blood, but that boy's face!

"'Tell father,' he'd said, 'that I hoped to make a name, hoped to make him proud of me; but perhaps, Mr. Sidney, he'll like this better; this is the kind of man he understands. I knew I'd be killed because I'd never have had the nerve to shoot twice—never; perhaps this will please him.' Then he told me where to find a roll of money in his pocket. 'For father,' he said."

"And the old man?"

"Out at the old place; spends his time reading over and over all the papers the boy left; all sorts of little poems and stories; I'm having a little volume of them printed; some touches of genius here and there; it will please the old man. Yes, two or three of us have taken up the mortgages, and we'll keep him and the old servants going as long as he lives."

"And Kreener?"

"We could not prove enough to hang him, but we put him in the pen. It was not self-defence, because Kreener shot first, and I would as soon have expected to be killed by a sucking dove as by Archie Wilding. My wife often begged me to steal the boy and bring him home to her; called the old man a pagan; she's gone all to pieces over it. Yes, he hit Kreener, shot after he got his death; he didn't know, poor child; but Kreener lost an eye by it!"

SOME REMNANTS

Down in the dim pine country, where here and there old clearings or deserted fields make good cover, a huntsman stood in the shadow on the edge of the barren and looked out. For weeks he had been working from the South Atlantic coast inland, through the loneliest country, he thought, that man's foot had ever trod; from the beautiful port that had no shipping, through the shadowy swamps and the wide-spreading live oaks, up to the dim, far-reaching vistas of the pine barren. And now it seemed that he had reached the center from which all the desolation emanated.

An old, large, white-columned house with a few primeval trees about it, and leading straight away from the entrance, the remnants of an avenue. There were no signs of fences; the outbuildings were tumbling down and the house was dilapidated, yet it had dignity. Perhaps it was its desolation, perhaps it was its aloofness; he could not decide; but it was impressive. Doubtless this was the homestead of the plantation over the waste fields of which he had been shooting; and the huntsman went nearer.

The windows on the front and the side toward him were all closed, save where a blind was missing; the front door seemed to be fast shut; the whole place looked absolutely forsaken; nevertheless, he made his dog come to heel as he approached silently over the coarse grass. He was quite close when a little sound from the dog stopped him. He turned and saw the eager look and lifted nose of the creature, and stepping sidewise instead of forward, he discovered on the low piazza, behind one of the big pillars, a white-haired woman seated in a large country-made chair. Her head was lifted even as the dog's was, and her expression was as eager; but although she looked straight at him with wide-open eyes, she did not seem to see him. One moment the huntsman paused; then he turned and went softly back to the shadow of the wood.

There was no one in the camp save the Negroes working under him in this advance expedition, and as he sat alone, with only the stars for company, the picture he had seen in the afternoon haunted him. In a few days his work had approached much nearer to the old house, and during the noon rest he once more made his way through the pine woods, this time coming out at a nearer point. He stopped suddenly, leaned his gun quickly and softly against a tree, and pressed his dog to the earth with his foot.

All the windows of the house were wide open; in front of the cavernous hall door sat the blind lady, and on the piazza near the top of the steps stood a middle-aged woman holding what appeared to be a flagstaff. The butt of it rested on the floor; from the upper end fluttered some dark brown rags, and the woman, holding it a little away from her, was looking down the avenue as if watching for something. The huntsman followed the direction of her gaze, and far away he saw an object moving that gradually developed into a man.

At first he could only discern that the man was tall; then that he seemed to be marching rather than walking; then that against his shoulder the man carried a stick as if it were a sword. It was like a little boy playing soldier. Presently, turning on his heel and marching backward, he began to give orders as if a body of men followed him. On he came, nearer and nearer, sometimes marching straight ahead, sometimes facing his company and stepping backward, giving his commands in a clear, distinct tone. His clothes were poor, his shoes were common brogans, and his hat was straw, yellow with age and of an antique shape.

His voice sharpened with excitement as he neared the house. He halted his company, put them at present arms, then facing the woman who held the flag, he took off his old hat with a sweep that was fine, and stood looking at her radiantly, while the sun made a halo in his snow-white hair.

The huntsman kneeled down almost on his excited dog, muzzling him with his hand.

In her turn, the lady seemed now to be making a speech; then she presented the pole and the rags; the blind woman rose to her feet, clapping her hands feebly, while the tall officer, waving the flag in front of the company, swung his hat with a hip-hip-hurrah! Three times that lonely cheer arose, echoing and reechoing back into the dusky woods; then he put the company at parade rest, and mounting the steps, carrying the flag with him, took the hand of the woman and led her into the house.

The huntsman did not move, nor did he let the shivering dog stir. Presently the heroine of the scene came out again, and after leading the blind woman in, proceeded to shut the front door and all the windows.

She appeared at the upper windows, shutting them, and the big house took on once more its forsaken look. Then the huntsman rose, and slipping his hand under the dog's collar, took his gun and made his way back to the camp.

That the extraordinary scene he had witnessed meant something went without saying, but what? and who could enlighten him? Those old people could not just be playing, could not just be trying to amuse themselves down in this lonely country. Impossible! It took deadly earnest so to penetrate with reality the behavior of the actors—to make a scene so vivid. That man was absolutely sure that he had a company behind him, felt really enthusiastic when he cheered all by himself; and the blind woman's applause was true, as true as was the stately speech and flag presentation of the other woman. Did they do this thing often? the huntsman wondered. As his men had all worked up the country with him, and were as much strangers to this place as he was, his only hope for information was the railway station five miles away; he would have to go there in a day or two to receive supplies for his camp, and he would try to find out then.

The next day at noon, leaving his dog and gun in camp, he went again to the edge of the barren, and found the same scene being enacted. The blind woman sat rocking gently; the other woman, in her limp black clothes, stood waiting and leaning a little on the flagpole as she looked down the avenue for the tall man and his phantoms. When he was near enough to see her, she straightened from her tired pose and threw her head back. On he came, marching with such energy, giving his orders with such force, that this time the huntsman felt almost as if he saw just what the man saw! The speeches were made, the lonely cheers rang out, the blind woman clapped her approval, and the actors marched into the house, leaving the company as before, at parade rest.

The morning after this it was cloudy, and by noon a fine rain was falling. Would the presentation of the flag go on in spite of the weather? Would those old people come out in the dampness, and leave that company without shelter in this penetrating drizzle?

Under the gray sky and the drifting mist the old place was absolutely ghastly. The moss on the foundations looked more living and encroaching; a gutter broken off halfway down the side of the house showed to cruel advantage, and the pools of water gathered here and there, and flowing one into another, pointed out how surely, if slowly, the old place was washing away.

But the lady with the ragged flag was at her post, and the tall man came marching up between the remnants of the avenue, waving his stick and splashing through the rain puddles. The lonely cheers echoed forlornly, and the applause of the blind woman sounded faintly from within. Then everything was shut up, and the drifting mist seemed to settle more closely about the old house, and the drip of the rain from the leaves was the only sound to be heard.

By evening the rain was pouring in torrents—an unvarying stream of discomfort, and the open wood fire in the big, barren office of the inn at the railway station would have seemed doubly comfortable to the young huntsman if he could only have driven from his mind the memory of the house out in the wilderness. The host, Captain Monty, a one-legged veteran of the Civil War, had received him with a reserved hospitality, as if in meeting one of a higher station than his usual lodgers he felt impelled to show that he had once known better things.

Nor did the huntsman find his host to be a garrulous old person. Instead, although perfectly civil, he was difficult to talk to, and they had exchanged very few words when, after supper, the new guest was ushered into the office, where, about the fire, a few local loungers and one or two traveling tradesmen were gathered. Here the conversation was general and intermittent, and the huntsman determined to wait for the dispersal of these people before he displayed his curiosity. While he waited, he talked to Captain Monty's little grandson, who seemed to be in attendance on his maimed grandfather, and who now, while the old man was stationary, sat tailor-fashion on the floor, working away with an old knife.

It was not long before the idle company began to say good night; then, by way of an opening, the huntsman handed the little boy his knife, which was a much better instrument than the one the child was trying to use. The little creature looked at the stranger wonderingly, at the knife admiringly; then with a smile he nodded to his grandfather, and the huntsman, glancing up, found the old man looking at him kindly. There was silence after this save for the fall of the rain and an occasional whisper from the fire.

"You don't grow tobacco about here," the huntsman began at last, by way of leading up to planting and planters, and so to the old house.

"Cotton's our staple," the captain answered.

"I've been shooting about the country a good deal," the huntsman went on, "and this seems to have been a rich neighborhood."

"Yes, we were pretty well off."

"It was a pity," said the huntsman.

Captain Monty looked at him for a minute; then he said, "Yes, a great pity," and relapsed into silence.

Once more the sounds of the rain and the fire and the little boy's knife made themselves heard, until at last the huntsman said, "War is an awful thing."

"Sherman told us, 'War is hell,' and it's true," and the old man took his pipe from his lips. "And the South," he went on, "is just now getting as far out as the station called purgatory."

The huntsman smiled, but Captain Monty shook his head. "That may sound funny," he said, "but purgatory isn't funny. We've got used to tragedies in the South, but we haven't got used to laughing at them yet." Then, as if to explain his seeming rebuke, he went on slowly: "There's an old lady not far from here who's still watching for her boy to come home, and he'd be a man of fifty odd. He sat down on the roadside to rest when we were marching back from Pennsylvania. I hailed him as we passed. 'Sick, Tom?' I asked. 'No,' he answered, 'only tired. I'll be on in a minute.' And that's been more than thirty years."

The huntsman was leaning forward in his chair as if intending to drop in a final question, when the little boy, who had stopped work to listen, said slowly, "Old Mrs. Shore makes me run down the road sometimes to see if Tom's coming."

The huntsman turned on the child. "Does she live in that old house with the great big pillars, and is she blind?" he asked quickly.

"What do you know about that big house and the blind lady?" the old man interrupted.

"I've seen her."

"Mrs. Delgado," the little boy put in, looking from one to the other of the men as if something strange might come next.

"Yes, that's her name," and there seemed to be some distress in the old man's voice. "She's the married sister."

"And who is the tired woman with the flag, and the man who marches up the avenue?"

"How'd you find it all out?"

"Why, I see them," the huntsman answered. "They do it every day. I don't like to interrupt, and so I wait under the trees until they finish." He paused a moment, then added, "I begin to believe that the company is really there."

The old man put his hand over his eyes and drew it down over his face, down to the tip of his long white beard. "So you've seen it all," he said, "all." Then he twisted up the ends of his mustache. "All."

The child on the floor put down his knife and stick, while the huntsman, afraid that even at the last moment the old man might yet not tell the story, said quickly, "Well?"

"Well, there's no harm to it."

"I didn't suppose there was—much."

"There isn't any," the old man answered sharply. "The Blaneys were the best sort of people."

"Yes?"

"Yes, the very best sort, and as you seem to be suspicious, stranger, I'll explain. Arthur Blaney raised a company and fitted it out himself, and Miss Patty Blaney, Arthur's cousin,—they were engaged,—made a flag for us, and the day before we left we formed over yonder where the roads used to branch, and marched to the Blaney plantation for the colors to be presented. There was no railroad here then," dropping from an irritated into a reminiscent tone, "and all this about here was fields—this was my father's place," with a wave of his hand to the whitewashed walls, while the little boy looked around him reverently, "and the fields were green, and the birds were singing and the flowers were blooming, and the earth smelled fresh from the rain of the night before." He paused for a moment.

"When we got to the Blaneys'," his voice was strictly narrative again, "the young ladies were on the piazza, in white, with flowers in their hair, and Miss Patty holding the flag, and Arthur's father standing there. And all to the right and left were tables out under the trees, with a feast for us. In the days that followed," for the first time looking straight at the huntsman, "we were glad sometimes for the corn that dropped from the horses' troughs.

"So Miss Patty presented the flag, and Arthur received it, and we cheered ourselves hoarse and marched away. We went straight to Virginia and fought steadily, most of us going under, and after Second Manassas Arthur was missing. I saw him charge—then he seemed to disappear. To save our lives we couldn't trace him, and we gave him up for dead. When the end came the few of us who were left straggled back, and I brought the flag—a few bloody rags on a patched-up pole— you've seen it—and gave it to Miss Patty.

"One day the next fall—a bone-dry, blazing day—I was riding down the road on a mule, when I saw a man. The country road here was so deadly still and lonely then that any kind of a thing on the road would attract attention, and a man behaving as this one did would make you stop and examine. So I pulled up. He was pretty far off, but you could see long distances then, and I could see him plainly. He would take off his hat and wave it, then shade his eyes with his hands, and look and look all about him steadily, then throw up his arms and fall on his knees down in the dust of the road as if in despairing prayer. I watched him for a little while, then went nearer. Presently he came farther down the big road to where the road to the Blaneys' used to branch off, and where the old finger-post still stood.

"When he got there he stopped short and looked at the finger-post; then he went nearer, and felt it up and down until he seemed to find something on it that he wanted. He looked all around him once more, straightened himself up and put his old stick to his shoulder like a sword. In a minute he began to give orders as if forming a company, and my hair began to stand on end. He called the roll name by name,—living and dead side by side,—and I was there, too, in that line of ghosts! The order came to march, and I turned my mule aside, down into the ditch, to let that company go by! I seemed to see them, I seemed to hear them, but they did not interrupt the sunshine—they raised no dust as they marched away—they left no footmarks in the sand.

"Presently I came to myself, and wiped the cold sweat from my forehead. It would kill Miss Patty and the old man. There were no fences left to stop me, and I rode across the old fields as hard as I could go, and tumbled off my mule at the side door. Having but one leg, and having left my crutch at home, I was hampered, but Miss Patty heard me and came out. The minute she saw me she turned deadly white.

"'Arthur!' she whispered. "I nodded. She turned as if to run, but I held her. 'Wait!' I said. 'He is—' "She pulled away. 'He is—he is Arthur!' and her voice broke with a sob as she ran.

"By the help of walls and chairs and a walking stick I found in the hall I got to the back piazza, where old Mr. Blaney, Arthur's father, was sitting. He looked up kindly. 'Well,' he said, 'what news?'

"'Strange news,' I answered.

"'My boy!' and he tried to get up.

"'Wait!' I said, 'wait!'

"'Dead?' I shook my head.

"'He's well in body,' I said at last, 'in body, and he's—coming—' Then I could not stay there any longer watching that old man's agony. I hobbled to the hall again, down the length of it toward the front, and there, through the open door, I saw Arthur marching his company up the barren road that used to be the avenue, and Miss Patty—Miss Patty walking along-side—clapping her hands! She ran into the hall where the old flag leaned in the corner, and took it out, and stood on the piazza as she had stood that May day six years before.

"The company was put at present, and Arthur turned. His face was drawn and haggard, but he took off his ragged hat with the same old sweep, and looked up at Miss Patty with the light of heaven in his eyes. I heard a little groan, and there was old Mr. Blaney holding on to the wall behind me!"

He paused, and in the dead silence a gust of wind drove the rain against the windows like a blow, and roared fiercely across the chimney top. Captain Monty started, looked quickly over his shoulder, as did the huntsman, and the little boy's eyes were like big stars. A window blind slammed, and the men came back to the present, looking steadfastly into the fire.

"He was lost that day in the road," Captain Monty went on; "lost because every landmark had been cut down or burned, and that's what made him so distressed until he found the sign- post, and found all the names cut there before we marched away. Yes, he was lost, and he had wandered long, for his bare feet were hard with walking, and the sore places were tied up with rags he had torn from his clothing, and his bones stuck out through his rags."

Once more the old man put his hand up over his eyes and drew it down slowly over his face, down to the very tip end of his beard, looking silently into the fire. The wind roared and blustered, the rain beat persistently against the windows, and the little boy, with his work and knife forgotten, watched his grandfather with years of experience showing on his little face.

"Perhaps you see what I mean by purgatory?" Captain Monty said at last. The huntsman nodded.

"All the old settlers know about it, but I believe I'm the only one in the country who's ever seen it, for nobody," the old man went on, "would go there to spy on them. Not meaning any offense to you, sir, for you happened on it by accident, and you don't seem to have laughed, either. And ever since that day in the road we've all done our best for Miss Patty. 'Tisn't much they need. Old Mr. Blaney died long ago, and Miss Patty takes care of her widowed sister, the blind lady, and Arthur. And the first warm spell in February Arthur begins to march, and marches every day until the time comes for the Confederate reunion; I take him and the old flag to that, and we all line up and let him have a real company. And after the reunion he doesn't begin to march again until the next spring."

"I'm glad of that for Miss Patty's sake," the huntsman said.

"Yes, even faithful Miss Patty couldn't stand it the whole year. But I'm sorry," added the old man, "they're going to cut the new road right in front of the house, for it will lay them open to the public, and

I've been afraid all along that just what has happened to you would happen, and it might be some one who would laugh, and what would we do if Arthur became violent?"

"Does all that far pine land belong to the Blaneys?" the huntsman asked.

"Of course."

"Then I'm working on their land on the right of way from the last tract."

"You?"

"I'm one of the engineers of the new road."

"The mischief!"

"Yes, and I can run the road clear the other side of the place, if you say so, and must pay for the right of way, if you'll price it."

"God bless you! oh, God bless you!" and the old man reached his hand to the engineer.

The rumble of a train was heard, and Captain Monty rose, while the little boy ran to get a lantern that they might go over to the station.

The grandfather carried the umbrella and the child carried the lantern. They waited a moment on the piazza, and the engineer heard the boy's clear voice. "If the gentleman buys the road, grandfather," he said, "then Miss Patty won't be sorry. Don't you remember she cried when we carried her the groceries? And don't you think *some* good times are coming now, grandfather?"

Then they splashed away to the train to look for possible lodgers.

THE WRECK

He could live in the old boiler for a few days; at least, until he could find out certain things that he must know.

It had been a horrible wreck, and it had happened on Christmas eve. He remembered as a child the awful crash—the cries, the screams. Numbers had been killed—crushed, scalded, caught in the wreckage and burned to death. It had seemed to make the spot accursed, and the Negroes had shown such terror when sent to work within an acre of where some of the unidentified dead had been buried, that his father had thrown that bit of field out, and instantly, almost, it had shot up into a dense growth of pines.

Then his father had built a fence round the graves, and had put wooden crosses at the heads and feet of them. "Somewhere—Sometime—Somebody loved them," was the record he had had cut on a stone that had been set up in the midst of the enclosure.

Just outside this enclosure had lain the old boiler of the locomotive, from which the pipes had been taken; a black mass that had seemed to him in his childhood smallness to be large, and dark, and mysterious. His mother had had the little enclosure attended to, going herself with the Negro gardener to see to it, and the children used always to go with her. For him especially the place had a fascination, drawing him quite up to it sometimes, even when alone; then, seized by a nameless panic, he would run with all his speed, breathless and terrified, across the fields to the quarters, from which point he could walk home to the big house with some show of manliness.

At Easter they had carried flowers to the graves of the nameless dead, and at Christmas time, too; and oh, the Christmas times at the old place! The grand preparations for weeks beforehand; the smell of spices, of rich brown mixtures full of raisins, currants and citron, that presently came forth as huge fruitcakes or as rich mince pies! The great turkeys that were fattened; the rich old hams that were put into soak; the piles of oranges that appeared! Then in the early dawn the singing of the Negroes under the windows; music that, coming before the light, and in the midst of dreams, had never seemed quite real, but as though, like the music to the shepherds on the plains of Bethlehem, it were some kind of far-off heavenly melody!

Then the stockings round the nusery fire; the delicious breakfast! As he sat alone in the darkness he moistened his parched lips! After that came the distribution of presents to the whole plantation; then the Christmas dinner! He seemed almost to smell the terrapin soup; to see the crisp brown turkey and all the other delicious things that for so long the children had been smelling! And the long, long table, that, wide as it was, looked endless, with all the children and aunts and uncles and cousins, and all their children; and he, the youngest, in his high chair, sitting close to his mother at the end of the table. Arthur, the eldest, sat with his father at the other end. Katie and Tom were distributed. Those were feasts fit for royalty. Then, later, the Christmas tree, and in the last hour, given to the children, the father read "A Christmas Carol," when the children pitied extremely Mrs. Cratchett's one goose and small pudding, and sniffled audibly over Tiny Tim; rejoicing vigorously when Tiny Tim did *not* die! And the wonderful day would end with Tiny Tim's "God bless us, every one!"

And now it was Christmas time; was it? Yes, tomorrow, the next day, would be Christmas eve. Was there any one left at the old place to keep it? What a happy home it had been—how simple, how true, how gentle and kind!

The Civil War; and after, when they returned, they found the old house still standing, and in the quarters a few old Negroes, almost starving. His father had been killed, and on his death in the last year of the war, Arthur, a boy of fourteen, volunteering in his place,—another pair of hands to hold a musket,—had been wounded and hopelessly crippled—Arthur, the beauty of the family, and he had been beautiful!

But his mother's spirit had not failed her, and with the two younger boys and one girl, she had set herself to win a living from the old plantation.

Curiously enough, the strangers' graves had been left intact. He himself had gone there the first thing, had been glad to see the old boiler, grown red with rust, and had mended the fence. The wrecked boiler had made him seem more at home than the old house even, for no change had come to it save what in any case time and weather would have brought. The pines had grown very tall, it seemed to him then, and very dense, and he had cut a path to the spot and had made the old boiler his favorite haunt. The remoteness, the quiet, the sound of the wind in the pines, of the water that flowed from the swamp, had meant much to him and to his boyish dreams.

After the long day's work in the hot fields it had been always cool and shadowy. And the life, for a season, had been exciting—the lurid dangers of the reconstruction days; the pride in the first crop and the constant guarding of it; the joy in the first cow, in the first mule. The pathos of the first Christmas, when a rice pudding had seemed a feast! But his mother had read to them once more the story of "Tiny Tim," and the solemn end had come home to them—"God bless us, every one!"

How patient and skilful and thrifty his mother had been! Then how gradually they had traced their old furniture, carried away to all sorts of places, and had bought it back from the Negroes, or from the poor whites to whom it had been given in exchange for food by the old Negroes left on the plantation. Not all, but a great deal had been secured. Then the fun in cleaning and in recovering it. Their mother had turned all into play; had made the old home lovely once more in a simple way. Then they had become able to hire hands; then—

He sat down on the side of the railway, and crossing his arms on his knees, leaned his head down on them. Then—then had come idleness, yes, and the child of idleness, discontent. Home had seemed small— poor—dull—beside his dreams. The world, he had announced, the world he must see! He had claimed a share of what had been made. He—he had claimed money from his mother! "Give me the portion that falleth to me!" he had demanded. Then, like the prodigal, he had gone away.

He rocked his head from side to side on his arms. "Mother!" he whispered. "Mother!" If he sat still in the darkness and let the train go over him, would any one give him a burial? Would any one care for him? Times had changed. People were in a hurry now; too much in a hurry to care for the accidentally dead, as his father had done, and his mother. His body would lie there until the trackwalker found it, and it would be—what? What would be done with it? There would be nothing by which to identify him; nothing to show that he had ever been other than his worn clothes and ragged shoes would seem to prove.

He got up. If he sat there much longer he would die of cold before any train could reach him. The December wind was piercing, even here in the far South. Colder than he ever remembered it. Had the climate changed with all else? How often he remembered helping his mother to pick flowers—roses—quite up to the new year. He could see her now with her basket and scissors going in and out among the flowers. For very soon after their return the flowers had been made to bloom once more in the desolated garden. His mother had been a wonderful woman. Had been? If she were not now, why was he tramping all these weary miles? She would be old, very old, but why not there? If not, he would not make himself known, for no one but a mother would be able to welcome such a creature as he had become. Suppose there was no one there? His mother might be dead, the place sold!

"No, oh, no!" and a sob broke from the man as he walked. "Not so cruel as that!" A sound of flowing water came to him. He stopped.

That must be the river! He must be near the culvert where the stream from the swamp flowed through into the river. He looked up to the strip of sky above the railway. It was covered with clouds, and the wall of forest on each side increased the blackness. "'In the dead vast and middle of the night,'" he quoted.

Then again the sound of the water came to him. He must go carefully. Nearer came the sound of the water. He could not see a step before him, and he got down on his hands and knees. So he must go until he crossed the culvert. He had a piece of candle in his pocket, but it could not possibly stay alight in this wind.

As he remembered it, it was a long culvert. If the train came, would he be strong enough to drop through and hang until it had passed? He was weak with hunger and sickness, and weary with walking. Or would there be space enough on the outer edge of the track for him to lie flat? But why care? Why this sudden valuing of his life? The thought of his mother had done it, had turned his footsteps homeward. He must live until he reached the old place that now was so near; until he found out if that mother still lived. If not—his thoughts stopped and he crawled on slowly in the darkness.

He could feel no thrill from the earth, nor any sound reached him to tell of even the most distant train; nothing but the cry of the rushing water that he was nearing. Deep, brown, clear water he remembered it, running out from the swamp. He paused and put his hand down between the ties in front of him. Yes, the next movement would put him over the water.

Should he go on? Should he wait for daylight? He was too tired, too weak with hunger; a few more hours would find him unable to go. On he crawled; the rushing water was under him now, and even if a train should be coming, he could not hear it! He began to tremble, and a cold sweat broke out on him.

"O God," he prayed, "have mercy!"

208

For years he had not prayed; was it the old surroundings, the old
memories, the nearness to his mother, that had once more brought holy
words to his lips; once more wakened the faith of his childhood?

The sound of the water had changed now; it was no longer rushing,
but had fallen into a deep gurgle; he must have reached the middle of
the culvert. Halfway across! Back or forward, it made no difference
now; just as far to one end as to the other. He must hasten. With a little light how quickly he were on the other side! On he crawled. There,
that was a much wider space; walking, he would have gone through
into the deep, gurgling water.

How swiftly the great river would have carried him out to the sea!
And his mother would not have known; nor have sorrowed any more
than through all the long years since he had left her. But soon he
would see her, hold her dear small hand that work could never harden;
look into her sweet eyes that sorrow nor trial could ever dim. And he
had left her!

"I am no more worthy to be called thy son," he whispered; "no
more worthy." But oh, he must get there—must see her once more—
crawl to her feet if only to die—die there with her forgiveness! She
would forgive.

What was that? He paused; a thrill under his hands! A train—which
side—O God, which side? What matter? He must go on—must—he had
come a long way on the trestle! He tried to hasten; he put out all his
strength. There! He could hear the oncoming roar! He looked over his
shoulder, and far down the cutting, between the black walls of the forest, he could see the great yellow eye of the engine! Courage! His
mother was just over yonder, across the fields to the right! He would
crawl toward the right; he might be able to lie flat along the outer
edge; or if he was to meet death, he would meet it as near to his
mother as he could.

"Mother!" he called out in the grim darkness. "Mother!" On—on he
crawled, so slow—so slow! The oncoming light struck far ahead. There!
There! Only a little farther—there was the solid enbankment—the
bushes! He rose to his feet—ran for his life; tripped, fell, rolled down
the embankment, and lay there very still with his feet in the dark water
while the train rushed by.

After a while he stirred and opened his eyes. Where was he? What
had happened? Where was the light that had seemed to burn him?
Slowly all came back to him, and he felt round him cautiously. The gurgle of the water was very close—his feet were in the river! He drew
himself carefully backward, felt the firm earth, the bushes; felt the em-

bankment rising on one side of him. He must go back to the railway, for, as he remembered, the swamp lay for some way yet on both sides of the road. He still was weak and trembling with the shock of his danger—he was indeed worthless!

He was walking again on the road, such weary walking from tie to tie. How glad he would be to reach the field where the old boiler lay; it would shelter him from the cold wind. Would there be any lights about the old home? In the dangerous reconstruction days a light used to be kept burning all night that they might not be taken unawares; but now would there be a light?

At all events, he would not go near the house tonight; he must watch a little, must manage to get some food to live on for a day or two until he found out something certain. No, he must not go to the house; he must shelter himself in the old boiler. He felt in his pocket; yes, he had still the bit of candle and the matches he had begged from a boy at the last farmhouse he had passed that afternoon. It was well, for he might find strange company in the boiler—creatures of the woods and the swamps, and he would need a light.

Suddenly it seemed to grow brighter. He looked about; the swamp had ceased, and fields lay on the left of the road. He stopped. On the right there was still a heavy growth. He could venture down the side of the embankment, because he remembered that the swamp extended no farther on one side of the road than on the other. This growth on the right must be the pines that had come up in the forsaken spot where the strangers were buried, where the old boiler lay, or used to lie. Had it rusted away? He had not thought of that!

He left the road and felt his way to the wood. Yes, here was the outer fence, a rail fence; he climbed it and made his way among the thick-growing pines. His foot caught in a vine. He stumbled forward and caught on something. He felt it, he put his arms over it, he kissed it, and laying his head down on it, he sobbed like a child. "I'm at home," he whispered, "at home!"

He struck a match, lighted his bit of candle, and looked about him. How strange! It looked as if it were a carefully kept spot. The boiler—the boiler had been painted! A shining coat of black paint covered it. And inside! He got down on his knees. There was a floor laid across, and on it there were doll beds and tables and chairs, and in the chairs were dolls, seated in solemn order. There was a table set, and on the table there was some broken bread, some bits of meat, and did his eyes deceive him? There was a little basket with an orange in it and some biscuits! "The children," he said, "the children!"

He turned where he knelt and looked about. The feeble ray of the candle showed him the fence about the graves, looking strong and new and painted white, and not far away he saw a swing, and then a seesaw.

"The children," he said again, "the children!"

He looked again into the boiler. If he moved their little toys and crept in he could sleep comfortably; but he might oversleep, and then the children would find him. He would lie down outside, under the boiler, toward the fence; he could hear them coming and creep away. No. There was not cover enough there for a bird. He must go into the bushes. But the food—he must take the food the careless little things had left; they could run into the house for more; mother would always give them more. Mother—he stopped to think. She was not their mother; if she were there, she would be their grandmother. The children; not Katie and Tommy and George—no, but some other children. Whose children? Strangers?

"God have mercy!" he pleaded. He covered his face with his hands. A moment he stayed so, then rose. His candle was going. How pathetic the little playthings looked in the flickering light, and the solemn dolls arow, all staring straight in front of them! And the orange, the biscuits? The blood rushed to his face. He must take the food—he must! The orange, the biscuits, and even the broken bread on the table! Then he crept away into the bushes on the other side of the strangers' graves.

"Oh, but, Mary, where are the biscuits we left?"

"And the orange!" chimed in another voice. The man crouched lower in the bushes. Early he had wakened, and, cold as it was, he had bathed in the river; it was as if he were striving to wash away his misdeeds. Then he had waited, warming himself in the brilliant sunshine, still hungry and weak but somewhat rested. He was looking now, peering through the thick bushes, his eyes shining. There were three little girls, an older boy, and a Negro woman carrying a basket.

"Maybe the squirrels have eaten it."

"Squirrels nothin'!" the boy put in, bluntly. "Here are tracks—plain as daylight."

The nurse and the little girls crowded round him. "Sho' 'nough!" the woman said.

"Then we can't leave the Christmas tree for the dolls!" wailed the children. "And grandmama won't come down!"

"It's a tramp," said the boy. "He was hungry, that's all, and he's gone. Nobody wants doll toys and trash like that!"

"'Tain't trash!" the little girls cried. "And he might eat up all the party!"

"Of course he's gone," the boy declared. "No man would wait here to pick up doll crumbs! Fix your tree and hurry up; then we can go back for grandmama."

Thus urged, the children set to work. A small pine bush was set up in the boiler, and the tiny presents hung on it. "And we'll light the candles when grandmama comes," they said. "And there comes Jake with the table!"

A Negro man appeared, carrying a low table and another basket. The excitement became intense when the table was put down just outside the boiler, and the cloth spread. Then the "party" was set forth. Ginger cake and oranges, milk and bread and butter—yes, and cold rice waffles!

The man in the bushes stared eagerly. Just what he and Katie and Tom used to have for parties. Would any one but his own mother be apt to furnish forth these identical things that forty years before he had had for his childish feasts? Whose children were these? Who was "grandmama"?

"Now," the children cried, "now the dolls!" And each staring effigy—more or less scarred veterans, with here an arm and there a leg or the half of a head missing—was stood up on its respective chair, or on piles of blocks, and leaned forward against the table.

"How fine!" the children cried, clasping their little hands, and the youngest began to jig about the table.

"Suppose we put the tree on the table," one suggested.

"Oh, no!" the others cried. "We won't cut off the presents till tomorrow—till the very Christmas day; and the dolls can enjoy looking at the tree all night."

"Yes, we'll have the party today and the tree tomorrow; it'll be more interestin'."

"Yes, it will. Now we'll go for grandmama!" And the whole party started off.

The man covered his eyes with his hands. He could not look at the food and not take it. He shivered a little. The grandmother was coming—and he thinking of food! The grandmother—who was she? Suppose these were strangers? And yet there had seemed something familiar about the children.

Tom's children would not be living here—but Arthur's children! Arthur, crippled by wounds—he would naturally bring his wife home. They might be his children. If only they had called each others' names, he might have known them by that. Tom, Katie, Arthur, George. Would any of them have been named George? He bent lower in the bushes. Arthur had been devoted to him.

Far off he heard the children's voices coming. The grandmother would be with them. He began to tremble from head to foot as one in mortal terror. Nearer they came, dancing and capering about a small, pretty old lady, straight and somewhat stately. A white shawl was drawn over her shoulders and a white scarf thrown over her head. The big boy carried a gun, and the Negro woman a low chair.

"O grandmama, it's fine!" the children cried. "You'll be so s'prised!"

The man did not look up—he could not; but all the hunger of his soul and body seemed to have gathered to his ears, that strained to hear the sound of that grandmother's voice. If it were she, how could he bear it?

"Isn't it lovely?" "Isn't it fine?" "Isn't it great?" the children cried. "And grandmama's chair must go here at the head!"

There was so much chatter that if the grandmother had spoken she could not have been heard. She took her seat at the low table, and the children sat on the dry pine needles on the ground. "Say grace," they urged.

There was a pause; then a voice as soft as sleep, as gentle as a child's sigh, came to the trembling waif:

"Comfort the suffering; forgive the erring; feed the hungry, Father, for the dear Christ Jesus' sake. Amen." A hush seemed to fall—a hush over all nature as the sweet words fell and a peace that stopped the trembling of the man.

"Forgive the erring!" The voice that had sung him to sleep in his cradle; that had taught his childhood; had pleaded with his manhood; had loved and comforted all his days! "Forgive the erring!"

The children chatted on, eating the party, feeding the dolls, and through it all the grandmother's clear voice and cheerful laughter. The man put his forehead on the earth. Break in on her peaceful life? Come back to jar the even tenor of her days? A black shadow in her sunshine? Why had he waited until disease had touched him—until death seemed to beckon him? Why come to be a burden? Better go jump into the river. "Forgive the erring!"

"And the tramp didn't steal the party," one of the children said, suddenly.

"The tramp?" the grandmother asked.

"Yes, we found his tracks; he'd eaten up everything! We were afraid, but Georgie said—"

The man started. "Georgie?" When he listened again the grandmother was saying, "Poor fellow, he must have been dreadfully hungry to have eaten doll crumbs."

"Oh, but there were a lot of biscuits and an orange!"

"Four biscuits, Katie."

"How do you know it was a tramp?" the grandmother went on.

"Saw his tracks," Georgie answered, "so I brought my gun."

"My dear boy!"

"To defend us."

"He would not hurt an old woman and little children. He did not take anything but the food?"

"No, nothing; not a doll nor anything."

"Of course not—a man!" George said, loftily.

"Suppose we leave something here for him to eat," the grandmother suggested. "You children run to the house and help Diana fill the basket and bring it down. You know that I have a boy out in the wide world—we don't know where he is—"

"Oh, yes, Uncle George," the children cried, "who used to love this old boiler!"

"And maybe, sometimes, he is very poor and hungry; so I want to feed all hungry people—"

"So do we! so do we!" the children cried. "Come, Georgie, come, Diana, let's get some party for the poor tramp man!" And seizing the empty basket, they ran off toward the house, whose chimneys could be seen beyond the fields and trees.

The grandmother and the dolls remained at the table, the grandmother sitting with folded hands and looking out toward the empty fields. The children's voices had faded away; the silence was intense.

"Mother!"

The old lady lifted her head.

"Mother!"

She rose and looked about her. So often in her dreams he had called her. Was she dreaming?

"Mother!"

"My son!" Then a figure rose out from the bushes and stood looking at her. Very still they stood, these two, with the graves of the strangers between them. "George,"—it was little more than a whisper,—"my child!" And she held out her arms.

The man stumbled toward her, catching at the trees as he went, falling on his knees before her, his arms about her waist.

"Mother, mother!" His sobs seemed almost to rend him.

"Child, my child!" And her soft old hands were resting on his gray head as he leaned against her. Her eyes were shining; a gentle flush came on her face; her lips were smiling softly. "My son! my own son!" The sobs were softened, and at last he looked up. "Mother?"

"I am here, son, thank God!" And with her delicate handkerchief she wiped his eyes. "I am not surprised," she said. "I've known always that you would come. I've heard you calling—calling in the night. Last night it was so loud, so clear, I got up and went to the window, and I prayed that you'd come home to me. Come," making as if to lift the tall man. "Come, your room is ready—has been ready for years. Arthur and his motherless children live with me, and tomorrow Kate and Tom, with their families, come over for Christmas. Come, all will welcome you."

It was as if she told him casually all the family news, taking him into the fold once more. Then she added, "Thank God, oh, thank God!"

And drawing his hand through her arm, she led him.

"So long I've prayed, and waited, and watched," she went on. "I knew the Lord would bring you home, bring you safe at last."

"A useless wreck, mother."

"My darling child! Son!"

The children were awed, yet enchanted. Uncle George had been hungry—had taken the doll crumbs! It was like a storybook, and it all had happened to them.

The children had gone to bed, and the wanderer had taken a low chair close to his mother, his arm across her knees. "Last night," he said, slowly, "I was on the culvert. It was dark, I had to crawl on my hands and knees lest I should fall in, and a train came. I prayed, mother, for the first time in years, and I called aloud to you."

"I heard you, my son."

"I was so cold, and I wondered if the old boiler was there. I thought that I could creep in and get shelter from the wind. I was afraid it had rusted away."

"I had it painted years ago," the mother answered. "You used to go there so often—your favorite place."

"Two wrecks, mother."

"The one, a joy to the children," the brother Arthur said; "the other, a joy to us."

There had never been a more joyful Christmas in the old house. There had never been wanderer more welcomed, and at the Christmas dinner the boy George said, "Grandmother looks quite a girl today."

"I am so happy!" she cried. "So very happy!"

And pausing, as if looking back over all the war, and want, and grief of her life, she said, "God has been so good to me—so good! What He has sent He has given me strength to bear; what He has taken away He will keep safe; him that was lost He has restored. God has been so good to me!" And from each one there came a soft "Amen!"

SQUIRE KAYLEY'S CONCLUSIONS

There is a certain family likeness in all small country towns that is quite consistent with a wide divergence in manners and customs, and one thing common to all is a "leading citizen." He is generally a good man, for after all it is the upright who best weather the storm and find permanent haven in the faith of their fellow men.

The town of Greenville, like all her family, was extremely self-important, and when her "leading citizen," Mr. Joshua Kayley—commonly called Squire Kayley—was sent to Congress, Greenville became absolutely sure of the large place she filled in the public eye, and felt glad for the rest of the world that a teacher should go out from such a place as Greenville. In return, Squire Kayley felt deeply grateful for the honor done him; was proud of his town, of his county, and of his State, and went to his post determined to do all possible credit to his native region.

As has been intimated, Squire Kayley was an upright man; he was also a modest and an observant man, honestly desirous of thinking and doing right, and when he reached Washington he found much food for thought. He did not make many remarks during his term of office, but in a quiet way he made many investigations, and arrived at some astonishing conclusions. He found, amoung other things, that the West and the South were looked on as being uncivilized because of what in those regions were called "difficulties," not to speak of lynchings and other modes of supplementing the law.

He found out, also, that in quieter regions, instead of "a word and a blow," people brought action for "assault and battery," and "alienating affections," and "breach of promise," and the rest of it—delicate matters which in his experience had always been settled by a bullet or a caning. Not being a blood-thirsty man, he pondered much on these things, and determined at last that he would try the experiment of making his native town more law-abiding. It was a herculean task, and he had serious doubts as to his success, but he was determined to try, for although Greenville could not boast that every man in her graveyard had died with his boots on, she could nevertheless bring to mind a long list of sons who had begun their march on the "lonely road" well shod.

He was sitting on the hotel piazza with a number of his constituents one afternoon after his return home, and while a Negro handed about glasses filled with a topaz-colored mixture, crushed ice, mint, and straws, Squire Kayley told this story:

"A man up yonder," he began, "made some remarks about another man, a stranger from another region of the country; a few days afterwards the man was on the cars when the stranger walked up to him and taking him by the nose, pulled him all the way down the car."

"Gosh!" exclaimed one listener.

"Did you stay for the funeral?" asked another.

"He didn't shoot," Squire Kayley answered, "he brought in a charge of assault and battery, and got two thousand dollars damages."

His audience groaned.

"You needn't groan," the Squire went on, with a steadiness in his tone and words such as a man puts into his actions when he is about to light a fuse—"that fellow had a level head. He had followed so quick that his nose wasn't hurt, and two thousand dollars is a lots better poultice for a man's honor than a fellow man's blood."

A dead silence followed this remark, and Squire Kayley, tilting his chair back against the wall, pulled gently at the straw in this glass. After a few moments a young fellow sitting on the railing of the piazza asked:

"An' you'd sue for damages, Squire?"

"I ain't sure, Nick," Squire Kayley answered, slowly. "I hope I won't be tried, but I think the fellow had a level head."

"An' two thousand dollars is a heap er money," said another young fellow, thoughtfully.

"'Tain't so much the money, Loftus," the Squire answered, "as not shedding blood. They're lots more peaceable up yonder than we are, and they haven't got it by killing each other, either; and they're lots richer, too, and a good deal of it has come through being law-abiding."

"Dang my soul, if you ain't changed!" cried an old fellow, jerking his rocking chair round so as to face Squire Kayley. "I'd noticed thet you'd smoothed your words a heap, an' had cut your hair short, an' shaved your face clean, but I hedn't looked for no fu'ther change, an' this is too much when you say you'd let a feller pull yo' nose an' be satisfied with two thousand dollars."

"I'd let you pull it for one, Uncle Adam," Squire Kayley answered, smiling.

There was a general laugh, but not a hearty one, for their leading citizen was announcing doctrines that would have branded any other townsman as a coward.

"There was another man," the Squire went on; "a fellow began to carry on with his wife; we'll suppose that he did what he could to stop it, then, after watching a while and seeing that things were hopeless, he brought action for alienating his wife's affections, and gained his suit and five thousand dollars."

"Damn it, man, you didn't think *thet* was right?" Uncle Adam cried again, growing very red in the face, while the other listeners looked at the Squire pleadingly, as if imploring him not to commit himself beyond redemption.

"Why not?" the Squire asked, taking another pull at his straw— "nothing could heal the hurt the woman had done him—and a woman as far gone as that didn't deserve to have blood spilled for her—and to leave her on the other fellow's hands, at the same time taking away his money, seems to me the most dismal punishment on the face of the earth."

"But, Squire, could you have held yourself?" cried Nick.

"I ain't sure," the Squire answered, again, "and I won't be tried, being a bachelor; but that fellow had a level head."

Loftus did not venture to remark again on the money, and Uncle Adam and the others having sunk into wondering silence, the Squire went on:

"There was a fellow engaged to a girl; first thing she knew he was married to another girl; she sued for breach of promise and got her money."

"Fur God's sake, Joshua Kayley!" Uncle Adam pleaded, for the third time, and now with a tone of despair in his voice, "you wouldn't er let yo' daughter do thet?"

The Squire shook his head. "No," he said, "seeing I'm a bachelor, I wouldn't; but I *do* draw the line there. I don't know what I'd do to a man who should ill-treat my daughter, if I had one—but *she* shouldn't do anything; all the same, the girl had a level head. And I'll tell you," he went on, rising to his feet and waving his glass to emphasize his words—"I'll tell you that the people up yonder have got the right end of the stick. You'll not get peace nor honor by killing people, and you'll not make money by paying lawyers to defend you in murder trials—and we don't gain credit nor bring capital to our country by riots and difficulties; and they call us barbarous and uncivilized, they do, and we've got to change—we've got to become law-abiding. I love

Greenville, and I love you all, and you've all got to help me change this town. God knows, and you know, that I ain't a coward, and if you could hear them talk about us and our ways, and read their papers about us and our doings, you'd try to help me;" and he resumed his seat.

There was a moment's silence, then Uncle Adam brought his hand down sharply on the arm of his chair.

"It's no use talking', Josh," he said, "we ain't been raised that way, an' we ain't a goin' to change into no pulin' complainers to the law, nor patch up our dishonor with money. Why, Josh, even the niggers would scorn such talk, an' for the land's sake, stop it!"

There was a chuckle from the doorway, where the Negro waiter had paused to listen.

Squire Kayley turned. "You there, Sam?" he said. "I'm glad of it, you can help me, too; you can go and tell the niggers what I say, and tell 'em I'm right."

The Negro bent double over his waiter as if with restrained mirth. "Lawd, Boss," he said, "'tain't no use talkin' to niggers; it's too easy furrum to shoot en run, en dat's w'at a nigger 'll do ev'y time."

"An' the whites 'll shoot an' stan' to it!" cried Uncle Adam; "an' you've gone all wrong, Josh."

Squire Kayley shook his head.

"No, Uncle Adam," he answered, "I'm right. People, and 'specially boys, seem to think that there's some kind of glory in defending what they call their honor, and half the time it's bad temper or bad liquor. But there's no glory in a cold-blooded lawsuit, and if they knew that they'd have to go into court and have their lives and their characters turned inside out, they'd control themselves a little better."

A tall young woman, very much overdressed, was seen coming down the street on the other side. Nick slipped off the railing on to the pavement, and, stepping across quickly, joined her. The group on the hotel piazza was silent, watching the couple out of sight.

Then Uncle Adam said:

"It beats me why Nick Tobin's wife is forever passin' this hotel. To my certain knowledge she's been by three times today."

"Maybe she has business downtown," suggested the Squire.

"Loftus Beesley's smilin' like he knows," was another suggestion.

Uncle Adam nudged Loftus.

"Not long ago," he said, "we mighter thought it was 'cause Loftus was a settin' her."

"Well, she's gone," said Squire Kayley, sharply; "and I can't see how it's our business what she's gone for."

Uncle Adam looked at the speaker for a moment, the color mounting to his face.

"It seems to me, Joshua Kayley," he answered, "thet you're losin' yo' mind. If I choose to make it my business who passes this hotel, I'm goin' to make it my business; an' if I choose to say thet Nick Tobin's wife spen's her life gaddin' roun' these streets, I'm goin' to say it; an' I'll add thet when Nick's in town she *does* spen' her time on the streets, an' when he's travellin', or with his firm, over in the city, she spen's it at home receivin' the boys. An' fu'thermo' Loftus is one o' them boys; an' I'll instruct you again—Nick suspicions it, an' he leaves the Seelye boys, his own cousins, on guard when he's gone, 'cause Nick's got no man to help him, an' the girl's own people can't do nothin' with her—now, what do you say?"

"That I'm mighty sorry for Nick," Squire Kayley answered, quietly; "he's a good fellow, a little hasty, but straight, and the least his friends can do is not to trifle with his wife behind his back, nor make her the subject of public comments; and I'll stand by Nick, and I'll stand by her for his sake. We all ought to."

Loftus moved uneasily, then joined Uncle Adam, who had risen, and, with a very much disgusted expression, stood looking down on Squire Kayley.

"I wish yo' new doctrines good luck, Josh," the old man said, sarcastically; "but I'm an ole bottle, an' the preacher says new wine busts ole bottles, an' I'm 'fraid o' bustin' if I takes in any mo', an' then you'd bring a suit for damages, so I'm goin'."

Squire Kayley laughed.

"You can't make me mad, Uncle Adam," he said, "and you can say anything you please. Some day you'll see that I'm right."

Of course Squire Kayley's new doctrines were the town's talk in a few hours, and the women with one accord took his part.

Squire Kayley was right, they declared, was always right, and if he had broken up that hotbed of scandal that collected every afternoon on the hotel piazza he had done a good work. Women scarcely liked to pass the hotel, and although Letty Tobin deserved to be talked about because of her scandalous behavior with Loftus Beesley, still they were glad that the Squire had spoken plainly, even if in so doing he had taken Letty's part. Further, if he could persuade their sons and husbands to stop bullying each other, they would look on him as their deliverer from many anxieties and evils, and they would try to help him.

The next thing Greenville knew, an action for assault and battery was brought by Sam, the waiter at the hotel, against Uncle Adam Dozier, the autocrat of the hotel piazza.

The excitement was intense.

Of course Sam had come at once to Squire Kayley, and of course Squire Kayley could not refuse the case. He did his best to persuade Sam from it, for Uncle Adam had often before whacked Sam with his walking stick, but though perfectly amiable, Sam stood to his point.

The town was in a fume. Squire Kayley's popularity wasted like snow under a July sun, and there were no words capable of expressing Uncle Adam's sensations, nor any reputable printer who would have put his language into type.

The women, hitherto solid for Squire Kayley as the man in town who stood next to the clergy in the matter of uprightness, were divided, for though they detested Uncle Adam as an old reprobate with an unscrupulous tongue—still, the case was a Negro against a white man, which brought many feelings other than justice into full play.

However, through it all, Squire Kayley was "Quiet and peaceable and full of compassion," and he gained his case, and Sam his money, and Uncle Adam, having exhausted his vocabulary, took out his vengeance in an ostentatious and belligerent avoidance of the Squire.

But time, humanity's one patent medicine that really cures all, soothed Uncle Adam, and as Sam had discreetly disappeared, the old man resumed his position on the hotel piazza, where each day he used Squire Kayley's new doctrines as a peg on which to hang an ever-enlarging book of lamentations over the old times, and declared that since Sam's victory "every nigger in town was tryin' to git licked, which would be mighty good for them but for the money which the Squire hed attached. For everybody knew that a thrashin' was a nigger's bes frien', while money was a pitfall of danger"—but that "the nex' time *he* hit, he'd hit to kill, then Josh Kayley could have the pleasure of puttin' him in the penitentiary." Furthermore he said that he hoped "thet no other Greenville man would ever go to Washington if it was goin' to ruin him like it had ruined Josh. Josh had gone away an old-time gen'leman. but only the omniscient Almighty knew what he had changed into 'fore he got back." The occurrence had its effect, however, as object lessons always do, and, as the Squire observed, "Uncle Adam had ceased his gentle play with his walking stick."

Greenville resumed its deadly stillness after this, until the first cold snap in the autumn waked up the young people to a sense of the beauty of dances and candy pullings, causing them to drive long distances to country places or to neighboring settlements to find a sufficient amount of amusement.

Of course Mrs. Grundy waked up, too, and while allowing them to have the most unquestioned freedom, the gossips kept a viciously strict account of the young people's fallings from grace, and especially were their eyes fixed on Letty Tobin, Nick's wife.

That Letty was beautiful no one denied, and her marriage to Nick Tobin had been an astonishment to all who knew her. Nick himself had been somewhat surprised, for up to the moment of her acceptance she had treated his loyal service as something of a joke, giving all her favors to other young men, especially to Loftus Beesley, who, for Greenville, was rich.

Nobody understood this sudden change of front, and all prophesied that the marriage would never take place. But it did, and in his love and gratitude Nick swore that if love and devotion could make Letty happy she should never have cause to repent her choice. And work he did, even Letty's mother declaring that he "spoiled the girl to death."

As Nick "traveled" for a firm in a neighboring city, he could be very little at home, which was declared to be "unfortunate," especially as Letty lived alone, declining even the company of her own sisters, who, doomed to the country, would have been very glad of a change to town.

Nick's comings and goings were uncertain also, but he came home as often and stayed as long as possible, meanwhile leaving to his cousins, Ben and Reub Seelye, the care of his wife and his home.

They had been married for a year now, and Nick had not yet entirely recovered from his surprise at his luck, for, besides being a modest fellow, his mind was as slow as his temper was quick. But when the first cold snap came, and all the young people of the town waked up to the delights of this weather that was so ideal for merrymaking, Nick was away, and Ben Seelye found himself very unhappy about his cousin's wife and about the talk that was so rife concerning her.

There was nothing that he could have proved, and yet he knew, and every one else knew, that things were not as they should be, and that Loftus Beesley was the man.

One morning Ben walked into Squire Kayley's office, pale, and somewhat breathless.

"What's up?" the Squire asked, at once, not even suggesting that his visitor should be seated.

Ben held out a telegram. "Nick's coming," he said, "and Letty's not here."

"Where is she?"

"We all drove over to Pinehollow last night to a candy pulling," Ben explained, "and some of us stayed over all night at Colonel Bolles's; but this morning when I reached town I found that Letty had not come. She and Loftus left Bolles's a little ahead of me, and took the road home, so that I felt safe; but John Brewin says that she and Loftus turned off on the Valley Creek pike, and told him to tell me they'd be back by five o'clock—and—and Nick is 'most here now!"

"Well?" queried the Squire.

"Well, it'll be death to somebody," Ben answered.

The Squire walked about a little bit with his hands in his pockets, then paused to look out of the window.

"It shall not come to that," he said, at last; "there's no harm in the girl's going to a picnic; and if you'll meet Nick and tell him about it quietly, it'll be all right."

"If it was any other fellow but Loftus," Ben answered.

"Is Nick jealous of Loftus?"

"I don't know; but Loftus is so careful when Nick's at home that it makes a fellow think, an' when Nick's away, not a day passes but he sees Letty."

"And I've known that girl since she was a child," the Squire said, as if to himself, again pausing to look out of the window. After a moment he turned—"If she comes at five," he continued, "we can smooth it, but a girl who deceives her husband systematically may not come home at five."

Ben groaned.

The Squire sat down again, and there was silence in the little office until the Squire roused himself with a deep sigh.

"Well," he said, "you go and meet Nick and explain things as lightly as you can, and if she does not come at five you bring Nick here; I'll be here late this evening." And Ben went off.

Five o'clock found Nick and Ben waiting patiently at Nick's house; at six o'clock Reub Seelye joined them; at seven, Nick was lying on his bed, tied, with Ben seated beside him, while Reub went for Squire Kayley.

"He tried to kill himself," Reub said, "an' we had to tie him."

When Squire Kayley entered the room Nick was attaching every oath he had ever heard to Loftus Beesley's name, and doing it with a deliberate, monotonous carefulness that was almost rhythmical and truly awful.

"That's no good," the Squire said, quietly, standing over him with his hands in his pockets, "and I'm ashamed to see you lying here tied like a beast. Untie him, boys."

Nick got up and shook himself.

"You've got no right to behave as if your wife had sinned," the Squire went on; "any accident might have kept them; if you loved her you'd not treat her with this dishonor."

"She's been two days, an' this'll be two nights, with Loftus Beesley!" Nick cried.

"True; but last night she was with all the party at Colonel Bolles's, perfectly respectable and legitimate, and now she may come in at any moment and give a perfectly clear account of herself; and even if she does not come until morning, she may be stopping with some friend—"

Nick struck his hands together.

"Then she'll have to stop away altogether!"

"Not at all," the Squire returned; "you must give her every chance to clear herself; she's young, and beautiful, and fond of admiration and gayety, and that kind of woman has a thousand temptations that a quieter kind never dreams of. She had the choice of every unmarried man in this town—" the Squire hesitated a moment, then added—"even of your humble servant, and out of all she selected you—"

Nick turned quickly—"You, too, Squire?" he asked.

The Squire nodded. "And I love her enough still," he added, "to insist that justice be done her."

The evening wore on. The town clock struck nine—then ten—then the Squire sent Reub Seelye out to the house of Letty's mother, to see if she was there.

It was a long ride, and until Reub returned, after midnight, the Squire managed to keep Nick quiet, but when a negative answer came Nick was almost beside himself, and Squire Kayley had to compromise, giving up the point that Nick must let his wife come home, and advising, instead, that he should pack all Letty's belongings, and in the morning send them to her mother's house and leaving Ben Seelye to meet the couple, come to Squire Kayley's place outside the town. For, at any cost, Nick and Loftus must be kept apart.

"Don't receive her," he said, "but give her a chance to clear herself."

"And Loftus?" Nick snarled between his teeth.

"What's Loftus done?" the Squire asked—"Letty's not the kind to be led—nor driven."

"If Loftus blames her I'll kill him."

"No, we are not going to have any bloodshed," the Squire went on; "if you can't hold yourself, I'll hold you. If I can't do any better I'll put you in jail."

Nick laughed long and loud, then burst into tears—"I love her so!" he cried, "I love her so!"

"Of course you do," his mentor answered. "And first thing you know it'll be all right."

Daylight found Reub Seelye, with Letty's trunks, being driven out to Mrs. Purdy's; Squire Kayley and Nick on their way to the country, and Ben Seelye, with a note in his pocket, and the key of Nick's house, on his way home to breakfast.

But, alas! as the day wore on and Ben did not come with news of Letty's arrival, Nick became almost wild; then the Squire tried to soothe him into quiet with talk of a divorce.

"You think she's too far gone to shed blood for," Nick said, at last, his voice grown low and weak from weariness—"that's what you said about that other woman at the North; you want me to sue Loftus for his money, and let him have Letty? Great God!"

"Do you want her?"

"But Loftus," Nick reiterated—"leave her to Loftus!"

"Humanity's strange," the Squire began, slowly; "let 'em have what they want, and ten to one they don't want it. Letty belongs to you, and that makes her the one thing on earth that Loftus wants. You belong to Letty, and that cheapens you in her sight. Let her go—that minute your value will double, and, like Esau, she'll shed many and bitter tears for what she threw away. Let her go; and Loftus will wonder what it was that made him so crazy. There's nothing makes a man feel so God-forsaken as to be left to follow his own evil courses—as to say to him, 'You've hurt me beyond help—take what you've been striving for and go your way'—and right then and there the tip-top apple on the tree that he's been fighting for turns to dust and ashes in his mouth, and he can never—never—never get you and your maimed life out of his heart. But just lift one finger to revenge yourself, and you lift the burden from his heart on to your own. Let 'em go, boy, wash your hands clean of 'em, and after a while peace will come to you—peace such as you've never dreamed of. But not to them, they'll have entered on a new lease of tribulation—for 'what ye mete, it shall be measured to you again.' I'm not much of a preaching Christian," he went on, in a lower tone, "but there's one thing I've read in Scripture—just a few words—'Are not all these things written in Thy book?'"

Nick sat silent, his arms crossed on the table and his head bowed on them. No food had passed his lips, and he was faint and weary, and for a little while he seemed to see as Squire Kayley saw, and so he fell into the deep sleep of exhaustion.

Just as the sun was setting Ben Seelye rode slowly into the yard and around to the stable, and the Squire stepped out very carefully, so as not to waken Nick.

"She's come," Ben said, "an' when she read the note she laughed a little, then she turned right white, and gave it to Loftus—"

"And Loftus?"

"He looked like a rooster with his tail feathers pulled out, an' said he thought he'd better leave town for a while, and then he looked at me and sorter straightened up, and asked Letty—'What do *you* want me to do?' an' she said, 'Leave town;' then he turned to get into his buggy, an' I told him he'd better drive Letty out to her mother's, 'cause the servants were gone an' the house locked up, an' all Letty's things were out there waitin' for her. It was pretty bad; but they did what I said, an' I rode my horse right behind 'em through the town, an' everybody stared, an' nobody spoke, not even Uncle Adam Dozier. It was bad. Loftus leaves at seven o'clock, if Nick 'll only sleep till then."

Never in the annals of Greenville had there been such excitement as when Nick Tobin sued Loftus Beesley for alienating his wife's affections.

The whole town and county—men, women, and children—rose in a solid, clamoring body against Squire Kayley. Women who had often torn poor Letty's character into ribbons now rallied around her, declaring that to bring a woman into such unheard-of publicity, into court, subjecting her even to the evidence of her Negro servants, was to destroy not only all the old and time-honored customs, but to subvert society.

Uncle Adam proclaimed that any man in Nick's position who did not shoot his rival was a coward, and that if Squire Kayley had not meddled, it would all have been arranged as of old; Loftus decently buried and his money left to his family, Nick could have come back, and everybody would have been his friend; and Letty—well, Letty would have been a "grass widder" with a bad name. Now Squire Kayley's methods had turned the two sinners into hero and heroine, and the injured man had become an object of pity and contempt, who deserved all he got!

Every sort of compromise was suggested, but Squire Kayley was determined to teach a lesson once and for all to his native town, and he did it—an awful, searching, withering lesson that revealed to mothers, and fathers, and brothers the perilousness of the liberty which they accorded their young daughters and sisters; which revealed to the women the views of themselves as given in the talk of the men who formed their society; which revealed to the men their own unloveliness as seen by purer eyes and an unanswerable logic; an awful, withering lesson that was as if the whole town had been driven into the Palace of Truth, there to endure a day of terrible judgment.

Through it all Squire Kayley kept Nick away, traveling, as usual, for the firm that employed him, while Loftus met the public eye only when the dreadful engine of the law dragged him into view, showing him in all sorts of false and pitiful guises. The Squire was virtually ostracized, but he had the courage of his convictions and the spirit of the martyr, which every man should have who undertakes the work of reform.

At last it was over. Loftus had to sell most of his possessions to pay costs and damages; Letty hid herself in her mother's house, while Nick, traveling incessantly, did not hear the half that was said, and paid no heed whatever to the money that was now to his credit in the Greenville bank. The town subsided, having become "sadder and wiser," and Squire Kayley's reward, for he had declined all fees, was to see that when expeditions were organized, at least one mother went to look after the young people; and that brothers and fathers took some heed as to who escorted their sisters and daughters; further, the girls themselves were seen less often on the streets, and it became a great breach of social observance for any woman to pass the hotel.

All this soberness was gall and wormwood to Uncle Adam Dozier, who having, through the fall of Squire Kayley, regained the position he had lost because of his defeat by Sam, bloomed once more into the hotel-piazza orator of happier days, and from this altitude he made one declaration which raised a puzzling question for the people of Greenville.

"Josh Kayley is the most immoral man in this town," he declared, boldly; "he is attempting to reduce everything to a money value, an' says thet even our mos' sacred affections kin be paid fur. It's wrong— it's damned wrong; an' I say thet the man who kin spen' the money gained through the ruin of his wife is a poltroon an' a sneak! But Josh Kayley ner no other man kin bring *us* to sich er pass—no, sir, I tell you the end is not yet, an' you'll see I'm right—wait, an' you'll see!"

So Greenville, a little at a loss between the practical ills as exemplified by Uncle Adam, and the theoretical ills as exemplified by the Squire, waited. In a convict-worked coal mine two prisoners labored side by side, a Negro and a white man. In the dim light cast on each by the other's lamp the Negro showed a contented, rather cheerful face, and worked skilfully, while the white man, young and comely, was haggard and hopeless, and worked clumsily. The Negro watched him furtively, but a guard stood near, for the white man was a new prisoner, and the Negro did not speak. After a while sounds of laughter came from a group nearer the opening, and the guard moved on; then the Negro said:

"Fur Gawd's sake! Marse Nick, whar's you come from?"

For the first time the white man looked at his companion. "Sam," he said, "you here?"

"Yassir, Marse Nick, I git yer kase o' dat money what Marse Josh got fumme f'um ole Marse Adam Dozier. Over to Duserville a gal fool me kase o' dat money, en her mammy had er funerl to perwide, an' I come yer—yassir. An' you, Marse Nick—you got yo' money, too, sir?"

"Yes, I got my money, too, Sam," the young man answered, wielding his pick deliberately, "an' I gave it all to your Miss Letty; she never had worked, an' I wasn't satisfied to think about her workin'."

"Yassir, Marse Nick, en den, sir?"

"An' then I heard 'bout the things your Marse Loftus had said 'bout her on the trial, an' so I killed him; for I thought the trial was 'tween me an' him, not her, an' while I was killin' him I told him why I did it; not 'cause he'd hurt me, but 'cause of what he'd said 'bout my wife on the trial. I told him so—I got him by himself, an' I told him; then I killed him—killed him slow, him, my old friend."

"An' Marse Josh!" the Negro was breathless.

"I told the Squire that I'd tried my best to do his way, but no man could say the things Loftus had said about my wife on that trial an' live. I was sorry to disappoint the Squire, for he's right in the main, but my case was diff'runt."

"An' Marse Adam Dozier?"

"He said I was right, an' a gentleman, but I told him no, that the Squire was right, but my case was diff'runt."

HANDS ALL ROUND

Preston was in a turmoil. Never since the war of Secession had there been such an upturning, such excitement, such despair and anger. The mothers, and sisters, and sweethearts were hopeless; the grandmothers were heartbroken, the fathers were indignant, and all because of Francis Newman.

Lying in the heart of a rich upland country, Preston had come into being as a resort for the planters of that district. It was on a watercourse, as were all the older towns of the country, and as long as watercourses were the ways of traffic, Preston was wealthy. But railways had taken away that glory, and the town had dwindled somewhat. It still held itself as a center of civilization and culture, however, and prided itself, and justly, on the number of public men it had given to the country, and on its social status. It was a true and laudable pride until the Civil War, when Preston was the camping ground for both armies, and its desolation was complete.

When all was over the people came drifting back, the soldiers came hobbling home, and the thread of life was taken up once more. Much of the land in the district lay idle, much changed hands; the old generation of planters died off; their sons, lacking money, lacking all advantages, became small farmers, struggling to live and pay taxes; and around the town there grew up a black belt of African suburbs. It was depressing.

A railway waked them up later on, and things became more prosperous. Mr. Newman re-opened the bank, and many new ways were developed of making ends meet. Schools were established, churches built, several people actually became able to send their children away to colleges, and though on a greatly diminished scale, Preston felt itself prosperous once more. But not for long. A financial crash shook the country, and times became screwingly hard. Later, free silver rent the town in twain. Mr. Newman, the banker, stood for sound money. Captain Alderley, who had come out of the Civil War with one mule and a Mexican dollar; who had had to cut down his inherited acres into a farm; mortgaging some, selling some, renting some, and actually making money on none, led the free-silver party, and the black suburbs were divided.

Yellow fever came next, creeping up to their very doors, and business was paralyzed. Cotton went down to four cents, and their hearts grew heavy within them. More than thirty years of toil, with only ruin at the end! Meanwhile, a "cloud no bigger than a man's hand," appeared above the horizon—a cloud not heeded in Preston. What was the Cuban question by the side of the problem that was rending the poor farmers; the problem of what they were going to live on when it took the whole cotton crop to pay the taxes? But the cloud grew bigger and blacker, and young Francis Newman came to the front as a storm center.

He was a tall, slight young fellow, with features that might have been cut in cameo to represent any of the classic heads that the world has ever produced, and eyes of so intense a blue, of such eager gaze, that a light seemed ever burning behind them, and yet, so earnestly preoccupied was their expression, that one was never sure that, though looking full at you, the young fellow's thoughts were not compassing time and space. He had been one of the fortunate ones who had gone away to college; who had also been across the water, but who coming home, had endeared himself to the town by saying simply that he loved Preston best of all, and was quite willing to spend his life there. He seemed to enjoy the simple entertainments, the picnics, the sewing society festivals and teas, for the raising of church funds. He gave teas himself, or made his mother give them every Saturday afternoon after bank hours. This was a new departure in Preston, for the young men walked in the old paths of hunting and such things as were called "manly sports," where women were not expected. They came to the teas, however, and joined the Tennis Club that Francis instituted, and also the literary and book club; Francis in his turn joining the local military organization, the Preston Grays. Preston was very proud of her company; the best blood in the county was in it, and to Preston this meant of course the best blood in the United States! Francis went into this heart and soul, and made the organization a social feature. The Grays found themselves giving dances in flag-draped halls, and picnics in a tented field, and they liked it, and Francis, before very long, was elected Captain. It was a proud day for his mother, and strangely enough, no other mother seemed to be jealous.

Indeed, the young fellow became a social center; a source of interest and pleasure, and everybody loved him, and he loved Captain Alderley's daughter Ann.

So things had gone along, driven by Francis' energy, in spite of hard times, of gloom, and of sad prognostications, until all the more frivolous organizations being in order, he instituted a society for the prevention of cruelty to animals. The town drew a long breath at this; then the men laughed, and the women applauded. It caused a good deal of discussion, but the young fellow pushed it through, and people began to find themselves rebuked for their treatment of beasts of burden. This seemed to be an infringement of their rights as free American citizens, and they resented it; but Francis held on his way and managed to keep his popularity. His father said, laughingly, that Francis was ruining him buying old animals from the Negroes. But Francis fined them, too, on occasion, and between his liberality and justice he found himself becoming an authority down in the African suburbs.

In a quiet way Francis was renovating Preston, and bringing it up to date. He was putting his own generation in touch with their own kind out in the world, and doing it steadily and with a purpose; but he was wiser than his years, and said nothing about it.

When the Cuban war cloud came up, Francis took his stand for universal freedom, and the arguments were hot among the young people. Wherever a group gathered, there discussion raged; even the Negroes became interested, and came to ask "Mister Frank" to tell them about it. Francis acquiesced at once, and going down into the black suburbs he held a public meeting and explained the situation.

Then his mother remonstrated; his father looked startled, and Preston frowned. Was the social favorite sinking into a politician bidding for the colored vote? This sort of thing was excusable at election times when the vote was running close, but to go down into the Negro quarter except on such occasions was a most serious thing. What did it mean? And people began to look askance.

The question grew, and the town broke into two factions, Captain Alderley heading a conservative peace party and Francis preaching liberty and progress. It was no longer Democratic and Republican, but national isolation as against a modern spirit of universal brotherhood.

"Spain has a right to chastise her own colonies," Captain Alderley declared.

"No person nor nation has a right to do wrong," Francis answered. "You have no right to cut off your own hand, if it makes you a less useful citizen."

The conservatives laughed. Not free to do what they would with their own? What crazy nonsense! What would the world come to under such teaching as this?

And among the older people the feeling was growing stronger and stronger against Francis. The young people were with him still. His mother pleaded with him. "You are my only child," she said. "If this war should come I could not let you go. I know war and its miseries as you cannot know them. It has ruined two generations in the South—we cannot sacrifice another. I saw so many march away who never came again. My son, I could not let you go."

"Yes, mother." And he laid his head against her knee as he sat on the floor by her chair. "You will let me go because it will be right."

"And Ann?"

There was a moment's silence, and then he answered, "I have no claim on Ann."

The excitement about the "Maine" quieted down; the spring rained itself into being, fresh and green, and people began to smile at their recent fears, when throughout the land the wires shivered with a declaration of war! The nation drew a long breath and a scattering cheer went up that ended in a sigh. Where would it lead—when would it end, and after all, who had done it?

Francis seemed to pause, too, for a little time; then the call for volunteers came, and he began to spend his afternoons and evenings in riding about the country talking to the members of the company, and the women began a rebellion.

"Go to Cuba to fight for half-castes," they said, "to die of yellow fever! Francis Newman was crazy, it *should not be!*"

Business fell off; prices rose; tea, and coffee and flour, the very necessities of life; and the old ladies began to talk as if the whole thing was Francis Newman's fault.

And Francis, while as sweet as ever to the old ladies who blamed him, made speech after speech to the company, but he did not ask them to volunteer.

Then one day three Negroes, dressed in their best, came to the bank to see "Mister Frank." The clerks peeped through their various little windows trying to see, and Mr. Newman looked out from his private office which commanded everything, and there was anxiety in his expression.

Francis did not appear at the tennis club that afternoon, which met out at Captain Alderley's, and the young people missing him dreadfully, wondered. Ann Alderley did not like it at all, for Francis had a way of making things go, and his absence had caused her turn of the tennis club to seem a failure. Having a spirit of her own, she decided at once that Francis was less and less satisfactory every day. He was too full of fads; it amounted to nervous restlessness, and it would be well to put some of the various organizations into other hands than his. A one man power was never wise.

The next day the news that Francis had forsaken the club to go to a public meeting of the Negroes in the black quarter, came out, and the shock to the town was almost as great as the declaration of war had been, and each asked the other what in the world it meant!

What it meant was that the Negroes had come to Francis to say that they wanted to raise a company to volunteer for the Spanish war, and he had agreed to go down and talk to them about it. The meeting was held in their church, and Francis sat in the minister's chair, the minister sitting on the step below him. He told them quite frankly that of course they could not come into the white company, and that being captain of that, he could not take charge of them, but that if they would give him a list of the names of all who wanted to go, he would try to get a regular army officer to come to Preston and muster them in. "Teck de names down now, Mister Frank," was suggested, and writing materials were handed him.

It was not a very agreeable afternoon in the crowded, ill-ventilated church, especially as his thoughts would wander off to the tennis party at the Alderley's and what Ann was thinking of him, but his sense of duty took him through, for behind this, as behind all his other schemes, he thought he saw the advance of the town. Preston must move forward, and how was progress possible while ignorance and brutality hung as a fringe about her outskirts?

That night he told his father what he had been after, and that he wanted leave of absence to go to Washington the next morning, and before the town had got wind of his last move, and so of course before the talk of the town had come down on his devoted head, Francis was away.

But the talk was furious, and Mrs. Newman, whose feelings went with the townspeople, was distressed beyond measure, and she pleaded with her husband to interfere.

"Francis must live his own life," Mr. Newman said.

"But he loves Ann Alderley, and the Alderleys are furious."

Mr. Newman smiled. "The surest way to win a woman is against her will," he said. When Francis returned there were tears in his mother's eyes, and so for greeting he kissed her eyes, answered his father's smile with a smile, and went away with him down to the bank.

If Francis felt any change in the attitude of the townspeople he made no sign, not even when Ann Alderley passed him with the slightest possible sign of recognition; but told the Preston Grays that he asked them as a military organization to call on Lieutenant Wardwell of the regular army, who was coming to Preston, and who would be his guest.

This news fluttered the town a good deal; not since the sixties had Preston seen a blue uniform, and they wondered what it portended. Not to touch the Preston Grays, of course, for they were militia—what then?

Then a Negro coachman gave warning, saying that he was going to enlist, and that the gentleman who was going to stay at Mr. Newman's was to enlist all the Negroes who wanted to go.

An officer for Negroes! and to stay at the Newmans!

The sensation seemed an unpleasant one to Preston, and Captain Alderley said plainly that he would neither call on nor receive Mr. Wardwell. That the time had come when a line had to be drawn against Francis Newman's vagaries, and that he would take the lead in drawing it. Personally, he was extremely fond of the young fellow, but he lacked balance, and must be made aware that he had offended the feelings of his fellow townsmen.

But Captain Alderley was puzzled as to how he was to make his opinions felt, for the community had no opportunity to so much as see Lieutenant Wardwell, much less to snub him or Francis. They seemed to be tremendously busy, taking only a little time in the afternoons and evenings, when they would go driving about the country together. To say the least, it was irritating, and society began to change from an attitude of objection to one of pique. And the girls also felt themselves injured. For the first time since Francis Newman's return to Preston they found themselves left out in the cold; while everything seemed to revolve around Lieutenant Wardwell and the war. The young men could talk of nothing else, and seemed to be at the Newmans during every spare moment.

"Mrs. Newman was keeping open house for the Grays," they said, "and the army was the best kind of a place for the Negroes; the discipline was the very thing."

"And you'd fight side by side with them?" Captain Alderley asked his son angrily.

"The English have native regiments in India," was answered.

Then Ann, flashing into anger, cried, "I'm ashamed of Francis Newman, hobnobbing with Negroes."

Her brother laughed teasingly—"He has rather let the girls go," he said.

The war spirit was growing, and the conservatives were boiling over. Then suddenly great words flashed from point to point—this time the wires thrilled, for the words were Dewey's victory!

Preston was in a state of the greatest excitement, for a summons had gone out to the Grays to meet that night at the public hall for enlistment.

The elder women wept, "Oh, God!" they said, "another war!" and the town rose in opposition, and Captain Alderley took the lead.

Everybody must be at the hall, he said, to vote this movement down, and himself rode ten miles into the country to bring in ex-congressman Hillyer to speak against Francis Newman.

And Francis seemed to be just as eager. He ordered the Grays to be there in full uniform, and to march into the hall in a body, where at the front, benches would be reserved for them. He asked the Mayor to preside; he asked all the clergy, the teaching force, the lawyers, Captain Alderley and Mr. Hillyer to sit on the platform; all the leading men, indeed, save his father, whom he asked to stay in the audience with his mother. The excitement was intense. The hall was packed and jammed, people sitting even on the steps that led up to the platform, and the gallery was black with the suburbs. A hum of eager talk rose and fell until the Preston band struck up "Dixie" and there came the tramp of marching men. The women shivered, and the men pricked up their ears like old war horses. On they came up the aisles in columns of two, into the reserved benches, paused a moment, then sat down as if moved by one spring, and Francis and Lieutenant Wardwell took their places on the platform.

In spite of itself Preston was thrilled. The little band brayed on; old griefs welled up as fresh as they had been thirty years before, and eyes were wet remembering the buttonless old gray coats that were folded away, worn, and ragged, and stained with dull brown stains! And Mrs. Newman grasped her husband's arm with hands that were icy through her gloves.

The music ceased, and Francis handed the Mayor a slip of paper. He glanced over it, then nodded and rose. "It was not usual," he said, looking about encouragingly on the expectant audience, "for a town to be called together on such an occasion; men usually decided such things for themselves; but just now so much was involved, and the conditions were so new, that no one was willing to trust to any one man's judgment, even for himself, until both sides of the question had been presented, and in pursuance of this policy," looking down at Francis' slip of paper, "he would like to hear from Captain Alderley."

Captain Alderley started, and a flutter went over the audience. This was unexpected, for Mr. Hillyer had been brought there to speak, and of course this change was Francis Newman's doing. Captain Alderley's eyes flashed and a flush came on his face; he had been taken at a disadvantage and he was angry.

He would not flinch, however, and he rose slowly; a commanding figure, tall and gaunt, and gloomy.

"I am not a public speaker," he said, drawing himself up to his full height, "for my school days were spent on the battlefield; my manhood, in gathering up the fragments that remained after the fiercest conflict of modern times. I've had no leisure to do anything but to fight misfortune to the death; I've had no training save in the school of endurance, and I did not expect to speak to you," his voice trembled with feeling, his deepset eyes were burning, and his clean-shaven, rugged face was set as if carved in stone. He had caught his audience, and Mrs. Newman wondered if Francis would have to go alone!

"I'm not a public speaker," Captain Alderley repeated, "but the case seems to be so simple, the reasoning so plain, that even I may be able to set it before you clearly. We are asked to send our sons to a war that does not concern us in the least; to shed our blood to free a people whom we are not at all sure are capable of self-government. We shall have to protect them or annex them; the first will take an enormous amount of money, the second will load us down with another race of irresponsible, incapable voters. We are taxed heavily enough now, God knows; and the political corruption due to this irresponsible and venal vote, is already a shame to this nation!" He was stopped by a round of applause, and cries of "Right! right!"

The Grays sat with eyes steadily to the front; Mrs. Newman wiped her dry lips, and Mr. Newman looked at his son anxiously.

"I say," Captain Alderley resumed, "that I do not believe in this war and we have been foolish to interfere. We have gained one victory, and what is the result? We have to send an army across the Pacific. We will take islands that we do not want; we will entangle ourselves in all the miserable difficulties of Europe and Asia; we shall have to make foreign alliances, and keep up an enormous standing army! It is folly! rank folly! And we are asked to send our best blood—for it is always the best who answer to a call like this that seems to be noble—we are asked to send our best, the only hope of the future, to sacrifice themselves to a bad climate, in a bad cause! Have we not suffered enough!" he cried raising his clenched fists above his head—"Have we not endured enough! Fathers and mothers, one generation was well nigh swept away, and those of us who were left to struggle on, maimed in body and spirit; poverty stricken, and almost hopeless; those of us who have survived these terrible years, who have reared our sons and daughters by dying daily to all that was easy and pleasant in life; must we now say to our children, 'Go, go and die yonder, because some ringleaders have invested in Cuban bonds! Never!" he cried, stamping his foot—"Never!" and he sat down amid shouts and cheers, wiping his forehead and looking defiantly at Francis.

Again Mrs. Newman wiped her dry lips; the Grays still looked straight to the front. Mr. Newman shifted his position uneasily, and the Mayor looked at Francis. There was a moment's pause, then the young fellow came forward.

"Your Honor," he said with a little bow to the mayor, "Ladies and gentlemen, and the Preston Grays." There was an intense look in his eyes that hid the quiet sweetness of his voice, and the hand that rested on the hilt of his sword gripped it as if in holding his sword he held himself. "Especially the Preston Grays," he went on, "for it is your question. Each generation has its problems that it must solve, or try to solve, and our generation, you and I, comrades, have come face to face with our problem." The silence was intense, and the low solemnity of the young man's voice held the people strangely. "It is not a question of whether Cuba is able to govern herself," he went on; "it is not a question of taxes and annexation, of irresponsible voters and political corruption—it is not a question of a standing army in the far east, or of Cuban bonds, nor of what has been, or may be suffered, the only question is—our duty. And this duty is the grandest that has ever faced a nation—the duty of freeing the world!"

A sigh as if of surprise went over the audience.

"Cuba and the Philippines are but the entering wedge," he went on, his voice rising. "Once having interfered, we must free them; once having freed them, we must protect them; this will drive us into foreign alliances, and the mother country is our natural ally! Do you not see?" he paused a moment looking over the audience.

"Do you not see?" he repeated, "the grand, the wonderful vision of the Anglo-Saxon race standing shoulder to shoulder for the order and the freedom of the world! Who would dare to stop us!" he cried,

"Who would dare to stand in our pathway? Right is might, and the end is inevitable!" A great wave of applause stopped him. He was as white as a sheet, and his eyes gleamed like beads of steel. He caught his breath for a moment, then went on.

"I am not persuading you to go," and his voice had become very quiet, and once more his hand grasped his sword hilt—"I am only telling you what I see; I am only asking you to see the duty that is looking us full in the eyes. The noblest, the most glorious duty that has ever faced any generation since time began! The world is ripe for this change—the 'whole creation groaneth and travaileth'—the movement has begun, and to try to stop it is to try to change destiny! From every quarter comes the demand for freedom. Dare we disregard this demand? Dare we turn deaf ears to this cry! *Dare* we! Before the eyes of all the nations of the earth we stand a monument to liberty—we, and we alone, hold this great gift—the gift of freedom, in our hands! We *must* grant it—we must hand it on to all who ask—'to give is to live—' we *must* give! And will the gift be any the less glorious because stained with our blood!" Cheer after cheer rang through the hall—the people were beside themselves, and Captain Alderley looked like a stone image. "What if we fight every day of every year for a thousand years," the young enthusiast went on—"if in the end the thing is achieved? What if our blood cements only the first foundation stone? What grander end can we ask than to die in such a cause? And the time will come when every nation of the earth will be represented in this great army of freedom, in this world war. All nations and all peoples—and the blood on the battlefield is all of one hue!" He paused, and there was a dead silence. Then he began again, more slowly, looking straight at the Grays.

"Comrades," he said, "you have heard, and you must choose. Will you remain a hide-bound, forest-clearing nation, or will you march out with the gift of freedom in your cartridge boxes? For me, I enlist for the war!"

In an instant the Grays were on their feet, every man holding up his hand—and again the people broke into shouts of the wildest enthusiasm. In the midst of the confusion Captain Alderley hammered on the Mayor's table for silence.

"Mr. Hillyer has come a long distance to speak to us," he said sharply, "and we will now hear him. Our friends of the Grays can have time to reconsider while he speaks."

It was like a douche of cold water. Everybody sat down except Francis, who withdrew a little to one side as Mr. Hillyer advanced.

Mr. Hillyer looked about for a moment, then smiled at Captain Alderley. "I'm like Balaam," he said; "I've been brought here to down
my enemies, and I can't do it." A laugh went round, and Captain Alderley flushed. "I've had the question presented to me in a brand new
light by our young friend, Captain Newman, and I've come over to the
war party."

The Grays led the applause. "We *do* hold the gift of freedom, and I
don't see how we can withhold it from those who ask. For the rest, I
cannot deny the vision of our young seer. It is an improbable vision to
me, but I cannot deny it, and the millennium *may* come his way; but
my friends, it will be the millennium sure enough when we see the
American eagle sitting on Easter eggs!" A roar of laughter went up,
and Francis grasped Mr. Hillyer's hand. "Thank you," he said, "thank
you, and now Captain Alderley—" but Captain Alderley had hurried
away.

The next afternoon Francis rode out to the Alderleys and found the
Captain sitting alone on the front piazza. Tying his horse he went in,
and the Captain rose to greet him. "I've come to say good-bye," the
young man began; "are Mrs. Alderley and Ann at home?" "Mrs. Alderley is sick in bed," the Captain answered. "I'll send and see if Ann is at
home," and he went into the house, leaving Francis looking out sadly
on the tennis court. Mrs. Alderley's illness meant that the eldest son
was in the Grays. Presently his host returned, and resumed his seat,
keeping a gloomy silence until a servant came to report that Miss Ann
had gone out, and Francis saying good-bye, wondered if she had
avoided him purposely. It was a bitter thought for a last thought and he
rode away slowly. It was a shady old highway that he turned into presently, with vine-grown fences on either side, and pleasant vistas into
green forest depths and across bright fields. Francis knew every foot of
it and looked about him from side to side, as if bidding it all farewell.
He checked his horse to a slower pace; he was coming to a stile at the
beginning of a woodland path, where he and Ann had often played as
children, and talked when older—the dear old stile! Then though
watching, he seemed to come abreast of the old haunt suddenly—and
Ann was standing on the other side! He drew a sharp breath, in an instant he was off his horse and standing before her. "Did you run away
on purpose, Ann?" he asked quickly—"did you come here—" She
looked up; her eyes were flashing—"Yes, I came here to meet you,"

she said gaspingly—"to tell you that I *hate* you! We are poor, and you know it. We need brother. Mother is heart-broken—father is crushed— and I—oh!" "Hush!" Francis cried, grasping her arm, leaning over the fence to look into her eyes—"don't be so cruel; I've loved you ever since you were a little child. Oh, Ann, you'll be so sorry soon!" "Sorry!" she cried, bringing her hands together, sharply, "what a poor little word—" "But if I come again, you will forgive me, Ann?" She turned on him quickly. " *When* you come again!" she cried. Francis sprang over the fence. " *If* I come again," he repeated. " *If*, Ann," with his hands on her shoulders. "When—when—when!" she cried, and burst into tears.

AFTER LONG YEARS

I had made arrangements with a friend to produce a book on "Homes," he to do the writing, I the illustrations. We were to travel as we would; if the pictures were done first, the writing would be fashioned accordingly; if the writing were first, the pictures should illustrate.

In pursuance of this plan we had loitered along the Maine coast, we had camped in the Adirondacks, spent Christmas at home, and had dallied a little in New York. But January found me restless, and leaving Harry to follow, I once more set out, this time traveling down the Atlantic coast, hunting for places where neither war nor progress had laid a devastating hand. Such spots were few, but they existed, and I was determined to find them.

In February I reached a town that must once have been a center of wealth, for although all was simple, yet the houses were spacious and the garden enclosures extensive. These old homes were mostly turned into lodging houses, or if lived in by the owners, they occupied as few rooms as possible. The hotel, which was moderately comfortable, was filled with excursionists from the cold hill country, or by idle tourists.

The town, however, was pathetic in its decay, and the country was level, monotonous, sad. The long gray moss that draped the trees, the dense swamps that even an intruding railway could not render commonplace, and the long roads of white sand leading back interminably into the dark reaches of the pine barrens! Not even the lovely yellow jasmine, nor the wild azaleas, nor the pale wild violets that covered all the low places, could, with all their profuse effort, render it cheerful. Sad it remained, but appealing, and I determined to stop and indulge my vagrant fancy by exploring in every direction.

It was an exquisite morning, with just enough cool crispness in the air to stimulate one, and arming myself with lunch, as well as with my tools for work, I mounted a patient beast I had hired, and following a Negro servant's advice, took my way along the least used of all the roads that led from the town.

241

"I wish to thank you... for allowing me to make these pictures."

"Des you go 'long, suh," the man said, "tay you come to de fust road w'at tu'ns to de lef', den you go 'long dat road tay you come to nurrer road w'at tu'ns to de right, en you foller dat tay you come to a fence, en dat's de oldes' place I know. My mammy en my daddy usen to b'long to dem people, en de house ent been tech,—no, suh,—kase my mammy claim de house en hole it tay de wah is done en she mawsa is come home. Dey ent rich now, no, suh, but de house ent been tech."

To the left, then to the right; but I had no idea of the distance between these turns. On I jogged, the road seeming to grow longer, the woods thicker, until the tall pines leaning toward each other left only a strip of golden- blue sky far above me. On and on, meeting no soul— nothing. How lonely it was, and how did these people endure it!

At last the turn to the left—a duplicate road that seemed to stretch as interminably. What if it did? I had all time before me, and that in a restful country where people did not rush.

Presently in the distance I saw an object emerging from the woods. As it was the first moving thing I had met, I stopped to look—a mule, with some kind of vehicle, and walking beside it a person. They came nearer; a load of wood and a white boy, slight and tall with rapid growth, young and very blond. His clothes were whole, but outgrown everywhere, his hat was aged, his shoes of the commonest; but his clear eyes, as blue as the sky, met mine serenely, and without trace in them of interest and curiosity.

Meeting in this wilderness, I had a wish to break the silence, to speak to this first bit of humanity; but he did not pause a moment, and to my greeting returned only a quiet bow, absolutely civil, but one that put an immense distance between us, and although I watched him until he became one with the shadows, he turned no backward glance. I decided at once that the boy did not belong to the "poor whites," even if his clothes were shabby and his occupation necessitous.

Interested and curiously attracted, I rode on to find that where he had come into view was the road turning to the right, the last turn before I should reach the fence, and presumably the house. Another long stretch of wilderness intervened, however; then I was rewarded by the sight of the fence crossing the road at right angles, beyond which the light was strong, promising a clearing. As I drew near I saw a well with an old-fashioned pole and bucket, and a Negress drawing water. She stopped to look as I rode up to the fence,—there was no gate,—

and returned a "Mornin', suh!" to my greeting. "This is Mr. Heath's?" I asked, pointing to a house some distance away, that, hidden as it was by trees, filled me with joy.

"Will any one object if I draw it?"

"I dunno, suh. Mas' Percy is gone to town, en missis en mawsa nebber sees nobody."

"I don't wish to see any one," I answered. "Only to sit out here and make a picture."

"You woan' hu't nuttin', suh?"

"Of course not—no. What is your name?"

"Tenah, suh. I live yer. I do de cookin'en washin'," she went on, as if pleased to talk, "en my husban' he he'ps Mas' Percy wid he work, en Mas' Percy let we hab house en big patch fuh plantin'. We's doin' berry well, en Mas' Percy is doin' berry well. Two mo' niggers is teck lan' fum Mas' Percy dis spring. Dat's de house, en dey usen to be berry rich."

"And I may make a picture?"

"I t'ink so, suh. I doan' like to 'sturve missis, en Peter is 'way down in de fiel'—ef you woan' hu't nuttin'?"

Renewing my promise, I tied my horse, and making no motion to cross the fence, followed it toward the front of the house. A "tabby" house, as they are called, that once had been washed yellow, with wide-spreading piazzas all about its two stories, with many windows looking out in all directions, and brick steps flaring broadly as they descended to what had once been a shelled walk.

Oleanders grew on each side of the steps, and there were signs of an old garden. Near the house some roses were cared for; yellow jasmine climbed up the tapering round pillars of the piazzas, and from the front, as far as the eye could reach, stretched the level marshes, with here and there a glint of water.

The house was not grand, but it had a large simplicity, a dignified solidity, and its broad piazzas seemed a mute assurance of an open-hearted hospitality. Besides this it possessed a repose I had not met elsewhere, and that delighted me.

Tenah still stood by the well watching that I did not "hu't nuttin'," and so stood until, finding an advantageous view, I sat down on the trunk of a fallen tree and began work. I made two sketches, eating my lunch between times, then packed up, determining that I would come again and do it in color.

Tenah came to the fence as I untied my horse, and I told her that I would return.

"Yes, suh," she answered, "en I'll tell Mas' Percy say you ent hu't nuttin'."

Very near town I passed the fair-haired boy. This time he was riding; he had sold his wood, and the packages in his wagon looked like provisions.

The next morning I was eager for my work. The memory of the delightful color of the house, golden in some spots, and in some spots green with dampness, the dark shingles, the blue sky, the deep hue of the live oaks, the rich background of the pines, the wonderful distances across the marshes! What a picture it would make if into it I could put the spirit of the place that seemed to look at me from every window, that seemed to whisper to me in every movement of the leaves! Knowing the way made it seem shorter, and I found everything undisturbed save that Tenah was not at the well. I heard faint cries of "Gee-haw!" and supposed that "Mas' Percy" was in the fields; and as there was no warning against trespassers, I took position on the log and began work. I was soon absorbed, and heeded nothing until the creaking of the well pole disturbed me. I looked, and saw the fair-haired boy of the road. So he lived here. Was he Mas' Percy?

He did not turn in my direction, and I stopped work to observe him. He was worth drawing, his manner and bearing were remarkable, and he was barefoot. Presently a Negro man came up and took off his hat; then I knew the boy was Mas' Percy. I returned to my work, but the old house was no longer so interesting. The boy, so poor that he could wear his shoes only when going to town, had usurped the first place.

He went into the house, and after some time came out again. I caught a glimpse of a slight woman, who followed him to the piazza. He made a gesture of protest, and the woman, glancing in my direction, retreated. Then the boy, crossing to the other side of the enclosure, jumped the fence and disappeared. I felt sure that the next day I should be warned off, but I was not.

Twice again I met the boy on the road, and each time he gave me the same serene look, the same quiet bow, and each time I became more desirous of knowing him.

One morning a telegram came; my father was coming down, would join me, probably that evening. This would put an end to my romance of the old house; but this last day I would go again to take a last look, and make up, perhaps, one more story about these unknowable people; also I would make a drawing of the well.

I had nearly finished the sketch when I saw the boy approaching. It was ridiculous how pleased I was, and how excited. He should speak to me, and as he laid his hand on the pole, I rose.

"I wish to thank you," I began, "for allowing me to make these pictures. My name is Branston." At the mention of my name he let the pole go.

"Branston?" he repeated. "Have you ever heard of Brockley Branston?"

"My father's name," I answered, "and mine!"

Without another word he walked away quickly to the house, leaving me amazed. This was really romantic. Would he come back? It was all I could do not to jump the fence and follow him; but in a few moments he came back and began to let down the rails.

"My father wishes to see you," he said, "and will you come in?" In a moment I was over the partly lowered fence and following him. Round to the front of the house we took our way, up the front steps, across the broad piazza, and in at the most lovely of doors. In the wide hall we stopped, and I was asked to sit down, the boy disappearing farther down the hall.

I looked about me at the broad stairway, at the old furniture, simple, fine, dilapidated; at the bits of silver on the enormous sideboard,—for the hall was evidently both dining room and drawing room,—at the fire on the hearth at one side, and felt my wishes realized. It was all I had expected.

A door opened and I rose. The lady of whom I had caught a glimpse was coming down the hall. She suited the house—she was worn, but she was fine.

"I am Mrs. Heath," she said, giving me her hand, "and I am glad to welcome you. In a moment my husband will come and tell you the story. It is singular."

"I shall be—" I began. Then a rolling sound made me turn, and I saw a most extraordinary contrivance—an arm chair mounted on a pair of carriage wheels that looked absurdly large for their work, the back legs of the chair being lengthened to rest on the floor when not moving. In the chair sat a gentleman, and pushing it was the boy, who now had put on his shoes and coat, and had brushed back his waving yellow hair.

"This is my father," he said quietly, and there was a light of beautiful love and pride in his eyes. The gentleman held out a white hand to me.

"Your father's son," he said, "if you are the son of my Brockley Branston—"

"He was a colonel in Grant's army—" I began. Instantly he put his other hand over mine, that he still held.

"Does he still live? Sit down, my boy. You must stop and break bread with us; I have much to say. My wife and son are as glad to see you as I am."

I took my seat between him and Mrs. Heath, Percy still standing behind his father's chair, watching him as if filled with a great pride in every word he said.

"You have a look of your father," Mr. Heath went on, "who was so good to me. On a battlefield we met. I was wounded in the back and left for dead; he lay beside me, unconscious. Numbed by suffering, I watched his white face idly. Presently he opened his eyes. 'What's happened?' he said, vaguely.

"'We are left for dead,' I answered. He turned and looked at me.

"'You look dead,' he said.

"'So do you,' I returned.

"'But I'm not,' and he sat up and began to feel himself. 'Good as new,' he went on, 'but you—' turning to me again.

"'I'm done for!' and trying to move, I lost consciousness. When I came to myself I was in a tent. Your father stood over me.

"'Not done for yet,' he said, laughing.

"'You are good!' I answered.

"'Not a bit,' he returned. 'I've adopted you as my thank-offering. Now go to sleep.'

"That was only the beginning," Mr. Heath went on. "Everything was done for me that kindness and skill could compass, and after a long time I reached a point where I could walk, and had begun to wonder when I should leave the hospital for a prison, when one day your father came in with a strange look on his face. I rose quickly to meet him. 'The war is done,' he said, gently, and laid his arm about my shoulder, 'and, Heath, old fellow, try to believe that it's all right.' Instead, I sobbed on his shoulder like a woman, and he stood there holding me like a woman.

"He was not rich, but at once he made arrangements for sending me south, delaying his own return home to do it, and when at last all was settled, he put me into the train with a basket of food and a military pass. I looked the last on him—God bless him! Then, like a boy, I began to investigate the pockets of my new suit. Suddenly I stopped. I felt myself a thief. I owned no purse, yet here was one! I drew it out guiltily—hesitated. Fifty dollars and a scrap of writing—'I wish I could double it, old fellow.'"

Mr. Heath paused a moment, then went on: "I reached home—a devastated country, a beggared people, and so many missing! It was a cruel time, but my wife and little daughter were well, and my faithful old nurse had claimed this place for me, and as if freedom had not come, lived with us to her death. My strength came back to me, and with that fifty dollars as capital I hired a mule and began to sell wood. We came near to starvation, but we did not quite reach it. At last things began to pick up. I was able to mortgage the place, and with the money I fenced in land for planting and began to feel safe, when my daughter died, and my back gave out—the old wound, you see. Since then—" he turned and looked up at the boy.

"We have not starved," the boy answered, smiling down on his father, "and now once more are prospering." Then the boy turned away, going down the hall, and Mrs. Heath followed.

"He was only ten," Mr. Heath went on, "when I gave out, and he and his mother kept things going. He built this chair," touching the wheels that supported him, "and has done everything."

"He is a beautiful boy," I said.

Mr. Heath nodded. "And has but two ambitions—to pay off the mortgage on the place, the deeds of which go back to the crown, and to return this." He held out an old-fashioned purse.

I started back. "Mr. Heath!" I cried.

"My boy is right," he said. "He was radiant when he discovered you. I have not known where to find your father, but, indeed, the last addition to the amount has just been made. Percy has had it turned into gold. You must take it."

"Never!" I said. "I cannot!"

"Your father would."

"Then let him!" I answered, sharply. "He comes tomorrow."

"Your father?" and Mr. Heath's face seemed to lose ten years. "You will bring him out at once?"

Then Mrs. Heath and the boy came back, but I was too much upset to enjoy the little luncheon that Tenah brought in, and I left as soon as possible.

It seemed to me the most heartrending story, that poor fifty dollars gathered through all these years of toil! Impossible! I would lay the case before my father, and of course he would not take the money. I was so full of the story that I hardly greeted him when he came that night.

"So you've found Heath," he said. "Of course I'll go there. As to the money—"

"You cannot take it!"

"The only thing to do is to take it. Wait!" He raised his hand. "I'll take the mortgage, too. It will never be foreclosed; and having come down to lease land for a hunting club, I'll lease from Heath. Is it not better to gratify the boy's ambition? And you shall have the gold to hang up in your studio—or round your neck—anywhere you like, only I must take it."

We drove out the next day. The meeting between the men was beautiful; and Percy, who had held me at such a distance, kept close to my father, seeming to hang on his words. The old times were talked over, the purse presented, and my father put his arm round Percy's shoulders.

"This is fine," he said, his voice breaking a little, "and I shall give it to my boy, so that looking on it he may realize what real work means." Then with a little laugh, he added, "I wish you were a girl, Percy. I'd like you for a daughter-in-law!"

So it was all arranged. The mortgage was secured and rapidly paid off, as the land for the club was leased on the most liberal terms possible. By the next autumn, when we came down to open the clubhouse, I had the satisfaction of seeing Percy clothed like other people; and when the spring came again, all of the great tract that was not leased to the club was once more put under cultivation.

Standing looking out over the marshes, Percy said slowly, "I love every stalk of marsh, every inch of earth, every tree and stump on this old place, and only God knows how glad I am to feel secure in it!"

"And all of it out of your own hard work," I answered.

He shook his head. "Say rather out of your father's heart, and—" smiling at me—"out of your book on 'Homes'."

"Good for me!" I cried, and I turned to greet Mrs. Heath, feeling happier about my great book than I could possibly have done even if the wonderful plan had been carried out; but my friend Harry having decided on matrimony, the book had died without a struggle.

"WE PEOPLE"

A turbid river filled to the brim by winter rains, and red with the clay of the hills, swept on its way between high banks, between pleasant fields, by dense canebrakes, by silent swamps where its haste seemed stilled for the moment, and its tawny rush eddied slowly in and through the clear brown waters that stretched back and back; but drawing again from out the dim primeval reaches in sucking, swirling eddies, it swept on once more between the rice-field dams, down to the sea, making in the bright water a great semicircle of ugly redness.

Just where this river left the hills, it spread out wide and shallow, leaving in the middle, parallel with the shore, a long, narrow sand bank that even the heaviest freshet could not cover, instead sending its floods spreading over the low-lying fields on either side. Nothing grew on the sands of this bar, its pale brown length stretched unbroken by any smallest shrub or cane, and but for a heavy post at the upper end, from which ferry ropes stretched to either shore, one would have doubted if the foot of man had ever touched this spot. To the Negroes, this bank was haunted. To the Whites, it was historic ground, regarded with pride that yet had a touch of deprecation in it, while mothers, and wives, and lady-loves even, looked on it with a sort of Spartan endurance.

"The river will not try to wash that bank," old Mrs. Weatherly had said once; "it's beyond cleaning, that 'Field of Honor' is; my husband fell there, and the blood of my eldest born soaked into that sand; buckshot at twelve paces—bullets at ten!" and with the last clause of her speech begun so bitterly, her old eyes flashed and her white head reared itself proudly.

Lying midway between two states, the bank was a famous duelling ground, and a meeting on the "Sand Bar" meant certain death to one man at least. A line fence, strayed cattle, a random word, a misconstrued smile, passing a vehicle and giving the dust of the road, even precedence on a hitching post, had been sufficient "Cause"; that was, until the call of the Civil War, the tragedy of defeat, the struggle for existence when every white man was needed to stand shoulder to shoulder in the race struggle, had given the hot blood other outlets. Duels had become rare occurrences even though the "Code" still held, and the unspeakable stigma of cowardice blotted out the good name of any man who hesitated before a challenge or a shot fired in revenge.

A mile or more from this "Sand Bar," the town of Highfield was now in a state of intense excitement. The Negro question had drowsed into temporary quietude, broken only by an occasional lynching or a growl of indignation over a minor Federal appointment given to a black, and political differences were for the moment between white men. A letter had appeared, written by a descendant of the old aristocracy, in which a man, Doby, lately emerged from unknown sources, but yet of the soil, had been arraigned in no measured terms. The letter stated that money meant for special philanthropic purposes had been diverted, and Richard Boulton, as a trustee for the fund, had made public this fact, together with his investigations of all the transactions concerning the fund; tracing to the man Doby, all the unaccounted for, or falsely accounted for monies, and declaring that they had been spent in winning a late election which had placed the said Doby in a high office of the State. Doby's friends, men like himself of the farmer class, who had for Boulton and his class the most unmitigated hatred, were in a state of intense indignation. This letter said that they had made way with public money, they had bribed, had sold offices, and lowest of all, the unpardonable sin in Southern eyes, they had touched the pitch of the color line, had tampered with the Negroes, had trucked to the leaders, black and white, of the black race. All this had been laid bare in Boulton's letter just as the political forces were girding themselves for the beginning of a political campaign for Governor.

Boulton, a quiet gentleman overseeing his cotton fields, had, up to a few months before, been an unknown factor in political circles. He had been selected as being a politically inoffensive person, as one of the trustees for certain funds, and also had been appointed chairman of the committee to look over the accounts. He had begun at once the work of investigating what on the surface had seemed a well-managed State charity. Very quietly he had taken up his task, but very conscientiously, becoming every day more interested in his discoveries, more sure of the power he was gaining and which, possibly, would help him to cleanse his State government of what had long been recognized as a low and disgraceful element. He had consulted his only brother, whose share of his father's estate was in rice fields on the coast, who had confirmed his decision that it was his duty to make known what he had discovered.

"It will make trouble for you," Edward had said.

"Of course, and I consult you because my trouble will necessarily touch you."

"Very serious trouble," and Edward looked anxious.

"A shot in the back, most probably. The fear is that Doby, himself, will not do the shooting. If he *will* do it and in consequence be hanged, I will have accomplished something; but that is not the point. You agree that I must make known what I have discovered."

"Without doubt. Shall I come to Highfield?"

"No, that would look as if I were taking precautions. I shall not make it a personal attack. I shall just point the facts, the conclusions will draw themselves. I shall print it in the shape of a report. I can't make a personal attack on a man I would not meet on the 'Sand Bar'."

Ned turned quickly. "You would not fight!"

"Of course, if Doby were a gentleman."

"Gentleman! His political position raises him to a fighting level."

"Nothing can do that but birth."

"Your friends will not agree with you there."

"Perhaps."

"After all the past, Dick, you'd fight?"

"I would."

"I'd give my life to dredge that 'Sand Bar' off the face of the earth, to do away with this barbarous blood code!"

"What would you put in its place?"

"Law."

"Suppose a man insults you?"

"Libel!"

"Suppose a man slaps your face?"

"Assault."

"Suppose Doby shoots me?"

"Murder."

"Suppose your women are insulted?"

"Libel."

"Good Lord!" And Dick turned away. They were standing on the bank of the rice fields, looking out on the same turbid river that up in the hill country parted that it might flow around the "Sand Bar," and Dick now looked out over its swirling current in sorrowful silence. At last he turned, "Don't say these things to any one but me, Ned," he said.

"If I could protest to all the world, I'd do it."

"I'll make a bargain with you: I'll promise not to fight Doby, promise even if my friends think that I should, if you will promise not to expose your name to the comment these views would incur."

"I can't promise that—I must protest if the chance come to me."

"You should be a parson."

"I come down here sometimes Dick and look out over this river, and feel that it is red with blood!"

"Clay from the hills. Old man, your liver's out of order. You live too much alone; you're hysterical."

"Promise you will not fight?"

"Promise you will not declare your views."

"My views are righteous."

"You'd never be understood—you'd be disgraced."

"But I'd be right. Promise me not to fight?"

"There was a moment's silence, then Dick went on. "No, as Doby is the man to receive the report, I'll hand it in to him; the law requires its publication. He will tamper with it before publication. In a public letter I shall demand the full report; if he refuses, I shall, as I have said, print it myself, as a report, and let things take their course."

Then Boulton went away home, again, and all had happened just as he had expected. A minimum synopsis of the report had been published, with some complimentary remarks as to the careful work done by Mr. Boulton, and regrets that he had discovered one or two serious but unsuspected abuses that should be rectified at once. This was followed by a private letter to Dick Boulton, thanking him for the careful work done, and telling him that as a slight token of appreciation, some road improvements which his brother had asked of the State authorities should be put through at once. Also some embankments should be built along a creek which divided, and sometimes overflowed the fields of Richard Boulton.

Dick Boulton's answer was the publication of this letter in two newspapers, along with the demand for the publication of his full report. No answer coming, he himself published the report, and this it was that caused Highfield to stand on tiptoe of excitement. The newspapers throughout the State took up the matter. "Behold an honest man who dare take a stand!" they cried. Then letters of congratulation, commendation, thanks, came pouring in on Boulton, but Doby made no sign to Boulton, going instead to the lawyers.

"You can sue him for libel, if it is libel," the lawyer said. Doby moved uneasily in his chair. "I'll send a challenge," he answered. The lawyer shook his head.

"I'll challenge him all the same," Doby declared, "and if he refuses, I brand him as a coward!"

"I don't think that will do any harm to a Boulton."

"Will you take him my challenge?"

"I don't think that I can, Mr. Doby."

"Damn it then, you needn't!" and Doby flung out of the office, while the lawyer whistled softly.

The challenge was sent, and it reached Dick Boulton as he sat on his wide piazza smoking and talking to a friend, a neighboring planter named Weatherly. "Who is it?" Dick said, taking his pipe from his lips to get a better look at the horseman who was coming under the trees. Weatherly turned a little.

"Why—why, its that scoundrel Dickson, Doby's henchman! What the devil does it mean?"

"Possibly the idiot has sent an invitation to the 'Sand Bar'."

Weatherly leaned forward a little. "Don't the fool know that you're the best shot in the State?"

"I doubt it."

"His political position will permit you to meet him."

"I don't think so."

"I do, most emphatically."

"You surprise me; are you in earnest?"

"Most assuredly."

Dick shook his head."

"It's the only way to save your own life," Weatherly urged. "Let me act for you?"

Again Dick shook his head. "You'll have to if this is a challenge."

"No" There was a pause, then Dick went on. "Our friend does not seem to observe," he said slowly, "that no servant has been sent to take his horse." But Weatherly had no answer. He was smoking furiously, and the visitor, tying his horse to the branch of a tree, came to the foot of the steps.

"Mr. Boulton?" he said.

"Yes," Dick answered, taking his pipe from his lips while the man mounted the steps.

"I am Mr. Dickson." Taking off his hat.

"Mr. Dickson," Dick repeated.

"And bring a note from Mr. Doby."

"Mr. Doby," Dick repeated. Dickson drew a note from his pocket.

"Will you kindly put it on the banister, Mr. Dickson?" and Dick pointed with his pipe to the broad railing that ran round the piazza on which his feet rested.

"It requires an answer, and quick!" Dickson said angrily, putting on his hat defiantly. Dick took his feet from the banister, letting his chair come down on its four legs, and reaching for the note, tore it across and laid the two parts carefully on the railing, Then once more tilting back his chair, he said, "That is the only answer I have for any communication from Mr. Doby; Good evening, Mr. Dickson," and he began to smoke once more.

Dickson looked silently from one to the other, then taking up the torn note, turned towards the steps. "It's a challenge," he said, pausing on the top step.

"And you've had Mr. Boulton's answer," Weatherly put in quickly.

"He won't fight?"

"He can't fight Mr. Doby."

"Can't!"

"If you and Mr. Doby do not understand this answer," Weatherly went on, "you may ask any gentleman in the county what it means and it will be explained."

"All right, but there'll be more to this!" Then Dickson went slowly down the steps, mounted and rode away.

Dickson told the story, and the town and county laughed, then grew grave. The next county took it up, a mountain county from which Doby came, "Doby wuz a gen'l'man, good's anybody," they declared. And things began to look serious.

Boulton's friends warned him. Even Miss Weatherly, who was engage to his brother, rode over to implore him to take care.

"What shall I do, Kate?" he asked, "wear a coat of mail? Leave the country? Shoot Doby on sight?"

"He'll shoot you."

"If he'll only do it himself, he'll be hanged for it, and I'll have done good missionary work."

"No, Ned will have to shoot him—and—"

"Then you'd not marry Ned?"

"Nonsense! 'twould be just retribution; but it would kill Ned."

"I think you mistake Ned; if he thought a thing right, he'd do it, and it would not kill him."

"Don't discuss it. You must not be shot!"

"I'll do my best; I promise not to call on Doby, nor to ask him to dine here, nor to do anything to him in any way. I've exposed him as a rascal and thief, and I have declined his challenge. The politicians are doing the rest. The next elections will go against him and his party, I think."

"Then he'll surely shoot you!"

"Very probably he'll try to, and I've asked your advice as to what I shall do?"

The girl sighed and turned away, stroking the flank of her horse—for she had not dismounted—and Dick, with his arm over the horse's neck, looked up at the lovely curve of her averted face, at the red-gold of her hair.

"I'll do anything you say, Kate," he went on slowly, "even to running away."

The girl laughed nervously. "What nonsense you talk!"

"Honest. I'll run if you say so, if it—it will save you pain."

"I've come to talk common sense," she answered hurriedly. "I wrote Ned to come, but he will not—says you'd rather he did not—and that he agrees with you."

"Of course, to lay in a stock of brothers would be worse than running away. Besides, your brother is here. We've been always three brothers together."

"Yes."

"What then?"

"Do you go armed?"

"Of course not."

"Dick!"

"I've no reason to shoot Doby, and if he shoots me he'll give me no chance to defend myself. But don't worry, here comes Dan," as Weatherly rode up from the gate. "I'd take a good gallop with you, if my horse were saddled, or if you will wait?"

"No," the girl said quickly, "you'll have to ride back alone!"

Dick laughed. "I'd better get old Judy to take care of me once more," he said. "The old soul is still quite chirpy. She's coming now to ask you in for some purpose—coffee, most likely. Well, Mawm Judy?" as the old Negress approached.

"I come, suh, fuh ax Miss Kate en Mass Dan fuh come in, suh, en teck some 'freshment, please, suh?"

"Good idea, Mawmer. Come, Kate."

"'taint nuttin much, ma'm," old Judy went on, "but 'taint to say right fuh unner to go 'way dout nuttin—not fum my Mass Dick' house—no ma'm," and while Kate dismounted, the old woman hastened round to the back entrance in order that she might welcome them in due form at the front door.

The Boultons had lived always on the coast, this cotton plantation having been only a sort of camping place for the summer, until in the division of property, Dick had taken it for his portion, leaving the old home and the rice fields to Edward, as the eldest son. Thus, the interior of Dick's home was simplicity itself, and most emphatically bachelor quarters. Old Judy, once a slave and his mother's maid, and later Dick's nurse, had stuck to Dick's fortunes, and had followed him to the red-clay country, for which she had the most open contempt. But she looked after Dick carefully, and now had set forth in the old silver that had fallen to his share such coffee as she had learned in her youth to make, and bread and butter and preserves such as are produced only from the recipes of our grandmothers.

"You live like a king, Dick, and Mawm Judy spoils you."

"No, m'am, Miss Kate, no, ma'm, I ent sp'ile um, but I'se berry scare furrum."

"Dick looked up quickly.

"Yes, suh, Mass Dick," she went on, folding her hands together under her apron, and rocking her body a little—"I's yerry Toby en Peter say es dat po' buckra Doby, is gwine shoot unner. Yes, suh, en I cahn sleep in de night, en ebbry day I watch down to de big gate, suh, tay I yerry unner horse comin' down de big road. I know how Prince put 'e foots to de groun' en w'en ole Judy yerry um 'plunckety-plunckety-plunckety' down de road, den old Judy run home so unner cahe see um; but now I git too scare, en I come fuh ax Mass Dan fuh watch unner. Please, suh, Mass Dan!" and flinging her apron over her head, she hurried out of the nearest door.

The three looked at each other, and Kate wiped her eyes. "I do love the old time darkies!" she said, choking a little, "Let Dan stay with you, Dick."

Dick shook his head, looking down at his coffee, which he stirred slowly.

"It would do no good, Kate, thank you; if anything happens, it will happen in the open street or on the road, and if we need not cry over spilled milk, surely we need not cry before the milk is spilled? Poor old Judy!"

The feeling in Highfield grew more tense as the politicians rang the changes on Doby and his party, with always Dick and his letter and report as a background, with always the laugh over the answer made to

Doby's challenge, with cartoons of Doby sitting forlorn and waiting on the Sand Bar. Dick's friends, meanwhile, hovered about him in a quiet way, doing regular picket duty among themselves so as to prevent even the most casual meeting between Dick and Doby, and more than once led Dick away from some street or corner when word had come of Doby's presence. If they could be kept apart until after the elections, the newspapers would drop the subject and the danger might be tided over.

Dick, himself, went on his quiet way as usual, smiling a little at the persistence with which some friend or acquaintance would meet him whenever he went to town, and ride with him. He knew too, how often they changed his route of travel, having always some excuse to persuade him down one street instead of another, or into one shop rather than another, and gave way to them. He was quite willing to save bloodshed if it could be done in a proper way, so he left himself in the hands of his friends.

But one day as Dick turned the corner of a street with Weatherly, Doby stepped out of a shop near the other corner of the block. He did not see Dick for a moment. Then he stopped, but Dick and Weatherly neither slackened nor hastened their steps, walking leisurly, talking quietly, Dick with one hand in the pocket of his loose riding coat, in the other, his riding whip. One second Doby paused, then advanced, while a crowd seemed to spring from the ground, so quickly men gathered to see the meeting. Doby walked rapidly down the middle of the pavement, and Dick seeing his intention of forcing a collision, stepped to one side. In a second, a shot rang out. Dick staggered. Weatherly sprang towards Doby crying out—

"You know he's not armed!"

Men rushed forward, but Doby fired two more shots, one into the prostrate body. A cry of rage broke forth, and Doby stood at bay!

Dick rose on his elbow and lifted a quieting hand. "Don't touch the coward!" he said; the crowd parted and Doby walked away.

Slowly and carefully Dick was carried to his home; Ned was sent for, and Kate Weatherly and Dan took up residence at "Cotton Top." Old Judy moved noiselessly to and fro. The worst had come. The strain of fear was over. Now the best must be done to save him. The bullets were extracted, the flow of blood stopped, and there was a flash of hope that Dick might live.

"You must do nothing but breathe, old fellow," the Doctor said, "and if you do that carefully, we'll pull you through yet."

Dick smiled a little to Kate who knelt by the low bed, and she whispered, "You must not even smile." Then she stayed there, his eyes holding her. He never took them off her—wistful if she moved in any direction—contented when she took her seat and fanned him softly, or put the bits of ice between his lips. Dan, Ned, and two physicians kept unceasing watch, but only Kate could keep the patient to the perfect quiet that was ordered.

Ned made her go to rest the second night at midnight, and himself took her place. Her last words were, "Keep very still—" then in a whisper—"for me, Dick?" Dick closed his eyes and lay like one dead, save that he swallowed the ice they put between his lips. Towards morning he grew restless. The doctor laid his hand on his pulse and called sharply for the stimulant! As Dan reached for it, Dick spoke out quite loud and clear.

"You must let the law take its course, Ned," he said.

"You must not speak," the Doctor ordered.

"Promise the law shall take its course!" Dick repeated.

"Hush, Dick!" The door opened and Kate came in. The Doctor raised a warming hand.

"Let her come," Dick spoke again quite clearly, "I'm dying now." Kate came forward quickly. Judy came from behind the bed. Dick looked up at the old woman. "God bless you, Mawmer," he said, "Take care of Mass Ned," then he laid his hand in Kate's.

"Drink this!" the doctor cried, but Dick was dead.

The trial was looked forward to with intense excitement, and there seemed to be no doubt in any mind of Doby's conviction. He had shot without warning an unarmed man who had not made even a motion to touch him, on the contrary had stepped off the pavement to give him passage way. Doby's lawyers demanded a postponement and a change of venue, on the grounds that in Highfield county Doby would not have a chance. The postponement was not granted, but the change of venue was, and that against the protest not only of the prosecuting lawyers, but of the community, and the trial was changed to the next county. Indignation ran high; in the that county, Doby's birthplace, where he had bought up every vote at every election, where there was not a man of higher standing than Doby himself, where the feeling against Boulton and his class was bitter, there was scarcely a doubt but that a jury selected there would clear Doby. And then—

"Then," said Kate Weatherly promptly, "Ned Boulton will be under the necessity of shooting Doby on sight."

"I don't know," Dan answered her slowly, "Dick's last charge was 'Let the law take its course. He said it twice."

"And we have," Kate answered, "Doby should have been lynched on the spot!"

"There's a prejudice against gentlemen doing that kind of thing."

"There was not at New Orleans at the Mafia lynching. Uncle Harry marched in that procession."

"Yes," Dan answered slowly. "What does Ned say?"

"Nothing, so far, but in case of acquittal he will have no other course."

"I don't know," and Dan shook his head slowly, remembering Dick's extraordinary order as to the law.

"I'll not stay to hear Ned maligned!" and Kate left the room indignantly.

The trial was called, and Dick Boulton's friends went in a body to take possession of the very dirty and small, but only hotel in the next county town. The landlord, being a friend of Doby's, hesitated. Instantly Ned Boulton hired an empty house in the village, and taking a camp outfit and servants, he made the party as comfortable as was possible. Kate Weatherly and old Judy having been subpoenaed, went also, and the townspeople, headed by the landlord who had hesitated only because he wanted to set the highest possible price, denounced them as "Too good to know folks—damned swellheads, and the sooner the State got rid of that kind, the better—" words that coming to Boulton's lawyers, made them shake their heads.

The trial began, and Doby's plea was self-defence. That Mr. Boulton had his right hand in his coat pocket as if holding a pistol, and had stepped aside as if to get a good shot; that he, Doby, had always heard of the Boultons as people who shot for anything or nothing, and thought that his life depended on his getting in the first shot.

Witness after witness was brought to prove that it was the surprise and comment of the whole community, both town and country, that Boulton would not go armed, that he had said openly and often that he had nothing for which to shoot Mr. Doby, that his duty had been to show Mr. Doby's rascality and that further than that he did not know Mr. Doby, that on being challenged by Mr. Doby he had torn the challenge in pieces.

"Why!" shouted the opposing lawyer.

"Because the 'Sand Bar' is dedicated to gentlemen only!" was shouted back, and a hubbub arose among Doby's friends, while the hue of Doby's face deepened to purple.

"That Mr. Boulton," the witnesses went on, "had said that it was no use for him to carry arms, as Mr. Doby would probably shoot him in the back."

"But he didn't!" was shouted.

"And in any case Mr. Boulton would not be allowed a chance to defend himself."

"And he wasn't!" came in a satisfied growl.

"Also, Mr. Boulton had said that if Doby shot him he would be hanged, and the State be rid of a vile element."

"Damned if it will!" came clearly, and the Judge called to order.

Two days were given up to witnesses, and one to the speech of the lawyer for the prosecution, through all of which the jury sat as impassive as wooden images, and Dan Weatherly, turning to Ned Boulton said,

"I believe they've empanelled twelve deaf-mutes!"

Ned nodded, "Bought," he answered.

The Judge made his charge, the jury filed out, and in less than fifteen minutes returned with the verdict of "Not Guilty!" There was a moment's silence while Doby looked in terrified apprehension at the friends of Boulton. Then a cheer broke from Doby's friends, and the Court room was cleared.

"You'll come over tomorrow," Kate had said to Ned at parting—for the whole company of friends had at once taken up the line of march for their homes—and the next morning found Ned dismounting at the Weatherly's door.

Kate seated on the piazza, came to the steps to meet him. "Worn out," she said.

"And very lonely," Ned answered. "With Dick gone, my life seems cut in two. Won't you marry me at once, Kate?"

The girl looked at him curiously. "How can you think of such things now?" she asked.

"Because I am so lonely—because, somehow, you seem to me to be a part of Dick." She turned her head away, moving a little. "I've loved you all my life, Kate; you've put me off so often, why put me off again?"

"You wish to marry me before the finale?" and she turned to look at him.

"The finale?"

"Doby!"

"The finale came yesterday."

"Ned!" she cried, and wrung her hands together.

Ned tried to take her hands, but she stepped back. "What do you mean?" he queried.

"Mean!" "Have you no blood in your veins!"

"Kate!"

"Are you a man!" she went on, her voice rising. "I seem a part of Dick to you, Dick lying dead, his blood crying out to you! He said let the law take its course. Was he trying to conceal your weakness?"

Ned stood stock still, his face growing white and set, his eyes fixed on her, then he said slowly, "You mean—you wish—me—to murder—?"

"Murder! No more murder than shooting a mad dog that attacks you!"

"Kate—a woman—you're beside yourself!"

"Beside myself! Where are all your traditions! Have you forgotten that out here on the 'Sand Bar' your father shot his friend for smiling— accidentally smiling—as your mother passed—and you stand quiet over a dead brother!"

Ned slipped his hands slowly into his pockets and looked out across the old garden to the dense woods. "I will not commit murder," he said quietly.

"Doby expects it."

"Our ideals differ."

"All your friends expect it."

"Then they do not know me."

"You'll be branded a renegade."

"According to the code of men—murder is a sin against God."

"I shall de—"

"Kate!" he cried.

The girl moved back, then came quickly close to him, laying her clasped hands on his breast. "Do you love me?"

He did not answer.

"You will be disgraced."

"That will not count if you stand by me?" and he put his arm about her. She moved from him a little, and his arm dropped at his side.

She looked at his white face, his wistful eyes, his lips that trembled, then she, pausing on each whispered word, "Are—you—afraid—" Like a shot his arm flashed up. She sprang back.

He covered his face with his hands. A little while they stood so, then he took his hands away. "Good-bye," he said, and turning went towards the steps.

"You'll be branded a coward!" she cried after him.

"He stopped and looked at her. "But not a murderer." Then he went slowly away.

The whole countryside waited breathless, but nothing happened. The newspapers all through the land scored the trial, the judge, the jury, the whole State. All agreed that the judge and the jury had been bought and that Doby should by some means be shut off from the doing of further evil. Then one paper lamented the necessity that would compel Mr. Edward Boulton to shoot Doby, which doubtless, would result in something like a feud; "or, perhaps, the esteemed and eminent judge who had cleared the worthy Doby, would hang Mr. Boulton, Mr. Boulton being a gentleman, and this, after having compelled Mr. Boulton to do the dirty work which the law was paid to manage. It seemed a pity that Mr. Boulton's friends would not relieve him of this disagreeable duty to the public by organizing a lynching party. This was a rare case when gentlemen could do such a thing and it would surely be the friendly thing to do. Nor could it be taken up, as numbers would paralyze the law. Mobs were never hanged, not even small mobs, and while their hands were 'in', why not attend to the judge and the jury as well. No other judge would follow up the lynchers, much less hang them if found."

Ned Boulton read this article slowly, then destroyed the paper.

Kate, meanwhile, had told Dan of the position taken by Ned, and Dan went the next day to see Ned, whom he found seated at Dick's table going over Dick's papers.

He looked up. "Well, Dan," he said, "sit down; there are cigars, and there's a flask. I want you to have that flask, by the way, it was Dick's."

"Thanks," and Dan took up the flask, turning it over slowly in his hands. "I've come to talk to you about Doby," he went on abruptly, "Everybody expects it, you know."

"Yes," Ned answered quietly.

"Well?"

"I will not."

"Will not?"

"No."

Dan rose. "Dick could have killed Doby." he said slowly.

"Yes."

"Did you tell him not to fight?"

"I did all in my power to prevent it."

Dan turned away. "Good-bye," he said, but did not offer his hand.

"Good-bye," Ned answered as he folded another paper. Dan paused a moment, then laid down Dick's flask on the table and left the room.

Ned went on with his work, steadily, far into the night, then threw himself down to rest. He must be very careful how he approached people after this; he had better not see his old friends when he passed them. The next day he rode into town and caught a glimpse of Doby hurrying round a corner; he met the judge also, whom he had known well, but he would not so much as see the man, and the judge crossed the street. It would take him two weeks more to finish with his brother's affairs, Ned thought, then he could go home and live his usual quiet life. Kate and Dan had taken the position that all his friends would take—he must do without friends.

Dan Weatherly was suffering bitterly. Dick and Ned had been as his own flesh and blood, but of the two, he had loved Ned the better; the grave, courteous, single-hearted gentleman; but now? Was it some foolish fad! It would disgrace him, and what was worse, disgrace his class. Even Doby would laugh him to scorn.

"Why didn't I slap his face," he said to himself. "What would he have done? It might have stirred his liver. What ails him?" Remembering Dick's words as to letting the law take its course, he had all along been afraid of Ned's taking some strange course. Poor old Dick had known all this and had insisted on the law in order to screen his brother. No one but Ned understood Dick's charge to mean the abiding by the verdict; no one would ever understand such tame submission! Every man he met alluded to the case in some way. "Of course I'll stand by Boulton;" and another, "I'll be glad to help Boulton pick off any number of Dobyites;" and again, "Boulton won't act, I suppose, until he has put all his affairs in order, but I'll come when he calls; tell him, will you?"

Dan already felt the bitterness of the contempt that would fall on his friend, the silence of the awful ostracism that would surround him for all his days. People thought this vengeance was only a matter of time, and they would not grant him much more time. Then Dan saw the article suggesting that Mr. Boulton's friends should relieve him of the dirty work of ridding the earth of Doby. Dan sat quite still, then read the article again.

Old Judy came in smiling, to where Ned Boulton was finishing his breakfast. "Hab some mo' aigs, Mass Ned?"

"No, thank you, Mawma," but Ned did not look at her.

"Is unner done breakfuss 'ready, Mass Ned?" coming close to him.

"Yes, Mawmer," looking up in surprise at her nearness. "What is it?"

"Peter is scare to det, suh!"

"Peter?"

"Yes, suh. 'E git scare in town, suh, w'en 'e gone fuh de paper."

"What do you mean!"

"Yes, suh—yes, suh," backing away, "Dey's done shoot dat Doby!"

"Ned sprang to his feet. "Who? Where!"

"Ober by de big hill, suh. Doan look at me like dat, Mass Ned, I dunno nuttin, suh!"

"You do!" He caught her arm.

"I fine dis under de do', suh," fumbling for her pocket, "En I wait tay unner done eat, suh—"

"Make haste!"

"Den Peter come tell me say dey's done shoot Doby!"

"Make haste!"

Unner scare me tay I cahn fine meh pocket, suh. Yez um, en nobody ent know bout dis, suh."

Ned snatched the sealed envelope from her hand, and tore it open. He drew out a sheet of paper—a newspaper clipping fell to the floor; the old woman picked it up and watched her master while he read.

"Only the two to whom you betrayed yourself, know of your 'views'—to the rest of the world you remain still a man among men. For Dick's sake, who I believe would have fought but for you, for your name's sake, for the sake of a class that never yet has been disgraced by cowardice, this thing has been done. To protest will be to betray me."

"Unner drop dis, suh." and Judy handed him the newspaper clipping. "En ole Judy is berry glad, suh."

But Ned did not heed her, he was reading the clipping, the article suggesting that Mr. Boulton's friends relieve him of killing Doby. He finished, and dashing the papers on the floor, strode out of the room. Old Judy watched him until he was in his own room, slamming the door, then hastily, she picked up the two papers and the envelope. She paused a moment looking searchingly about the room: quickly she stepped to the fireplace and carefully, pushed the papers into a crack behind the mantelpiece, glancing back over her shoulder the while.

"Dey's done loss now," and she nodded. She carried the remains of the breakfast away to the kitchen; a Negro man was eating at a table, and looked up as she entered.

"W'ah 'e say, Mah?"

"Nuttin."

"W'ah 'e do?"

"'E gone out en slam de do'—bim!"

"'E bex kaze 'e ent hab chance fuh shoot dat Doby heseff."

"Cose 'e bex"—making a great clatter with the fire—"'e been cleanin' 'e pistol dese t'ree day, but 'e ent hab chance fuh shoot; cose 'e bex, po' Mass Ned!"

Again excitement rose to fever heat, and Doby's county threatened vengeance, but on whom? Mr. Boulton had been spending that evening in town with his lawyer; every hour of his day could be accounted for, so that he had nothing to do with it; nor did any one know when or where Doby had been captured. He had left his home after breakfast, and had never been seen until found the next morning huddled together at the foot of a tree with twelve bullets in his body. Some Negroes living out near the big hill had heard horsemen pass down the road at midnight, twelve men, one riding in the middle was tied. They counted from behind the fence, were afraid to go out, and it was raining a little.

"There is nothing to be done," declared an extra of the Highfield *Courier,* "it is a just retribution, the protest of an outraged community, the unspoken criticism on a bought judge and a 'fixed' jury. The law has failed but the people have not! The pity is that the judge and jury too, have not been attended to, and the sooner the matter is dropped the better."

Ned read the extra, and walked slowly down the avenue, hatless, his head bowed, his hands clasped behind his back. Again old Judy watched him, then drawing the papers from their hiding place behind the mantelpiece, she went quickly out to the kitchen. She looked about cautiously; she made a deep hole in the very heart of the fire, and thrust the papers in.

"W'en 'e ax furrum," she said to herself, "I tell um say—'unner t'row de paper on de flo' so I bu'n um.' Ef 'e bex, I cahn hep it—dat paper is come fum Mass Dan, kaze I see um ride up to dis house 'fo' daylight, en gone 'way gen dout knockin'. Mass Dan know say Mass Ned ent gwine shoot nobody. Lawd, Lawd! Ef my ole Mawsa know dis t'ing dis day, 'e woulder come back fum dat San' bank in de ribber en scare Mass Ned to de't'! I know, Mass Dick know, en Mass Dan is done fine out, say po' Mass Ned ent to say like *we* people."

THE LAST FLASH

Along a road a little procession was moving, headed by a clergyman in a white surplice and carrying a service book in his hands. Behind the priest came a four-wheeled wagon; the wheels had been freshly washed, and the horses had been curried, and the driver was very careful how he drove, for in the wagon there was a large coffin wrapped in an old Confederate flag and surrounded by wreaths and crosses, all of red or white flowers. Each side of the wagon marched six men, the guard of honor—all gray-haired, some bent, some limping; behind the wagon came a boy who wore on his little sleeve a broad black band, and in his arms he carried an old-fashioned sword. His round, pink face was very serious and he held the old sword close to his breast as if it were very precious, not moving a hand even to brush away his hair which sometimes the wind blew into his eyes. Behind him came eight young men, the pallbearers. A few vehicles followed, all that the town could boast, public and private. On the path that ran along the roadside a long procession of people moved, old and young, rich and poor, walking two and two. The procession of people was longer than the procession that marched in the road, some people being ahead of the priest.

It was very quiet, only the creaking of the vehicles and a low murmur that might have been the talk of the people who marched, or that might have been the wind in the tops of the big trees of the wood, for the wind was blowing—not very hard as yet but it was rising—and the people said to each other that they thought it would rain before night. It always rained after a good person died, many of them believed, though they did not say it, so that the footsteps of the righteous might be washed away and not be desecrated. And the old general had been a good man. Yes, they thought it would rain before night.

In the depths of the wood was the graveyard where the Negro gravediggers, resting on their spades, stood each side of the grave. A white man was there, too, the town carpenter, who also took charge of funerals. Across the grave were two beams of wood and by each beam stretched a stout rope. The crowd flowed in and around the grave; the

"There! How natural it looks!" and seizing the thread, the old lady kissed it.

vehicles drove as close as possible, and the big coffin was laid on the two beams. The family stood closest, mostly women, with their arms about each other and their black veils hiding them. The little boy with the sword stood at the foot of the grave; the priest at the head. The coffin was lowered, the service was read, the prayers repeated with bowed heads. A hymn was sung while the grave was filled in—an Easter hymn:

"Alleluia! Alleluia!

The strife is o'er, the battle is done!" quaveringly at first, until all the people joined in. The grave was "shaped"; the flowers were laid on it by all the friends until it was quite covered. The priest lifted his hand and gave the blessing; then from out the crowd there stepped a thin old man carrying a bugle. In his buttonhole there was a bit of red ribbon, on his breast a bronze Cross of Honor. He was one of those who had walked beside the coffin. He laid his old, gray, campaign hat on the ground, then stood up very straight. He put the bugle to his lips and lifted his head a little, and his eyes were fixed on the tops of the tall trees. He was so old, could he blow his bugle the people wondered? He had asked to blow "taps" for his old commander; could he do it?

How clear it rang out—how far it seemed to go—to echo—to come back from the solemn woods! And the old bugler stood there, still looking up, still listening!

There was a sudden movement in the crowd; it had begun to rain. But nobody hurried until they were out of the graveyard.

The war in Europe had killed the old general, they said; he had got so excited about it and his heart was so weak. A heated argument between him and a strange man he had met in the post office, a traveling man; before the end of the argument the general had fallen dead. His old wife had been with the general at the post office, and she had tried to catch that big man! Others had done it, fortunately, else the little old lady would have been killed; but she sat on the floor and held his head in her lap until the wagon had come that would bring him to his home; but the traveling man, without so much as speaking to a merchant about what he had come to sell, left on the next train. The village children watched him so, and followed him so closely, he was glad to get away. "A German," the children whispered, "and the Germans are trying to kill all the people in the world, and he killed the old general!" and they threw stones at the train as it moved away.

But the general's old wife sat by the little fire that, winter or summer, burned always in her room, and did not speak. When people came to see her she only looked at them; even her children and grandchildren could not rouse her. "His voice was so loud," she would whisper, "so loud and so angry—a wicked man!"

She did not go to the funeral; she did not seem to know about what was taking place. Day after day she sat over the fire silent. The family was in despair. One day her daughter, called out of the room, dropped the newspaper she had been reading and the headlines caught the eyes of the old lady.

"Terrible Battle Raging!" she read. "Latest from the Front! Awful Carnage!"

She grasped the paper and began hurrying about the room. Her granddaughter came in.

"They are fighting!" the old lady cried, "and I must meet Arthur! Come, help me get my things!"

The granddaughter ran out to her mother and together they came into the old lady's room. "Arthur's things must go into that trunk," she said, pointing to a small, old trunk in the bottom of the closet.

"Yes," her daughter said, fearing to contradict her, while the granddaughter thought it strange that such and old man as her grandfather should have such a beautiful young name.

"His socks!" the old lady cried; "I darned them yesterday, but there are so few!"

The daughter turned quickly. "Every one is knitting socks for the soldiers," she said; "why not you? You told me that in the war you knit a pair a day."

The old lady paused. "I did," she said, and with a half-folded garment in her hands she stood a moment as if thinking. Then—"I will!" and she dropped the half-folded garment on the floor. She went to an old-fashioned wardrobe and pulled open a drawer. "My needles are here," she said, her little old fingers busy among small bags and bundles all laid away in camphor. "Here, two sets; I can keep one going with wool and one with cotton." Then to the granddaughter who stood watching in wonder: "Run and get me some thread; I shall try to bring a dozen pairs to Arthur."

The granddaughter ran to the shops to get the thread and the daughter wiped her eyes. "Poor, poor soldiers," she said; "they'll be so glad to get the socks."

"Yes," the old lady answered proudly; "and the way I turn the heels they never wrinkle; no man has ever a blistered heel from the stockings I knit. And when I'm tired knitting socks I can scrape lint! Hunt up some old linen for lint; and we can tear and roll bandages, too! And gloves! Not knitted gloves, but out of chamois skin, I will make those, too. Strange that I should have thought the war all over and my work all done, and the 'Terrible Battles' still raging—still raging—how awful—how awful! The fatherless children, the desolate widows! Raging battles—the dead and the wounded all piled together in the burning sun, in the rain, in the snow—and I thought it was over."

The granddaughter came running in with the wool thread in hanks, the cotton in balls.

"There! How natural it looks!" and, seizing the thread, the old lady kissed it. "I thought it was all over and my work all done. I'll knit and knit!" Swiftly she knitted, sharply the glittering needles clicked and the stockings grew beneath her skilful fingers, while sometimes she quavered "The Bonnie Blue Flag" and sometimes an old love song, "Lorena."

One day the old bugler came to sell some eggs. "Did you think the war was done?" she asked. "I did, but now the war is still raging; still there are terrific battles, and I am knitting—knitting for the soldiers. The general has joined his command. Are you going, too, with your bugle?"

"Yes, ma'am, I'm going, too."

"And again you'll be bandleader?"

"I hope so, ma'am," and as he went away he drew the back of his hand across his eyes.